"ARE YOU A SPY, GINA?" DOMINICK MURMURED, HIS LIPS AGAINST HERS.

"I'm not!" she protested.

"You were eavesdropping." He kissed her again, slowly and thoroughly, until her knees went weak. "For what purpose?"

"I'm worried about you. Don't get involved in that crazy scheme to overthrow Charlemagne. In any time, in any place, they kill traitors."

"So you're worried about me, are you?" His thumbs flicked across her nipples.

Gina cried out, a wild, aching sob that Dominick silenced with another kiss. His arms encircled her. His large palms caught her hips and pulled her hard against him, letting her feel his desire.

Gina almost forgot about eighth-century political plots. Still, she wanted to plead with Dominick to stay out of harm's way. But she knew he'd never agree. Charles was his king, and Dominick was going to step right into the middle of the intrigue.

And unless Gina could discover a way back to the twentieth century—fast—he was going to take her along with him. . . .

TIMESTRUCK

FLORA SPEER

LOVE SPELL BOOKS   ✦   NEW YORK CITY

A LOVE SPELL BOOK®

May 2000

Published by

Dorchester Publishing Co., Inc.
276 Fifth Avenue
New York, NY 10001

ISBN 0-505-52378-7

The name "Love Spell" and its logo are trademarks of Dorchester Publishing Co., Inc.

Printed in the United States of America.

TIMESTRUCK

Chapter One

New York City
7.45 A.M.
Friday, December 31, 1999

"Not so fast!" The landlady planted herself squarely in front of her tenant, blocking Gina's rush through the hall of the old house to the outside door.

"I can't stop to chat right now," Gina said, even though she was certain that conversation was not on Mrs. Benson's mind. "If I do, I'll be late for work."

"Your rent is due." Mrs. Benson's manner was decidedly hostile. She was a short woman on the far side of middle age; and at the moment she looked like an angry little bulldog.

"Legally speaking, I don't have to pay you until the first of the month," Gina said.

"Legally speaking," Mrs. Benson snarled right back at her, "tomorrow is a holiday. The banks will be closed all weekend, and from what I've heard, they won't open again until the end of next week. If we're lucky, that is. Some say this here XYZ problem will stop all the computers. That means, on the stroke of midnight there'll be no electricity, no water, and probably no food in the stores. I got shoppin' to do before then."

"It's Y2K," Gina said. "Actually, I don't think there will be much of a problem at all. Most large corporations, including banks and public utilities, have made the necessary corrections to their computer programs. It's only small companies and individuals who are expected to run into trouble with their computers."

"You sound just like them government agents I've been seein' on the TV talk shows," Mrs. Benson said. "You don't believe them, do you? Or maybe you do, since you work on computers all day, every day. But I don't trust the government—not here in the city, not the people in Albany, nor the folks in Washington, neither. And I sure as hell don't trust them infernal computer machines. Disaster— maybe even the end of civilization—is comin' at midnight tonight, and I expect you to pay your rent today. In cash."

Gina resisted the urge to ask what Mrs. Benson was planning to do with cash if she really expected civilization to end. The woman's attitude was so illogical and so ill-informed that Gina wanted to laugh. She shivered instead, as an odd, chilling sensation crept over her.

No wonder she was cold. The old brownstone

building that Mrs. Benson had turned into a boardinghouse, renting out sparsely furnished rooms, with bathroom down the hall, to a motley collection of tenants, was always chilly, and the front vestibule, where Mrs. Benson had cornered Gina, was the coldest place of all, thanks to the door opening and closing so often.

"Mrs. Benson," Gina said, straining for patience, "if you want the rent money, you'll have to let me out of here so I can go to work. I'll be paid at noon, and I promise I will cash my check at the credit union right there at Y2K Computer Systems. The moment I get home this evening, I will knock on your door and hand you the cash. I've never been late before, have I?"

"There's always a first time," said Mrs. Benson. She squinted at Gina, screwing up her wrinkled face as if to make herself appear even fiercer.

"Not this time," Gina retorted sharply. She ventured a step in the direction of the front door, and Mrs. Benson, making no secret of her reluctance, moved out of the way, letting Gina finally make good her escape.

"Home, sweet home," Gina muttered sarcastically as the door slammed behind her. "The kind every woman dreams of." She paused on the front step to turn up the collar of her hip-length black leather coat before she stepped off briskly in the direction of the subway. She told herself the sudden moisture in her eyes was caused by the cold and the city's gritty, sooty wind.

"You're late," said Gina's boss, frowning at her. She was a tough woman who seldom smiled. Gina sometimes wondered if she slept in her dark, severe business suit.

"My landlady imagines civilization is going to end on the stroke of midnight," Gina explained. "I had to reassure her that she will get my rent money before that happens."

"Ignorant fools," grumbled the boss. "I'm sick to death of these millennialists and their end-of-the-world scenarios, and even sicker of all the publicity about tonight."

"I guess it's natural to be afraid of something you don't understand."

"If you say so." The boss handed Gina a sheet of paper. "Here's the printout on the list of calls you're to make today. If you're efficient and don't run into too many problems, you ought to be finished by six or seven. That'll give you plenty of time to celebrate the new year. At least I and my employees won't be expected to work all weekend long, unlike the people in some companies I could mention."

"You are planning to hand out the paychecks today, aren't you?" Gina asked, ignoring the comment about celebrating. She had nothing to celebrate, and she wanted to be sure she hadn't made a mistake in promising to have the rent money by the end of the day. Sometimes the holidays messed up even the most basic routines of everyday life.

"Scared the computer will go down?" asked the boss.

"I'm not," Gina said. "Mrs. Benson is."

"Stop back here at lunchtime, and you can pick up your check then. But don't be late; I'm leaving early."

"I'll be here."

The first two names and addresses on the print-out were located in midtown Manhattan. Both were fairly simple problems with personal computers, and Gina made short work of them. The third address was on the Lower East Side. Gina took the subway, which seemed to be running at half speed. One of the passengers loudly complained that the Y2K problem was already beginning to affect the subway machinery, which would shut down completely at midnight, if it didn't grind to a halt before then. Other passengers looked uneasy. Gina shrugged and kept her mouth shut.

The nearest subway stop was several blocks from her destination, so she had to walk. By the time she reached the address it was almost noon, and she was hungry and irritable. She'd had only a quick cup of coffee for breakfast, and if she didn't get back to Y2K Computer Systems, Inc., in time to pick up her paycheck and cash it before the credit union office closed for the day, she wouldn't have money for lunch. Or for dinner. Or a place to live, if Mrs. Benson had anything to say about it.

"It's just plain stupid," Gina muttered to herself as she checked the address again before pulling open the door of a decrepit office building. "Everybody has known about this problem for years, even people who don't have computers. Why would anyone wait so long to fix it?"

She jabbed the *Up* button for the elevator, then waited impatiently. Down in the basement a loud, rumbling sound began and drew slowly nearer.

Gina glanced around the dreary lobby, alert as only someone bred in a large city can be to the possibility of an intruder intent upon robbery, or worse. The lobby was empty. There weren't even any pedestrians to be seen on the street beyond the smudged glass door. But then, as Gina was uncomfortably aware after the last fifteen minutes of walking, the day was so cold and windy that no one who didn't need to be would be outdoors.

She heaved a long, irritated sigh. The world outside was typical of late December, all gray and bleak. Inside the office building wasn't much better. The lobby was decorated—if *decorated* was the right word—in dull brown and beige, without even a holiday wreath. It wasn't a place where anyone would want to linger.

"Come on, come on," Gina said to the lumbering elevator. She tapped the toe of one high-heeled, fake-suede boot on the dingy linoleum floor. "I haven't got all day."

As if in response to her words, the door slid open to reveal a grubby-looking elevator.

"Doesn't anybody ever clean this dump?" Gina grumbled. She stepped inside, taking care not to brush against the walls. Her coat was secondhand, but it had cost a week's wages, and she knew she was going to have to wear it for years.

Three stories above street level the elevator stopped with a jolt that almost unbalanced its lone passenger. When the door opened Gina discovered she would have to step up a good ten inches to floor level. The realization did nothing to alter her growing conviction that the last, miserable day of the old year was going from bad to worse in a hurry.

"There must be a law about elevator safety," she

said under her breath as she planted one foot on the floor and hauled herself upward. "I bet the owner pays off the inspector so he doesn't have to fix this machine."

There were only three doors in the third-floor hallway. One of them bore a stenciled sign announcing her destination: THE BROWN DETECTIVE AGENCY. Gina turned the knob and walked into a small, cluttered office.

It looked exactly as she expected, a sleazy place where the majority of clients were probably women who wanted to hire detectives to dig up information about their adulterous husbands. Gina was glad she didn't have a husband to worry about.

After a quick glance around the unkempt room, she understood why the computer had been neglected until the last possible moment. Obviously, nobody cared about the office equipment—or the appearance of the employees.

"Well, hello there." A man wearing a stained sweatshirt and sporting an untidy beard looked up from the tabloid spread across the reception desk. Behind him a door stood ajar. It looked as if a larger office lay back there, with gray midwinter light coming through a couple of windows.

"What can I do for you, pretty lady?" asked the bearded man, letting his gaze sweep over Gina in a way that was all too familiar to her.

She wished she had worn trousers instead of a short black leather skirt and opaque black pantyhose. In fact, she wished she had worn an old-fashioned nun's habit that covered her from head to toe. Gina hated it when men looked at her the way

Mr. Hairy-Face was doing. She was glad she was through with men. No one was ever going to break her heart again. Or empty her bank account and max out her one and only credit card, either.

"Virginia McCain," she said crisply, and deliberately did not offer her hand to shake. She didn't want to touch him; she was sure his palm would be sweaty, and he'd try to hang on to her fingers too long. "I'm from Y2K Computer Systems, here to fix your equipment."

"You're kidding, right?" Mr. Hairy-Face leered at her. "You look as if you could have another reason for being here. I'll be glad to help you."

"Do you have a problem with women?" Gina demanded, making her voice hard and cold. When the man's eyebrows rose in surprise, she continued, "Having ignored the issue of Y2K until much too late, you called last week, begging for our help."

"Not me," said Mr. Hairy-Face. "That must've been Bob Brown who called. But he's not here. He's taking a few days off."

"Why am I not surprised?" Gina bestowed her best icy glare on the man. "Do you want me to fix the computer or not?"

"Yeah, sure, go ahead. I can't send out the January bills till it's fixed. It's in there." Not bothering to rise from his chair, Mr. Hairy-Face tilted his head in the direction of the inner office. His next words were filled with insinuation. "Are you going to need anything special from me, honey?"

"Nothing, except to be left alone while I work." She marched past him with her nose in the air. "By the way, I am not your honey. Call me that again, and I'll sue you for sexual harassment."

16

"Yeah, right." Mr. Hairy-Face stood up at last and took a step in her direction as if to intimidate her. He was several inches taller than Gina and a lot heavier. She kept glaring at him until he grinned at her, almost as if he knew how hard her heart was pounding in alarm. "I'm leaving now. It's time for my lunch break. If anyone calls or comes by, tell them I'll be gone for about an hour.

"By the way, *honey*," he added, shoving his face much too close to hers, "I was only asking if you wanted me to bring back anything for you to eat or drink."

"Close the door when you leave. I don't want to be interrupted," Gina responded.

She waited until he was gone before she entered the inner office. There she leaned against the door, letting out a long, shaky breath. Then she noticed there was no lock.

"Oh, well, with any luck I'll be out of here before the creep comes back, and I won't have to deal with him again," she said to herself, still using her tough voice.

Despite her desire to complete the job she'd been sent to do and leave, she stayed where she was for a minute or two, leaning against the door for support and despising herself for her weakness. Though she felt like swearing, she refused to let herself utter a single four-letter word.

She had been six years old—she couldn't recall whether she was living in her third or her fourth foster home—when she decided that she was never going to use the kind of language the people around her used. She didn't understand the impulse; she just knew she wanted to be different, so she decided she would always speak proper English and would never resort to cursing. It was her first small rebellion against the circumstances of her life.

Unfortunately, she was the only person who thought she *was* different from any of the other foster children. Everyone else saw just a skinny, sharp-faced kid with black hair that was too curly and big eyes that people teased her about, calling them cat's eyes. As soon as she was old enough to get a part-time job and earn enough money, she solved the hair problem by visiting a stylist and having the unmanageable curls cut into an ultra-short, spiky style. She had kept the same style ever since, no matter what the fashion trends were. That taming of the apparently untameable was her second act of rebellion.

Her third revolt was her decision to call herself Gina instead of Ginny, the nickname others invariably used.

She couldn't do anything about her green eyes, but few people teased her these days. Gina was too street-tough now for teasing. She never let anyone see her real feelings. Half the time she didn't even let herself know her real feelings. Life was easier that way. If she thought about how alone she was, how empty inside, without a place where she belonged or anyone who cared about her, whom she could care about in return, she'd never get any work done. Which, she told herself, was what she ought to be doing right now—working, instead of daydreaming. Dreams weren't going to pay the rent.

She surveyed her surroundings, discovering that

while the inner office was neater and cleaner than the reception area, it was no more cheerful. There was an oddly unused look about it, almost like a haunted room in an old house, in spite of the perfectly ordinary furnishings. Beige file cabinets and a bookcase stood against one wall, and the floor was covered with wall-to-wall brown carpeting. The desk in front of the windows was plain dark wood, its swivel chair upholstered in brown.

The office was unnervingly quiet, with no noise coming from the street outside. Shafts of pale sunlight slanted through the windows in shifting patterns as the clouds blew across the sky. Gina shivered, trying to shake off the eerie effect of sunlight, shadow, and complete silence, telling herself her reaction was the result of Mr. Hairy-Face's suggestive leers.

"I wish I were somewhere else," Gina whispered so intensely, it was almost a prayer. "I wish there were someone—ah, forget it. No one cares. No one ever has. No one ever will. Get over it, Gina. Live with it. Do the job, and clear out of here."

There were no papers on the desktop, no pencils or pens, no *In* or *Out* box, not even a paper clip. The computer she was to repair sat squarely in the middle of the barren surface.

"That's odd," Gina muttered, frowning. "If Mr. Brown is a neat freak, why is the reception area such a mess?"

Shrugging off the peculiar discrepancy between inner and outer offices, she dumped her purse on the floor beside the swivel chair, then pulled off her coat and draped it over the chair back.

"OK, let's see what we've got here." She quickly

discovered that the computer was plugged into a relatively new surge protector, which in turn was properly connected to the wall outlet. Wiring to both the keyboard and the printer appeared to be in good condition. When she pressed the switch, the display lit up, and the self-test sequence began to run. The familiar, soft noises of a working computer eased her tense nerves a little.

"So far, so good." Proud of her typing skills, Gina preferred to use a keyboard rather than a mouse. She derived great pleasure from the sensation of her fingers flying over the keys. She sat down in the swivel chair, pulled the keyboard closer, and waited for the screen to turn blue.

The Y2K problem that so terrified Mrs. Benson had resulted from the need to conserve expensive space in a computer's memory. Traditionally, only the last two digits of a year were used when recording dates in a computer program. Thus, when the year 2000 arrived, some computers were going to read the new year as 1900. Others would stop working altogether.

As Gina had assured Mrs. Benson, most large corporations and governments had already made the changes necessary to eliminate the problem. Unfortunately, there were no hard facts available on how many computers were *not* Y2K compliant. Predictions on what would happen at midnight ranged from airplanes falling out of the sky and elevators tumbling dozens of stories to the ground, to the stock market crashing and causing a world-wide depression while nuclear missiles launched themselves at predetermined targets, to nothing much happening at all. In Gina's opinion, the biggest problem of Y2K was the uncertainty, that allowed all kinds of shady characters to make money from the fears of the uninformed.

But whether the world entered the new millennium with disastrous results or with a snore, for a small business like The Brown Detective Agency, the issue was economically crucial. No bills could be sent out until the date on the computer was adjusted, so that charges made to clients would be properly listed. In addition, if income tax information was incorrectly dated, and tax payments weren't made on time, the agency would soon be in trouble with the IRS.

The computer Gina was dealing with was one of those programmed to reset itself to an earlier date. From the information showing on the monitor, it looked as if the automatic resetting had already taken place, which was strange. The year was showing as 1972. Even more puzzling was the time of day, which was displayed as 11:57:06 P.M., exactly twelve hours late. But it didn't matter. The system was so simple, not to say primitive, that it wasn't going to take long to reset both the date and the time.

"I'll be out of here in half an hour, forty-five minutes tops," Gina told herself, and began to type in her first command.

It was then that she made the mistake. For someone whose fingers were as nimble on the keyboard as hers were, and who was as knowledgeable about computers as she was, it was a mystery to her how it happened. Afterward, when she thought about those few crucial moments, all she could remember clearly was sitting there, staring at the screen where *792* appeared, and realizing that, instead of typing in the correction she intended, she had inadvertently transposed three of the numbers from the wrong year—and she had already hit the *Enter* key.

She was going to have to start over again to reset the program. She'd have to give up her lunch break, and she was going to have to rush to pick up her paycheck in time to cash it before the credit union closed. It was definitely not a good way to end the old year.

In desperation she hit the *Escape* key twice, hoping against all logic that she could erase the error she had made. Nothing much happened. The computer continued to display the date as 792, though the time had advanced to 11:59:10 P.M.

"The third time is the charm, so I'll try it once more," she said, and pressed the *Escape* key again.

The time display changed to 12:00:00.

"It's not midnight. It's not even noon yet. What's going on?"

As the time display changed to 12:00:01 A.M., the computer exploded. It happened silently and in slow motion. The screen simply split open before Gina's face, and a red flame enveloped her. She tried to scream, but she could not draw in enough air to make any noise at all.

She thought she was about to die, and for an instant thoughts of all the things she still wanted to do in her lifetime whirled through her distraught mind. Then the fiery redness was gone. In its place was a cold black tunnel through which she was being sucked. She couldn't move, couldn't breathe, and her last conscious thought was that, contrary to everything she had read or heard about the death experience, there was no light at all at the end of this particular tunnel.

1:30 P.M.
Friday, December 31, 1999

"Honey, I'm home!" The bearded man stuck his head around the door frame and peered into the inner office. "What the— Gone already? That's the thanks I get after I bring you a cup of coffee?"

He glanced around the empty room, then stared at the computer. The screen displayed a list of names, addresses, and charges—all the information he needed to start billing clients. On closer inspection he saw that the dates were correct.

"All right! She did fix it." Taking a swig from the cup of coffee he had intended for Virginia McCain, he sat down at the computer. "Now I can print out the January bills. Bob Brown is going to be very happy about that."

Being careful not to spill coffee on the keyboard, he set to work, alternately typing commands into the machine and sipping the hot, bitter liquid. Within a few minutes he had forgotten all about Virginia McCain.

When late evening came and Gina still hadn't returned to the shabby boardinghouse where she lived, Mrs. Benson grumbled for an hour or so. Precisely at midnight, knowing her rights as a landlady, she went into Gina's single room and packed up her few belongings. She stacked the boxes in the basement, where she kept the effects of any tenants who left without paying their rent. It was a common enough occurrence, especially with young people, who, in Mrs. Benson's opinion, were almost always flighty and unpredictable.

Sometimes renters came back later and paid what they owed, plus interest, so they could get their belongings back. Most of the time the stuff just accummulated until Mrs. Benson called in a local charity organization to haul the boxes away.

She wasn't overly concerned about Gina, although she was greatly annoyed at not receiving the rent on the room. She was also disappointed in the young woman. Sometimes people you didn't think would turn out to be deadbeats, were. It was now clear to Mrs. Benson that Gina McCain was one of them.

Chapter Two

For Gina, time had stopped. Unable to breathe or move, she was being sucked through that cold black tunnel for what seemed like an eternity. She wasn't experiencing any pain, but the dark emptiness and the lack of any sense of direction combined to produce heart-pounding terror.

Abruptly, with no warning at all, the darkness ended, and she was bathed in light. And with the awful clarity that sometimes occurs during nightmares, she knew she was falling from high above the earth. She wasn't plummeting downward, she was just drifting, softly and gently, like a feather borne on a current of air.

Still, she was certain that when she finally hit the ground, she was going to die. Oddly, though, now that she could use her eyes again, she wasn't afraid. What she felt was curiosity, so as she slowly turned head over heels, she took the opportunity to look around.

She was seeing through a mist that softened every object. Perhaps the haziness was due to oxygen deprivation after not being able to breathe for so long. Or maybe her vision had been damaged by the computer explosion. It didn't seem to matter which it was. Since she wasn't able to *do* anything about what was happening, she just accepted her predicament.

The blue sky above her contained a few streaky white clouds. Off to one side was a range of mountains, tall, jagged peaks topped with snow tinted pink and gold by a sun that appeared to be rising. Below her stretched a thickly wooded landscape. In some places the forest had been cleared and the land planted in neat rows. Born and bred in a big city, Gina wasn't sure what the crops were, and she couldn't tell the exact time of year, but the leaves on the trees indicated either spring or summer.

She did like all the different shades of green, and the way a silver stream meandered through the land. Seen through the softening mist, the landscape was prettier than Rockefeller Center in the springtime. She wondered idly if there were any hyacinths growing down there. She always liked the blue hyacinths planted beside the fountains at Rockefeller Center.

Without any effort on her part she turned over again, and this time she noticed a structure directly below her, set in the largest of the cleared areas. A wooden palisade surrounded a group of buildings made of pale, creamy stone. Right in the middle of the enclosed space was a two-story building with a higher tower at one corner. As she revolved in the air, Gina glimpsed what looked like a garden, with a few small trees and neatly laid out beds of colorful flowers.

If it were possible to breathe, she would have sighed, for she experienced an intense longing to explore that handsome central building and to sit in the garden under the trees when they were in bloom. It was a ridiculous idea. She knew nothing about gardens, and she didn't know if those were the kind of trees that ever bloomed. The longing she felt was the futile, last-minute daydream of a woman about to perish. And yet, so strong was the emotion that tears started in her eyes as she relinquished the thought.

She kept looking at the garden until she suddenly realized that she was about to crash through the red-tile roof of the big building. The tiles were just a few feet away. She was falling faster now, and she discovered that she could breathe again. She filled her lungs with one frantic gulp of air and let it out in a last, despairing shriek as she fell through the roof.

"No!"

Gina landed hard on a bed. She was aware of a mattress bouncing under the sudden impact and of a sound like that of ropes creaking. Someone was occupying the bed, and her precipitous arrival knocked the breath out of him. She heard his gasp. Of course it was a man; with her luck, it would be a very angry man.

She had fallen face down, but she was quickly

tossed over onto her back, with the man firmly on top of her, holding her thighs between his. Her wrists were wrenched up over her head and pinned there by hands so strong they were like iron shackles. With her body pressed against him from shoulder to thigh, she could feel that he was a very *manly* man, and he had a deep, loud voice. His outraged roar almost broke her eardrums.

"What in the name of all the saints are you doing? I was asleep!"

Gina was so astonished to find herself still alive that she couldn't speak at first. She looked upward, bemused, to find the ceiling of the room intact, with nary a sign that she had just crashed through it. She blinked a couple of times before she realized that the jolt of her landing had banished the mist obscuring her vision. With perfect clarity she saw her coat drift *through* the ceiling and watched it float down to cover both her and the man under a swath of black leather.

With another roar the man threw off the coat, just as Gina's heavy purse thudded to the floor beside the bed. There was still no sign of a hole in the ceiling.

Early morning light was pouring through a pair of windows at one side of the room, so Gina was able to see with unusually sharp vision the man who held her pinned to the mattress. He was staring at her as if he could not believe what his eyes beheld. Still holding on to her wrists, he shifted position so his astonished gaze could take in all of her, from her short dark hair to her black turtleneck sweater and black leather miniskirt, to her black tights and boots. Then he moved on top of her again and looked directly into her eyes.

Gina stared back into silvery gray eyes that were like mysterious, bottomless pools of ice water. His lashes and eyebrows were brown, but his hair was blond, cut to just below his ears. He was a handsome man, with a long, straight nose and a square jaw, and he had definitely been working out regularly, because he was a mass of hard muscle pressing down on her skinny body.

His mouth was beautiful. Perfectly chiseled lips curved upward to meet a tiny line at either side of his mouth. Gina guessed he was a person who smiled a lot. She caught a quick whiff of a slightly piney fragrance. He smelled good, too. Her nose seemed to be working overtime, just like her eyesight.

The unknown man's weight on her was not unpleasant; it was almost welcome. For just a moment Gina reacted to his closeness with unaccustomed warmth, relaxing a little in his grasp, almost as if she trusted him. Her lips parted in an involuntary invitation. She moistened her dry lips, and she saw how he watched the slow movement of her tongue.

That was the instant she remembered what she hated most about men.

"Get off me, you jerk!" She heaved with all her strength. The man didn't move an inch. To her fury, he just grinned at her. Then, slowly, as if to make it plain that the action was by his choice and not by her command, he rolled to the side of the bed and sat there.

"Who are you?" he demanded. He was no longer shouting. His voice was lowered to a pleasant level, but his eyes were narrowed, and Gina realized he was regarding her as if she were an enemy. "You are not one of the maidservants. I have never seen you before."

She couldn't blame him for being annoyed. After all, she had dropped into his bedroom while he was sound asleep. She disliked being wakened abruptly, and it was pretty clear that he felt the same way.

"Who are *you?*" she asked, rubbing her forehead with one freed hand, trying to clear her mind. What, exactly, had happened?

"*What* are you?" he countered.

"What do you mean, what am I? You have eyes. Can't you see I'm a woman?"

"I can see that you *appear* to be a woman. I also note that you bear no weapons, unless you carry a knife hidden in those very impractical boots."

"Where am I?" she asked.

"In my bedroom," he said. "I assumed you knew as much. Answer my questions. Who are you? Did Fastrada send you?"

"Who is Fastrada?" The instant she spoke she could see that he thought he had made a mistake. It was apparent to her that he wished he hadn't mentioned that peculiar-sounding name.

"Wait a minute," she said. "What kind of language is this we're talking? How do I know how to speak it, and how do I know it's not English?"

"I understand now," he responded. "You are mad. Who but a madwoman would dress as you do? Who else would claim that she doesn't recognize the language she is speaking as if she was born to it, or dare to say she doesn't know who is the queen of Francia?"

He put out a hand to touch her arm. Fearing he'd try to restrain her again, Gina scrambled to the wooden footboard of the bed, as far from him as she could get. It was impossible to get out on the opposite side from him, because the side of the bed was pushed against the wall. In fact, the bed looked like a studio couch or one of the fancy daybeds Gina had seen in upscale furniture advertisements.

"What I need to know," the man said, his words drawing her attention away from consideration of his bed, "is how a madwoman found her way into my private chamber without being stopped by the guards. Do you understand what I'm saying to you?" he added in a gentle tone, as if he didn't want to upset her.

"Don't patronize me!" she shouted at him. "You want to see mad? I'll show you mad! Let me out of here. So help me, if this is some kind of trick, I'll sue you for everything you've got."

"You are the one who leapt on top of me," he said quietly.

His reminder of the way she had arrived in his room quelled her brief bout of belligerence. Gina was suddenly too terrified to think rationally. She had no idea what was happening, or where she was, or who the handsome weirdo in the bed was. He ought to be ashamed of himself, talking so calmly to a woman he didn't even know when he wasn't wearing a stitch of clothing.

"Oh, dear," she whispered, gaping at the unclothed, obviously very strong man whose mus-

31

cular presence on the edge of the bed was preventing her from escaping. He didn't seem to be aware of his own nakedness, but she was having trouble keeping her eyes focused above his waist. "Do you think you could get dressed?"

"That is the first sensible thing you've said. It's an excellent idea, too."

His smile was devastating. It lit up his face and made his eyes glow. She could almost forgive him for calling her a crazy woman. She watched with great interest as he rose to pick up a loose woolen tunic and pull it over his head. The way his shoulder muscles rippled was truly fascinating. It wasn't until he had the plain blue garment on that she realized she should have seized the opportunity to escape from the room while he was distracted. But if she did escape, where would she go?

"Please tell me where I am," she said.

"I will do so, if in return you will tell me how you came into my bedchamber unchallenged by my men-at-arms."

"It's a deal." That wasn't exactly what she said. In the strange language they were speaking, which she understood perfectly, though she could speak nothing but English, the word she used was closer to *compact* or *firm agreement*.

"You are in Francia," he said.

"That tells me exactly nothing. Where in Francia?" Though she said *France*, the word came out as *Francia*, and she knew somehow that the word she'd wanted to use didn't exist yet. What was going on?

"This household is in Bavaria," he said.

"That explains the mountains." She had seen the

movie version of *The Sound of Music*. In her confused state she was eager to seize on any hint of the familiar. "Are we near Salzburg?"

"Nearer to Regensburg."

"I don't know that place."

"Don't you?" He looked at her as if he didn't believe her. Or as if he still thought she was crazy.

"Tell me how I got here."

"That," he said, "is something you have agreed to explain to me."

"I'm afraid I can't explain it. I was hoping you'd know."

"Conversation might be easier if you reveal your name," he said with a faint smile. "I am Dominick, lord of these lands, loyal noble to Charles, king of the Franks."

"Do they call you Dom or Nick?" she asked, stalling for time while she tried to figure out if he could be the crazy one.

"Dominick will do," he replied with a firmness that told her not to try to use a nickname.

"I'm Virginia McCain," she said. "People call me Gina." She spoke absently, not looking directly at him, her gaze on the object that stood propped against the wall at the end of the bed where Dominick's pillows were. It was a long, wide, ornately decorated scabbard. The shape rising above the scabbard was unmistakably a sword hilt. It would be easy enough for Dominick to reach out and grab the sword if he were attacked while in his bed. He could have used it against her. But he hadn't.

"Where do you live, Gina, when you are not creeping into the bedchambers of sleeping knights?" he asked.

"I'm from New York," she answered, her throat dry and her eyes still on the huge sword.

"I know of Yorvik, in Northumbria," Dominick said. "Alcuin came to us from Northumbria. If you are a friend of his and you are in Francia to see him, why are you not in Regensburg? You will find Alcuin there, with the king. You see, I am trying to convince myself that you are not entirely mad and that you have a reason for visiting me so unexpectedly," he ended with an encouraging smile.

His teeth were white and even. He really was a handsome man. Gina tried to force herself to stop admiring him so she could pay attention to what he was saying.

"That's the second time you've mentioned a king," she told him. "The last king of France that I know of had his head chopped off on the guillotine. I think it happened a couple of hundred years ago, while the Scarlet Pimpernel was trying to save the aristocrats. I don't know much about history and literature and all that liberal arts junk. I graduated from a technical high school." Seeing his bewildered expression, she stopped to catch her breath. She was talking too much because she was so scared.

"I already know you think I'm crazy," she said, lifting her chin in defiance of the quaver in her voice. "Well, I'm beginning to think you're nuts, too. Maybe both of us are locked up in the loony bin, and we just don't know it."

"I am not an acorn." He looked deeply offended.

"That's not exactly what I said. It's the way your language translates. What is this language, anyway?"

"Frankish." He was frowning at her.

"Let's start all over," she said, and made herself smile at him as if she wasn't ready to die from terror. "According to you, we are in Bavaria, speaking Frankish, and you are Dominick, lord of this place. Does it have a name?"

"This is Feldbruck." He was still frowning at her, but he displayed no sign of impatience. He just stood there beside the bed, wearing nothing but his thigh-length tunic, his eyes on her face as if he was trying to decide whether she really was a madwoman or just a lost and confused traveler. His bare legs were long and straight, his feet narrow and elegant. And clean. So were his hands.

Gina repressed the urge to stretch out her own hand and touch him. Then she marvelled at herself for wanting to get that close. She usually made a point of staying well out of the reach of any man.

"All right," she said, trying to make sense out of what had happened to her. "Now, you say you have a king named Charles. Does he have a number after his name? Real kings usually do, you know."

"He is Charles, son of Pepin, and he does not need a number. There is no other ruler like him." The words were spoken with quiet pride.

"Son of Pepin? That's a name I do know. When I was a kid, there was a Broadway play about Pepin." A chill went down her spine. "Dominick, what year is this?"

"It is the Year of Our Lord 792."

"That number! It's the same number I mistakenly typed into the computer. What have I done to myself?"

"What is a computer?" asked Dominick.

35

"A . . . a machine. If my suspicions are right, there is no way I can possibly explain it to you. You don't even have electricity. Or indoor plumbing." She twisted her hands together to stop them from shaking.

"I don't wish to alarm you, but it's plain to me that you are not in your right mind," Dominick said in a soothing tone of voice. "After speaking with you, I think I understand why. I see how unpleasantly thin you are, and how closely your hair has been cut, most likely to conserve your strength. Those signs, added to your confusion, must be the results of a debilitating sickness. Perhaps you contracted your illness during the past winter, when the weather was so unusually cold and snowy. What I do not understand is how or why you left your home, how you traveled here to Feldbruck, which is far from any other settlement, and how you got past my guards and into my room."

"I fell through the roof," she said.

"The ceiling is undamaged," he pointed out with calm reasonableness. "Or are you a sorceress?"

"No, definitely not," she gasped. The next thing she knew, he'd be burning her at the stake. "I don't know anything about magic."

"I choose to believe you," he said, "for now. I do wonder how you know your name—if Gina really is your name—while making no sense at all when you attempt to answer my other questions. But I assure you, I will learn how you reached Feldbruck, whether you came here with companions, and, if so, where they are. More important, I will learn *why* you are here."

"No one came with me," she said. "I'm alone. Completely alone."

His eyebrows rose in unconcealed disbelief. He looked at her as if he was trying to read her very soul. Gina kept her eyes locked on his, even though he was making her more afraid than she already was. She didn't dare tell him what she was beginning to believe, that the computer in The Brown Detective Agency had somehow sent her into the distant past.

She decided that until she could figure out how to get back to the last day of the twentieth century, there was only one thing to do. She was going to have to go along with Dominick's false conclusion and pretend to be a dazed creature recovering from a dreadful illness. Considering how confused she felt and how little she knew of the time and place where she found herself, acting dazed wasn't going to be difficult.

Chapter Three

"You cannot continue to wear those garments," Dominick said, casting a disapproving eye upon Gina's short black skirt. "There is a trunk in one of the storerooms that ought to have a dress or two in it that you can wear."

"Oh, really? Do you keep extra clothing handy in case a woman drops in on you unexpectedly?" She couldn't believe she'd said that. She sounded positively jealous. But she wasn't. She couldn't be. It was just that her nerves were badly jangled. She didn't care how many females came to see him.

"It doesn't happen very often," he responded dryly. "I will call one of my servants to help you." He began to pull on a pair of rough woolen trousers with a drawstring at the waist.

"I don't need help," Gina told him, watching

39

with compulsive attention as he pulled the drawstring close around his narrow midriff. "I can dress myself."

"But not very well, as your present costume proves." He tucked his trousers into boots of soft brown leather, then belted his tunic. "Please remain in this room until I return. I fear your present appearance will shock my people, should anyone see you."

"You forgot your sword," she said when he opened the bedchamber door. "Aren't you afraid I'll use it against you when you come back?"

He looked at the sword propped against the wall, and then he looked at her as if he was seriously considering the possibility.

"If you use both hands, you might be able to pull it from the scabbard," he said. "I doubt you are strong enough to lift it without breaking one of your delicate wrists. Certainly hands as small as yours are incapable of wielding so large a blade forcefully enough to cause much damage. However, you are welcome to try."

With that he was gone, leaving her to wonder whether he had intended an insult with those cracks about her delicate wrists and small hands. She was as strong as any woman her size. If he tried to touch her again, she'd prove how strong she was. She'd jab him in the eye and knee him in the groin, and when he doubled over she'd whack him in the back of the head with his stupid sword.

She reached for the sword hilt, wanting to have the weapon handy just in case he came back with the wrong idea in mind. Then she stopped, looking at her outstretched hand. It was small, and her wrists were tiny, just as he'd said. Could he possibly have meant his words as a compliment? Did men in this time and place actually say things like that to be nice?

She circled one wrist with her fingers, the way Dominick had held it against the mattress. His hands were much larger than hers, and she knew from trying to wrestle herself from his grasp how strong they were. She held out both hands, fingers spread wide. She wore no jewelry, not even a watch, and her nails were filed short, but they were neat, and she used hand cream every night. Her hands were her livelihood, so she took good care of them. But she had never thought of them as attractive or delicate.

"Don't be silly," she warned herself. "If he's paying compliments, it's because he wants something, and you know what it's likely to be."

With that thought in mind, she slid the sword out of its scabbard. She needed both hands to do it, just as Dominick had warned, and the weapon was so long and so heavy that when she held it straight out she could barely lift it to shoulder height. Nor could she hold it that high for more than a moment or two. She laid it on the bed. As she did so she noticed for the first time that the sheets were of finely woven linen and the quilt was so lightweight that it almost drifted out of her hands when she lifted it. A tiny fluff of feather poked through the bright blue fabric.

"Dominick is not a poor man," she murmured, smoothing the quilt into place.

He had called himself a knight, and the lord of Feldbruck. She went to the open windows to look at his land. Now that the mist was gone from her eyes, she was seeing with a clarity that only added to the strangeness of her situation.

The mountains—the Bavarian Alps, from what Dominick had told her—filled the horizon with their imposing mass. Next came the forested foothills in shade upon subtle shade of green, then the cleared area that was Dominick's farmland, and closest of all, the tall wooden palisade. Gina's unnaturally sharpened eyesight showed her the bark remaining on the upright logs that formed the palisade. Just inside the fence was a small orchard of trees bearing diminutive green fruits. The garden she had noticed while falling from the sky was out of sight on the other side of the house.

As for Dominick's bedroom, the walls were plastered and whitewashed, and the window and door frames were made of a smooth, golden wood. The twin windows were unglazed, with sturdy shutters that could be closed in bad weather. A table under the windows held a basin and a pottery pitcher full of water and covered with a folded linen towel. Opposite Dominick's bed were two wooden chests with intricate designs carved into the tops and sides. They looked like hope chests, and one of them had pillows ranged against the wall to form a seat. The other chest was topped by several books.

That was all the furniture, yet the room was comfortable in a thoroughly masculine way. She was sure Dominick didn't want or need fancy curtains, or rugs on the floor, or a dust ruffle on the bed.

Giving way to curiosity, Gina picked up one of the books and tried to flip through it. But the volume was too heavy for her to flip the pages, and it felt different in her hands from books she knew. The binding was leather, apparently stretched over a pair of thin boards. The pages were not paper.

"This must be parchment," Gina said, touching a page with respect. Her wondering gaze fixed upon the miniature painted figure of an angel with red and green and blue wings, who was holding up the first large letter of the page. The angel's halo shone with real gold applied to the parchment with incredible care. "Someone painted these decorations and wrote out this entire book by hand," she murmured in awe.

Since she could speak Frankish, perhaps she could read it, too. She studied the unfamiliar script, and after a few minutes she deciphered a couple of words. The book wasn't in Frankish, however. Gina wasn't totally uneducated in the liberal arts; she knew Latin when she saw it. Dominick read Latin books.

"So, he's not only well off and a nobleman, he's well educated, too."

She stood there, holding the first handmade book she had ever seen, while she looked out the windows at the wooded Bavarian landscape and tried to adjust to the incredible yet indisputable fact that she was in a time totally different from her own.

One part of her mind began to scream frantically, hysterically, that she wanted to return to the time where she belonged, even while another part of her being was responding to the beauty of the countryside and those soaring, snow-topped mountains.

There was also a part of her that responded to

the man who had treated her kindly and was trying to help her, even though he believed she wasn't in her right mind. He had been annoyed when she woke him out of a sound sleep, but what person, man or woman, wouldn't be upset to have a complete stranger come crashing out of nowhere? Once he recovered from his surprise, Dominick had proven to be downright nice.

"He's a man. Don't trust him," she warned herself. Still, there was a quality about Dominick—something deep in his silvery eyes and in the quiet, assured timbre of his low-pitched voice—that told her he could be trusted.

He was such a gentleman that he actually knocked at his own bedroom door when he returned. He brought with him a middle-aged woman whose sturdy form was clothed in simple brown wool, her skirt reaching to her ankles. Seeing the woman's cheerful expression and dancing blue eyes, Gina relaxed a little.

"This is Hedwiga, my chatelaine," Dominick said. "She sees to my comfort, and she will take care of you, too."

"If you will come with me, Lady Gina," Hedwiga said, smiling, "we can choose some new clothing for you."

Lady Gina? That wasn't the exact title in Frankish, but to Gina's mind that was how it translated. She wondered what Dominick had told Hedwiga about her and how he had explained her sudden appearance at Feldbruck. Gina could tell she was going to have to be very careful what she said.

Hedwiga was waiting. Gina gathered up her coat and purse, then looked to Dominick for some hint as to how she ought to behave. He only smiled benevolently and allowed Hedwiga to lead her away. She was oddly reluctant to leave Dominick, but at least the tension she felt in his presence dissipated once he was out of sight.

Dominick watched the woman who called herself Gina leave his bedchamber. He kept his smile in place until the door closed, in case she decided to look back at him.

She was a spy. Unless she really was a madwoman, which he considered unlikely after talking with her, he couldn't imagine any explanation other than spying for her sudden appearance in his bed. Whoever had sent Gina was a person lacking in subtlety and without any real understanding of Dominick's character.

The first candidate who sprang to mind was Queen Fastrada. Gina denied having been sent by the queen, but then, she would deny knowing Fastrada if she was that she-devil's agent. Fastrada was perfectly capable of setting a trap for Dominick. She had tried it once already, with his wife. Perhaps Fastrada was making a second attempt to ruin him.

There was also the possibility that one or more of his fellow nobles could be conspiring to draw him into a rebellious scheme. Dominick was aware of the resentments smoldering just below the peaceful surface of Frankish life. Even in isolated Feldbruck he had heard the rumors.

He considered several ways to discover proof of who had sent Gina to him and why. He decided to begin with the simplest method: being kind to her and encouraging her to talk in hope that she'd mis-speak and thus provide a hint as to her purpose and her accomplices.

If sympathy failed, he'd threaten dire punishment unless Gina told him what he wanted to know, and he'd hint at mercy if she cooperated. It was unlikely, yet possible, that one of his own people was involved and had helped Gina sneak into his bedroom. If that proved to be the case, he'd find out who it was, and then he'd drag Gina and her accomplice to Regensburg in chains and turn them over to Charles. If he could prove that Charles's queen was involved in the scheme, so much the better. He owed Fastrada retaliation for what she had tried to do to him.

If nothing else worked, he'd seduce Gina and then coax a confession from her in the aftermath of passion. It wasn't a method he preferred, but he'd do it if he had to. Whether the devious and bloody-minded queen of the Franks or a rebellious nobleman was behind Gina's appearance in his home, Dominick's honor and his life were at stake, along with the welfare of Feldbruck. To preserve what he cherished, he was willing to relinquish the private vow of celibacy he had made to himself when his marriage ended.

He recalled the way Gina's slender body had softened beneath his as he held her down on his bed. She was so delicate, yet so fiery in spirit. There was passion in her. He knew it instinctively. Yet she seemed so innocent, so lost and alone. He tried in vain to remember the last time a woman had made such an impression on him.

With considerable bitterness he reminded himself that the chances were good that, far from being innocent, Gina knew exactly what she was doing. Worse, if she proved not to be Northumbrian but Frankish-born, as he suspected from her speech, and if she was involved with any rebellious nobles, then she was a traitor.

Dominick was and always had been completely loyal to his king. Duty and honor both required that he find proof whether Gina really was a spy, and if she was, who her associates were and what they intended. Upon leaving her a short time ago he had ordered a band of his men-at-arms into the countryside in search of any strangers found loitering or camping on his lands without reason. Once he had collected the evidence he needed, he'd take Gina to stand trial before Charles. And if she was found guilty, he was going to watch her die.

Hedwiga conducted Gina to a chamber several doors down the corridor from Dominick's room. It was furnished in much the same style, though the eiderdown quilt on the bed was bright red instead of blue, and there was only one wooden chest, which sat in the middle of the floor.

"Dominick ordered it brought from the attic storeroom," Hedwiga explained. "Since you haven't brought a clothing chest of your own with you, you will use this one. Now, let's see what's in here. I haven't looked inside since Lady Hiltrude left us, but I put a lot of lavender and sweet woodruff in the folds of every garment when I packed them to discourage any moths."

"Who is Lady Hiltrude?" Gina asked.

"She was married to Dominick, though not for

long. The silly girl divorced him and went to live at the convent at Chelles. Said she'd rather be a nun than wife to a man like him. Can you imagine such a thing?"

"The convent at Chelles," Gina repeated, to be certain she hadn't misunderstood. She said no more, though she was absolutely dying to ask what the departed Hiltrude had meant by *a man like him*. As Dominick's wife, Hiltrude would have known all his dirty little secrets. Every man had them, as Gina knew too well. Apparently Dominick was no better than any other man, despite his gentlemanly veneer. Having discovered what he was really like, his wife had left him. Gina experienced a stab of disappointment at that realization.

"Well, of course, Chelles is a nice place, or the king's own sister, the Lady Gisela, wouldn't live there, would she?" Hedwiga said. She pulled a green woolen gown from the chest and shook it out, smoothing away a few wrinkles and checking the fabric. "Not a sign of moths. I always say if you store clothing properly, it will last for years, and then you can use it again for someone else. Let me see, now, there must be a shift or two in here, and some stockings, too. While I'm looking, you take off what you're wearing," Hedwiga ordered. She spared a disapproving glance for Gina's black outfit before she leaned over the open chest again and began to pull out more items of clothing.

When she realized that the kind of underclothes she wore were nonexistent in the year 792, Gina decided to keep on her bra and briefs. She did, however, remove her boots and heavy winter tights and put on a pair of soft leather shoes that tied with leather thongs. She found them a lot more comfortable than her high-heeled boots.

She agreed to wear the short-sleeved linen shift Hedwiga handed to her, thinking the green woolen gown would be scratchy against her bare skin. The linen flowed softly over her body, and Gina's oddly acute senses welcomed the touch with unfamiliar, sensual pleasure. When she put the dress on over the shift, the wool proved to be so finely woven that it didn't scratch at all.

The dress was too big through the torso but, according to Hedwiga, too short by several inches. Gina thought ankle length too long and said so.

"You cannot wear the skimpy garments you had on," Hedwiga told her sternly. "Not even the shameless women who ply their trade in the worst part of Regensburg would consent to be seen in such clothing. Lady Gina, you must be properly dressed."

There really wasn't any answer Gina could make to that. Hedwiga knew better than she what was proper attire for the late eighth century. She let Hedwiga fasten an embroidered fabric belt around her waist, which made the dress fit a little better.

"It's too bad about your hair," Hedwiga said, trying unsuccessfully to fluff Gina's rudimentary curls, "though, of course, it can't be helped, and it will grow again, in time. Mine was cut short once, too, when I was very sick."

"Oh?" Gina remarked, hoping Hedwiga would keep talking. The woman knew everything Gina needed to know to pretend that she belonged in the eighth century.

"When I was fourteen, I developed a dreadful

fever and a bright red rash all over my body," Hedwiga said. "My mother feared I would die, until the doctor bled me twice and insisted that my hair be cut right down to my scalp to save my strength. According to him, the strength of the body flows into the hair. As you can see, the doctor was right. I recovered and am perfectly healthy now. So will you be healthy again."

"With no antibiotics—no medicine," Gina corrected herself when Hedwiga seemed perplexed.

"Well, one can use potions made with herbs," Hedwiga said, "but there is nothing better than a doctor who knows what he's doing. Do you always paint your face that way?"

Gina responded somewhat defensively to the sudden change of subject. "This is nothing—only mascara and eyeshadow and a little powder. The lipstick I put on this morning is probably worn off by now. You should see some of the women in New York. They wear lots more makeup than I do. Oh, dear." She stopped, judging by Hedwiga's expression that she was talking too much.

"The ladies at the royal court paint their faces," Hedwiga said, frowning her disapproval. "I suppose it's the custom in Northumbria, too."

"Northumbria? Oh, right." Apparently Dominick had repeated his mistaken assumption that Gina was from a place called Yorvik in Northumbria. Since she knew nothing about such a town, she decided it was time to change the subject again, before Hedwiga could begin asking questions about her supposed home. "Thank you for the clothes. Is there anything I can do for you in return?"

50

"You are a guest," Hedwiga responded, patting her arm in a kindly way. "What's more, you've been sick. You ought to rest until you are completely recovered."

"There must be some little thing I can do." Once she was out of the bedroom she intended to investigate Dominick's house with the idea of trying to find a way to get back to New York.

"Well, there is a basket of mending," Hedwiga said.

"I'm sorry. I don't know how to sew," Gina said.

"Can't sew? How strange. I thought every girl was taught at a young age to make neat stitches."

"Customs are different in Northumbria," Gina said, seizing on the first excuse she could think of.

"I see." Hedwiga thought for a moment. "I suppose you could work in the kitchen. Mixing and kneading the bread will probably be too strenuous for you, but you could help to chop the vegetables and cook the stew."

"I can't cook," Gina confessed. "I never learned how." She could see that Hedwiga was beginning to wonder if there was any womanly chore Gina *was* able to perform. In her own time and place Gina considered herself quite competent. With her computer skills, she could always find a job, even if she wasn't paid very much. But it was rapidly becoming clear that in the eighth century she possessed no useful skills at all.

"You are too frail to assist with the laundry," Hedwiga said. "Scrubbing and wringing out sheets and clothing is heavy work. But I suppose you could help to spread out the smaller pieces to dry."

"I'm sure I could do that," Gina said, eager to agree to something Hedwiga suggested.

"Come along, then. First I will show you the house, so you won't get lost."

From seeing the main building as she drifted downward through the air, Gina remembered that it was built in an H-shape, with covered walkways on its inner sides. Now she learned that Dominick's chamber was on the upper left part of the H. There were several other bedrooms on the second level, and a large great hall directly below, on the ground level.

The crossbar of the H contained a formal reception room and an office for the overseer of Dominick's farmlands. The remaining wings housed the servants and men-at-arms, with stables set off to one side, near the entrance gate of the palisade. The kitchen and laundry were in a separate building directly behind the great hall—according to Hedwiga, an arrangement intended to lower the risk of a damaging fire.

The laundry was a hot and steamy place, with cauldrons of water boiling over open flames. A pair of women, sleeves rolled above their elbows, labored over soapy tubs. Another pair rinsed the laundry in separate tubs, wringing out the finished pieces. Meanwhile, three teenaged boys lugged pails of hot water from the cauldrons to the tubs.

"Ella," Hedwiga called to a rosy-cheeked girl, "Lady Gina is a guest, but she has offered to help us. I want you to show her what to do with the finished laundry."

"I'd enjoy some company, and especially help with the sheets," Ella responded, grinning at Gina with easy friendliness. "There's a basket ready and waiting for us."

The wrung-out laundry was piled into an oval wicker basket with handles at either end. Ella seized one handle, Gina took the other, and together they carried the heavy load through the back door of the laundry. They came out of the hot room onto a swath of grass edged all around by bushes. With Ella providing instruction, she and Gina shook out each piece of wet laundry and spread it over the bushes to dry in the sun. The sheets and other large items they spread on the grass.

"Doesn't everything just get dirty again as it dries?" Gina asked.

"We shake any loose leaves or debris off the bushes and then sweep the grass first thing on laundry day," Ella explained.

"Why don't you string a line and hang the laundry on it?" Gina asked. "That's what people do where I live. I've seen lots of clotheslines strung from building to building."

"The wind would blow everything away," Ella said with a laugh. "It's better to dry the linens spread flat, with clean stones to hold down the larger pieces."

There was a basket of stones in the drying yard, and these they laid on the corners of the sheets to keep them in place. A second and third basket of wet clothing and linens arrived, carried to the yard by the other women and left for Ella and Gina to see to.

Gina found the work unexpectedly satisfying, in large part because Ella was such a pleasant, chatty companion who did not ask disconcerting questions. Ella was willing to talk about herself and her own life, so Gina encouraged her to chatter. Soon she knew all about the fifteen-year-old Ella's budding romance with Harulf, who was one of Dominick's men-at-arms.

"Be careful," Gina warned, recalling herself at that age. "Sometimes men take advantage of young women, and sometimes they mistreat girls."

"Not Harulf. Besides, no man would dare, not here at Feldbruck. Dominick wouldn't allow it."

The total conviction in Ella's voice made Gina cease her attempts to spread a sheet flat in the brisk wind so she could stare at the girl.

"Really?" Gina said. "Dominick makes other men behave themselves with women? That seems unusual."

"If you knew Dominick well, you wouldn't think it at all unusual."

"Yet I understand Dominick's wife left him. From what I've heard, Lady Hiltrude would rather live in a convent than with him."

"She claimed it was because Dominick was ruled a bastard," Ella said, shrugging as if such a statement was unimportant. She didn't notice that Gina was gaping at her, openmouthed, and she continued to spread a pair of men's linen underdrawers on a bush while she talked. "If you ask me, I think all of that was just an excuse. I think the truth is that Hiltrude was afraid to have children. Some girls are. But if that's the case, they shouldn't allow their fathers to arrange marriages for them, now should they? It's upsetting to their parents and cruel to their husbands if they change their minds later."

"Even crueler to call the husband a bastard,"

Gina said in hope of eliciting still more information about Dominick.

"Everyone here at Feldbruck thinks the new rule is a bad thing," Ella said. "It's unfair. So many people were hurt by it, and some even turned against the Church because of it. But that's the way it is when the pope makes rules for lesser folk. I suppose in time it won't matter so much. Eventually, everyone who was affected by the change will be dead."

Gina couldn't ask what the new rule was without betraying her total ignorance of life in eighth-century Francia. She didn't have the chance, anyway, for Hedwiga appeared, stepping carefully around all the laundry Gina and Ella had spread on the grass.

"Well done," the chatelaine said, nodding toward the empty baskets. "Ella, you are needed in the kitchen."

After Ella took her leave and hurried off with the empty laundry baskets, Hedwiga turned her attention to Gina.

"Your face is flushed," Hedwiga said. "You've been in the sun too long."

"I've enjoyed it," Gina responded truthfully. "Ella is a very nice girl."

"We appreciate your help," Hedwiga said, "but you must rest now. We don't want you to fall ill again. I suggest an hour or two in your room, where it is cool." She made the suggestion sound like an order.

"I'd rather sit in the garden," Gina said. "Will you tell me how to get there?"

"Go through the kitchen and across the great

hall, then out of the hall by the side door," Hedwiga said, adding, "but be sure to stay in the shade."

"I will."

The garden contained four oblong beds of plants, each edged with stones, and there was a sundial in the middle, where the gravel paths intersected. The trees were taller than they had appeared from the air, and the flowers were brighter in color and more riotous in growth, spilling out of their neatly defined beds and tumbling into the paths. Gina could almost feel their need to grow without restraint, and she wondered at her odd, distinctly emotional reaction to a few simple plants.

She discovered a stone bench under one of the trees and sat on it, leaning back against the tree trunk and closing her eyes for a moment to block out one of her newly sharpened senses. Her fingers still tingled from handling wet sheets and underclothes, and she remained keenly aware of the textures of linen and wool against her body.

As she sat there quietly, she was struck by how peaceful Feldbruck was compared to New York. No one was shouting or quarreling. No car horns or radios were blaring or sirens wailing or trash trucks clattering. Instead, she heard insects buzzing. She heard laughter in the distance. And she could smell the garden. She took several deep breaths, then opened her eyes and looked around, trying to adjust to the fragrances and colors that impressed themselves on her mind with glorious intensity. It was like coming alive for the first time, with the world bright and new around her.

Often she had peered into New York florist shops

with longing, and she always paused at street-corner flower stands to look at and smell the blooms they sold. Seldom had she been able to indulge herself in the extravagance of fresh flowers, and she didn't know the names of many. Roses, daffodils, anemones, and her favorite, hyacinths, because their fragrance was so lovely—that was about the extent of her horticultural knowledge. She wasn't sure what she was seeing in Dominick's garden. The only plant she recognized was a clump of white Easter lilies, and she definitely smelled mint. Other than that, the beds before her were a mystery.

Bees droned their way from flower to flower, multicolored butterflies flitted here and there as if they were very busy, the sun beamed down, and Gina discovered within herself a contentment that was the fulfillment of the longing she had known while gazing down at the garden as she fell from the twentieth century to the eighth. Now that she was actually in the garden, she was able to set her many fears aside for a little while and take pleasure in the beauty that lay before her. For a few minutes she was happy.

She heard a step on the gravel path and knew it was Dominick even before she turned her head to look at him. She simply *sensed* his presence, and the sight of him gladdened her heart—the same heart she usually kept tightly guarded against any wayward emotions.

"This is for you," he said, handing her a leafy stem on which three pink flowers clustered. "Be careful of the thorns. Every rose has them, you know."

"These don't look like any florist's roses I've ever seen. They have only five petals." She bent her head, sniffing at the flowers. "What kind of roses smell so sweet? It's like holding a bottle of expensive perfume in my hand." Struck giddy by the scent, she inhaled again.

"The fragrance makes the prick of the thorn worthwhile," Dominick said.

He sat next to her on the bench, so close that his sleeve brushed against hers and she could feel the warmth of his arm. To her own surprise, Gina experienced no compulsion to move away from him.

"Thank you, Dominick. No one has ever given me flowers before."

"I find that difficult to believe," he said, his gaze on the garden, rather than on Gina. "Roses don't last long. Lovely things seldom do."

He looked so wistful that she wondered if he was thinking of the wife who had left him in favor of a convent. Knowing the subject was none of her business, still Gina tried to think of a way to mention it. Ella's remark that Dominick had been ruled a bastard intrigued her—and that was a subject that *did* touch on her own life. Besides, she told herself as her fears returned, the more she knew about Dominick and his world, the more likely she was to discover a way to return to her own time and place. Before she could begin, however, Dominick took control of the conversation.

"Now that you are properly clothed," he said, "I would like you to reveal how and why you suddenly appeared at Feldbruck."

"Why do you want to know?" To her own ears

she sounded rude, but as far as she could tell, Dominick didn't take offense. He just smiled a little, his chiseled lips curving upward in a tantalizing way. His smile and his gift of roses combined to make Gina's insides twist with guilt. If she was ever going to get back to New York, she had to be ruthless about pumping him for any scrap of information that might help. She couldn't afford to be sidetracked by his kindness.

"Gina, what is wrong?" Dominick put a hand over hers, and she did not pull her fingers from his grasp. "If you are in danger, if you are being forced to act against your will, I can protect you. Please trust me."

"I can't tell you. I wish I could," she whispered, certain he'd never believe her story. "There is nothing you can do."

With a frown marring his handsome face, he removed his hand from hers. The loss of the warm contact between them produced a longing that unsettled Gina almost as much as did her displacement in time.

"Very well," he said quietly. "I'll not intrude on your privacy. Should you change your mind—"

"I won't," she said, turning away to hide her face from him. She didn't want him to see the tears his persistent kindness had caused. "I can't."

"As you wish. But know this, Gina: I stand ready to help you, by armed force if need be. If there is truly nothing I can do, then I am willing to listen, and to keep your secrets. I do not betray my friends."

He left her then and headed into the house without looking back, leaving her filled with yearnings she was afraid to examine too closely. Instead, she thought about what he had said.

Dominick was the strangest man she had ever met. How could he think of her as a friend when he hadn't even known her for a full day, when he knew nothing about her? Could there be people in this time who actually refused to betray a trust?

Never in her life had Gina known someone she could depend upon completely. In her experience, everyone always had a private agenda, and letting Gina down at a crucial moment was usually part of that agenda.

She almost dared to hope that Dominick was different. Perhaps if she stayed in the eighth century long enough, a time would come when she could tell him the truth about how she had reached Feldbruck. But not yet. Not yet.

However, she had discovered a way to connect with him. She didn't like being manipulative, but she couldn't see that she had any choice. She would tell Dominick about her past, leaving out the fact that she had been born in a different century. Then she would encourage him to talk about his own life, and she'd listen carefully for any information that might help her to get back to New York.

Judging by what Hedwiga and Ella had told her, she and Dominick had a lot more in common than he knew.

Dominick left the garden with a new possibility to consider. It hadn't previously occurred to him that Gina could be forced into a scheme she didn't want to be part of out of fear for her life, or for the life of someone she loved. If she was being coerced, and Dominick could prove it, when he took her to the royal court he could plead with Charles to save her life. The eagerness with which he contemplated the opportunity to prove her a victim rather than a conspirator shook the very foundations of the orderly world he had built for himself over the past few years.

He told himself he had no choice in the matter. He was honor-bound to uncover the real reason for Gina's presence in his home.

Chapter Four

At Feldbruck the main meal was at midday. Dominick's entire household gathered in the wood-panelled great hall to feast on game birds roasted on a spit over the kitchen fire, a vegetable stew, and a tart made of custard flavored with walnuts and dried apples.

Only Dominick sat in a chair. Everyone else was on a bench or a stool, including Gina, who was given a place of honor on the bench next to Dominick.

There were no forks. Gina stared at the wooden bowl in front of her and at the spoon that looked as if it was made out of cream-colored plastic, and she wondered how she was expected to eat without a knife or fork. Dominick came to her rescue.

"Since you have no knife of your own, I'll cut

63

some meat for you," he said, reaching for the platter of roasted birds a servant had set before him.

Gina watched as he neatly sliced a piece of breast meat from one of the birds, then speared it on the point of his blade and offered it to her. She did the only thing she could; using her fingers, she lifted the meat off Dominick's knife and ate it. Then, since there were no napkins, she licked her fingers. Everyone around her was doing the same, except for the men-at-arms, who were eating directly from their knives. Gina tried to be dainty about licking her fingers, and she guessed she was succeeding, for no one remarked on her table manners or lack thereof. The vegetable stew was easier to deal with.

"What is this spoon made of?" she asked, lifting a mouthful of the tasty stew to her lips.

"There is a man here at Feldbruck who is skilled in making many useful objects out of horn," Dominick answered. "Each autumn after the butchering is done, he collects the horns from the slaughtered animals, cures them, and spends the winter carving new utensils."

The explanation made sense to Gina. She had once read in a magazine that horn spoons were preferred over silver for eating caviar. The salt in caviar tarnished silver but did not affect horn. She chuckled to herself at the thought. She had never tasted caviar, and she wasn't likely to do so here at Feldbruck. Still, she couldn't regret that particular loss, for to her newly awakened taste buds all the food served at Dominick's table was delicious. The fresh, homemade bread was especially good, dark and chewy and still warm from the oven. It was better than any bread she had ever tasted in the twentieth century. She ate three thick slices, much to Hedwiga's approval.

"The more you eat, the sooner you will be completely well again," the chatelaine said. "You are much too thin for good health or good looks."

"That's a switch," Gina murmured to herself. "And here I thought a woman had to be thin to be beautiful."

After the meal began, a heavyset, middle-aged man arrived in the hall and took a place at the head table, where Dominick, Gina, and Hedwiga were sitting. Dominick introduced the man to Gina as Arno, the overseer of Feldbruck farmland. The two men fell into a serious discussion of crops. From then on, neither paid much attention to Gina, which was fine with her; she found Dominick's household an interesting place, and she entertained herself by trying to guess what each person in the hall did for a living.

As the meal ended Ella approached Gina, bringing with her the man with whom she had been sitting at one of the lower tables.

"This is my Harulf," Ella said, blushing a little.

Harulf was a brawny fellow with pale brown hair and a luxuriant mustache that drooped down on either side of his mouth in a style that many of the men-at-arms wore. Gina noticed how he regarded Ella with something close to adoration. When Harulf spoke to the girl his voice was soft, and his touch on her arm was gentle. Observing the way Harulf treated Ella, Gina decided that perhaps her new friend was right and Harulf was one of those rare men who wouldn't hurt the woman he claimed to love.

"Friend," Gina said softly, testing the word, and the idea. "If even a fierce man-at-arms can have a kind heart, which I think Harulf does, then why can't I have a friend in Ella?"

After the remains of the meal were cleared away, Hedwiga told Gina and Ella to fold and put away the laundry they had spread out to dry during the morning. That meant they had to pay a visit to Dominick's room, to store his shirts and clean underclothes in the wooden chest on which his books rested.

Dominick wasn't there. Gina had heard him telling Hedwiga that he and Arno were going to ride out to inspect a newly cleared field that was being prepared for planting with a late-summer crop. Gina stood looking around his room, still amazed to see no sign of her precipitous arrival through the ceiling plaster. She was intensely aware of Dominick's presence in every item, every stick of furniture in the room. His sword was gone. She supposed he was wearing it. Everything else was just as she had seen it at daybreak—or would be after she replaced his books.

Kneeling beside the clothing chest, she picked up the books one by one, stroking their leather bindings as she restacked them on the lid Ella had just shut. She held the book containing the painting of the angel against her bosom, thinking of angels flying. Then she thought of the way she had floated slowly through the air to end her fall uninjured, in the room where she now was, almost as if a supernatural force had guided her to a safe landing at Feldbruck.

Sure, Gina thought cynically. *It was the angel in*

charge of computer explosions. Get hold of yourself, girl. You don't believe in all that mushy New Age stuff. There was nothing supernatural about it. You made a mistake on the computer, and you have to figure out a way to correct it so you can go back. Nice as Feldbruck is, you don't belong here.

Was it possible that the way for her to return to her own time lay through Dominick's room? It was the place where she had entered the eighth century; might it also be the place from which she could leave? Through the ceiling? But how? She stared up at the ceiling, looking for a sign, a piece of evidence. Then, for a moment or two, she wondered if there was something about Dominick that had brought her to this particular time and place.

"Gina?" From the doorway Ella regarded her with a puzzled expression. "Are you coming? We still have to put the sheets away in the linen room."

"Yes, I'm finished." Gina set down the last book and rose from her knees. She paused long enough to glance around at Dominick's belongings once again, then shook her head. "I have to stop thinking about him. No man is worth twisting myself into knots, especially not a man from another century. If I have any brain left at all after what has happened, I'll concentrate on getting out of here."

"What did you say?" Ella asked.

"Just that I have to stop daydreaming and begin thinking seriously about what I intend to do next," Gina answered.

"That's always a good idea," Ella said with a laugh.

* * *

The evening meal was bread and cheese, washed down with ale or wine. Gina didn't care for the ale, but she did like the wine. It tasted like slightly fizzy grape juice, and it didn't have much kick to it. She knew better than to ask for a cup of hot tea, which was what she really wanted to drink. She seriously doubted if the people gathered in the great hall knew that China or India existed, so it was a pretty sure guess that they wouldn't know about tea.

Having imbibed three cups of wine for whatever courage they would impart, Gina left the table soon after Dominick did and followed him out of the hall to the garden.

The sun was low in the sky, casting a golden light on the rustling tree leaves and sending long violet shadows across the beds of herbs and flowers. The brisk wind that earlier had made laying out the laundry difficult was now a gentle breeze. The evening air was cool yet with a hint of summer warmth to come.

Gina saw Dominick bend to smell the lilies. Then he straightened, and though he hadn't looked in her direction, she knew he was aware of her presence, just as she had known that morning that he was in the garden.

"It's my favorite time of day," Dominick said. "Work is finished until tomorrow, Feldbruck is at peace, and soon the stars will begin to shine."

"Were you born here?" she asked, coming to stand beside him. "Have you lived here always? It seems to me you love this place."

"I do love it, perhaps because I won these fields and woodlands by my own sword at a time when there was nothing left except my sword that I dared to call mine. The first time I rode through the gate, I felt as if I was coming home. What Feldbruck is today I have built by my own effort and with the help of the people who were living here when Charles granted the land to me at the end of the Bavarian campaign."

"You sound like a pioneer who ventured into a new land to build a new life," she said. "From what I have seen of your people, they like and respect you, which means you are a good landlord." Then, before she lost her nerve, she launched into her scheme to learn as much as she could from him, in hope of discovering how to return to New York City. "Earlier today you said you'd listen and keep my secrets if I wanted to talk."

"So I will." He faced her, the lowering sun behind him turning his blond hair into a fiery halo. She couldn't see his expression, but his voice was gentle. "You may speak freely to me. Shall we sit where we did this morning?"

"If you don't mind, I'd rather walk. I'm a bit nervous. I don't usually talk about my past. It's not a nice story. In fact, it's pretty awful." He did not respond to what she said. She began to walk down the gravel path, and Dominick fell into step by her side. Because of what she already knew about him from Hedwiga and Ella, the first part of her story wasn't terribly difficult to tell. She didn't think he would be shocked by it. "My parents weren't married. I never knew either of them. I was told that my mother was very young and my father deserted her as soon as he learned I was on the way, so she gave me up for adoption."

Gina paused, frowning a little. The words she was speaking were slightly different in Frankish, so the tale didn't seem quite as stark and unpleasant as it did in English. Dominick's reaction helped to explain the difference.

"That is a situation common to Francia, as well as to your homeland," he said. "Here in Francia, children whose parents cannot raise them are usually given as oblates to convents or monasteries, to be trained into the religious life as they grow up. Occasionally, childless couples will adopt children, usually the offspring of deceased relatives. There are some unwanted children, fortunately not many, who are simply abandoned, left to fend for themselves."

"Well, I was adopted by a couple who had no children of their own," Gina said. "For the first three years of my life I guess I was among the wanted children. I'm sorry to say I have no memory of that time. When I was not quite four, both of my adoptive parents were killed in a car accident."

"They were riding in a cart?" Dominick asked, looking puzzled. "Why weren't they on horseback? Were they farmers?"

"No, they . . . they lived in the city. It's difficult to explain. Let's just say the cart overturned. I was only slightly injured, but I was left an orphan, with no other family, so I was put into a foster home."

"Fostering is not unknown in Francia," Dominick said, nodding his understanding. "Often nobles send their sons to live in each other's households for a time. The custom helps to build friendships, so the nobles don't fight among themselves as frequently as they once did. Then there is the

70

palace school, where intelligent boys can be sent to learn their letters and counting. That's a kind of fostering, too, with Charles as the foster father. Nor is it unknown for him to take in the orphaned offspring of his nobles and raise them with his own children."

"That isn't the kind of foster home I'm talking about," Gina said. "The government paid people to take me in. Actually, I was moved around quite often. Some of the foster families I was sent to were kind enough. It really wasn't their fault if I had the feeling I ought to be somewhere else. Then there were the other foster parents, the ones who never should have been given a child to care for."

Perhaps it was the edge of bitterness in her voice that made Dominick pause on his way along the path and look hard at her. "Were you beaten?"

"Oh, yes. Often." She couldn't repress the anger or the emotional fatigue that drained her whenever she recalled those unhappy days. The reaction came from years of going over and over that period of her life, wondering what she had done wrong. She had never found a satisfactory answer. "Beatings and worse. Some of the other children were as nasty as the grownups. Especially the bigger boys." She paused, gritting her teeth at the memory.

"Anyone who mistreats a person who is smaller or weaker is a coward," Dominick declared. "Was there no one to whom you could complain?"

"I was too afraid. While I was still little, I hoped someone would notice the bruises and help me. But no one ever did, and after a while I lost hope. As soon as I was old enough, I began living on my own. I worked at a part-time job while I was in high school. I've been supporting myself since I was sixteen."

She was a little surprised at herself for revealing so much emotion. She had learned early in life that men weren't interested in how she felt. Dominick's understanding response startled her.

"It is a terrible thing to be unable to trust," he said softly. "To know that you are alone and unloved."

Though he didn't comment about the details of her story that did not fit into his Frankish world, Gina reminded herself to speak more carefully in the future. Then she slammed the door shut on the emotions that were threatening to break out into tears, so she could launch into her fact-finding mission.

"You know about being left alone, don't you?" she asked very deliberately.

"It's no secret that I have been declared illegitimate." Dominick's voice turned cooler. "I assume that is what you have been trying to learn from me by recounting your own story. I wonder why you did not simply ask. I also wonder what else you are determined to discover. However, you have eliminated one possibility I was considering."

"What possibility? What are you talking about?"

"I was wondering if someone you love was being threatened."

"I don't know what you mean. I don't love anyone, so there's no one whose safety I'd worry about. Why did you think so?"

"Gina, I want to know who sent you to Feldbruck, and why. Was it Fastrada? If it was, you must tell me. I am trying to help you."

"I never heard of anyone named Fastrada until you mentioned her earlier today. Dominick, everything I've just said to you is the truth."

"It may be. I hope it is. But I don't believe you have told me your entire truth."

"My life has taught me to be cautious," she said.

"I understand. If Fastrada has sent you, she chose her agent well." His hand touched her cheek, his fingertips stroking gently across her skin until he held the nape of her neck.

Gina reminded herself with unusual forcefulness that she did *not* like men, and for good reason. Then she admitted to herself that she did rather like Dominick. She enjoyed a quick mental vision of him with sword in hand, defending her against some of the cruel bullies of her childhood. She wondered what his reaction would be if she told him everything about herself.

While she was considering doing just that, Dominick leaned forward and placed his mouth on hers. Gina was so startled that she gasped and opened her lips. Dominick held the back of her head a little more firmly and kissed her a bit harder.

There was no force involved. There was only Dominick's warm mouth on hers, his tongue teasing along the edge of her lips, and his fingers splaying into her short hair. He wasn't holding her tightly. She could have wrenched her head away, could have protested what he was doing. That she stayed where she was and allowed him to continue kissing her was an amazement to her own mind.

When he finally drew back and she saw the light in his silvery-gray eyes, she began to tremble. To her horror she wanted him to kiss her again, this time with his arms around her and her body close to his. For a woman who had firmly and permanently rejected the idea of a man's intimate embrace, the spark of desire that Dominick engendered in her soul was terrifying.

"Who are you?" Dominick asked, his voice just above a whisper.

"I told you this morning," she said, attempting icy reserve and failing miserably, "I am Gina McCain."

"No," he insisted, still using the same soft voice. "Except for the fact that you are an orphan and were unkindly treated during your youth, you have told me nothing important."

"My childhood may not be important to you," she exclaimed, "but it is to me!"

"You become evasive whenever I mention the reason why you are at Feldbruck," he said. "Perhaps if I answer your questions, you will be willing to respond more fully to mine. What do you want to know?"

"Are you serious?" she inquired.

"Completely. Be forewarned, though. I will not reveal any secret I am sworn to keep, nor will I betray any oath I have taken. But I have nothing to hide." He paused, folding his arms across his wide chest, watching her as if he expected her to do something wild and foolish. "I am waiting for your first question."

"Why were you ruled a bastard?" she asked, careful not to reveal who had been talking to her. She harbored a strong suspicion that, in spite of his kindness, Dominick didn't trust her at all, and she didn't want to get Hedwiga or Ella into trouble for gossiping with her. "What is this strange new rule the pope has proclaimed?"

"There are few Franks who don't know the answers to those questions."

"I am not a Frank. I've told you so several times already. Explain the new rule to me."

"It's simple enough," he said. "The rule has three parts. The Church has ordained that no marriage is legal unless it is blessed by a priest. Children born of marriages not so blessed are illegitimate. Bastards cannot inherit." His voice was flat, betraying no emotion.

"If they made a rule," Gina said after a moment of thought, "it must mean there were a lot of unblessed marriages."

"That is so. It was the old Frankish way," Dominick responded. "By tradition, the two families agreed to the marriage, the man and woman stated before witnesses that they wanted to live together, and there was a feast to celebrate the union. The next day the bride received her *morgangabe.*"

"A morning gift, after the wedding night," Gina translated the last word to be sure she understood it correctly.

"Exactly. We called the arrangement *friedelehe*, and all Franks accepted it."

"Common-law marriage," Gina said.

"Frankish marriages were made that way for centuries, and no one saw the need for priests. Nor did we ever consider any child a bastard. The parents might err, they might choose not to marry at all, but the child was not to blame. All children inherited equally from their parents."

"Even girls?" Gina asked.

"Of course." He looked surprised by the question. "Why shouldn't girls inherit?"

"The more I learn about you Franks, the better I like you," Gina said. "What you are telling me is, the clergymen in Rome saw a system that was working just fine, so they tried to fix it. Why? For money and power? I'm sure the priests receive gifts in return for bestowing these newly required marital blessings. And the power part of the deal is obvious: priests now have the final say about who marries whom."

"You have an interesting way of stating facts," Dominick said with dry humor.

"Am I right that your parents were married by the old *friedelehe* system?"

"They were."

"Couldn't they simply have had their marriage blessed to make it legal when the new rule went into effect?"

"My mother died when I was still a baby," Dominick said, "so there was no way to prevent the Church from ruling me illegitimate. My younger half brother is more fortunate. My father's second wife, being deeply religious, insisted upon a priestly blessing before she would go to my father's bed."

"I get it," Gina interrupted. "Your father's second marriage was acceptable under the new rule, and any children born to that marriage could inherit from his estate, but you couldn't, even though at the time you were born, you were considered legitimate. Your status was changed when the rule went into effect."

"Just so."

"The Church should have included a grandfather clause. It's grossly unfair to change the rules in the middle of the game." Those bits of twentieth-century slang translated very differently, indeed, into Frankish. Dominick considered her outraged statement for a few minutes before nodding his agreement.

"I am not the only person so treated. I have a friend—" He paused before continuing in a slightly different way, as if he had thought better of what he originally intended to say. "Many Franks, men and women both, resent the change. Children of powerful families were disinherited and there was no recourse. Still, Charles insists we must all abide by the Church's order."

"But you showed 'em," Gina said. "You didn't have to inherit what you have. You earned land and a title for yourself." And, apparently, lost his overly scrupulous wife when the rules were changed.

"So I did," he agreed, smiling at her choice of words. "I showed them."

"What happens if you have children? Can they inherit from you?"

"Oh, yes," he said, "so long as I am married to their mother, and the marriage is properly blessed."

"What a crock!" She saw his incomprehension; then he laughed.

Gina was fascinated to learn there were unjust rules in Francia, but for all her questioning, she still hadn't uncovered any information that would show her how to return to her own time. In fact, everything she had learned since arriving in Francia was so *un*technical that she was beginning to wonder if she would ever find her way to the twentieth century.

She *had* to discover the key that would send her back. She couldn't stay in Francia. She didn't want to stay there. Then Dominick smiled at her, and she recalled his kiss—and she was no longer so sure she wanted to leave.

Chapter Five

Hedwiga was determined to teach Gina how to sew. Gina didn't think she'd ever learn the knack of it. Her stitches varied wildly in length, and seldom could she keep them in a straight line.

"With perseverance you will improve," Hedwiga said. "There is always so much mending to do that we are glad of even the simplest seam."

"I don't see how anyone could be glad to wear this," Gina responded, holding up the linen undershirt she was repairing for one of the men-at-arms. The original seam at one side was torn, and she wasn't making a very good job of mending it. "I've sewn it crooked."

"Dominick says you will be staying at Feldbruck for some time," Hedwiga informed her. "Use the opportunity to learn the skills you should have acquired when you were younger. You won't regret it."

"Dominick told you I was staying?" Gina's fingers went still with the bone needle caught in a thick fold of linen.

"He said you will be here until he travels to court later in the summer. He will take you with him to Regensburg."

"How nice of him to tell me his plans for me," Gina said so tartly that Hedwiga sent a reproving glance her way before returning to her own pile of sewing.

On laundry days Gina helped Ella in the drying yard, and she worked in the kitchen, too. More than a hundred people lived at Feldbruck, and nearly all of them came to the hall for the midday meal, so there was always a lot of peeling and chopping to be done in preparation for the vegetable stews that were an important part of most meals. With her nimble fingers Gina soon mastered the technique of using a kitchen knife. She spent several hours each day cutting up cabbages, carrots, turnips, and parsnips.

The actual cooking was another matter. Gina thought the open fires dangerous and shied away from them. Hedwiga scoffed at her fears, but, in a departure from her usual bossiness, she left Gina to peel and dice, or to make salads from the lettuces and other leafy greens, the herbs, and even the flowers that grew in the garden. Gina was surprised by how popular salads were and by how often fish from the stream or poultry from hunting served as the main course. In her imagination people in the Middle Ages spent every mealtime gnawing at huge beef bones or carving greasy slabs of pork from whole roasted pigs. The diet at Feldbruck was remarkably well-balanced.

She was also surprised by Hedwiga's insistence on kitchen cleanliness. After the preparations were completed for each midday meal, Hedwiga instructed Gina to scrub down the big chopping block in the middle of the kitchen so flies and maggots wouldn't be attracted to it. When Gina was finished, Hedwiga checked to be sure the wood was cleaned to her satisfaction.

Hedwiga kept track of personal hygiene, too, refusing to accept excuses about the chore of filling buckets at the pump outside the kitchen and then heating the water. Everyone at Feldbruck was expected to use the bathhouse at least once a week, and there was always a good supply of soft, homemade soap in wooden bowls, with plenty of dried herbs handy to scent the water. No one complained when Gina bathed more often.

The days slid by peacefully. One week passed, and then a second. Gina could tell by the fit of her green dress that she was gaining weight. Oddly, it didn't bother her. She was sure some of her new bulk was added muscle from all the manual labor she was doing.

But she was no closer to learning how to return to New York, and that did bother her.

She didn't see Dominick as often as she would have liked. He was frequently gone all day with Arno, the two of them riding off to make sure the crops were doing well and, as Ella told Gina, resolving farmers' complaints or judging disputes. Acting as judge was one of Dominick's many duties, for, as lord of the district, he was Charles's representative in legal matters. When Dominick was at home he was always busy, though as she learned one day, his activities weren't entirely confined to administrative duties.

In her eagerness to discover how to return to the twentieth century, Gina used every spare moment to explore Feldbruck in hope of finding a clue. Hedwiga didn't seem to mind. She took Gina's curiosity as a sign of her restoration to good health and readily answered all her questions. And, as long as there were no chores waiting, she allowed Gina to wander about at will.

On a sunny afternoon in the middle of her third week at Feldbruck, Gina finished in the laundry and left by the outside door. Directly in front of her on the other side of the drying yard stretched the orchard, where apple and pear trees grew. She was planning to locate a shady spot where she could sit and think out a strategy. She was beginning to fear that if she didn't get back to New York soon, she'd never find the way.

As she started for the orchard, she heard off to her left the clash of metal on metal, followed by men shouting. When she stopped to look in that direction, she saw sunlight flashing on a bright object. And she saw an unmistakable blond head.

"Dominick!" Without a moment's thought she ran toward him, increasing her pace as men continued to shout.

At one end of the main building was an open area where the ground was hard-packed from many booted masculine feet trampling it. There, a dozen or so men-at-arms stood in a rough circle, leaving plenty of room for the two men in the middle, who were fighting with broadswords. Both were stripped to trousers and boots, and Gina could see the sweat glistening on Dominick's shoulders and chest. He was breathing hard. Gina completely disregarded the other man; all she could see was Dominick and the danger he faced.

"Stop it!" Gina tried to force her way through the ring of men, only to be caught by Harulf's thick arm around her waist.

"No," he said. "Do not attempt to stop them."

"They're going to kill each other!" she cried.

"Since they are well matched, that is most unlikely," Harulf responded with remarkable calm. "However, if you should distract them, one or both may be injured." He looked hard at Gina, then, as if explaining the obvious, said, "You need not fear for Dominick's sake. They are only practicing, and each man knows how to avoid harming the other. Didn't you realize that?"

"Do you mean to say they get out there regularly and whack at each other with those awful swords?"

"Of course," Harulf answered. "How else is a man to stay in shape for fighting real battles?"

"It's just a game?"

"Today it is," Harulf said. "Tomorrow, or next month, or next year, the king of the Franks may call upon Dominick to provide battle-worthy troops. We must all be ready. That is our duty."

"I understand," she said, easing herself out of Harulf's grasp. He let her go readily enough, though he kept such a watchful eye on her that she knew he'd grab her again if she tried to reach Dominick. "It's just that those swords look so dangerous."

A cheer from the spectators caught Harulf's attention. Gina went up on tiptoe to see what was happening. She didn't know anything about fighting with broadswords, but after watching the action for a few minutes she began to notice that Dominick's reach was longer than his opponent's, and that he was very agile. Dominick was able to bend and stretch, to lunge forward or spin away on the ball of one foot, while the other man was stamping his feet and missing every time he swung his heavy blade. Then she heard Dominick talking to the man, giving him advice. And she suddenly realized why those in the circle around Dominick were paying such close attention to him.

"It's not a fight *or* a game!" she exclaimed. "It's a lesson."

"Dominick is the best teacher there is," Harulf responded, grinning at her. "He taught me most of what I know about sword fighting."

"I wish I knew enough to be able to tell just how brilliant he is." She regarded Dominick with new respect, seeing his physical toughness and the determined set of his mouth. In a sudden onslaught of beautifully controlled muscular power that even Gina could appreciate, Dominick drove his opponent back, and back again, and finally to his knees, leaving no doubt about who was the victor. Then Dominick took the defeated man's hand and clapped him on the shoulder and said something that left both of them laughing. The other men-at-arms cheered their approval before they broke up into smaller groups and began practicing with their own broadswords.

"As you see," Harulf said to Gina, "we all learn from such demonstrations."

"I do see," Gina said. "Thank you for stopping me before I made a complete fool of myself and embarassed Dominick."

"It was a natural mistake for a gently bred woman to make." Harulf patted her shoulder and walked away to join his friends.

Several buckets were lined up on a bench at one side of the practice area. Dominick went to the bench, laid down his sword, and dipped his hands into one of the buckets, scooping up water to splash over his head and chest.

Gina followed him, pausing a couple of feet away from the bench. As if he knew she was waiting, Dominick turned. His hair was soaked, water streaming down his face and neck, and his eyelashes were stuck together with moisture. Seeing him look so oddly young, so boyish and vulnerable, totally different from the determined male who had been working out with a heavy broadsword, Gina felt a catch at her heart. She barely resisted the impulse to brush his hair out of his eyes and offer to dry his face and shoulders. She simply stood there, lips parted, staring at him, her fingers itching to touch him, while he stared back at her in tense silence for a long, breathless moment.

"You should not be here," he said roughly, breaking the spell between them. "The practice yard is no fit place for a woman."

She almost told him that, where she came from, women went wherever they pleased. She thought better of it just in time and instead offered a polite excuse.

"I was planning to take a walk in the orchard," she said, "until I heard the shouting and came to investigate."

"Really?" His eyes narrowed with suspicion. "Well, now you know how well I can use a sword."

"Correction: If I understood anything about sword fighting, I would know how good you are. Unfortunately, I'm too ignorant on the subject to offer a serious opinion."

"I do not consider you ignorant on any subject," he said. With that, he picked up his sword and strode away.

"Now, what did you mean by that?" Gina asked, glaring at his back. "Was it an insult or a compliment? I wish I could figure you out."

The conclusion she reached after thinking about it for a while was that Dominick didn't trust her. Therefore, he wasn't likely to provide any more information to her, even if she asked specific questions. If he was actually planning to take her to Regensburg as Hedwiga claimed, it was probably for the purpose of turning her over to the king.

Aside from the complications to her life that surely awaited her in Regensburg once it became clear that she didn't have any credible reason for being in Francia, she didn't want to leave Feldbruck. It was the place where she had arrived in the eighth century, and she believed it was the place from which she must depart when she returned to her own century; specifically, from Dominick's bedchamber. With her bedroom only two doors away from his and no one else sleeping on the upper level of the house, she would be free after bedtime to examine Dominick's room inch by inch if necessary, if only he were gone.

She began to think of excuses to keep her at Feldbruck when Dominick went to court.

"Can you ride?" he asked her the morning after she had observed his demonstration of swordplay. They were in the great hall, breaking the overnight fast with brown bread and cheese.

"I have never been on a horse in my life," she said. "Why do you want to know?"

"You will have to learn to ride before we leave for Regensburg," he responded. "I should have asked sooner. I made the mistake of assuming that you came here on horseback, though the men I sent out to search for evidence of your arrival found no sign of a horse."

"I didn't ride to Feldbruck. I'm afraid of horses." She didn't know if she was or wasn't—she had never been close enough to a horse to find out— but Dominick had just provided her with the excuse she needed to keep her at Feldbruck and away from court. She didn't think her inability to ride would seem strange to him; it would simply be added to the growing list of other ordinary female accomplishments in which she was lacking.

Of course, if Dominick went to Regensburg without her, and she stayed at Feldbruck and got into his bedroom and finally figured out how to reach the twentieth century, then she would never see him again.

"Don't look so unhappy," he said. "It's a problem that's easily solved. I'll start you on a gentle mare. I have no pressing business today, so we will make a tour of Feldbruck lands."

"No, please, I can't."

"Nonsense." He smiled encouragement at her. "Anyone can learn to ride. Once you are used to being on a horse, you'll see how unnecessary your fears are."

"I don't *want* to learn to ride."

"I didn't ask whether you wanted to learn," he said, still smiling at her. "I told you that you are going to learn."

She could see he had made up his mind. She took comfort in the hope that she would be a complete failure at handling a horse. Perhaps she could manage to fall off without hurting herself. Afterward, she'd make a huge fuss and insist that she couldn't ride, and maybe he'd agree to leave her at Feldbruck. Then again, she thought, maybe he'd just tell her to get back on the horse and try once more.

Harulf was right about Dominick being a good teacher. As they walked to the stable, he explained a few basic facts about riding. The horse he selected for her was a passive creature that nudged Gina's shoulder and let her rub its nose and feed it a carrot when Dominick told her to make friends with it. He was remarkably relaxed about her ability to stay on the horse.

"Cela won't throw you," he said. "There is nothing for you to worry about."

"Easy for you to say," Gina muttered under her breath.

Until Dominick boosted her into the saddle, she hadn't realized just how high off the ground a horse's back was. The saddle didn't make her feel secure, either. It was smaller than those she'd seen in western movies, no more than a padded leather seat with a slight rise in front and back. There weren't any stirrups, either. Her skirt was hiked up to her knees, and her bare legs hung loosely down on either side. At least Dominick wasn't making her ride sidesaddle. She supposed she ought to be grateful for that.

Dominick leapt onto his horse as if no effort was involved, providing further proof of the physical agility Gina had already witnessed. The animal was much larger than Gina's mount, and, unused to horses though she was, she could see that the creature had fire in its eyes. Guiding his horse with his knees and a light hand on the reins, Dominick headed for the palisade gate.

"Don't leave me alone!" Gina yelled after him. "What do I do now?"

"Just follow me," he said, turning his head to favor her with one of his incredible smiles.

Actually, Gina didn't have to do much at all. Without any urging on her part, Cela began to follow Dominick's horse. Within a few paces Gina discovered she was too frightened to fall off as she had planned to do. With her luck, and from this altitude, if she dared a tumble, she'd probably break her neck. As she rode through the gate behind Dominick, she decided to postpone any "accidents" in favor of allowing him to show her his property.

They proceeded slowly until Gina felt a little more secure in the saddle. After watching the way Dominick rode, she straightened her back and began to use her knee and thigh muscles to keep her seat.

Gina already knew that Dominick was proud of his estate, and it didn't take long for her to see why. Feldbruck was an enormous holding, including vast tracts of untouched woodlands that sloped upward to the foothills of the Alps. The cultivated fields were on the level areas near the stream. Gina listened politely while Dominick explained how water from the stream was used for irrigation and pointed out fields of wheat, barley, and rye, then showed her row upon row of cabbage, peas, and root vegetables.

The tenants who worked the fields greeted Dominick with such familiar ease that Gina knew she'd been right to call him a good landlord. No mean or cruel master could elicit so many spontaneous smiles.

They rode for hours, until Gina's thighs and knees and lower back were aching with the strain of staying on her horse. When Dominick suggested they stop to rest for a little while, she assented gladly. Almost at once she regretted having agreed, for he slid off his horse and came to her, reaching up to help her to the ground. She didn't want to go into his embrace. Still, she didn't have much choice, unless she wanted to take the fall she had decided to postpone.

She could barely swing her leg over the horse's back, and she tumbled backward out of the saddle and into Dominick's arms. Laughter rumbled in his chest, though when he turned her to face him, he looked solemn.

"You will be stiff," he said, steadying her until she found her balance. "You made no complaint, so I forgot that you are new to riding."

"Or were you testing me?" she snapped at him. "Did you think I really did know how to ride?"

"When I am dealing with you, I never know what to think," he replied.

His arms were still around her, keeping her so close that Gina could feel the warmth of his body through his woolen clothes. His cheek brushed against hers. His arms tightened, and Gina's face was pressed into his shoulder. A lock of his hair tickled her nose. His lips were on her forehead, then on her cheek and her chin. She held her breath, wanting his mouth on hers and knowing she shouldn't want it. Her lips parted, waiting. . . .

"Walk for a while," he said, taking her by the shoulders and setting her apart from him. "You'll find movement relieves your aching legs. I will see to the horses and lay out our meal."

"What meal?" She couldn't see his face. His back was toward her. What was he trying to do to her, holding her so close and almost kissing her, then shoving her away like that?

They were in a clearing near the stream, in a spot where moss grew right down to the water's edge. It was a pretty place, with the sunlight shining gold and green through the shimmering tree leaves. The stream was wider than she'd thought, and it tumbled over half-submerged rocks, breaking into sparkling foam interspersed with dark whirlpools. Above the sound of rushing water Gina could hear birds singing.

Had Dominick brought her to this isolated woodland glade to seduce her? He wasn't paying any attention to her at the moment. He led the horses to the stream, then looped both pairs of reins over a bush. Gina watched him guardedly, frowning when he removed saddlebags from his horse.

"What meal?" she repeated.

"The midday meal," he said. "I brought it with me."

"Why?" She was afraid of his effect on her emotions, but she wasn't going to let him know it.

"We are too far from the manor to return for a meal, so I carried it for the sake of convenience," Dominick said. "There's cheese, bread freshly baked this morning, a small skin of wine, some nuts and apples. That should be enough."

"You planned this." She confronted him with her fists planted on the hips of her green woolen gown. Her hair was growing out, and the breeze caught at it and blew a curl across her forehead. She lifted one hand to push the hair aside, then put her fist on her hip again, watching him unpack the food and spread it on the moss.

"Of course I planned it," Dominick said. "Only a fool would set out on a long ride with no provisions."

"You arranged a long ride knowing I've never been on a horse before today? How thoughtful of you. What else have you arranged?"

"Join me," he said, holding out a hand.

She just stared at him, knowing he was bigger and stronger than she, knowing he'd catch her easily if she tried to run away.

Dominick's outstretched hand fell to his side. He watched her as if he didn't know what to make of her.

"You are the most suspicious, untrusting person I have ever known," he said. "Even at the royal

court, even in these days of Queen Fastrada spinning endless webs of intrigue, still, women there
speak more freely than you do."

"I don't have anything to say."

"Liar." His voice was soft, almost turning the
word into a verbal caress. "Sweet liar. Beautiful
Gina, how I wish you would tell me who you really
are."

She was rooted to the spot where she stood. In
spite of all the warning bells going off in her mind,
she couldn't move to save herself, couldn't flee
when he approached her and laid a finger on her
lips.

"Do not repeat your name again," he ordered.
"It may or may not be your true name. I want to
know who lives behind the name, behind those
lovely green eyes. You are a tantalizing mystery,
Gina. For what purpose did you come to Feldbruck?"

"If you ask me that one more time, I *will* go
mad!" she cried. "What's the matter with you? Talk
about *me* being suspicious! Do you imagine I'm
some kind of spy?"

"Are you?"

"How can you talk like that when I don't know
anyone in this time and place except you and your
buddies here at Feldbruck? What are you afraid of,
Dominick?"

"What do you mean, 'in this time and place'? "

"I'm a stranger here. That's all I meant." She
threw up her hands in exasperation. "Will you
please stop interrogating me? Let's eat." She wasn't
the least bit hungry, but she had to do something
to divert him. She decided to rearrange the food

he'd piled on the moss and try to act as if she was enjoying the picnic. She'd take care to keep her distance from him, too.

She wasn't used to tramping around in woodlands, so the first thing she did while attempting to stay away from Dominick was catch her foot on a tree root. She went sprawling onto the ground.

"Gina!" Dominick gathered her into his arms. "Are you hurt?"

"Let me go!" She wasn't hurt, but she was breathless, and the warmth she felt with his arms around her was enough to scare her silly. She pushed against his shoulders, then began to pound at him with both fists.

"Go where?" he asked, completely unaffected by her puny assault.

"I'll walk back to the house on my own." She continued to try to push him away.

"Have I mentioned the dangerous wild boars who live in the forest? Or the wolves?"

"There's a bore imprisoning me right here," she said, and she saw by the sudden laughter dancing in his eyes that he appreciated the play on words, though the terms were slightly different in his language. "You're a wolf, too," she added.

"Am I?" He was still chuckling.

"A mean predator."

"Understand this," he said, turning from humor to seriousness so quickly that she was shocked into wary silence. "If I were truly a predator, if I wanted to ravish you, I'd have done so when we first met in my bed. If I wanted to kill you, I could have whenever I pleased. No one at Feldbruck will question any decision I make, and since you claim to be

94

alone in the world, I don't even have to consider the possibility of revenge by your male relatives. I suggest you stop acting like a fool, Gina. It is insulting to be host to a lady who refuses to trust me. It is even more insulting when I am honestly trying to help you."

"You're right. I have been rude." She was no longer trying to push her way out of his arms. She sat quietly, letting him hold her. "I learned early in life not to trust men. Females will say and do spiteful things behind your back. Sometimes they'll slap you or pull your hair. A man will break your heart." She couldn't look at him. She just put her head down on his shoulder and wrapped her fingers around his strong upper arm.

"Who was he?" Dominick asked. "Your husband? Your betrothed?"

"I thought we were going to be married. He lied to me. There was another woman. He's married to her now. It's a proper marriage, blessed by a priest. There was nothing proper about our arrangement. I got home from shopping one Saturday afternoon to find he had taken most of the furniture from our apartment, all the cash in our joint bank account, and he'd gone to the limit on the credit card I let him use. It took me three years to pay off the debt."

"He stole all your possessions," Dominick said, translating her words into terms he could comprehend. "Worse, he destroyed your love, making you afraid to trust another man."

"That's a simplified version, but you have the basic facts right." Gina rested in Dominick's arms, letting relief wash over her, glad that he understood. Except, of course, that Dominick didn't know where or when the misadventure that broke her heart had occurred. She no longer thought of it as a love affair; it was simply a mistake she wished she hadn't made.

One of Dominick's big hands began to stroke her hair, smoothing down the short, springy curls. Gina nestled closer, craving his gentle touch. Then Dominick's fingers under her chin tipped her face upward, and his mouth came down on hers. She didn't resist; she didn't want to.

The next thing she knew she was lying on the moss, and Dominick's hands were on her breasts, caressing her. She opened her mouth, letting his tongue surge into her, wanting the taste and smell and feel of him, wishing she was unclothed, wishing she could stay with him always.

His kisses were incredibly sweet. They warmed her innermost body, stirring her in places no one had ever reached before. Slowly, ever so slowly, his gentleness opened a narrow crack in the door to her tightly guarded heart. Sensing his firm self-control, she allowed herself to trust him—only a little, but still more than she had trusted any man for years. She made no protest until his hand skimmed the bare flesh of her inner thigh. She knew what he was going to do next.

"Stop, please." She twisted, trying to get away from him. "I can't do this."

He let her go, and she crouched, gathering herself into a ball, trying to protect herself. It took only a quick glance at Dominick to see how aroused he was, and the sight increased her fear.

"I thought you wanted it, too," he said, his voice surprisingly calm.

Gina looked at him doubtfully, unable to believe he wasn't going to strike out at her in some way. He met her gaze squarely, observing her expression, and she saw understanding come to him.

"He did this to you, made you afraid of a man's possession." It was a flat statement. "That cowardly knave."

"I don't want your pity. Just keep your hands off me."

"Never in my life have I forced a woman. If you will allow it, I would like to hold you and comfort you. I give you my word, I'll do nothing more. I think you need comforting."

"No." She sat up straight. "Keep your distance."

"Will you at least eat something? You must be hungry after riding all morning. I know I am."

"Could I have some wine?" What she really wanted was a large shot of vodka to dull the pain of roiling emotions she couldn't explain to him—or to herself. She had seen no evidence of distilled spirits at Feldbruck, so she'd settle for wine.

Dominick filled one of the wooden cups he'd brought along and handed it to Gina. While she drank he drew his knife and set about slicing bread and cheese. She took the food he offered her, and he was careful not to allow his fingers to brush hers any more than was necessary. He didn't want to frighten her all over again.

In a way, the day was a complete failure. While showing Gina around Feldbruck, he had tried to draw her into talking about her own home, only to learn she knew nothing of farming or country life. Hedwiga had already informed him that Gina was ignorant of all aspects of housekeeping. Even if she lived in a city, she should have been familiar with cooking and cleaning, with laundry and sewing. Even if she'd been raised in a convent she'd have been taught those simple skills at an early age, for nuns and their pupils did not exist in prayerful idleness. Nor did Gina display any interest in prayer or other devotional acts.

When he embraced her, she responded with sweet passion, but only to a certain point. She was plainly terrified of anything more than kissing and holding and a few exploratory caresses. Either she was an exceptionally clever spy, as he had first suspected, or she was exactly what she appeared to be: a lost and untutored girl who had been badly hurt by a selfish, abusive man.

Despite all his attempts to probe both her past and her current purpose, Gina remained what she had been since he'd found her in his bed—an elusive, intriguing mystery. And Dominick, with his blood still aflame from their kisses, with the feel of her bare skin still tingling against his hands, wanted her as he had never before wanted any woman.

Chapter Six

Except for a few suggestions on horsemanship from Dominick, their return journey was silent. Gina was still too upset by her own emotions and too tired after her long first horseback ride to make conversation. All her remaining energy was concentrated on staying in the saddle. As they slowly made their way back to the manor, she promised herself that the first thing she'd do after she dismounted was hobble to the bathhouse, where she could sink into a tub of hot water and stay there until all the aches in her legs and hips were soaked away. Then she was going to skip the evening meal and sleep until morning.

Perhaps after a good night's rest she'd be able to cope better with her feelings for Dominick. She knew what she needed to do for her own safety.

She needed to convince herself that her reaction to him was purely a physical response to an attractive man. Then she needed to put her unwanted emotions away deep in her heart, lock the door, and keep it locked forever.

The problem was, she was no longer sure she could do that. Dominick's understanding response to the story of her unhappy past, coupled with his willingness to let her leave his embrace even though he was sexually aroused, had changed her attitude toward him in a way she didn't fully comprehend as yet. The man was capable of amazing self-control. He didn't even seem to be angry with her for refusing him. And he hadn't hit her.

By the time she and Dominick turned into the open gateway of his home, Gina was reeling with emotional and physical exhaustion. Thus, she didn't notice at once how many people were gathered in the courtyard. Not until Harulf caught her horse's reins and made Cela stop did Gina begin to pay attention to what was going on around her. There were half a dozen men-at-arms she'd never seen before, and more horses than usual. She saw Dominick leap off his mount and hasten to where Arno waited at the door of the formal reception room. The two of them disappeared inside. Gina looked to Harulf for enlightenment.

"Shall I help you dismount?" Harulf asked her. "Ella told me to look out for you. When you and Dominick were gone for so long, she said she was sure he had taken you over every hill and stream he owns, and you'd be stiff after riding so far your first time on a horse. Benet, come here," Harulf called to a boy who stood nearby. He tossed Cela's reins to the boy, then held up his hands to catch Gina.

"Thank you." For the second time that day Gina fell off a horse and into a man's arms, but this was not at all like falling into Dominick's embrace. Harulf was a robust, handsome fellow, but he was in love with Ella and simply helping her new friend. He held on to Gina's shoulders until she was used to having her feet on solid ground again. Her hands on his forearms, she smiled up at him. "What a nice man you are."

"Remind Ella of that," he said. "Can you stand alone now? Benet will see to your horse. He's one of the grooms, and a good one, too. If you are going to continue to ride, you'll want to learn how to care for Cela, and Benet will be happy to show you what to do. This isn't the time, however. We have guests. Only two, but they are an important pair, and you will probably want to wash and change your gown before the evening meal begins. Ella told me to say that." He ended his speech with a self-conscious grin.

"Harulf," Gina said, looking across the courtyard, "what are those two animals that are being led into the stable?"

"Those are donkeys," Harulf answered. "Priests ride them."

"The guests are priests?"

"One is. The other has refused for years to take his vows. Ella will tell you all about it," Harulf said. "Will you be all right now? I should be on sentry duty."

"Go ahead, then," Gina told him. "I don't want you to get into trouble on my account."

"I won't," Harulf said. "Not for the sake of a guest. Dominick will understand."

They parted, Harulf turning toward the wooden gatehouse and Gina heading for the hot bath her overworked muscles demanded.

To Gina's surprise, Ella was waiting for her in the bathhouse, ready with soap and a pile of clean towels and a robe for Gina to put on after she was dry. The big wooden bathtub was draped with a sheet to prevent splinters and filled with steaming water. The moist air smelled of lavender and thyme.

"What luxury! But how did you know when I was coming?" Gina asked as Ella helped her out of her clothes. She slipped into the herb-scented water with a blissful sigh.

"Because of our unexpected guests, the sentries were on the alert for Dominick's return," Ella explained. "They sent word to Hedwiga as soon as you were sighted. I suggested you could use some help to get cleaned and dressed and into the hall as quickly as possible, and Hedwiga agreed."

"You told Harulf to meet me at the gate," Gina murmured. "I appreciate that. Thank you for caring about me."

She could easily have been lulled into sleep by the warmth of the water, but Ella wouldn't allow it. Never had Gina been in and out of a bathtub so fast. Even so, while Gina washed herself, Ella used the time to explain who Dominick's guests were.

"The priest is Father Guntram of Prum," Ella said in a reverent tone. "He's a very holy man. It's an honor to have him here. And such a long journey from Prum, too."

"Who is the other man?" Gina asked while soaping her hair. "There were two donkeys."

"That's because Pepin can't sit a horse without

pain," Ella said. "Even slow travel on a donkey is difficult for him."

"Pepin?" Gina asked, reaching for the pitcher of rinse water. "Do you mean King Charles's father is here?"

"No, that Pepin is long dead. This Pepin is Charles's eldest son. He was named for his grandfather before—well, before his parents noticed his deformity."

"What deformity?"

"He's called Pepin Hunchback," Ella said.

"You're telling me the heir to the throne is physically disabled? That is good to know in advance." Having rinsed her hair, Gina grabbed the towel Ella offered and began rubbing her head with it.

"Pepin's not the heir," Ella said. "How could he be? He can't ride a horse or lift a sword for more than a few moments, and thus he cannot lead the Franks into battle. A man so physically weak can never be king. Charles's heir is Carloman."

"Carloman?"

"Charles's oldest son by his third wife," Ella patiently explained.

"That would be Queen Fastrada?" Gina guessed as she stepped out of the bathtub.

"Oh, no," Ella said with a laugh. "Fastrada is Charles's fourth wife. The first two he divorced, and the third, Hildegarde, died. Hildegarde was Carloman's mother. Pepin's mother was Charles's first wife, though the Church claims they weren't really married because no priest blessed the union. There now, you are all clean."

"Just in time, too," Gina said. Having dried her arms and legs while Ella talked, she pulled on the loose robe and collected her discarded clothing, preparing to leave the bathhouse. "Another few minutes of explanations and I'd never get your royal family straightened out in my mind. And I thought the British royals led complicated married lives! So, when the Church proclaimed its new rule a few years ago, Pepin was declared illegitimate, just as Dominick was?"

"That's right," Ella said. She opened the bathhouse door, letting in cooler air that banished the warm and steamy atmosphere. "We must hurry. You don't want to be late."

When they reached Gina's room, a new gown was spread out on the bed, with a clean linen shift to wear underneath.

"Of course, it's one of Lady Hiltrude's gowns. Hedwiga altered it for you to take to Regensburg," Ella said. She picked up the shift and slid it over Gina's head.

The gown was bright blue silk with bands of green and blue embroidery edging the wide round neck and the long sleeves. There was no waistline; the skirt flared out from Gina's hips into swirling ripples of fabric.

"It's beautiful." Gina spun around, watching the way the skirt moved. "I feel like a princess."

"Lady Hiltrude never looked so pretty in it," Ella said, tugging the bottom of one loose sleeve into place. "She always wore such a sour face. You are almost always smiling. That makes all the difference."

"Me, smiling?"

"You probably don't notice, but it's true," Ella said. "It's too bad you don't have any jewelry to set off the dress." She looked at Gina as if expecting her to produce some.

"I've never been much for jewelry," Gina said. "I don't like the cheap stuff and can't afford the good stuff, so I do without."

"In that case, you are ready." After pausing only long enough to listen to Gina's heartfelt thanks, Ella departed for the kitchen.

Gina was grateful to have a few minutes alone in which to prepare herself to meet the royal elder son who had been displaced as heir by his able-bodied, Church-approved younger brother.

In his tunic and trousers of plain dark wool, Pepin Hunchback did not look much like a prince to Gina. She guessed he was a year or two younger than Dominick, and with his pale hair and blue eyes he was certainly handsome, though he gave the impression of having little physical strength. That was natural enough, given his so-called deformity. Gina didn't notice it immediately. Not until Dominick glimpsed her and beckoned for her to join the group of men clustered in the middle of the hall, and Pepin turned around, was she able to see the physical problem that meant he could never be king of the Franks.

One of Pepin's shoulders was noticeably higher than the other, and the distortion had evidently twisted his spine so that he walked with an odd, sideways gait. He tended to balance himself on one whole foot and the big toe of the other foot.

"Lady." Pepin bowed over Gina's hand. "I feared Dominick would invite only men to his table. How pleasant to find you here."

Gina didn't know whether to curtsy or call him "my lord" or "prince." She settled for a simple "Thank you, sir," and Pepin didn't seem to notice anything amiss.

"Here is Father Guntram," Dominick said, indicating a tall, skeletally thin man in a dark monk's robe.

The priest Ella had declared a great holy man bestowed a fierce and disapproving glare on Gina, then pulled Pepin aside and began to speak with him in a low voice.

"Ella told me who they are," Gina said to Dominick.

"And warned you not to be offended by Pepin's appearance," Dominick said. "I'm glad she did. You hid your reaction well."

"Why should I be offended?" Gina asked. "Pepin can't help it."

"You have a kinder heart than many ladies," Dominick said.

"Not really. I just don't see any point in blaming a person for something that isn't his fault, that he'd change if he could."

Seeing the way Dominick was looking at her, as if he wanted to put his arms around her right there in the hall with all his people and his guests present, Gina decided to change the subject promptly. Tearing her gaze from Dominick, she glanced toward Pepin and his traveling companion.

"I don't think the priest likes me," she said.

Before Dominick could respond to her claim, Pepin left Father Guntram's side and rejoined them. Gina noticed the priest's disapproving expression, and some imp of mischief made her smile at Pepin with extra sweetness. She didn't think many women flirted with him, and she was delighted when he smiled back.

"Will you be staying long at Feldbruck, sir?" she asked him.

"Only one night," Pepin said. "We are on our way from Prum to Regensburg to see my father. It has been a long and painful journey, and I want to end it as soon as possible, but I could not come so far without stopping to visit Dominick."

"If you are staying in Regensburg for more than a few weeks, we'll meet again there," Dominick told him. "You are always welcome at Feldbruck, but it is far out of your way. Knowing how much you dislike travel, I wonder why you didn't seek me first at court and come here later if you didn't find me."

"Indeed," said Father Guntram in a cold voice. "That would have been the sensible thing to do, as I have told you many times along the way, Pepin. Hear how your friend agrees with me."

"You are always sensible, Father." Pepin reacted with quiet dignity to the priest's insulting manner. "Whereas I am not the most sensible of men, as you so often remind me. I conceived a great longing to sit far into the night with Dominick, drinking his excellent wine and reliving our youthful days together at the palace school."

A most unreligious snort was Father Guntram's response to Pepin's remarks, followed by an angry lecture on the virtue of exercising good sense on all occasions. Gina looked from the darkly frowning priest to the almost angelically blank face of the listening Pepin. It didn't take a genius to see that something was seriously wrong between the two of them. In hope of a clue as to how she ought to react to the tension, she glanced at Dominick, only to find that his usually expressive face was almost as devoid of emotion as Pepin's. Dominick's bland silence further aroused her suspicions.

"How far away is Prum?" she asked him while Father Guntram was still ranting at Pepin.

"It's west of Cologne," he said, "and south of Aachen. A long day's ride from either place, and several weeks from Feldbruck at the speed Pepin must travel."

Gina tried to recall the map of Europe, picturing where Feldbruck was and where Cologne was.

"That's hundreds of miles from here!" she exclaimed. "Ella told me that riding is difficult for Pepin, yet he rode all that distance on a donkey."

"And?" Dominick watched her closely, as if he was waiting for her to reach a conclusion.

"Well, I'd say Pepin wants very badly to speak with you."

"So would I." Dominick's response was so soft that Gina barely heard it. While she looked at him, noting the frown that drew his brows together and wishing he'd reveal what was on his mind, Father Guntram finished his lecture, and Pepin bowed his head as if in complete acquiescence to what the priest had said. But from the way Pepin's hands were fisted at his sides and the stiff manner in which he held his crooked back, Gina suspected he was not as passive as he pretended to be.

That evening's meal was not the usual simple fare of bread, cheese, and cold meat left over from midday. Hedwiga produced several hot, roasted chickens that Gina was sure were sacrifices from the chatelaine's treasured flock of laying hens. There was a huge salad of garden greens and herbs sprinkled with violets and rose petals, plenty of fresh bread, and even a bowl of newly churned butter, which was a special treat fit for a king's son.

Pepin praised the food, thanked Hedwiga for her efforts on his behalf, and ate little. Father Guntram uttered no word of thanks but stuffed himself until Gina wondered how he kept his lean figure if he routinely ate that way.

It was not a pleasant meal. Father Guntram's dark presence cast a shadow over the high table and, to a lesser degree, over the tables where men-at-arms and servants sat. Conversation was stilted, consisting of remarks about the weather, the difficulties of travel, and the chances of a good harvest. Gina detected undercurrents, but she didn't know enough about Frankish society or about Dominick's guests to understand what they were.

As soon as she could do so without being rude, she excused herself and fled the hall for the garden. It was quickly becoming her favorite spot at Feldbruck, especially at twilight, when all the floral and herbal fragrances released by the heat of the day combined into a single, complex perfume that was borne aloft by the gentle evening breeze. Gina meandered slowly along the gravel path to the sundial at the center of the garden, where she paused to inhale the sweet air.

A loud, haranguing voice coming from the direction of the great hall disturbed her peace. Almost certainly it was Father Guntram speaking.

"What is your problem, anyway?" Gina muttered, glancing over her shoulder toward the door to the hall. She saw a slender figure silhouetted there, and Father Guntram's voice grew louder. Fearing that the priest, too, was planning to walk amid the flower beds and wanting to avoid him, Gina hurried past the sundial to the shelter of the trees at the other end of the garden. The sun was below the mountaintops, night was falling, and the shadows were growing darker by the minute. She was sure no one would notice her.

No sooner had she reached the trees than she heard footsteps on the gravel and the voices of two men, one of whom her heart recognized at once. It was not Father Guntram, but Dominick and Pepin coming along the path. She stepped forward to join them, then halted. The quiet, intense way they were speaking told her they were in the garden seeking the same privacy she had sought.

She knew what she ought to do, which was slip quietly through the trees to the open area where the garden ended. From there she could turn left and walk, unseen, around the wing where the great hall was, and enter the house through the kitchen door.

Whatever Dominick and Pepin wanted to say to each other was no business of hers. She knew that perfectly well, yet she remained where she was, hidden in the deepening shadows of the trees, shamelessly listening to a private conversation.

"I can bear no more," Pepin said. "My father knows that the last thing on earth I want is to become a priest. I don't have the vocation, and I never will, yet he insists I must profess my vows.

He has commanded Father Guntram to preach at me every day until I give in and obey. They say it's because Charles fears me that he wants me out of the way."

"They?" Dominick's quiet voice interrupted Pepin's passionate outburst. "Who are 'they'?"

"The Bavarian nobles. They have invited me to join them."

Gina heard Dominick's firm footsteps pause. Pepin's limping gait continued a few more paces. Then a sudden movement in the dimness told her Pepin had swung around to face his friend.

"Are you speaking," Dominick said, "of the nobles who swore fealty to Charles after Duke Tassilo of Bavaria was deposed and imprisoned? The same nobles who, in return for their oaths, were permitted by Charles to retain their lands and titles?"

"Yes," Pepin responded fiercely. "Tassilo and all his family were sent to monasteries and convents for the rest of their lives. It's a habit my father has, his way of appearing merciful when other people prove inconvenient to him. It's what he wants to do to me."

"Tassilo was more than inconvenient," Dominick said. "He was a traitor, over and over again, and Charles forgave him so many times that most people lost count. It's a wonder he wasn't executed years ago. When Tassilo was finally defeated in battle after his last revolt and then deposed, most of his nobles cheerfully turned their backs on him and swore themselves to Charles without a bit of hesitation. Pepin, don't be taken in by those deceitful men. If they could so easily forsake their sacred oaths to their first lord, and then break their oaths

111

to Charles, they will also break any oaths they swear to you."

"But don't you understand? I can use them to gain what should be mine," Pepin said, all eagerness and excitement. "Once I am king, I'll have the power to control them. They will obey me."

"As your father controls them?" Dominick asked scornfully. "As they obey him and keep their word to him?"

"I am the firstborn son!" Pepin cried. "My rights have been denied me!"

"Is that the argument they used to win you over? You have known from your earliest childhood that you are physically unfit to be king of the Franks," Dominick said. "Furthermore, you are legally a bastard. Therefore, the Church will not accept you as king. Surely you understand that you cannot rule Francia without the backing of the clergy."

"I am no more a bastard than you are!" Pepin exclaimed bitterly. "We were both born into legal marriages."

"Forget your illegitimacy, and your deformity, though I assure you, others will not forget either, not for a moment," Dominick said with brutal honesty. "Tell me this, Pepin: in your wildest dreams, can you imagine Charles meekly giving up his throne? If you want to be king, you will have to kill your father."

"No. It won't come to that." Pepin sounded breathless. "We are going to capture him and send him to a monastery, just as he has done to so many other men."

"Charles will never allow himself to be taken alive. If you think otherwise, then you know nothing about your father."

"Dominick, please, I came here to ask you to join us. You are my oldest friend. I want you with me."

"Because we are old friends, you know how I lost my inheritance from my father and later won Feldbruck by right of arms, fighting with Charles in the war against Tassilo," Dominick said. "If you are my true friend, how can you ask me to endanger my hard-won lands and my people by betraying my king?"

"When I am king of the Franks, I will confirm you in your estate," Pepin cried. "And when we divide Tassilo's treasure, I'll see that you receive your full share."

"Ah," said Dominick. "Tassilo's treasure. Now I begin to understand. That is what your false friends, the disaffected nobles, really want, isn't it?"

"Always after a campaign," Pepin declared, "the lands and possessions of the defeated have been divided among the men who followed Charles into battle. Tassilo's treasure is the single exception. The entire gigantic hoard was given to Fastrada, that greedy bitch. And did she distribute it as she ought to have done? As any decent queen would do? No! She kept it all for herself."

"It seems to me there are noblemen as greedy as the queen." Dominick spoke with remarkable mildness after Pepin's uncontrolled emotion. "Hasn't it occurred to you that many of the men who now claim a portion of Tassilo's treasure are the same men who fought for Tassilo, against Charles and the Frankish army? Why should they think taking an oath to Charles after the war is over gives them the right to any part of the treasure?"

"Then there is my younger brother, Carloman,"

Pepin said as if Dominick had not spoken. "When my father made Carloman king of the Lombards, he had the little brat rebaptised, as Pepin!"

"I know," Dominick said gently. "Charles wants the Lombards to associate their new king with a great Frankish ruler."

"First I was denied the right to succeed my father," Pepin said. "Then I was unjustly declared a bastard. And now, as a final insult, my very name has been taken from me. These are wrongs no man can forgive."

"You would be wiser, and happier, not to dwell on such matters," Dominick said. "Your immediate, dangerous problem lies with the dishonest nobles who are trying to use you against your father. Pepin, I think you do not understand how difficult it is to be a king beset by contentious nobles and to try to keep peace among them."

"I understand that Charles the Great does not love me at all," Pepin retorted with bitter assurance. "Are you with me, Dominick? Are you still my friend?"

Gina heard this discussion with growing horror, not for Pepin's sake, but for Dominick's. Regardless of whether he joined Pepin's rebellion, Dominick was involved in the scheme merely by listening to Pepin's offer. If the plot failed, or if Dominick was caught, he'd be executed, probably in a very painful way.

While Gina was trying to decide what to do, she noticed a motion at one side of the garden. Her eyes had adjusted to the fading light, allowing her to make out a tall figure in a dark robe. With Dominick's safety foremost in her mind, she acted immediately.

"Dominick," she called, stepping out from the

trees, "there you are. I've been looking all over for you."

"Gina?" Dominick's boots crunched on the gravel as he spun around to peer in her direction. "Have you been spying on us?"

"Certainly not. I just came to kiss you good night." She caught Dominick's neck with one hand, pulling his head down. With her lips against his ear she whispered, "Father Guntram is hiding in the shadows, listening to every word you say."

"And you weren't?" he responded, also in a whisper.

"I'm on your side, Dominick."

"Which side is that?" he whispered back.

"Is something wrong?" Pepin asked, his normally pitched voice sounding loud in the darkness.

"Just a tender good night," Dominick said, and kissed Gina hard on her mouth before turning back to his friend. "Pepin, it is growing late, and you will want to resume your journey at first light. You and I should also say good night."

"Will you at least think about the plans I've told you of?" Pepin asked, sounding tense and worried.

"My friend, I always consider your words seriously," Dominick responded. He put an arm around Gina's waist, keeping her near. "I will see you in the morning before you leave."

"Good night, then," Pepin said. "I know I don't have to tell you not to speak to anyone else about what we've discussed here."

Pepin started for the hall, and Gina saw his slight, twisted form silhouetted against the light spilling from the door.

"Good night, Pepin," she called after him.

Dominick's right arm tightened around her waist as if to warn her not to say anything more. His left hand caught her chin, holding her so she couldn't turn her face aside. To anyone watching them, as Father Guntram surely was, they probably looked as though they were enjoying a brief romantic encounter.

When Dominick bent his head, it wasn't just fear of what might happen to him that made Gina tremble; it was also the memory of their time in the glade beside the stream. His mouth brushed lightly over hers.

"Now I know for certain that you are a spy," he murmured with his lips against hers.

"I'm not. I just happened to be in the garden," she protested, keeping her voice low. "I know I shouldn't have stayed hidden, but when I heard what you and Pepin were saying, I was too embarassed to reveal myself."

"You were eavesdropping."

He kissed her again, slowly and thoroughly, until her knees went weak and she clung to him to keep from falling.

"So was Father Guntram eavesdropping," she gasped as soon as she was able to free her mouth from his. "He still is. You can't deny that I warned you he was lurking about."

"For what purpose did you warn me?" His lips were scorching along her throat, and his hands grasped her ribcage on either side of her breasts. The heat of his palms made her heart flutter like a captive bird. "Surely, dear Gina, you had a reason for speaking up when you did."

"I'm worried about you. Don't get involved in

116

that crazy scheme of Pepin's. In any time, in any place, they kill traitors."

"So, you're worried about me, are you?" His thumbs flicked across her nipples several times. Gina cried out, a wild, aching sob that Dominick silenced with another kiss. His arms encircled her, his large palms moving steadily down her back to catch her hips and pull her hard against him, letting her feel his desire until Gina forgot all about political plots and treacherous nobles and resentful royal sons.

"I have decided what to do," Dominick told her some time later. He was still holding her hips firmly against his, and Gina was quivering with an urgent need she had never known before, but he spoke coolly and calmly, as if completely detached from any emotion. "I must travel to Regensburg as soon as possible, and you are far too dangerous for me to leave behind. But for now, you are to go to your room and stay there until morning."

When he released her, she thought she'd faint. She wanted to scream at him that he was committing a major mistake if he joined Pepin's harebrained scheme. She wanted to pound on his chest and pull his hair and say she hated him—and then throw herself into his arms and plead with him to remain at Feldbruck.

She knew he'd never agree to that. Pepin was his friend, Charles was his king, and Dominick was going to step right into the middle of their intrigues. And unless she could discover a way to get back to the twentieth century—fast—he was going to take her along with him.

Chapter Seven

Gina lay awake for hours that night, worrying. Though she felt a deep sympathy for Pepin, she thought he was foolish to allow himself to be used by the disloyal nobles. To her way of thinking, it was not an act of friendship for him to involve Dominick in a scheme that was probably going to end up with both of them being killed.

"And me, too," Gina concluded. "If the authorities start asking questions, they're going to learn I don't have a past or a family in this time. They'll think I'm hiding something important—and I am, but not state secrets."

The danger to Dominick and herself was upsetting enough. Even more terrifying was her realization that Dominick, with his tenderness and his passion, was beginning to destroy her personal defenses. She didn't want to become emotionally involved with him, for she knew from past experience that heartbreak lay dead ahead if she allowed herself to care for a man. Her reaction was panic and a desire to flee before her heart could be broken again.

As the first faint glimmer of dawn lit the sky, and the snowcapped Alpine peaks began to glow with a soft peach tint, she made up her mind. Before Dominick dragged her off to Regensburg, she was going to check his bedchamber from floor to ceiling in an all-out effort to find a way back to the last day of the twentieth century. If she found it, she would use it, because if she remained in the eighth century much longer she was likely to lose both her life and her heart—and she couldn't decide which prospect was more frightening.

Having reached her decision, she fell asleep and did not waken until Ella knocked on her door to tell her Pepin and Father Guntram were about to leave. Gina was in no mood for dressing up, so she threw on her everyday shift and the well-worn green woolen gown, splashed cold water on her face, raked her fingers through her thick, short curls, then hurried to the courtyard.

There, by the gatehouse, the men-at-arms were making final preparations for their journey. Pepin was already mounted, looking uncomfortable on his donkey. Father Guntram, also mounted, was a frowning presence close by Pepin's side.

"We'll meet again in Regensburg," Pepin said to Gina. He held her hand a bit longer than he should have, and he looked from her face to Dominick's closed visage. "I know you are going to be a good friend to me, Gina, just as Dominick has always been."

"Have a safe trip," Gina said, finally succeeding in pulling her fingers free of his grasp.

Father Guntram bade Dominick a curt farewell, pointedly ignored Gina, and led the procession out of Feldbruck with Pepin and six men-at-arms following.

"Are those the king's soldiers?" Gina asked, watching the men-at-arms.

"They belong to one of the Bavarian nobles," Dominick answered curtly. He began to walk away from her in the direction of the stable.

"Is it an honor guard, or is Pepin a prisoner?"

Dominick paused, but he didn't turn to face her.

"Pack your belongings," he said. "We leave for Regensburg early tomorrow morning."

"You will catch up with Pepin by tomorrow night," she remarked. "According to Ella, he can't travel very fast. Why didn't you tell him to wait and leave with you? I'm sure he'd rather have you to talk with than Father Guntram."

"I have no desire to travel with Pepin," he said. "We will not catch up with him along the way. We are taking a different route."

"Dominick, will you kindly turn around and look at me? I don't like talking to your back."

He spun on his heel, and Gina saw how closed and hard his expression was.

"You're still angry about last night," she began.

"I am angry about many things," he said. "Do not think to send a message about my plans, not to Pepin or to anyone else. No one leaves Feldbruck until we ride out tomorrow."

"Why would I want to send a message? I don't really know what's behind all the plotting, and, furthermore, I don't care." That was far from true, but she was so worried about Dominick's safety that she couldn't stop herself from snapping out an insult. "If you want to risk your neck in a stupid scheme to take over the kingdom, that's your problem, not mine."

"It will be your problem, and your neck, if you are involved," he said. "After last night's eavesdropping episode, I cannot trust you."

"Gee, that's too bad. I was just beginning to trust you," she snarled the words at him, because she could see the doubt and the pain in his eyes when he looked at her, and seeing it made her heart ache. She didn't want to feel the way Dominick made her feel, all soft and tender inside, trusting and foolish, ready to be hurt again. The conflict between what she felt for Dominick and her need to keep herself safe from emotional pain was driving her crazy.

"I will be occupied for most of the day, making arrangements for Feldbruck during my absence," he said. "I'll speak to you this evening about what I expect of you during the journey and at Regensburg."

He gave her a hard look and stalked off, leaving Gina angry and exasperated—and longing to throw herself into his arms and explain everything to him. She was afraid to do it, afraid he wouldn't believe her. He didn't trust her, so he'd never accept her story about traveling through time. She had to protect herself from caring about him. The only way to do that was by leaving Feldbruck the same way she had come.

Dominick had said he'd be busy all day. That meant he wouldn't be in his bedroom. Keeping a safe distance from the kitchen, where Hedwiga was assigning morning chores to the servants, Gina hurried up the stairs to the second level of the house.

Dominick's bed was still unmade, the quilt tossed back as he had left it upon rising. One of his books lay open on the wooden chest. When Gina glanced at it she noticed the page was the one containing the painting of the angel with multicolored wings and a real gold halo. She lightly brushed a finger over the angel, feeling the texture of the paint and the smoothness of the parchment.

"I wish you could help me," Gina said with a sigh. "I wish you could help Dominick, too. As it is, he'll be better off without me to worry about, and I know my heart will be safer if I can get far away from him."

Ignoring the whisper in her mind that said she didn't want to leave Dominick and never see him again, she kicked off her soft shoes and climbed onto his bed, balancing herself with one hand against the wall. On the day of her arrival in Francia she had fallen straight down through the roof tiles and ceiling directly above the bed. There had to be some sign of her passage.

By standing on tiptoe and stretching her free arm, she was just able to reach the ceiling. It was definitely solid. She felt the plaster, pressing as hard as she could and jumping up to knock on it. Then she moved along the mattress, keeping herself steady with a hand on the wall, continuing to test the ceiling as she worked her way from the head of the bed to its foot.

"How did I get through the roof? Did the molecules of my body somehow pass through the molecules of tile and plaster, like a special-effects gimmick in a science-fiction movie? But this isn't science fiction. It's real. It happened."

She caught her breath when she heard footsteps in the corridor. If one of the servants was coming to straighten the room, she'd lose her chance to explore it. And with Dominick determined to take her with him to Regensburg, she was unlikely to have another opportunity.

In a frantic final attempt to find the opening, she flung both arms high and jumped.

Her left hand disappeared into the ceiling. There was no shattering of plaster, no chalky flakes sifting onto her head. Her hand simply vanished up to her wrist. At the same time, she felt a definite sucking action on her arm.

A small hole opened above her, allowing just a glimpse of sky before the blue was replaced by the darkness of the tunnel. The tunnel was too small to accept her body, but she could see it slowly enlarging, and she could feel the suction increasing. Soon she would be able to enter.

She hesitated, withdrawing her hand, afraid to be pulled into that cold, black emptiness for a second journey through time. She wanted to return to the world that was familiar to her. She was convinced she must return. Yet some part of her resisted.

"Would you care to explain why you are standing on my bed?" said an unmistakable masculine voice.

"Dominick!" Gina turned to face him just as he looked up and saw the opening.

"What in the name of all the saints is that?" he demanded.

The tunnel closed. Without a sound it was gone, and the ceiling was smooth once more, as if the opening had never existed.

Dominick grabbed for Gina. When she tried to avoid him, her foot caught on the upturned edge of the quilt, and she spilled off the bed and into his arms.

"What are you doing here?" she gasped.

"Precisely the question I was asking of you. Need I remind you that this is my room and you have no right to be here? What were you doing? I will have an explanation for what I just saw."

"Put me down first," she ordered, knowing she couldn't think clearly when she was so close to him.

He set her on her feet but kept a tight grip on her upper arms. His eyes were gray ice, boring into her. For the first time since the day of her arrival she was truly afraid of him.

"Were you opening a secret door in the ceiling?" he demanded, shaking her. "I warn you, I am in no mood to listen to half truths and evasions. You are going to tell me, right now, who has employed you to spy on me."

"No one!" She tried to escape him, but he only held her more securely. "I don't know anyone outside of Feldbruck."

"You cannot expect me to accept that," he said, his grasp growing ever tighter on her arms. "Were you sent here to entice me into joining the traitors, in case Pepin's pleas failed?"

"No, certainly not. Dominick, let me go."

"I will not lose Feldbruck," he said, his mouth hard. "I keep what is rightfully mine."

125

"That's fine with me. I don't have anything to do with that dumb plot," she cried in dismay. The kind, humorous man she knew had vanished. In his place stood a warrior prepared to deal with any threat to what he held dear. Almost any threat; he couldn't possibly be prepared for what she could tell him if she dared. Feeling trapped and desperate, she said, "If I told you the whole truth, you wouldn't believe me."

"Perhaps I would. Perhaps I'd rather hold a kinder opinion of you than I do at the moment. Almost any explanation would be preferable to what I am thinking."

She stared at his grim expression, weighing the chance that he'd accept the whole truth against the risk that he'd kill her the instant she finished speaking.

"I am waiting," he said.

Gina's bravado collapsed. She couldn't bear to have him believe her a liar or a traitor or a lot of other nasty things. She wanted Dominick to think well of her, and the only way to achieve that was to tell him the whole truth. Not allowing herself time to consider what her longing for his approval meant, she began to talk.

"All right, I'll tell you. I was looking for a tunnel through time," she said, tearing her gaze from his face to glance at the ceiling above his bed. "I found it, too, but it vanished again when you interrupted me. Now I may never find a way back."

"Back where?" he demanded. "What tunnel?"

"When I arrived here that first morning, you asked how I got into your room," she said, trying

126

to sound calm and confident though her heart was pounding in apprehension over what she was about to reveal. "I told you I fell through the roof. That was the truth."

"I don't understand." He was still gripping her arms and still frowning.

"Neither do I. Dominick, I swear to you, I am not a madwoman. I'm telling you the truth as far as I know it. I have no explanation for what happened to me." She paused, took a deep breath, and continued, simplifying the story as much as possible.

"I was working with a complex machine when something went wrong. All I remember is a searing flame, then a cold, black tunnel. I thought I was dying, until suddenly I was falling through the air. I was so high that I could see all of Feldbruck, every part of it that we rode over yesterday. I was convinced I was going to crash into the roof of your house and be killed. Instead, I landed on top of you. The reason I came to your room this morning was to search the ceiling."

"When I first entered, I thought I saw a dark hole in the ceiling, but there is nothing wrong with it now," he said, glancing upward.

"That is frighteningly true," she agreed.

"You fell through the air?"

"It was a very strange sensation."

"On that first day you asked me where you were."

"The place where I had been working was not Yorvik, and not in Northumbria," she said, speaking slowly and carefully, aware that what she was about to reveal would be even more unbelievable than what he had already heard. "It was a huge city called New York. It is larger than any city you can imagine, and it's in a country that lies on the other side of the Atlantic Ocean."

"I've heard tales of such a faraway land, but no one has ever actually seen it."

"It exists, all right. But there's even more, Dominick." From his set face she couldn't tell what his reaction to her story was, but she had gone too far to stop before he knew everything. "I also came here from the future. To be exact, twelve hundred and eight years in the future."

He dropped his hands from her arms and stepped away, regarding her with horror.

"Was it witchcraft?" he asked. "Has someone placed you under a spell, and are you searching for a way to break it?"

"No. That's one of the few things I *am* sure of. It wasn't magic, it was the computer—the machine. Actually, very few people in my time still believe in magic or witchcraft. Even fewer believe in miracles. As I said, I don't have an explanation."

He looked at her for a long time, and the horror slowly faded from his face. Still, she couldn't read his expression.

"Do we Franks seem like barbarians to you?" he finally asked.

"Far from it. The people here at Feldbruck are the kindest, most generous and hospitable souls I've ever met. Dominick, everything I told you yesterday about my past life was true. I just didn't mention the dates."

"Can you tell me what will happen to Charles in the next few months?" he asked.

"If I knew, I would gladly tell you. Unfortunately,

I am almost completely ignorant about this period of history."

"I see."

"Do you believe what I've just said?"

"You are unlike any other woman I've ever known," he said slowly, as if thinking over her words.

"I'm sure I am," she responded.

"In the short time you've been at Feldbruck, I have learned you are not a madwoman, and you are far from stupid. Ignorant of Frankish customs, eager to ask peculiar questions,yes— and your story does explain your odd behavior and your lack of everyday knowledge." He was looking at her with a strange mixture of warmth and regret. "After listening to you yesterday, I am astounded that you have entrusted me with this part of your story."

"I'm a bit astounded myself," she said, venturing a weak smile. "You're the first man I've trusted in years."

"Well, I intend to prove worthy of your trust," he said. "Since you want to return home, I will try to help you. I have an idea."

"You have?" She didn't know whether to be glad or annoyed that he was so eager to get rid of her.

"While there is no sign of your entry through the ceiling," he said, "you haven't explored the roof have you?"

"If I found a ladder and tried to scale your house," she responded wryly, "your men-at-arms would likely ask a lot of questions. Not to mention what Hedwiga would say if she saw me."

"You don't need a ladder," Dominick said.

"Above us the roof slants at an angle, but the ceiling is flat. Between the two is an open space that is used for storage. An attic. Shall we see in what we can discover up there?"

She studied his face, trying to discern his real attitude. He cocked an eyebrow and watched her in return, and all she could see in him was a faint, rueful amusement at her hesitation.

"Yes, please," she said at last.

Dominick took her hand and pulled her out of his room and along the corridor to the end of the wing, where stairs led down to ground level. A smaller staircase climbed upward. At its top was a narrow door.

Gina was right behind Dominick as he pushed open the door and stepped into the attic. On either side of them the roof slanted right down to the floor. A small window at each end of the long, narrow space provided just enough light for Gina to see trunks and baskets piled along the eaves. A dusty straw pallet was spread near the door, a quilt folded on top of it.

"Someone has been here," Gina said.

"Probably servants looking for a bit of privacy," Dominick responded, making his way to the other end of the attic. "My bedchamber will be just about here. I can find no sign of anything awry. Come see for yourself."

Gina hurried forward to the spot he indicated. She banged on the roof with both fists and stamped her feet on the wooden plank flooring. Her efforts raised a small cloud of dust that made her sneeze, but they produced no evidence of her entry to Feldbruck or of the brief reappearance of the tunnel.

"I don't understand," she said. "There has to be a sensible explanation for what happened to me."

"Occasionally something happens for which there is no explanation," Dominick said.

"Are you telling me to just accept my lot and live with it?"

"I suppose I am."

"But I want to understand how this happened!"

"Why must you understand everything? I don't understand much of what you've told me. Nonetheless, I accept it on faith. Or perhaps," he added quietly, "I simply want to believe you are not a spy trying to entrap me. But, for many reasons, I do accept your story."

"Thank you for that." Sudden awareness of Dominick's presence and of how alone they were prickled along Gina's spine. She started for the doorway and the stairs, speaking over her shoulder as she went. "And thank you for letting me check out your attic."

"I am sorry you did not find what you sought."

He sounded so honestly regretful that Gina turned to face him. Watching him and not where she was going, she smacked the back of her head on the roof. She cried out and instantly felt the threat of tears. Why she was getting so emotional just because Dominick was being kind?

"Gina." Dominick's arm was across her shoulders, guiding her the few steps to the pallet. "Sit down."

She sat, wrapping her arms around her knees, and pillowing her head on them. Dominick knelt beside her, watching her anxiously.

"I'll be fine in a minute," she said.

The attic was quiet and comfortably warm. A

single bee was buzzing along the eaves, trying to find a way out. Dominick's fingers were in her hair, rubbing the sore spot. Gina sighed and relaxed a little. Dominick certainly did have a calming effect on her. When he pulled her head to his shoulder, she did not resist. Nor did she protest when he lowered his head and kissed her.

"Would it be so hard for you to stay in this time with me?" he asked.

"As far as I can tell," she said, "I don't have any choice in the matter. I don't know when, or if, that tunnel will appear again."

She fell silent, uncertain what she really wanted. The only sounds she could hear were the pounding of her own heart and Dominick's breathing. The bee was still.

"You had enough faith in me to reveal your strange story," he murmured.

"And you believed me," she said, leaning back in his arms to look into the warmth of his eyes.

"Gina," he whispered. His fingers stopped their movement through her hair.

Long, silent moments passed while the tension between them rose until it became unbearable. Gina ran her tongue across her dry lips and saw Dominick's gaze follow the motion. She couldn't think clearly, couldn't stop what was happening to her mind and her body. It had really begun on the day when she, newly arrived in Francia, had lain beneath him in his bed and felt his hard manliness pressing against her. She hadn't been able to shake the memory of that sensation; she had felt it again each time she looked at him.

She touched his face, conscious of the strong

132

bones of his cheek and jaw. She traced the outline of his lips. Dominick caught her hand and kissed her palm, and all of her fears dissolved. She had already trusted him with her life; now she was going to trust him with her body.

She let her head fall back against his arm while he kissed her throat, and she whimpered softly when his hands caressed her breasts. She wasn't sure how he so easily removed her dress and shift and his clothing. She only knew he was being infinitely gentle and patient with her, somehow understanding that her past sexual experiences had been unpleasant ones.

After another few minutes Gina closed the door firmly on the painful memories of her past. For the first time in her life she wanted to touch an unclothed man. With his eager encouragement she began to caress Dominick, taking pleasure in his muscular strength and the contrast between his smooth chest and hairier limbs, reveling in the hot moistness of his mouth and tongue when he kissed her, and, finally, aching to feel the hard length of him between her thighs.

"How I have wanted you," he whispered, returning every touch she bestowed on him with his own tender caresses. "Since the first day I met you, my beautiful Gina, I have longed to hold you this way."

She started to protest that she wasn't beautiful, but the words caught in her throat, for Dominick had just reached the hot, liquid center of her, and his fingers were working a magic she had never dared to hope for.

"Please," she gasped, her hands stroking down his back, trying to pull him closer. She was a great, throbbing emptiness, and only Dominick could bring her the release she sought.

He filled her so slowly that she feared she would go mad from the drawn-out pleasure of it. He withdrew and repeated the slow, sliding motion. And did it again.

Gina dissolved into a pulsating joy that went on and on as Dominick thrust faster and harder into her convulsing body, until she heard his gasp of pleasure and he went completely still.

It was a long time before she returned to the full knowledge that she was lying naked, in a state of complete physical contentment, on an old straw pallet in a dusty attic.

"This was no proper place to bed you," Dominick said, smiling down at her, "especially not the first time."

"It seemed like heaven to me." He had said *the first time*, as if there were going to be other times. The thought made her smile, too. She stretched, feeling Dominick's strong legs still tangled with hers, and lifted her face for his kiss.

"If I could find the way back to New York City," she murmured, "you could go with me. You'd be safe there."

His smile vanished. His face went perfectly still. An instant later he lifted himself away from her and reached for his tunic. When he spoke again, his voice was harsh.

"I belong here," he told her. "This is my home. And, whether you like it or not, Gina, you are still traveling to Regensburg with me."

Chapter Eight

"You can't tell me what to do." In the warm attic she stood naked, facing him in outrage. "I am a free and independent woman. I have rights. Don't imagine you can order me around just because you had sex with me."

"Let me give you a lesson about this century, since you claim to be a stranger to it," Dominick said. Flinging aside the tunic he hadn't put on yet, he planted his fists on his hips, assuming the posture of a male who was absolutely certain of his own power and dominance. "There isn't a person in Francia who will dare to deny me *my* rights. I am master here, and you will obey me. You gave yourself to me willingly. No force was involved between us. It seemed to me that what we did was more than the simple, lustful rutting your crude words imply, and, I confess, I enjoyed it greatly. Nevertheless, I will not be charmed by feminine wiles or coerced by foolish female anger. You *will* travel to Regensburg with me."

"You miserable male chauvinist!" Infuriated by his attitude, Gina lifted one hand to slap him. He caught her wrist, twisting her arm behind her back and forcing her against his unclothed body. She went rigid, fighting the effect on her mind of that sensuous contact of skin to skin.

"Is this how you treated your wife?" she snarled at him. "No wonder she ran away to a convent."

"What do you know of Hiltrude?"

The distrust was back on his face, making Gina regret her impulsive words. But she wasn't going to back down.

"I wear Hiltrude's clothes every day," she said. "Hedwiga told me that she divorced you."

"That is inaccurate," Dominick responded. "It was I who ended my marriage to Hiltrude. Would you like to know why?"

"Let me guess. Did she refuse to obey her master's orders?" It was a nasty remark, but Gina couldn't help herself. She did want to hear Dominick's version of the breakup, so it was a good thing he ignored her comment.

"Hiltrude was Fastrada's agent. Fastrada suggested our marriage to Charles and promoted the idea until he agreed."

"You could have refused to marry her," Gina said.

"Refuse the king to whom I owe my lands and title, the man who has been a second father to me, when he arranged my marriage to a nobly born and well-dowered virgin? I think not. In fact, I was willing. In those days I was not yet aware of Hiltrude's duplicity."

"Did you love her?" Gina asked.

"I tried. For a while I thought I did love her, until I learned she was involved in one of Fastrada's intrigues. The contempt and lack of interest in her that I felt when the truth was revealed told me I had never loved her at all."

"So you were a gentleman and let Hiltrude get the divorce," Gina said. "How did you manage it? I thought the Church didn't allow divorce."

"As the old Frankish customs give way to Church decrees, divorce does become more difficult," Dominick said. "Still, there are ways to end an unsatisfactory marriage."

"Murder?" Gina suggested, and Dominick responded with a mirthless grin.

"It has been done," he said, "though not by me. I'll touch no woman in violence. I merely offered Hiltrude a choice. I would send her to Charles in chains, under guard, with a letter describing her involvement with Fastrada. Alternately, she could request a divorce and go quietly into a convent, and I would say nothing about the queen's plan to ruin me through my wife. Hiltrude is intelligent enough to fear Fastrada's wrath if the story were ever told, so she chose the convent. She used my illegitimacy as an excuse the Church would accept, and after I agreed to donate her dowry to the convent where she chose to retire, our divorce was quickly granted.

"Having once been betrayed by a woman I took into my home and my bed," Dominick concluded his account, "I am not likely to allow the same thing to occur again."

"You said you trust me," Gina protested.

"No, I did not. I said I choose to believe your tale of travel through time, which is a different matter entirely."

Dominick's fingers were still fastened tightly around her wrist, pressing her hand and his against her back, keeping their warm, naked bodies close together, and Gina was finding rational thought increasingly difficult.

"I thought you cared about me," she said, rearing her head back so she could glare at him. "But you don't. My mistake. What's wrong with me? Why do I have to learn the same lesson over and over?"

She tried to pull away from him. Dominick slid his free hand down over her hips, holding her closer, letting her feel his renewed arousal.

"You hear, but you do not listen with your mind and your heart," he said. "I do not make a habit of bedding every willing female I encounter."

"What is that supposed to mean?" she demanded.

"That I find you unusual, fascinating, alluring. That I must go to Regensburg, and I don't want to leave you behind because I am going to need your help," he said, and smiled at her in a way that nearly melted her bones.

"How can I possibly help you?" she asked. "Never tell me you intend to join that band of traitors?"

"Of course not!"

"Good." She sighed with relief. "I didn't really imagine you were the kind of man who could betray his king."

"I intend to expose them," Dominick said.

"Will Charles believe you?" she asked. "It's his son you'll be accusing."

"There has to be a way to extricate Pepin from the influence of those wicked conspirators and save Charles from harm at the same time," Dominick said. "Before I can speak to Charles on this matter, I need proof that cannot be denied, and I must have evidence that Pepin is being used."

"I've never been good at sitting around twiddling my thumbs," Gina said. "Considering that I am apparently going to stay in the eighth century for a while, I'll want something useful to occupy my time. What could be more useful than routing out a bunch of traitors? I'm with you, Dominick. Just tell me what you want me to do."

She didn't add that if Dominick could expose the conspirators, he wasn't likely to be accused of being one of them. Keeping Dominick safe was a prospect that appealed to her strongly enough to make her forget her fears and, at least temporarily, her concerns about returning to New York. She'd worry about New York later.

"You do understand that there is a certain danger involved?" Dominick was searching her face as if to discover any hint of false intentions on her part.

"I am already in danger, just by knowing about the plot," she pointed out. "If we don't stop it, we could be trapped in the middle of it and both lose our heads. Literally."

"I do admire courage in a woman," he said. "Very well, then. When we reach Regensburg, I will introduce you at court. I'd like you gather information from the ladies you meet there. I can't question them; they'll think I'm seeking another wife, and that will place any young lady I speak to for more than a moment in an awkward position. But you, as a female and a stranger, will be free to ask almost anything you want."

"Not just of the young girls," Gina said. "I can talk with the older women, too. Old ladies love to give advice and to gossip, and unless they're completely dotty, they often remember details that other, busier people forget or consider insignificant. That was true of my landlady back in New York, and I suspect it's the case here, too. Now, tell me how we get to Regensburg."

"It will be difficult," Dominick murmured, and bent his head to nibble at her earlobe. "The journey will take at least a week if the weather is good, and for most of that time I won't be able to lie with you. I'm not sure I can contain myself for so long."

"Oh." Gina hid her face in his shoulder, breathing in the clean smell of him, feeling his wonderful strength beneath her cheek. He released the hand he'd been holding behind her back, and she put both her arms around his waist. She couldn't believe that less than half an hour after he had made love to her, he wanted to do it again—and that she was more than willing. She was eager, longing for the same glorious sensations and heart-stopping release she had experienced with him the first time. "I suppose we could lie together now. Couldn't we?"

"I was hoping you'd suggest it." His hands were on her breasts, coaxing the nipples into hard peaks.

Gina's gasp of pleasure went straight to Dominick's heart—and to his conscience. He prayed that he had judged her correctly, that her fantastic story was true, for if she was lying to him, more than his life was at risk. Far more important was the life of the king of the Franks. Pepin's life, also, for Dominick knew Charles well enough to know that being forced to execute his own son would break that noble ruler's valiant heart.

Dominick sank onto the pallet with Gina in his arms. He was aware that her desire for him was intense enough to overcome her fears about what he was asking her to do, just as his incredible longing to possess her had melted most of his suspicions about her.

Gina's arms were around him, urging him toward complete union. Driven by uncontrollable desire, Dominick entered her in a swift rush, not being careful with her this time, obeying his body's hot insistence. He saw her wonderful green eyes open wide in surprise, and a moment later he watched her shimmer into ecstasy. As he buried himself deep inside her with one final, forceful thrust, he hoped with all his heart and soul that she really was honest and true. For, whether she was or not, he didn't think he could live without her.

"My plan is to present you as a visiting Northumbrian noblewoman," Dominick said when they were dressed once more and back on the second level of his house. "However, no lady would show her face at court without at least one maidservant. Would you like to ask Ella to join you?"

"I don't know how to behave nobly at a royal court," Gina protested, "and I don't know anything about Northumbria."

"Just think carefully before you speak," he said. "If you must, use the confusion of thought resulting from your recent severe illness as an excuse, and point out your very short hair as proof that you were sick. I have every confidence in you."

Gina wasn't so sure that his confidence wouldn't prove to be misplaced. If she made a serious mistake, they could both lose their lives. She did seize on Dominick's idea that she should invite Ella along.

"Not just as a maid," she said to Ella later that morning, while the two of them were busy at their usual task of spreading out the laundry to dry. "I'm scared to death to go to a royal court. I'd like to have a friend with me." It didn't seem at all strange to think of the ever-cheerful Ella as a friend, though they had known each other less than a month.

"Harulf is to lead Dominick's men-at-arms," Ella said, her blue eyes dancing as she considered Gina's invitation.

"Well, then, you absolutely have to go with us," Gina told her. "It was Dominick's idea, so I'm sure Hedwiga won't mind."

Far from objecting, Hedwiga had altered more of Hiltrude's gowns for Gina to wear, and she supplied baskets to pack them into, which that could be strapped onto the pack horses that were to accompany Dominick's party.

There was such a rush to be ready to travel at short notice that Gina didn't see Dominick again

142

until evening, when she found him in the garden. She still wasn't completely sure of him, so she approached him with some hesitation.

"You look sad, Dominick."

"I may not see Feldbruck again until autumn," he said with his gaze on the distant mountains. "I don't like to be away from my land for so long."

"I understand," she said. "If I ever find a place to call home, I'm sure I'll be as attached to it as you are to Feldbruck."

In response to her words he took her hand and kissed it.

"You ought to go to bed," he told her. "We leave at dawn."

"I thought you'd want—I mean—I thought tonight—after this morning—" Her tongue stammered to a halt.

"Oh, I want," he said. "More than you know. The problem is a lack of time. I still have to meet with Arno for several hours and give final instructions to Hedwiga and to three or four other people."

"I wish I knew more about running a place like this, so I could help you."

"Thank you for that. I think you need your sleep." His hand brushed softly against her cheek. "I used you hard out second time this morning."

"I didn't mind at all," she said, grinning at him. "I enjoyed it. Very much."

"Oh, God help me. God help us both."

He caught her to him in a crushing embrace, holding her till she was breathless. Then he kissed her so long and so thoroughly that it was almost as if he was making love to her all over again. Standing there in the twilight with both of them fully clothed, the intensity of Dominick's passion was mind-boggling. Gina half expected him to pull her into the trees and take her there. She wished he would. Instead, he released her abruptly.

"Good night, Gina." He walked away from her so fast that he was almost running, and he disappeared into the wing of the house where Arno's office was.

"Dominick," she whispered, fingers at the lips he had just bruised with his passionate kiss. "You talk about feminine wiles? What about the masculine wiles you are using on me? I'm sure you know I can't resist you. Why do I have this awful feeling that you are going to get both of us killed before you're done?"

Chapter Nine

They left Feldbruck at dawn, as Dominick had commanded, and rode north with the Alps at their backs. Gina was again mounted on Cela, and since she still hadn't learned anything she needed to know about taking care of a horse, she was glad to see Benet and two other grooms riding along with their group and leading the pack horses. Harulf was at the head of eight brawny guards, all of them well armed.

As for Gina's lack of riding skills, she didn't have time to worry about that. Dominick was in a hurry, and Cela, apparently inspired by her equine companions, was moving far more quickly than on their first ride together. Gina just held on as best she could and hoped she wouldn't fall.

"The stream that runs through Feldbruck flows

into the River Inn, which empties into the Danube," Dominick explained as he rode beside Gina. "That's the route Pepin and Father Guntram are using—along the waterways. It's a longer journey, but easier for Pepin. They can travel by boat part of the time, and where they must ride, the roads are better, with more places to stop at night or if the weather turns bad. Rain and cold always make Pepin's back and legs ache."

"So we are taking the quicker and less scenic route?" Gina asked, a little breathless from the effort to stay in the saddle.

"Straight overland to Regensburg," he replied. "A rougher but more direct path."

"And you are making us travel as fast as possible because you plan to arrive a couple of days before Pepin does."

Dominick didn't respond; he simply gave her a long look she couldn't interpret.

When Gina had first reached Feldbruck, the trees and undergrowth were arrayed in soft, springtime shades of green and gold. In the weeks since then the landscape had blossomed into the full density of lush summer, and the fields displayed healthy crops almost ready for the early harvest. Gina had never seen so many shades of green.

When their company left the open farmland and entered the forest, the thick, leafy canopy above provided cool shade from the sun. Firs added a more somber note of dark green, along with a resinous fragrance that reminded Gina of Christmas. They were riding through a fairytale landscape of deep shadows and sudden, sunlit clearings, and of rushing streams that provided all the water they required for themselves and their animals. Only occasionally did they pass a settlement, and rarely did they meet other people.

"I've seldom been away from Feldbruck," Ella confided to Gina, "and never to Regensburg."

"Neither have I been there," Gina said.

"Aren't you excited? We'll see the king! And they say the queen is the most beautiful woman in the world."

Gina recalled Pepin's unflattering comments about Fastrada's character. "Beauty must be the primary requirement for the job," she said.

Unlike Ella, Gina wasn't looking forward to meeting either the king or Fastrada. After asking a lot of questions over the past few weeks, she had figured out that Charles, king of the Franks, was the famous Charlemagne. She had learned about him in eighth grade, and, if she remembered correctly, he had a reputation for being a benevolent ruler. In light of what she knew about the scheme to remove him from his throne and young Pepin's involvement in it, she tried to hold on to that thought.

The first night out from Feldbruck they slept in the forest. The men-at-arms built a big bonfire, which Ella said was to scare away wild boars. Gina hoped the fire also kept any lurking woodland outlaws at bay. She was relieved to notice that the men-at-arms were taking turns at sentry duty, though not so pleased to hear Dominick say he would also stand guard during a watch. She had hoped to have some private time with him.

They ate the cold meat, cheese, and bread Hedwiga had packed for them and shared a couple of skins of wine. After a long day of riding the simple fare tasted almost as good as one of Hedwiga's hot feasts.

Gina had never slept under the stars before. She decided camping out was fun, especially after Dominick finished his watch and, while the others slept, lay down next to her, put his arm around her, and let her use his shoulder for a pillow. She drifted into slumber with his lips against her forehead.

They were off again early in the morning after a breakfast of leftover bread and water from a nearby stream. Gina began to wonder where they would find their next meal. She needn't have worried. Dominick knew what he was doing. In late afternoon, just as it began to rain, they reached a wide river.

"It's the Isar," Dominick told her. "That's Landshut on the other side, where there is a monastery. We can stay in their guesthouse for the night."

"And say a prayer in the monastery church for the sun to shine tomorrow," Gina added from beneath the hood of the heavy gray cloak Hedwiga had found for her to wear. As she peered though the downpour, she could see a bridge just ahead of them. "At least we won't have to ford the river, though I don't think it would make much difference. I couldn't be any wetter if I waded across."

Dominick laughed at her remarks and rode on ahead. Gina followed him over the bridge and through the monastery gate into a courtyard with a stable on one side and a guesthouse on the other. The monk who met them and whom Dominick called by name guided the travelers into a stone reception room, where charcoal braziers provided a warmth that quickly dried their damp clothing.

Gina was so grateful to be out of the rain and near the heat that she didn't even mind the pervasive smell of damp wool and unwashed bodies. When she stretched out her hands to the charcoal, she saw that her nails could use a scrubbing with soap and a stiff brush. So could her knuckles. Somehow, the grime wasn't unimportant. She smiled ruefully, accepting that she was growing used to the inconveniences of the eighth century. She could bear inconvenience, so long as she was with Dominick.

The monks gave them hot vegetable stew and brown bread for their evening meal, and Dominick made arrangements to take along bread and cheese when they left the next morning. From what Gina heard of his conversation with the prior, she understood that he regularly made large donations to the monastery and thus was entitled to food and lodging whenever he came that way.

After two days in the saddle Gina was grateful for the narrow, hard bed in the little cell that she and Ella shared. She was so tired that she only missed Dominick's warmth beside her briefly before she fell into a deep sleep.

Since leaving Feldbruck they had been following a path with enough wagon ruts in it that even Gina could recognize it as a regularly used road. From Landshut they left the road and struck out directly north through deep, trackless forests, where the trees dripped the remains of yesterday's storm onto their heads and shoulders until all of them were as wet as if it were still raining. In fact, the sky had cleared in early morning, and whenever they came to a break in the trees, the sun shone through the mist, making the very air glow with golden light, as if the forest were enchanted.

"It's so beautiful here," Gina murmured. It was nearly midday, and Dominick had called a halt for eating and a chance to stretch their legs. He was standing next to her because the rocks and the ground were too wet for sitting. "I expect to see fairies pop out from behind every bush."

"In this part of Bavaria there are ancient legends about spirits of the trees and the waters," Dominick said. "Not to mention tales about the Norns."

"Who are they?" Gina asked.

"The Norns are three immortal sisters who sit beneath a great ash tree, forever spinning the threads of the lives of individual men and women into the ropes of fate."

"They really messed up the thread of my fate, didn't they? I guess they spun it into the wrong section of rope."

"Or perhaps they made a mistake the first time and then corrected it," Dominick said, his gaze holding hers. "I am certain of one thing, Gina. No mysterious, supernatural creature could possibly be more captivating or more magical than you."

"I hope you mean that." She looked into his eyes and saw only warmth and desire, with none of the questions or mistrust she sometimes noticed in him.

Then his mood shifted to humor.

"I warned you the journey would be difficult," he said, teasing her.

"Dare I hope it's almost over?" she asked, teasing back.

"Three more days and nights, if the weather holds," he answered. "During this journey we will travel even on Sunday."

"I can endure it," she said, smiling a little. "Can you?"

His answer was a low, sensual chuckle that stirred a dangerous warmth deep inside her. It was amazing how he could warm her heart with a look or a word or a quick touch that no one else saw. It was almost as if he was using the journey as a means of slowly seducing her. If that was his intention, he was succeeding.

Nonetheless, by the time they reached the road that led directly into Regensburg, Gina was heartily sick of being on horseback and more than ready for a long, hot bath, followed by a long, hot night with Dominick.

The road curved, and they came out of the trees onto a wide, cleared swath of land. There before them lay Regensburg and the Danube.

"It really is blue," Gina said, surprised by her first sight of the river. Then she added, "I didn't expect the town to be so large."

"It has to be," Dominick said, "to accommodate all the people who are obligated to follow Charles from place to place. Everyone from the queen and her ladies and the royal children, to Charles's closest advisors, to the teachers and students of the palace school, the counts who are presently in attendance at court along with their families and retainers, the scholars, physicians, bishops and ordinary priests, men-at-arms, cooks, seamstresses, and servants. They all come to Regensburg when Charles decrees it—along with the usual camp followers," he finished, glancing at her as if to see how she would accept that last item in his long list.

She was about to say that she'd never understand how any woman could do something so unpleasant for a living, when it struck her like a thunderclap that she no longer thought of sex as unpleasant. With Dominick, it was wonderful. She stared at him with her lips parted, and what was in her thoughts must have appeared on her face, for she saw his eyes widen. He moved his horse nearer to hers and leaned toward her.

"Later," he murmured. Then he nudged his mount and rode ahead to join Harulf, who was awaiting him with a question.

Feeling the need of a cooler subject to contemplate, Gina turned her attention from Dominick to the town they were approaching. Almost all the houses were built of creamy stone, and their red tile roofs were steeply slanted. There were lots of gardens; nearly every house in Regensburg had one. She had learned enough under Hedwiga's tutelage to recognize cabbages, lettuces, the leafy tops of carrots and beets, and several kinds of herbs.

A strip of young trees was planted along the river's edge for shade, and here and there she could see docks extending into the water with a few boats tied up at them. Men and women in bright clothing hurried along the dirt streets or gathered on the docks to watch the boats unloading. It was a colorful, attractive scene.

On a hill just a short distance from the river rose

a large church dedicated to St. Peter, with two tall square towers and door arches that Gina noticed were curved, not pointed like later Gothic arches. The palace, which was close by the church and built in the same sturdy architectural style, was simply stupendous. It dominated the town. From what Gina could see while riding along, the palace was a series of connected buildings of differing heights, of towers and gateways and long colonnades that were open to the river breezes.

She was surprised to learn that Dominick kept a house in Regensburg, with a few servants always there to maintain it and see to his needs when he was in residence. It was a clean, orderly house in a quiet neighborhood near the river. Gina was given her own private room next to Dominick's. Ella was to sleep in the female servants' quarters, and she seemed content with the arrangement. Gina wondered if Ella harbored plans to spend as many nights as possible with Harulf. Since Gina intended to spend her nights with Dominick, she couldn't criticize Ella for doing something similar.

As soon as they were unpacked the two young women retired to the small bathhouse at the rear of the building, where both of them washed away the grime and the aches of their week-long trip. Gina was back in her room, clad only in her shift while she dried her hair, when Ella hurried in.

"Dominick is in the bathhouse now," Ella said. "He wanted me to give you plenty of notice. You are to dress in your best gown and paint your face. We are going to the palace."

"What, now? The afternoon is almost gone. I thought we'd wait until tomorrow," Gina cried, seeing her plans for a leisurely dinner and evening with Dominick evaporate.

"Dominick said you'd understand why he wants to talk to as many people as possible tonight," Ella said. "I'm to attend you. Isn't it exciting?"

"Thrilling," Gina responded dryly. "I suppose it can't be avoided. Go and dress yourself, Ella. I can see to my own clothes."

"Are you sure?" Ella looked uncertain.

"Yes. Your hair is longer than mine. It will take you a while to dry and braid it. Come back when you're finished and tell me if I look all right."

What Gina really wanted was some time alone to brace herself to meet one of the most famous kings in all of history. She wished she knew more about Charlemagne, so she could talk intelligently to him. Then she decided he most likely wouldn't pay any attention to her. He'd be too busy with Dominick and the other courtiers.

Gina had brought to Regensburg the hairbrush, makeup bag, and mirror that were in her purse when it landed beside Dominick's bed a few seconds after she arrived in the eighth century. Small as the mirror was, she was glad to have it, for mirrors were a scarce commodity. The few she had seen at Feldbruck were made of polished metal that barely reflected at all. Using her mirror, Gina applied powder, eyeliner, mascara, and lipstick.

From the supply of newly altered clothing Hedwiga had packed for her, she chose a dress of deep burgundy silk with gold embroidery at the neck and sleeve edges, because it looked to her like the kind of gown a lady would wear to meet a king.

After pulling it over her head and tying the gold sash, she brushed her hair carefully, making it curl as much as possible. Once her preparations were completed, there was nothing left for her to do but grow more nervous with each minute.

Dominick and Ella appeared at her door at the same time, and Gina learned to her dismay that she was expected to remount a horse and ride to the palace.

"Can't I walk?" she asked. "Riding will ruin this lovely dress."

"The streets are too muddy for walking," Dominick said. "But I can take you up with me, and Harulf can do the same for Ella. You can sit sideways and thus spare your gowns from wrinkling."

"I'd like to ride with Harulf," Ella said at once. Gowned in bright blue wool, with her blond hair in twin braids tied with blue ribbons, she was looking exceptionally pretty, her cheeks rosy with excitement.

"I wish I could feel as cheerful," Gina said, watching Ella hurry ahead of her to meet Harulf. "Dominick, I assume you are going to insist on speaking alone with Charles, which means you'll be leaving me to fend for myself."

"I wouldn't dream of deserting you," Dominick said. "Nor can I request a private interview with Charles until I have unquestionable proof of the plot that's being formed and names I can supply when Charles asks for them."

"In other words, we are off to the palace to seek the very proof you need."

"Exactly. Pay attention to everything you hear or see while we are there."

As if Dominick had known what Gina was planning to wear, he was clad in a red wool tunic and matching woolen trousers just a shade or two lighter than her gown. His trousers were cross-gartered with strips of gilded leather, and he wore shoes instead of boots. His only other decorations were the gold chain and pendant of a count and a gilded leather belt with his plain, serviceable eating knife in its sheath at one side. Swords, he informed Gina, were not usually worn at court unless war preparations were under way. With his sword or without it, he was the most imposing specimen of manhood Gina had ever seen, and just standing next to him made her shiver with pleasure.

While she was lost in appreciation of his masculine splendor, he caught her by the waist and tossed her lightly into the saddle. Then, before she could begin to worry whether she was going slide right off without a leg on either side of the horse, he mounted and put an arm around her waist, holding her securely.

It was a remarkable sensation to be sitting so close between his thighs, and it quickly became obvious to her that Dominick wasn't indifferent to the position, either. Startled by his immediate physical reaction, she looked directly at him and found his eyes filled with laughter, though his face was perfectly solemn.

"I'd kiss you," he said, "but it would be most improper to do it in public and would likely smear your face paint."

"Do that, and I'll bite you," she retorted. She was rewarded by his hearty laugh.

Between Dominick's teasing and her own yearning, by the time they reached the palace gate Gina was ready to turn around and gallop at full speed back to his house.

"Feeling better?" he asked as he lifted her down from the horse.

"You teased me on purpose, to make me forget about being nervous," she accused him.

"Did it work?" he asked with a straight face. "Answer later, and punish me then if you want. When we are alone I'll let you do whatever you like to me. For now, remember that you are a noblewoman. Take my arm. Just put your hand on my wrist. Harulf, Ella, stay with us," he ordered over his shoulder.

This time his teasing wasn't enough to calm her nerves. Though intensely aware of Dominick at her side, Gina still couldn't forget where she was and what she and Dominick were trying to do. With her knees shaking and her heart beating double-time, she entered the great hall of the palace to meet Charlemagne.

Knowing he'd had four wives and several concubines, Gina expected the king of the Franks to look like a movie version of the similarly licentious Henry VIII, all beefy and bloated and missing a few teeth. She wasn't prepared for the tall, handsome man who stood in front of the throne set at one end of the long hall. Charles was simply dressed in a blue woolen tunic and trousers, with no jewelry and no crown. His hair was silver-blond, cut just below his ears, and he was clean-shaven except for a droopy Frankish mustache similar to the facial hair worn by many other men in the room.

Dominick had told her that Charles was past forty, and middle-aged spread was catching up with his midriff, though no one could have called him fat. In his mature features Gina could detect an older, slightly fleshier version of Pepin's more delicate face.

What impressed her most was the personal warmth that Charles radiated and the way his smile made her feel he was her friend when Dominick brought her forward to present her. This was no cold and distant royal personage; Charlemagne was a hearty, plain-spoken man who stooped to pick up the little girl who suddenly ran to him and threw her arms around his leg.

"My daughter, Theudrada," Charles said, and kissed the child. "Pretty 'Drada. Yes, Papa loves you. Have you children, Lady Gina?"

"No, sir, I'm not married," Gina responded. She was a bit surprised to notice at least a dozen other children standing about or playing near the throne. Most of them resembled Charles, so she assumed they were his.

"Perhaps your situation will change soon," Charles said, and he winked at Dominick. "I'm glad to see you back at court, my boy. We've missed you, haven't we, Fastrada, my dearest?"

Charles turned to the woman who sat in an ornately carved chair next to his throne. The infamous queen of the Franks appeared to be in her early twenties, and she was incredibly beautiful, with dainty facial bones. Her long hair, which she wore loose beneath a gold circlet, was a lovely honey shade, and her complexion was perfect, if a bit too pale for vital health. Her eyes were sapphire blue under the delicate arches of her neatly plucked brows.

Only on a careful second look did Gina see the lines of discontent near Fastrada's pretty mouth and the cold expression in her eyes when she regarded Dominick. A whiff of heavy jasmine perfume drifted to Gina's nose as the queen moved restlessly.

"I'm glad to find you well, my lady," Dominick said politely to Fastrada. "I note that you are more beautiful than ever."

"I am surprised to see you here at all," Fastrada retorted. She leaned back in her chair, sticking out her lower lip and looking for all the world like a sullen, sulky teenager. Transferring her attention from Dominick to Gina, she asked, "Is this your latest concubine?"

"Lady Gina is my guest at Regensburg," Dominick responded mildly.

"Indeed?" Fastrada's elegant eyebrows rose. Her voice took on a mocking tone. "I do believe I recall that dress. A friend of mine wore it the last time she was at court. A certain Lady Hiltrude. Really, Dominick, can't you afford to have a new dress made when you reward a woman for joining you in bed? Or, better yet, give her a piece of jewelry?"

"You are mistaken, my lady. I am no man's concubine." Gina spoke up loudly, too offended to tolerate the queen's rudeness another moment. Words tumbled from her lips in an angry rush, offering an explanation that was far from accurate. "In fact, Count Dominick has been extremely kind to me. I was set upon by robbers, and all my belongings were stolen. That's why I have no jewelry to wear and why I was forced to come here to court in borrowed clothes. It's also why my hair is so short. The robbers left me by the roadside wearing only my shift, and I caught a chill that quickly developed into severe chest congestion. Of course, the only thing to do was cut off my long hair to preserve what little strength I had left, and then pray I'd recover. I'm very grateful for the good care that Count Dominick and his housekeeper gave me. Together they saved my life."

"Gina," Dominick cautioned her when she paused to catch her breath, "you've said enough. Your praise is embarrassing me."

"Yes, Gina," said Fastrada, her lips curving into a nasty smile. "You have said more than enough to tell us that Dominick has been remarkably lax about seeing to the safety of the roads in his county and, no doubt, in apprehending and punishing the robbers who apparently flourish around Feldbruck. Such neglect of the land entrusted to him by his king is a serious matter and ought to be looked into promptly."

The threat in Fastrada's voice was unmistakable. Too late Gina recalled Dominick saying that the queen had once tried to ruin him. Now, in her eagerness to stop the unpleasant woman from continuing her public rudeness toward Dominick, Gina had provided her with ammunition to use against him.

"There are no more robbers left in the vicinity of Feldbruck," Dominick said to Fastrada. "They've all been caught and hanged."

"Really?" Fastrada shifted in her chair, thrusting

out her shapely bosom until her nipples were outlined against the fine silk of her gown. "I wish I'd been there to see it. I am passionately fond of witnessing justice done."

I just bet you are, Gina thought. *I've got your number, Queenie. You get off on hurting people. But what's a nice guy like Charles doing with a wife like you?*

Chapter Ten

"Fastrada, my sweet love," Charles said, "I thought you'd be glad to welcome Dominick back to court."

"Whatever made you think that?" Fastrada exclaimed. "He broke my dear friend's heart, then sent her off to a convent to repine. Who knows what misery your precious Dominick inflicted on poor Hiltrude while she lived at Feldbruck, or what disgusting demands he made of her?" Fastrada squirmed in her seat, the motion sending another cloud of perfume in Gina's direction.

"Hiltrude was Dominick's wife," Charles reminded her. "It was her duty to submit to his wishes."

"As you well know, my lady," Dominick said with quiet dignity, "it was Hiltrude who left me, claiming she could not bear to live any longer with a bastard. Since ours was an arranged marriage, and we'd not had time enough to grow fond of each other, I do not believe her heart was affected in any way."

For Dominick's sake, Gina hoped Fastrada did not detect the dangerous note in his low voice. Charles had noticed. He was staring at Dominick with a puzzled expression, and his mouth opened as if he wanted to say something.

"Charles." Fastrada leaned forward and reached toward her husband, wrapping her arms around his thigh the same way Theudrada had done. But Theudrada was a child, no more than three years old. Fastrada was a woman grown, and a queen. Surely she knew better than to touch a man so intimately while in public. Her slender arms were like pale snakes about Charles's thigh, and her face was pressed against him. When Charles smiled indulgently and tried to move away, Fastrada stroked one hand across his crotch.

Gina smothered a shocked gasp. All around her Charles's nobles were either staring at the panelled walls or gazing at their own feet. The crowded hall fell silent as everyone there pretended not to see what Fastrada was doing.

"I don't feel well," Fastrada whined. "Oh, Charles, help me to bed."

"I'll call a servant." Charles gestured to the elderly woman who was looking after the children. He gave Theudrada into her care, then bent to untangle Fastrada's arms from around his leg.

"No." Fastrada tightened her grip on him. "I want you, Charles. I need only you."

"Very well, then." Charles put an arm around his

wife's slender waist, and at last Fastrada released his leg, allowing him to lift her till she was on her feet. She leaned against him as if unable to stand on her own.

With the weary air of a man who knows he has barely managed to avert a wild emotional scene, Charles spoke to his courtiers.

"My poor wife has overtaxed her frail strength," he said. "Her devotion to me and to her duties as queen deserve our admiration. I will see her to her bedchamber and make sure she is resting peacefully, and then I'll rejoin you for the remainder of the evening." With that, he began to guide Fastrada toward a door at the rear of the hall.

"I don't believe what I've just seen," Gina said.

"I do," Dominick responded. "But then, I've seen it before."

"She shames him," said a voice from directly behind Gina. "Fastrada quirks her little finger and bends the greatest king in Christendom to her will."

Gina spun around to confront the speaker, an elegantly gowned, middle-aged woman with brown hair liberally streaked with gray. Pale blue eyes regarded Gina with interest before the woman turned her gaze on Dominick.

"My Lady Adalhaid. What a pleasure to meet you again." Dominick's manner was polite, his bow impeccable, yet Gina noticed the wary tension in him.

"Welcome back to court, Dominick," said Lady Adalhaid. "You are looking well."

"Thank you," Dominick said. "I am in perfect health." Despite his almost painful politeness, he did not ask after Lady Adalhaid's well-being.

"You always were in good health. It's one of your most attractive qualities." Lady Adalhaid's smile altered her plain, lined face, giving Gina a brief glimpse of the pretty girl she must once have been. "Would you like me to introduce Lady Gina to some of the other women? She will want friends if she's to remain at court for more than a few days."

"I would like that very much," Gina said quickly. Her curiosity was aroused by Lady Adalhaid's manner toward Dominick and by his odd response. More importantly, Gina saw in Lady Adalhaid's offer the ideal opportunity to gossip with the noblewoman and perhaps find out whether the ladies of the court knew about the plot to dethrone Charles.

Gina also saw her chance to make up to Dominick for her mistake in speaking her mind to Queen Fastrada. She was painfully aware that she had been foolish in not thinking through what she wanted to say before she opened her mouth to the queen. She couldn't understand why Dominick was frowning and looking so reluctant when she had an opening to the information he needed.

"It's quite all right, Dominick," said Lady Adalhaid. "I mean the girl no harm. Take yourself off to visit with your male friends for an hour or two, and then rejoin us for the evening meal. I doubt if Charles will return to the hall much before then."

"Gina . . ." Dominick began.

"I'll be just fine," she insisted, trusting him to understand the hidden message in her words. Dominick had investigative work to do, too. "Lady Adalhaid is right; you ought to talk to your friends. You've been complaining that you haven't been at

166

court for a long time. Here's your chance to catch up on all the latest news."

Still Dominick hesitated, looking as if there was something he wanted to say to her. He was probably going to warn her to be more cautious in her conversations.

"I promise to mind my manners and not offend anyone," she said, laughing to reassure him as she waved him away.

Dominick looked from her to Lady Adalhaid. Finally he left, taking Harulf with him.

"This is my companion, Ella," Gina said to Lady Adalhaid.

The noblewoman looked Ella up and down, as if trying to decide her actual social status.

"Stay within sight of us," Lady Adalhaid instructed Ella. "Lady Gina or I will call if we have need of you."

Gina was annoyed by Lady Adalhaid's curt order to a girl she clearly deemed no more than a servant—and someone else's servant, at that. On the other hand, Gina didn't want to antagonize a woman who could possibly provide vital information, so she kept quiet, contenting herself with a quick wink at Ella behind Lady Adalhaid's back. Ella grinned to show she wasn't insulted and dropped a few paces behind, as Lady Adalhaid had commanded.

"I am sorry the queen is ill," Gina said, hoping to elicit a remark or two about the royal marriage.

"Fastrada is not ill," Lady Adalhaid responded in a voice so low that Gina was forced to lean close in order to hear what she said. "She is a willful child who has been given too much power at too young an age. After bringing forth two daughters in three

167

years, her dearest hope lies in bearing Charles a son who will permanently secure her position."

"I thought Charles already had sons," Gina said.

"He has four, all of them by Hildegarde." Lady Adalhaid added in a whisper, "There was a true queen. Did you know Hildegarde?"

"Unfortunately, no. I only recently arrived in Francia."

"Ah, yes. Your journey was interrupted by robbers who seized all your belongings. How sad for you." Lady Adalhaid sounded as if she didn't believe the robbery story. "Where were you before you came to Francia?"

"Northumbria," Gina replied. "I was raised in a convent there." She thought that little detail was an inspiration. If she had spent years inside a convent, she couldn't be expected to know much about Northumbrian life outside the cloister. She reckoned without Lady Adalhaid's determination to learn all about her.

"Which convent?" asked Lady Adalhaid. "Where was it located?"

"I beg your pardon?" How many convents were there in Northumbria? Did Lady Adalhaid have actual knowledge of any of them? Where was Dominick? Gina looked around frantically, wishing he would suddenly appear to rescue her. She couldn't see him, which meant she was going to have to rescue herself. On the spur of the moment she decided to adopt Fastrada's method.

"Oh, dear." Gina clapped a hand to her forehead. "Would you mind if I sit down? It's this awful dizziness. It comes and goes, ever since the robbers hit me over the head."

"Certainly." Lady Adalhaid led the way to a bench at one side of the hall. There she sat and patted the wood beside her. "Sit here, my dear. I do hope you were properly cared for at Feldbruck. Perhaps you ought to ask Charles's physician to examine you. A bit of bloodletting can do wonders for almost any illness."

"Hedwiga is a very competent nurse, and she says I will recover completely without any further treatment," Gina stated firmly. "It will just take a little while, that's all. Hedwiga says I'll need to be patient."

"Ah, yes, I remember Hedwiga. An overbearing woman."

"Have you been to Feldbruck?" Gina asked, surprised.

"Once," said Lady Adalhaid. "Briefly. Dominick and I are old acquaintances."

"Did you know his parents?" Gina couldn't resist the chance to learn more about Dominick and his family.

"My dear, in Francia everyone knows everyone," Lady Adalhaid said with a superior smile that suggested Gina wasn't anyone. "Dominick's mother and I were friends as girls. After she died, Dominick's father and I were lovers for a time. You look shocked."

"Just surprised that anyone would admit a love affair to a complete stranger."

"Really? You are an innocent. I suppose that means you won't admit to me that you and Dominick are lovers."

Gina could feel the blood rushing into her face. She turned away from Lady Adalhaid, too embarrassed to meet her eyes any longer. Lady Adalhaid uttered a soft, knowing laugh and patted Gina's hand.

"Let us speak of something else," Lady Adalhaid suggested.

"Yes, let's." Gina's thoughts floundered about for a minute or two while her companion regarded her expectantly. The conversation wasn't going at all the way Gina wanted. She was supposed to be ferreting out information about the plot against Charles. Instead, all she had done was embarrass herself. She didn't think Lady Adalhaid was capable of embarrassment, which was a good thing, because it was time to get down to serious information-seeking.

"You mentioned that all Charles's sons are the sons of Queen Hildegarde," Gina said. "I thought he had another boy, from his first marriage." Did she only imagine it, or did Lady Adalhaid's spine stiffen a little at that remark? Certainly, the lady's smile was gone.

"You must be thinking of the hunchback," said Lady Adalhaid. "A pitiful fool, a creature of no importance."

"Pepin is still a king's son." Gina repressed the urge to snap out a few well-chosen words at the cold-hearted woman. If everyone at court reacted to him the way Lady Adalhaid did, it was no wonder Pepin was ready for all-out rebellion.

"Since you are new to court," Lady Adalhaid remarked, unperturbed by Gina's irritation, "I will pretend you did not say what you just said, and I will offer you a piece of valuable advice. Never repeat those words, or anything similar to them, within Fastrada's hearing. She cannot bear the sight of Pepin or even to hear his name spoken. In fact, if you are wise, you will never say anything that might upset Fastrada."

"Not even if what I want to say is the truth?"

"I can see you have much to learn. There are many subjects that displease Fastrada. Those who incur her displeasure suffer dreadful punishments."

"Yet Charles seems like a good man."

"He is." Lady Adalhaid's voice took on genuine warmth. "A wise and generous king."

"But he can't control his wife?"

"When Hildegarde died and Charles married Fastrada, he exchanged an angel for a devil. I am not the only person who thinks so. Fastrada exerts an evil influence on him."

"Because she is young and beautiful, and he's going through some kind of mid-life crisis," Gina mused aloud. "Relations between men and women never seem to change, do they? I suspect that Charles needs Fastrada to prove to himself and his friends that he's still the virile man he used to be. Meanwhile, Fastrada makes a habit of pawing him in public and then dragging him off to bed to keep his attention focused on her."

"Perhaps you are not as innocent as I first thought." Lady Adalhaid's serious expression gave way to a faint smile. "Walk carefully here at court, Gina, for your own sake and for Dominick's. Always think before you speak. And stay as far from Fastrada as you can."

"I'll take your advice. Now, weren't you going to introduce me to some of the other ladies?"

"Is there anyone special you'd like to meet?"

"I don't know anyone at all, so I'll leave the introductions to your discretion."

"There's a clever girl. Are you quite recovered from your dizziness? Then come along, and I'll present you to the ladies you ought to know."

"Well?" Dominick asked. "Were you able to learn anything about the plot?"

It was after midnight, and he and Gina were alone in his bedchamber, speaking softly in case any of the servants were still awake. After helping Gina to remove her court gown, Ella was in her bed—or with Harulf—and Gina was clad only in a soft woolen robe that opened down the front.

"Lady Adalhaid introduced me to at least a dozen women, and they chattered for hours while I listened," Gina said. "They were all young unmarried girls. I guess Lady Adalhaid assumed I'd have something in common with them. Anyway, I don't think those ladies are involved in anything more serious than deciding which gown to wear. If they've overheard their parents plotting, they either disregarded what they heard or they aren't interested. They remind me of the butterflies in the garden at Feldbruck, pretty, thoughtless things fluttering from blossom to blossom."

"The blossoms being the unwed noblemen who frequent the court?" Dominick said, chuckling at the comparison. "Those girls aren't as heedless as they appear. Most of them have been brought to Regensburg specifically to be married off, or at least betrothed. Their parents are busy in the background, arranging the marriages, and the more intelligent girls are dropping hints to Mama or Papa about which men they prefer."

"I was hoping Lady Adalhaid would introduce me to some of the older women who might have husbands involved in the plot, but every time I suggested I'd like to meet someone other than a giggly girl, she changed the subject."

"She's a clever woman. She is also one of Fastrada's closest companions."

"You must be joking! She warned me against the queen, told me to be careful of anything I say to her. I got the impression she doesn't like Fastrada."

"I wouldn't be at all surprised if she dislikes the queen," Dominick said.

"She doesn't like Pepin, either. She called him a fool. And she thinks Hedwiga is overbearing. Yet I don't think she's the kind of woman who just criticizes everyone indiscriminately. There must be a purpose behind the remarks she made to me. Dominick, why are you staring at me that way?"

"I am marvelling at your insight," he said. "Did Adalhaid reveal how well she knows me?"

"Actually, it was more a revelation about how well she knew your father." Gina felt herself beginning to blush. "I didn't ask. She told me. Now that I think about it, I wonder why she did that."

"You may be sure there was a reason." Dominick drew a long breath. "Did Adalhaid mention her daughter?"

"No. I didn't know she had a daughter. Come to think of it, she didn't say anything at all about her family, though she certainly did ask a lot of questions about mine. I followed her advice and guarded every word I spoke. Dominick, what is it? I can tell something is wrong here. We are supposed to be working together, so you'd better start talking."

"Adalhaid's daughter," said Dominick, "is Hiltrude."

"Merciful heaven!" Gina gasped. "Do you mean to say I just spent an entire evening with your mother-in-law?"

"Former mother-in-law," Dominick corrected her.

"Right there at court, where every person but me knows who she is—oh, I'll bet the gossips are having a fine time with that story! Why didn't you warn me?"

"I did try," he said. "But you were so eager to hurry off with her and begin spying on the ladies of the court that you weren't willing to listen."

"Well, there's an opportunity wasted. After I made such a fool of myself, I won't get a second chance to learn anything. The ladies will all be laughing at me. So will their husbands and fiancés when they hear about it. Not to mention their lovers. I understand from Lady Adalhaid that noblewomen frequently take lovers. I guess that means their husbands have mistresses. Nice society you have here."

"In fact, I believe you did learn something valuable," Dominick said.

"If you're trying to make me feel better, forget it."

"Why do you suppose Lady Adalhaid spoke so freely to you?"

"Oh, I don't know. It could be that she realizes I don't know what I'm doing here, so she can say anything and it won't matter."

"It's far more likely that she was trying to send a message to me, while taking care to be seen speaking to me for no more than a few moments and with someone else present."

"What message? That she doesn't like the queen? I'm not sure we ought to believe that. After all, the queen and Hiltrude were apparently close friends. That's why Fastrada urged Charles to arrange your marriage, isn't it? So she and Hiltrude together could ruin you? By the way, why does Fastrada hate you enough to want to destroy you?"

"When Charles led the Frankish army to war, I advised him not to make Fastrada regent in his absence. She was—still is—much too young to wield power wisely, and she is stubbornly certain that she is always right. Fastrada refused to listen to the advisors Charles left in Francia to guide her. Several of those men are no longer welcome at court. Some of them are dead."

"So," Gina said after a moment to absorb those unsettling facts, "Fastrada is trying to ruin anyone who spoke out against her? Can't you talk to Charles about this? He seems like a reasonable man."

"Not where his wife is concerned. Fastrada holds him in the palm of her hand. She is young and beautiful—"

"Beautiful is as beautiful does," Gina interrupted. "That's a saying one of my foster mothers often used. Judging by what I've seen and heard so far, Fastrada is an ugly witch."

"Don't let Charles hear you say so. Or Fastrada, either."

"I'm beginning to understand why you prefer Feldbruck to court," Gina said with a sigh. "Life at Feldbruck is much simpler, isn't it?"

"Seldom have I been able to speak openly to anyone at court." Dominick pulled her into his arms.

"Your honest presence is a joy and a delight to me."

"Gee, I was afraid I was more trouble than I'm worth," she murmured, cuddling against his chest. She was so comfortable there, safe and secure. That was not the kind of thought that usually came to her when she was close to a man, but Dominick was different from all other men. She could trust him, relax with him.

"I'm sorry I've been such an amateurish spy. I'll try to do better next time," she said, relishing the touch of his lips on her forehead and then on her nose and eyelids. "Were you able to learn anything about the plot?" she added just before Dominick's mouth came down on hers.

"Hmm."

She wasn't sure whether he was saying *yes* or *no* or simply expressing masculine pleasure at her eager response to what he was doing. Then she felt the pressure of his tongue against her lips and the hot surge of him into her mouth, and she forgot all about traitors' schemes and the childish, spoiled queen and her overindulgent husband. All that mattered to Gina was Dominick's strength and vitality and his fiery passion. Without removing his mouth from hers, he swept her off her feet and carried her to his bed. He lay down beside her and gathered her close, showering her face and throat with kisses.

Dominick smiled when Gina reached up to stroke his face and push back the blond hair that had fallen into his eyes. With growing anticipation he opened the folds of her robe and gazed in delight at her small, nicely rounded breasts. He bent his head to take one nipple into his mouth.

Gina yawned.

Dominick stared at her and laughed softly at himself. He should have known what would happen the moment she was lying down.

"I am sorry," she whispered.

"Don't be. You've been awake since dawn, and it's now past midnight. You rode for half the day, then spent long hours at an unfamiliar royal court. It's no wonder you're ready for sleep."

"You aren't," she said. "I can stay awake for a while longer."

"I am no animal to force you into compliance with my desires. We have tomorrow and the next day."

"Have we? How can we be sure?" she murmured, already half asleep.

"I am sure," he told her, shifting his position so her head was supported on his shoulder. She muttered something, then lay still.

After a full week of abstinence Dominick ached to possess her, yet he wouldn't, not unless she was wide awake and as hot and eager for him as he was for her. He was old enough and experienced enough to know he'd not perish from the hardness in his groin. It would pass, and the next time he took Gina into his arms, she'd remember his restraint. He would see to it that she was writhing in ecstasy and begging him to take her. And when he did, the bliss she'd confer on both of them would prove worth the wait.

Once he was certain that Gina was sound asleep, Dominick picked her up and carried her to her own room. He tucked her into bed, then paused to look down at her, struggling against the unaccustomed tenderness that suddenly filled his heart. Gina was nearly as tall as he and physically quite strong, yet when she slept she appeared fragile and defenseless. The hand that lay folded against her cheek was small and delicate. Her rosy lips were slightly parted as if inviting his kiss. Soft violet shadowed her eyelids. What Dominick wanted most at that moment was to lie beside her through the night and watch her wake when morning came, to see her emerald eyes open and a smile of greeting meant just for him light her face.

He sternly warned himself that this was no time for soft emotions. If he intended to serve his king as he was duty-bound to do, then unflinching resolve was what he needed.

He picked up the oil lamp that burned on the chest beside Gina's bed and walked out of the room, not allowing himself to look back. He stood in the corridor for a moment, listening. His house was quiet, as it ought to be at that late hour. Only one completely trustworthy man-at-arms stood guard at the door.

Ah, but on the docks along the riverfront and in the drinking houses of Regensburg, men were awake who would sell their own souls for a cup of wine or a few coins, men aware of the most surprising twists and turns of conspiracies supposedly unknown except by those involved in them.

Dominick caught up his dark cloak, wrapped it around himself, and pulled up the hood before he slipped out the door. He made a silent gesture to the well-trained guard, who nodded and said nothing. Then Dominick vanished into the darkness.

Chapter Eleven

"I don't think this is a good idea," Ella said for the fourth time. She was following Gina, both of them picking their way among the ruts and mud puddles of the unpaved street that led to the palace. "We ought to wait for Dominick to return."

"It's midday, and no one has seen Dominick," Gina responded. She lifted her blue silk skirts a little higher to avoid the mud being splashed in their direction by a horse whose rider wasn't paying attention to lowly pedestrians. "If he's not at home and not at the palace, then something has happened to him. And to Harulf, since he is missing, too. Aren't you concerned about him?"

"They may have gone hunting," Ella said with placid assurance. "Men often do, you know."

"If Dominick planned to go hunting, he'd leave a message for me."

They reached the palace gate. Gina gave her name to the guard and told him she was to meet Count Dominick.

"I haven't seen him this morning," the guard said, "but it's possible he entered by one of the other gates. You'll most likely find him in the great hall."

Dominick wasn't in the hall. Few people were, and none of them had a face Gina recognized.

"Ella, I want you to stay here," Gina said. "If Dominick arrives, tell him I'll return shortly and I'd like him to wait for me."

"I shouldn't leave you alone. Dominick won't approve. Where will you be?" Ella asked.

"Looking for Dominick, of course." Following Dominick's order, Gina hadn't said a word to Ella about the plot they were investigating, so she couldn't say anything more, and she didn't dare admit just how worried she was. She didn't like not knowing where Dominick was. She only felt safe when he was near. He was the one dependable person in her strange new life, the only other soul who knew what she really was. Gina wasn't going to let the size of the palace deter her. If Dominick was anywhere within its walls—anywhere from the throne room to the dungeon—she was going to find him.

Leaving Ella muttering and shaking her head at the idea of a young noblewoman wandering about unattended, Gina hurried out a side door of the great hall and into a courtyard. A few noblemen and some clerics in dark robes were there, but not

Dominick. Across the courtyard and through another door leading to a large reception room she went. There she paused to greet Ansa, one of the young ladies she'd met the previous night, and to be introduced to Lady Ansa's newly chosen betrothed. After offering her best wishes, Gina asked if either of them knew where Dominick was.

"I haven't seen him, though I haven't been looking," said the young nobleman, gazing fondly at his lady while he spoke to Gina. "He could be in one of the king's private chambers, perhaps with Charles himself." He tore his attention from the girl at his side long enough to indicate the direction Gina should take.

When the happy couple turned to speak to a friend, Gina slipped away toward the private wing of the palace. A short time later she found herself in yet another courtyard. This one boasted a cloistered walk around all sides, with thick stone columns supporting a series of the rounded arches routinely used in Frankish architecture. Stone paths crisscrossed the sunny courtyard, with colorful flower beds set into the open spaces. Gina paused to admire the pretty sight.

She was immediately glad of the impulse that had made her stop before venturing out of the shady cloister and into the sunlight. Fastrada and Father Guntram stood in the exact center of the garden, where all the paths converged. Seeing them with their heads together, Gina quickly ducked behind one of the wide columns. They were so deep in private conversation that they hadn't noticed her, and her soft shoes made no sound on the stones of the cloister floor to alert them.

Not a word of the low conversation between the priest and the queen reached Gina's ears. Still, she trembled with fear. If she was discovered, Fastrada would have good reason to accuse her of spying. Given Gina's association with Dominick, the queen would have a perfect excuse to call him a spy, too. Gina harbored no doubts about the queen's eagerness to cause trouble for Dominick.

"I have to get out of here, fast." She was so unnerved that she didn't realize she had whispered the words aloud until someone responded.

"An excellent idea, Lady Gina," said a soft voice next to her ear.

Before she could make any sound a long, inkstained finger was laid across her lips, enjoining silence. She looked up into a face that was seamed with lines of humor around the mouth and calm blue eyes. The man was very tall. His shoulders were stooped, as if he made a habit of bending to the height of shorter folk, and he wore a plain, dark cleric's robe. His thinning gray hair was cut short all the way around in the bowl-shaped style Gina had seen on other palace clerics. The man allowed her a moment to look at him and take in the fact that he was unarmed except for the bunch of stiff feathers he held in one hand, a collection that only added to his harmless appearance.

"Come," he whispered, beckoning. "Follow me."

Gina had no choice but to do as he asked. If she protested or made any sound, Fastrada would know she had intruded on a private conversation, and the queen wasn't likely to believe it was an accident.

With his inky finger now at his own lips, the

cleric moved to a door at the side of the cloister. Gina glanced backward to ensure that she and her companion were hidden by the thick stone column. She couldn't see Fastrada at all, and Father Guntram was facing away from the side of the cloister where Gina stood. A moment later Gina was through the doorway, and the cleric quietly shut and bolted the wooden door behind them. Then he beckoned again.

All was done in silence until they were two rooms away from the courtyard, safe behind a closed door in a small, untidy office where books and scrolls lay scattered across a large table, with more books piled on several stools. Shelves along one wall held rolled-up scrolls, a tag dangling from each. A hasty look at the tags revealed that they identified the contents of the scrolls. Gina turned to the man who stood observing her with an air of amused friendliness that told her she had nothing to fear from him.

"Who are you?" Gina asked. "How do you know my name?"

"I am Alcuin. I saw you in the great hall last evening when you were presented to Charles. You are fortunate that I chose this hour to procure a fresh supply of quills." He laid the feathers on the table next to a pot of ink. "The queen does not like to be interrupted when she is carrying on a private conversation."

"I wasn't going to interrupt. I stumbled into the garden by mistake. I was looking for—"

"For Count Dominick?"

"Do you know where he is?"

"Not at the moment." Alcuin poured wine into two cups and handed one to Gina.

She looked into the red liquid in her cup, then looked up at him, recognition dawning. Alcuin of Northumbria was one of Charles's closest friends and advisors. When she had learned about Charlemagne in school, Alcuin was also mentioned, though much too briefly for the classroom memory to be of much assistance now. Gina knew only that he was a great scholar who devised a script that was easier to read than the older writing style.

"I have been told that you are also a native of Northumbria," Alcuin said.

The mildly uttered statement brought Gina back to dangerous reality. With a few well-chosen questions Alcuin held the power to blow her cover—as the author of a twentieth-century spy novel might have said—by proving that she knew nothing at all about Northumbria. Perhaps the man wasn't as innocuous as he seemed.

"Courtiers do love to gossip, don't they?" Gina's hand began to shake. Fearing she'd slosh her wine all over his documents, she set the cup down, its contents untasted. Alcuin sipped from his cup and watched her.

"Actually, I come from a place very far away," Gina said, instinctively aware that she couldn't lie to him. He'd know it if she tried. "Dominick misunderstood the name of the city where I used to live." She fumbled to a halt, caught by Alcuin's suddenly penetrating gaze.

"Once, almost fifteen years ago, reckoning by the time in which I am living, I knew another woman like you," Alcuin said slowly. "Her name was India. Her lover was killed at Roncevaux along with Count Hrulund. After that, there was nothing to hold her in Francia any longer, so she returned to her own home. In *Connecticut*. I don't know how she did it, so I cannot help you to do the same."

"Are you saying what I think you're saying?" Gina cried in astonishment at the one, oddly pronounced word he had emphasized.

"I am merely saying that you remind me of an old friend. But then, I am an aging cleric who likes his wine too well," Alcuin answered. "I do think there is someone holding you in Francia. And I believe there are certain subjects that ought never to be discussed aloud."

"You're telling me I'm not likely to get home again?"

"Perhaps the decision is yours to make. That was the case for India."

"I don't understand."

"There are mysteries that mortals are not meant to understand."

"Dominick once said something similar. He said sometimes we just have to accept what happens and not worry so much about understanding *why*."

"I have always found Dominick wise beyond his years."

"Thank you for rescuing me just now," Gina said, feeling the need to change the subject before her whirling thoughts could drive her into a state of total confusion.

"It's not often a cleric has the opportunity to rescue a beautiful lady. Our unexpected meeting has enlivened a rather dull morning."

"What do you do in here?" Gina asked, surveying all the paraphernalia of medieval scholarship piled high on the table and shelves.

"I am working on a new translation of the Bible," Alcuin said. "I am also head of the palace school, and I correspond with many friends. That is why I was in need of new quills," he added, touching the feathers.

"It sounds like a lot of work. I shouldn't keep you from it. If you think it's safe, I'll leave now."

"Let me see." Alcuin headed toward the door. "Drink up your wine. It's too good to waste."

"This *is* good," Gina said after a hearty gulp.

"I serve only the best to my friends. India also enjoyed the wine from that vineyard." Alcuin stepped out of the room, returning a moment later. "The courtyard is empty."

"Thank you again." Gina started to leave, then turned back. "Alcuin, do you know Father Guntram?"

"I do." The cleric's kindly face was suddenly hard and cold as stone.

"I don't like him either," Gina said, guessing at the reason for his reaction. "But I do like Pepin. Have you seen him this morning? Could Dominick be with him?"

"Pepin has not yet come to Regensburg," Alcuin said. "We expect him any day."

"Not here? But, when I saw them at Feldbruck, he and Father Guntram were traveling together. Why is Father Guntram at Regensburg, but not Pepin?"

"I have been asking myself the same question since I saw the priest with the queen," said Alcuin.

"If you learn the answer, let me know," Gina said, heading for the courtyard. "I'll do the same for you, if I can discover what's going on."

"I can be found most evenings in the great hall," Alcuin's voice followed her. "Or here during the daylight hours. You are always welcome."

"I'll remember that."

By the time Gina returned to the great hall, Dominick was there, with a younger man whose blond hair and gray eyes lent him a striking resemblance to Dominick.

"I've been looking all over for you," Gina said, joining the two men.

"I intended to return home to fetch you in time for the evening feast," Dominick responded.

"Well, then, I've saved you the trouble." Gina thought he didn't look very pleased to see her.

"Women almost never obey orders," Dominick's companion stated in a challenging way.

"I have an unblemished record in that respect," Gina said, laughing in an attempt to lighten the atmosphere. Both men were frowning at her. "I take orders from no man."

"Lady Gina, this is my younger brother, Count Bernard," Dominick said.

"We are only half brothers." Bernard was glowering, looking ready to erupt into a tantrum or perhaps a full-blown battle. "Dominick, you are a fool to return to court. The queen still hasn't forgiven you for the way you sent Hiltrude off to a convent. She certainly isn't going to welcome your concubine amongst her ladies."

"I am *not* a concubine!" Gina cried. "And I wouldn't be one of Fastrada's ladies if you paid me."

"Gina, be quiet!" Dominick commanded.

"She won't obey you," said Bernard, sneering.

"She has already declared her refusal to accede to the wishes of mere men. Have a care, Dominick. Acting on your own initiative, you achieved only partial ruin. With this woman's assistance, you may well be completely destroyed." Uttering a rude sound that clearly indicated his disgust, Bernard walked away.

"I've done it again," Gina said, looking after him. "Wouldn't you think I'd have sense enough by now to keep my mouth shut, to just smile politely and say nothing when I'm insulted?"

"Silence would be best, considering you are ignorant of the various loyalties and dissensions among Charles's courtiers," Dominick responded. "Bernard likes me not at all, though before others he will bestir himself to hide his distaste for his father's bastard. He imagines his display of good manners makes him appear to be a better man. His mother is not so polite. Fortunately, she is not presently at court."

"That's good news. It means one less enemy for me to antagonize. Dominick, you will never guess who I met while I was searching for you. Please tell me Alcuin is a true friend."

"He is." Dominick's stern expression softened at the mention of the cleric's name. "Alcuin is so honest and valued an advisor and stands so high in Charles's regard that all Fastrada's wiles cannot dislodge him from his position at court. Where did you meet him?"

"He rescued me and spirited me away to his office when I was about to stumble into a secret conference Fastrada was holding with Father Guntram."

"That cursed priest is in Regensburg? Then where is Pepin?"

"That's what Alcuin and I were wondering. Personally, I think the queen and that unpleasant priest are up to no good."

"I agree," Dominick said.

"Since I've vowed to be more cautious, I guess I should ask, is it safe for me to be seen talking with Alcuin in public?"

"Of course." Dominick chuckled, his usual good humor restored. "Everyone talks to Alcuin, and drinks his wine, too."

"It's very good wine." Gina hesitated, reluctant to speak of what else she and Alcuin had discussed—the tale of a lady who had apparently visited Francia for a while and then, after her lover died and nothing held her in the eighth century any longer, returned to another time and place. Gina wasn't sure she wanted Dominick to know about that possibility. She was even less certain what, if anything, she wanted to do with the unexpected knowledge. She decided to postpone revealing what Alcuin had said about his friend, India.

"Dominick, where were you for half the day? I've been worried sick. That's why I was wandering around the palace. I was looking for you, terrified that something terrible had happened."

"As you can see," he said, "I am alive, unharmed, and free."

"For the moment. Have you been able to uncover anything of interest?"

"Several details," he said. "We will talk later, at my house, where there is no chance we'll be overheard. Here comes Lady Adalhaid. Gina, I warn you again, think twice before you speak."

"I promise I'll do better from now on." She touched his arm in a quick caress. Dominick responded by smiling at her in the way that always left her feeling weak and warm inside. "I'll stay awake tonight, too," she added, and laughed softly to hear his deep chuckle.

"I'll see that you do," he said just before Lady Adalhaid reached them.

Chapter Twelve

Queen Fastrada's chambers were unlike anything Gina had ever seen in real life. In a scene of barbaric splendor straight out of a Hollywood historical epic, the walls were draped with silk, low tables bearing gold or silver bowls of berries and early apples stood about the room, and pillows in bright colors were strewn over the wooden floor. The oil in the lamps was scented with jasmine, adding heavy perfume to the fragrances of the ripe fruit. Gina coughed, tried to repress a sneeze, and hoped that none of the queen's attendants suffered from severe allergies.

Fastrada lounged on a pillow-crammed bed that was pushed against one wall. She was wearing a blue silk gown with a red sash wound about her slender waist, and at least a dozen gold necklaces.

Her feet were bare. She looked downright unhappy. Or perhaps she was sulking. Gina had the impression that Fastrada often sulked.

"Did you have to bring *her* here?" Fastrada asked when Lady Adalhaid appeared with Gina at her side. "Why should I be expected to receive a low-born concubine?"

The other ladies in the room smothered giggles. Gina bit her lip and, true to her promise to Dominick, did not respond to the insult.

"My lady, you know that all unwed girls who come to court are placed under your protection," Lady Adalhaid said. "I am merely doing my duty in bringing Lady Gina to you."

"I've a mind not to receive her," Fastrada said. There was a certain gleam in the queen's sapphire eyes, a hint of malice that warned Gina to be on guard. "Then again, perhaps she will prove useful to me."

"I am sure Gina will be happy to serve you in whatever way you desire," said Lady Adalhaid.

It was on the tip of Gina's tongue to inform both Fastrada and Lady Adalhaid that she wasn't the least bit interested in serving the queen in any capacity. She thought about what she wanted to say, thought a second time, and held her peace, for Dominick's sake. As long as she had to spend time with Fastrada, she'd learn as much as she could about the plot in which Pepin was involved, as well as any schemes of the queen's devising. That was what she was at court to do, after all.

"Bring me my fan," Fastrada ordered.

There were three other noblewomen in the room, one of them Lady Ansa, and the instant the queen spoke they all began searching for the missing fan.

"Not you." Fastrada made a lazy gesture to indicate that the others should move away. "I want Gina to find my fan."

"Certainly," Gina said as politely as she could manage. "What does it look like?"

"What do you mean, what does it look like?" exclaimed Fastrada. "Don't you recognize a fan when you see one?"

"I meant, is it made of paper—er, parchment—or feathers, or silk, perhaps? Is it large or small? What color is it? Do you remember where you last saw it? Or when?" Gina began to look around the overstuffed room, trying to decide if she dared to toss a few pillows about or search behind the wall hangings or get down on the floor to peer under the tables.

"Your questions are rude," Fastrada declared. "I want my fan *now.*"

"I'm very sorry, but I've never seen the fan before, and I have no idea where you could have lost it. My questions are not meant to be rude. They are aimed at trying to find your cursed—your fan." Gina was close to losing her temper but not so close that she missed the way Fastrada's petulant mouth twitched at her barely restrained response.

So that was it. Fastrada was deliberately trying to make her say or do something that would get her—and Dominick, too, no doubt—into trouble. Well, she wouldn't give the spoiled brat the pleasure. She gazed at the luxurious furnishings, trying to think where in all the clutter a missing fan could be.

"Really," Fastrada said to Lady Adalhaid, "this girl is too stupid to be of any use to me."

While Fastrada was glaring at Lady Adalhaid, and the other ladies-in-waiting were huddled together as if they feared the queen's displeasure would be visited on them, Lady Ansa made a quick, surreptitious gesture, pointing to a pile of green and blue pillows. Gina looked in the direction Lady Ansa indicated and saw a bit of carved wood sticking out from beneath the bottom pillow. She seized it and pulled, until a flat, round, wooden fan came loose from the pillows. The action unbalanced the pillows, which tumbled over, spilling against one of the many tables and upsetting a bowl of small green apples.

"What are you doing?" Fastrada screeched, swinging her feet to the floor. "Clumsy, stupid— Out! Get out!"

"I found your fan." Gina made the best curtsy she could, which, since she'd never attempted one before, wasn't very graceful, and handed the fan to the queen. The moment Fastrada snatched it from her, Gina began to pick up the apples. Lady Ansa grabbed one that had rolled across the room and tossed it to Gina, who grinned her thanks.

Fastrada's high-pitched complaints ceased abruptly at a sudden movement behind Gina. Gina turned, her hands full of apples, and found herself face to face with the king of the Franks.

"What is wrong?" Charles asked, speaking to Gina, not Fastrada.

"I've been clumsy," Gina said, indicating the spilled apples. "I am sorry," she added to the queen.

"You miserable, impertinent—" Fastrada lifted

the fan she was clenching and slashed out, plainly bent upon striking Gina across the face.

Before the wooden fan made contact with Gina's cheek Charles caught his wife's wrist and took the fan from her.

"How pretty this is," he said, smiling at Fastrada. "Surely, my dearest, you don't want to break it. After all, it was a gift from me."

"I thought you planned to be busy all afternoon long," Fastrada responded, as if accusing her husband of abandoning her. "If you will no longer allow me to sit with you while you meet with your councillors, then I must find some way to entertain myself."

"It was concern for your health that led me to suggest you keep to your rooms this afternoon," Charles said.

"Don't expect me to believe such a flimsy excuse. The queen of the Franks has every right to involve herself with affairs of state. Indeed, that is my responsibility. I managed your kingdom very well while you were away at war."

"Now that I am home again, I thought to lift some of the burden from your shoulders."

"When I am not present, you permit your councillors to say whatever they please to you. I can think of several among them who ought to be tried for treason and executed—a long, slow death that spills every drop of treacherous blood." Fastrada's pale cheeks turned pink as she spoke, and she moved closer to Charles in a sinuous, undulating way obviously intended to catch and hold the king's attention. Gina could see that the ploy wasn't entirely successful.

"I have always ruled by allowing my nobles to express their opinions. Knowing that I have listened to them, they are usually willing to accept the decisions I make." Charles hadn't moved a single step, yet with his calm words he had distanced himself from Fastrada, and she seemed to recognize it. Her temper rose again.

"Did you discuss the hunchback?" she demanded, her lips curling in disdain. "Where is that laggard, Pepin? Why hasn't he come to Regensburg as you requested? *Requested*, not ordered! But your slightest wish should be a command to him! How dare he not obey you at once?"

"Gently, Fastrada. Pepin is my son."

"He is a disgrace! A bastard who shames you by his very existence. He ought to be grateful you allow him to continue to live. I cannot bear to look at him."

"Then you ought to be happy he isn't here, instead of complaining about his absence. In fact, I received a message this morning, sent ahead by Pepin to inform me that he and Father Guntram expect to reach Regensburg within a day or two."

"I suppose he is using his deformity as an excuse to travel as slowly as possible, when the truth is, he doesn't want to see you. The hunchback does not love you, Charles."

Gina longed to exclaim that Pepin did love his father but feared his father did not love him. She could not help wondering whether Father Guntram had poured that particular poison into Pepin's ears, while Fastrada created a similar belief in Charles's mind. It would be a good way to turn the two against each other, especially since they didn't see each other very often and thus had little chance to correct their mistaken assumptions.

"Enough, Fastrada. I'll hear no more on the subject of Pepin. Ladies," Charles said, turning to the other women in the room, "if you will kindly leave us, I'd like to speak privately with the queen."

As the women obediently filed out, Gina noted how informally they went. There were no bows, no curtsies, no walking backward out of the chamber as she had seen done in movies. Charles was a remarkably relaxed monarch, approachable and easygoing. If only his wife were half so pleasant.

"Ansa, thank you for your help," Gina said as soon as they were all in an anteroom. "Without it I never would have found that fan."

"It's a game Fastrada plays," Ansa said. "She loves to torment her ladies."

"Would she really have hit me if Charles hadn't arrived?"

"Oh, yes. We've all been struck at least a few times," Ansa said.

"Charles is kind to her," Gina murmured, hoping for an informative response.

"Kinder than she deserves," Ansa responded. She nodded toward the door to Fastrada's inner chamber. "We are free of all duties for the next hour or two. They won't want us loitering about. They won't be doing much talking in there, either. Fastrada is determined to present Charles with a son."

"Ansa, mind your tongue," said Lady Adalhaid. "An unwed girl ought not to speak of such matters."

"I won't be unmarried for much longer," Ansa said, giggling. "Then I'll say whatever I want. Gina, will you come with us? We're going to stroll in the outer courtyard."

"You mean, you intend to flaunt yourselves before the young men," Lady Adalhaid said, disapproval written on her face. "I will keep Gina with me. She requires training in court etiquette."

"I think Gina does very well," said Ansa with a saucy grin. "Gina, we'll meet again soon, I'm sure." Ansa joined the other ladies in their merry but hasty departure from the queen's apartments.

"Let us walk in a more private place," Lady Adalhaid said. She took Gina's arm, drawing her out of the anteroom and along a corridor, then through an open doorway, stopping when they reached the same secluded courtyard where Gina had earlier observed Fastrada and Father Guntram in secret conversation. Gina looked around expectantly, hoping to see Alcuin again, but both courtyard and cloister were empty. The sun was lower in the sky, and the red and yellow flowers in the little gardens glowed in the late-afternoon light.

"How peaceful it is," Gina said, feeling some remark was called for but not wanting to admit she had previously intruded on so private a place.

"I suppose so." Lady Adalhaid shrugged as if flowers, blue sky, and sunshine meant nothing to her. "Ansa was correct when she said you did well in the queen's presence. Fastrada can be exasperating. You must remember that she is still young. We hope she will learn to rein in her temper as she matures."

" 'We'?" said Gina. "Who is 'we'?"

"The other courtiers, and the ladies who attend her."

"Hasn't it occurred to any of you that, since she is so young, she may outlive her husband?"

"No! Oh, no!"

Lady Adalhaid turned her back to Gina, and Gina watched, fascinated, as the older woman's shoulders shook as if she was weeping, then rose and fell with several deep breaths. Gina noticed Lady Adalhaid's hands clenching and unclenching at her sides. And she recalled her first impression that this woman did not like the queen.

"What do you think Fastrada would do without Charles to quiet her tantrums and keep her in line?" Gina asked.

"I cannot bear to think of it," Lady Adalhaid whispered. "Charles is so virile, so full of boundless energy, that I cannot imagine a time when he is no longer with us. Life was difficult enough when he was away on the Bavarian border, fighting those wicked, heathen Avar tribesmen and then battling against Duke Tassilo, but we all knew he would return and then life would go on as it has done since he was first elected king."

"Dominick told me that you are Hiltrude's mother," Gina said, walking around her companion so she could look her full in the face.

"My poor girl." Lady Adalhaid's eyes filled with tears. "Fastrada insisted that Hiltrude marry Dominick. As you surely know, noble marriages are almost always arranged by the parents. In this case, Charles acted as one of the fathers. He had known Dominick since he was a boy and took an interest in him after he was disinherited. He granted Feldbruck to Dominick after the Bavarian war ended, so it was natural for Dominick to want an heir, and when Fastrada put forward my daughter as bride, Charles agreed. Since my husband is dead, the decision on Hiltrude's side of the family was mine to make. I foolishly acceded to Fastrada's demand. I have regretted it ever since. I know my dear girl was miserably unhappy."

"You cannot think Dominick was a cruel husband," Gina protested.

"I do not. But Hiltrude had taken a fancy to another man. At first she refused to marry Dominick. But the queen talked to her and changed her mind."

"I'll just bet she did," Gina muttered. "Fastrada sucked Hiltrude into a nasty plot to ruin Dominick."

"You know about that?"

"Dominick told me."

"I believe Dominick sent Hiltrude to Chelles for her own safety," Lady Adalhaid said. "Even Fastrada cannot touch her as long as she remains in that secure convent. But the thing is, Hiltrude does not have a religious vocation. She would far rather marry and have children."

"What about the man she loved before she was married off to Dominick?"

"Audulf has always refused to wed. And whenever we meet, he inquires about Hiltrude in great detail."

"What a mess. There's your daughter, stuck in a convent where she doesn't want to be, and there's a man who cares about her, but they can't be together as long as the queen is alive."

"Hush! Never say such a thing aloud," Lady Adalhaid whispered urgently. She stared at the columns of the cloister as if she expected to discover some-one lurking behind one of them, listening.

Gina wasn't worried. She knew, from trying to eavesdrop earlier that day, how difficult it was to hear anything spoken in the courtyard, and she and Lady Adalhaid had been talking very quietly.

"You haven't told me Hiltrude's sad story as a way of idly passing the time," Gina said. "What do you want of me?"

"I thought we could work together," Lady Adalhaid said. "Fastrada is involved in many plots. That's not unusual for a queen. Women married to powerful husbands are frequently asked to use their influence to help bring various projects to fruition or to promote the advancement of friends and relatives. But Fastrada's schemes tend to be particularly vile in nature. She cares only for herself and two or three of her male relatives. She will do anything to advance her family."

"Is that where Duke Tassilo's treasure went?" Gina asked. "To Fastrada's relatives?"

"Only some of it. Most of the treasure she kept for herself. The men who went to war with Charles deeply resent that none of it was distributed to them."

"It always comes down to money, doesn't it?" Gina said, recalling Dominick's remarks on the subject.

"I care nothing for Tassilo's treasure," Lady Adalhaid said. "I care only for my daughter, who is, in effect, a prisoner, as she dare not leave Chelles. And I believe you care as much for Dominick's welfare as I do for Hiltrude's."

"So you think we should join forces in hope of exposing Fastrada for the conniving, cold-hearted creature she is? And then what?"

"I know several young noblewomen who would make excellent queens. In the past, Charles has divorced two wives."

"Won't the Church object to a third divorce?"

"If Charles can be impressed with the extent of Fastrada's evil deeds, he will find a way to be rid of her."

"I hope you aren't talking about beheading," Gina said with a shiver. "I don't want to be responsible for anyone's death. Not even hers."

"Certainly not," Lady Adalhaid said. "Charles is too kindhearted ever to hurt a woman who has borne his children."

"That aspect of his character may prove to be our biggest obstacle." Gina began to laugh.

"What do you find so amusing?" demanded Lady Adalhaid.

"Doesn't it strike you as funny for the woman everyone thinks is Dominick's concubine, and the woman who was his mother-in-law and his father's lover, to work together as you've suggested?"

"It seems to me that we are natural allies," said Lady Adalhaid, "since we both have loved ones whom the queen hates."

"There is something you should know about me. Dominick has scolded me several times because I can't keep my mouth shut. I'm used to speaking my opinion without weighing the consequences. That doesn't make me a good candidate for secret work."

"Perhaps your concern for Dominick will lead you to exercise greater discretion."

"I can try to curb my tongue." Gina didn't actually agree to work with Lady Adalhaid. Nor did she mention that she would be discussing the conversation they'd just had with Dominick as soon as he and she were alone in private.

"As far as I've been able to learn," Gina said later that night, "Charles is not aware of Father Guntram's visit to Regensburg. The priest wasn't in the great hall this evening, and no one has mentioned him, so I am assuming that no one but Fastrada, and possibly a servant or two, knows he has been here. I'm guessing that Father Guntram will arrive with Pepin as if he hasn't seen Regensburg since the last time he came to court."

"Very likely," Dominick said, sounding distracted, as if something else was on his mind.

They were in his bedchamber. Gina had gone there to speak with him when he did not come to her room after they returned from the palace. She judged it was a couple of hours before midnight, and though the rest of Dominick's household had retired, she wasn't the least bit sleepy.

"What's your opinion of the offer Lady Adalhaid made to me?" Gina asked.

"Interesting," Dominick said as though he wasn't thinking about Lady Adalhaid. "Not entirely unexpected."

After the enforced celibacy of the trip from Feldbruck, followed by Dominick's advances toward her on the previous night and his teasing promise of that afternoon, Gina had assumed that he was planning at least a few passionate hours once they were back in his house. Now that they were alone together, she couldn't understand his preoccupation.

"What's wrong? Why are you shutting me out?" As so often happened, the words that came out of her mouth in well-spoken Frankish were somewhat different from what she intended to say. Still, the message was clear. "Have you learned something that you think is important? Talk to me, Dominick. Tell me what's going on."

"What is going on," he said, "is my amazement when I realize how long it has been since I've held you close."

"Well, you did try last night. That was my fault, not yours," she said ruefully. "I have promised to stay awake tonight, and I will."

"Gina." His lips touched hers lightly. "Beautiful Gina. You drive me mad with longing."

"You don't act as if I do," she said.

"No? Shall I prove to you how much I want you, how I have ached to hold you close, night after uncomfortable night?" Hands still on her shoulders, he drew her nearer, then wrapped his arms around her. "There are hours when you are all I can think of, moments when I believe I will die if I cannot bury myself deep inside you until I hear you cry out in delight."

"Oh, Dominick, don't you know I want you, too?" In newfound hope and trust she raised her face to him. His mouth came down on hers boldly, with no tentative, preliminary testing. Gina melted into him, freely giving what he demanded of her. His arms were tight around her, offering no chance of escape from his mounting passion. But then, escape from Dominick was the last thing on her mind. She welcomed him, she kissed him back, matching passion for passion.

He tugged at the sash of her woolen robe and pushed it off her shoulders so it fell into an untidy, and unheeded, pile around her ankles.

Gina caressed and stroked, then tore at his clothing, eager to feel the hard length of him in her hands. She rejoiced in his groan of pleasure when she was finally able to touch his naked heat.

They stood toe to toe for a long moment, simply holding each other, immobilized by the sensation of skin against skin. That didn't last very long, though. Wild desire, repressed for too many nights, seized hold of them. Dominick put his palms on Gina's buttocks, lifting her up and closer still. His mouth ground against hers. She folded her arms around his neck, holding on tight, afraid he'd let her go again. She couldn't bear to be separated from him for even an instant; she'd die without his body straining against hers.

The fell onto the bed together, Dominick on top. His hands were all over her, beginning with her hair, which was growing longer and curling around her face. He wove his hands into the curls, tugging gently. He moved on to caress her shoulders and breasts, pausing to tease her nipples till she cried out at the sensations he was causing deep inside her. Next he encircled her ankles with his big hands, then stroked her calves and thighs in a purposefully tantalizing dance of clever fingertips, until he reached the very core of her that was already, so quickly, hot and moist and ready to receive him.

She felt his mouth on her and screamed, so

flooded was she with heat and a building tension that she knew he was going to release—but not until he was finished tormenting her by kissing and suckling her breasts, by turning her over so he could place a hot, moist row of kisses all along her spine while his fingers were finding and teasing the sensitive places between her thighs. She moaned and wept and pleaded with him, and he chuckled and promised more to come.

"That's pleasant enough," he said when he held her face to face again.

"Pleasant?" she gasped, then found that she could not speak another word, for he was pushing his hardness against her and she was desperate to hold all of his great length.

"I like to see the look of wonder on your lovely face when I possess you," he whispered. "Gina, my dear heart."

The pressure and the stretching sensation intensified, and she murmured his name, lifting her hips to him, accepting his size with ease, for he had prepared her so well that she was already beginning to dissolve into him.

He withdrew a little, then thrust hard several times, and Gina's mind exploded into rainbow-hued fragments of light and color, into a pleasure so fulfilling that all she knew was Dominick filling her, and all she heard was his triumphant cry of release.

In the sweet, languorous aftermath, Gina lay thinking about the haunting urgency of Dominick's lovemaking. It was almost as if he feared they'd never come together again. Her twentieth-century experiences with men who promised one thing but did another came to mind to provide a possible explanation she did not want to consider in connection with Dominick. But consider it she must.

Dominick was lying to her. Or, more accurately, he was concealing something from her.

She did not doubt the reality of his passion for her. That had been honest and intense. But Dominick had used his need for her and had played upon her longing for him to direct her attention away from the intrigues they were supposedly investigating—the intrigues they had been discussing when the lovemaking began.

It did not require a great leap for Gina to reach the conclusion that Dominick had learned something of vital importance, something to do with the plot against Charles. He'd told her several times that he must have irrefutable evidence against the nobles involved before he could go to the king with what he knew. Gina thought Charles should have been alerted as soon as they reached Regensburg, so he could be on guard against attack, but she wasn't going to second-guess Dominick. He knew more about the workings of Frankish society, and more about the character of the king, than she did. If Dominick said Charles would demand proof, then he was probably right.

But they were supposed to be working together to find that all-important evidence. He owed her an explanation. She was hurt that he hadn't offered one, especially after she had told him everything she had been able to learn during her day at the palace.

He wasn't going to do any explaining while he lay

sleeping in her arms. She ran her fingers through his hair, and Dominick sighed. He briefly tightened his hold on her, then relaxed again. She'd have to wait until morning to confront him with her conclusions. In the meantime, she ought to get some rest.

She was just beginning to drift off when Dominick stirred. Slowly, cautiously, he slid out of her embrace and lifted himself off the bed.

So stealthy were his movements that Gina came instantly awake, though she pretended to be asleep. The only light in the chamber was the star glow from the night sky beyond the unshuttered window, so as long as she kept her eyes closed, she didn't think Dominick could tell that she was aware of what he was doing.

She heard him pull on his tunic and trousers and then his boots. She knew when he picked up his sword belt and the cloak he'd tossed down on his clothing chest upon returning from the palace hours earlier. She had thought the act odd, for Dominick was a neat man and usually put his belongings away after he used them. Now she knew he had wanted the cloak easily available because he was planning to sneak out.

He paused to look down at her, and Gina lay perfectly still, scarcely daring to breathe. When his lips touched her forehead in a brief kiss, she longed to grab him and demand to know what he was doing and where he was going. But she knew he wouldn't tell her. He would offer an excuse, perhaps even make love to her again to shut her up. Then he'd wait until she really was asleep, and he'd sneak out and do whatever it was he was planning.

Without her. After lying to her.

She wasn't going to let him get away with it. She was going to follow him and find out what he was up to.

She got out of bed and went to the window just in time to see his tall figure walk away from the house. Dominick wasn't heading directly for the palace. He had chosen a street that would take him past the palace and past at least a dozen houses of noblemen. He could be planning to stop at any of those houses.

Gina sped to her own room, stopping there just long enough to throw a woolen gown over her head. She had barely thrust her arms through the sleeves when she was pulling on and tying her shoes and snatching up her dark cloak.

She knew better than to leave Dominick's house by the front door. If she tried, she'd have to deal with the guard posted there, who was sure to ask questions about Dominick's guest going out alone so late at night. She'd lose too much time, and Dominick would be gone before she could get away from the house, assuming the guard was even willing to let her leave.

She hurried toward the back door, lifting a key from its hook as she passed through the kitchen. Then she was racing out to the walled area behind the house, where the bathhouse was, and the gardener's toolshed, and the door to the stable, which had its main entrance onto an alley at the far end of the property. Along one side of the backyard lay a kitchen garden, and there was a door in the wall, used by the gardener to bring supplies in and carry refuse out.

Gina halted only once, to be sure neither Benet

or the other groom who slept in the stable, nor any of the men-at-arms, were awake. Hearing no sound of anyone coming to see who was in the garden, she fitted the key into the door and pulled it open. There was no squeaking of hinges; Dominick's house was beautifully maintained. Thinking she might need to return in a hurry, Gina left the key in the door, pulling it almost shut behind her.

She stood in the dark, quiet road until her vision, already adjusted to the night, detected a movement in the direction Dominick had taken. She set out after him, keeping to the darkest shadows, being as quiet as she possibly could and praying she wouldn't run into any late-night carousers.

Chapter Thirteen

The road Dominick had taken slanted slightly upward, leading away from the river. Only a few people were out so late at night. A couple of drunken men in workers' clothing lurched across the road ahead of Gina. She halted, worried that she'd have to make a detour around them, thus possibly losing Dominick, who was moving rapidly through the dark. But Charles kept the town in good order. A watchman accosted the workers and bundled them off with stern admonitions about drinking too heavily. Gina waited only a moment or two before hurrying onward to where the road opened into a large open square in front of the church of St. Peter.

She saw Dominick stop as if he was listening, and she tried to shrink into invisibility. When he ducked around the side of the church, Gina followed him.

The church was built in the shape of a cross, with the main entrance at the foot of the cross. The transepts, or crossbars, were about three-quarters of the way down the long nave, and there was a door at the end of each. These were smaller and not as splendidly decorated as the bronze double doors at the main entrance. In the architectural style Gina was coming to know well, the walls were of thick stone, and the supporting arches and the small windows were rounded at their tops.

The solid bulk of the church loomed upward against the night sky. No lights showed at the windows. All was silent and serene, as a holy edifice ought to be.

Gina saw Dominick vanish through the door in the south transept. When she reached the door she found that he had left it slightly ajar, as she had done with the garden door back at his house. Perhaps he, too, wanted a quick route of return. The door was heavy wood with a big iron ring for a handle, and Gina was grateful not to have to pull it open and risk making noise. She was able to squeeze through the opening and into the dense darkness of the interior.

At first she couldn't see anything. She did hear muted scuffling sounds, as if several people were there and were attempting rather unsuccessfully to be quiet. As she stood still, trying to decide what to do next, a light flared ahead of her to her right, in the chancel. Gina started forward, staying close to the wall and being as quiet as possible.

The light was coming from a single taper on the

altar. The church was so huge that one candle flame did nothing to dispel the nighttime shadows, not even with its glow reflecting off the golden cross on the altar and a series of golden candelabra, each as tall as a man, that stood at the entrance to the chancel, bearing unlit candles. Still, there was light enough for Gina to make out a group of cloaked and hooded men, perhaps a dozen of them, perhaps more, huddled together beside the altar. She could not see any of them well enough to identify them.

On silent feet she moved toward the rounded chancel, and as she drew nearer she was able to hear what the men were discussing in hushed tones.

"We'll make it appear to be a brawl," said one man, "and stab him as if by accident. If we stick to our story that we were all drunk, no one person can be blamed for striking the fatal blow."

"We will all be executed," protested a second man.

"Not if we are ruling Francia," declared a third man. "When we hold the power, no one will dare to accuse us."

"Are we agreed, then?" asked the first man.

"Agreed."

"Agreed."

One after another, all of them assented to the notion of a false brawl.

"Well, then," said the first speaker, who was apparently in charge of the meeting, "when shall it be?"

"Tomorrow morning. Charles attends early prayers each day, so we can depend on him to be here then. We will strike just outside the church, before he sets a foot upon this hallowed spot."

"Aye, we've waited long enough."

"I've been told that Pepin should reach Regensburg by late tomorrow," someone remarked.

"Just in time to be crowned," said another, and several men laughed in an ugly way that made Gina's skin crawl with apprehension.

"Be sure to make the brawl look real," one man cautioned. "We don't want questions raised about it afterward."

"What questions?" scoffed another. "It will be just a stupid fight among a few drunken men who bitterly regret its accidental outcome. Afterward, we can each make a donation to the Church in repentance. Of course, our story will appear all the more realistic if one or two of us are actually wounded."

"Aye. I'll volunteer for a knife scratch on the arm—the left arm, you understand."

"Gerold, you may punch me in the nose," said another man. "Do it hard enough to make me bleed but not hard enough to break the bone."

"It will be a pleasure, my friend."

The sly remark drew general laughter from some of the other conspirators, as if they did not comprehend the deadly seriousness of what they were doing. Nor, apparently, did they see the hypocrisy of plotting in a church to murder their king, while at the same time voicing religious scruples that led them to do the actual killing outside, away from sacred ground.

By this time Gina was leaning against the stone wall of the transept because she was trembling too much from fear to stand up without support. She hadn't identified Dominick among the men at the altar, who all kept their hoods close around their faces, as if trying to hide themselves. If Dominick was present in the chancel, he was there as a spy, which meant his life was in terrible danger.

She couldn't recall enough history to know if the conspirators were going to succeed or not. She did know that it was her responsibility to get to the palace as quickly as possible and warn Charles. Fastrada wouldn't take kindly to Gina bursting into the king's private quarters in the middle of the night, but if she could locate Alcuin, he would believe her, and he had Charles's confidence. Charles would listen to him.

If she could reach the transept door and slip outside, she'd run all the way to the palace. She began to back away from the spot where she had been standing. She had taken only three steps when a large hand clamped down on her mouth and a muscular arm wrapped itself around her waist, pinning her arms to her sides so she couldn't fight.

"Don't make a sound," came Dominick's hushed whisper in her ear, "or we are both dead."

He didn't wait for a response; he lifted her off her feet, with his arm still around her and her back forced hard against his chest, and carried her away into the darkness of the nave. He wasn't gentle, and he didn't release her until they were hidden next to the tall statue of a saint.

Gina was too limp with relief and fear to struggle. She knew Dominick was right. If they were caught, they'd both be killed, and then there would be no one to warn Charles.

The meeting of conspirators was breaking up. Men were quietly walking toward the south transept door. One man was carrying the lone candle, its flame wavering as he moved. In another minute or two they'd all be gone, and she and Dominick would be safe. Gina held her breath, waiting.

"What's this?" exclaimed a muffled voice. "The door is open."

"I told you to close it," came another, impatient, voice. "We're lucky we weren't discovered."

"How do we know we weren't? In this darkness, anyone could be hidden, listening."

"If there's an eavesdropper here, we'll find him."

The barely heard voices made the threat of discovery even more terrifying to Gina. She heard the unmistakable whisper of steel weapons being withdrawn from their sheaths. The man with the candle began walking toward the nave. The others spread out, drawn swords at the ready. They were like dark, hooded ghosts prowling quietly through the church. The only sound was their soft footsteps.

Dominick pushed her between the saint's statue and the wall and held her there, his dark-cloaked back toward the searchers as if to confer invisibility on Gina and himself. His hand was no longer over her mouth, but she was too frightened to make a sound.

The quiet footsteps came closer. Suddenly, without warning, a sword was thrust behind the statue, the blade coming so close to Gina's left side that she could almost feel the coldness of the metal. She feared she'd faint from terror, until a soft call from the chancel drew the swordsman's attention elsewhere.

"Here, behind the altar! Look what I've found."

"Well, there is no one down here in the nave," said the swordsman.

His voice was so close that Gina almost screamed. She sank against Dominick, shaking, as the swordsman's footsteps moved back toward the chancel. The man holding the candle followed his friend. Dominick relaxed his hold on Gina, and she turned a little, so she could peek around the side of the statue and see what was going on.

"Well, well. I was right about an eavesdropper." The candle was set down on the altar again while the conspirators gathered to regard the little man in clerical robes who stood quivering before them.

"What have we caught?" asked someone. "Is it a priest?"

"No, no," said the little man. "I am not ordained. I'm only a deacon—Deacon Fardulf."

"What are you doing here?"

"I came to light the candles for Matins," answered Deacon Fardulf.

"Did you? And how long have you been hiding behind the altar?"

"Not long. Not long at all."

"What did you hear, Deacon Fardulf?" The anonymous voice held a threatening note that made Gina shrink back against Dominick's stalwart solidity.

"Hear? Oh, nothing, my lords. I am a bit deaf, you see." Fardulf made the mistake of crossing himself several times.

"You've just told a lie inside a church," said one of the swordsmen, setting the tip of his blade under Fardulf's chin. "That's why you crossed yourself, isn't it?"

Fardulf gave a terrified squawk, peering from one hooded man to another as if trying to recognize them.

"Strip him," commanded the leader of the conspirators.

"Please don't. Not here in the chancel, before the altar," Fardulf cried. "It wouldn't be seemly."

They paid him no heed but tore his dark robe from him, leaving him shivering and trying to cover his nakedness while they laughed at him.

"I say run him through," someone suggested.

"Not here," said the leader. "Shedding blood inside a holy church will surely damn us. Our plan would be ruined."

"Then let's take him outside and kill him there."

"I have a better idea," the leader said. "On your knees before the altar, Fardulf." He prodded the little man with his sword until Fardulf did as ordered.

"Now," said the leader, "swear by all the holy saints, by the sacred relics in the altar cross, and by everything you hold dear that you will never reveal what you've heard here tonight."

"I swear." Fardulf clasped his shaking hands together and bent his head. "Oh, I do swear most solemnly on all the saints and on the relics, and on my dear mother's grave, too. I will say nothing, my lords. Not a word."

"It's not good enough," protested one of the conspirators.

"I think it is," the leader responded. "Fardulf is a deacon, so he knows better than most men what an oath taken before an altar means. Don't you, Fardulf?" The tip of his sword poked at one of Fardulf's bare buttocks.

"I do know. I have sworn the firmest, most solemn oath possible," Fardulf said in a quavering voice.

"Let him live." The leader sheathed his sword. "It's time for us to be gone from here before anyone else appears. Remember your oath, Fardulf."

While the naked deacon crouched on his knees at the altar, the conspirators left their candle behind and melted into the darkness. Gina heard the south door close, and then the church was silent, except for Fardulf's sobs.

"Dominick, we have to get to Charles," Gina whispered.

"Wait a bit. One or two of those men may decide to come back and finish the deacon after all, just to be absolutely certain he doesn't speak."

They stood hidden behind the statue for what seemed to Gina to be hours, until Dominick finally released her and stepped into the nave.

"You were a fool to come here," he said, sounding angry.

"So were you," she countered. "If those men had seen you, they wouldn't have been as kind to you as they were to that poor, harmless little deacon."

"What do you imagine they'd have done to you?" he demanded, his voice growing louder.

"Who's there?" cried Fardulf, cringing against the altar.

"We're friends." Gina started forward. "Don't worry, we won't hurt you."

"A woman!" Fardulf tried in vain to cover himself. "Don't look at me. Oh, what shame!"

"You are not to blame for what happened," Gina said as firmly as she could manage, given her own recent terror. Stooping, she plucked Fardulf's robe from the chancel floor and draped it over his thin shoulders. "This is torn all the way down the front, but I think there's enough cloth for you to cover yourself. Would you like my sash to fasten it?"

"Thank you, no. My cincture must be here somewhere." Fardulf began to look around the chancel.

"Here it is." Dominick handed him the thick, knotted cord that clerics wore as a belt. Fardulf seized it and wrapped it around his narrow waist, thus securing the remnants of his robe.

"Are you all right?" Gina asked.

"How could I be?" cried Fardulf. "I have just been forced to swear a wicked oath. Oh, what shall I do?"

"There is a way for you to erase the shame of what has happened here," Dominick responded. "I once heard a bishop argue that an oath sworn under duress is no oath at all."

"What do you mean?" Fardulf stared at him as if seeing a faint glimmer of hope through his terror.

"Those men gave you two choices," Dominick said. "You could swear as they demanded, or refuse and forfeit your life."

"I did as they wanted. I am a wretched coward."

"Far from it. You made the wiser choice. I am assuming you did hear everything the conspirators said?"

Fardulf regarded Dominick fearfully and did not respond.

"I need you to bear witness to what happened here," Dominick explained.

"Witness?" Fardulf squeaked.

"We heard everything, too," Gina said, speaking gently to encourage him to forget his very legitimate fears. "The three of us, together, can convince Charles that our story of the plot is true."

"Charles? You expect me to speak to the king?" Fardulf cried.

"You don't want him to be murdered, do you?" asked Dominick.

"Never. He is a good Christian ruler and always generous to the Church. But I will have to find another robe before I can go to the palace."

"I want Charles to see you as you are now," Dominick said. "Let him know how roughly that band of traitors has treated an honest deacon."

"Charles will call you a hero," Gina added.

"Do you think so?" Fardulf stood a little straighter, throwing back his shoulders and lifting his chin. "In that case, let us be on our way."

"Don't you have to light the candles for Matins?" Gina asked.

"Oh, yes. I'd almost forgotten." Fardulf took the taper the conspirators had left, and, using both hands to steady his arm, he began to light the thick candles that stood on either side of the altar and at the foot of the chancel. "I wouldn't want anyone to say I've been derelict in my duties."

"No one could possibly claim that," Gina assured him. Then, to Dominick, she added, "As I told Fardulf, I am also going to Charles. I can back up the story you tell."

"It will be better if no one knows of your involvement in this matter," Dominick objected.

"Do you actually expect me to find my way back to your house alone in the dark?"

"Why not? You found your way here alone in the dark."

"I had you to follow," she said sweetly, and she saw in the candlelight the look of admiration he tried to hide from her.

"We will go out by a different door from the one the conspirators used," Dominick said to Fardulf. "They may have left a guard, in case anyone else was hiding in the church to overhear their plans."

At this Fardulf began to look frightened again. He pulled himself together when Gina smiled at him and touched his arm in a friendly way.

"We are depending on you," she said.

"It will have to be the north transept door, then," Fardulf said to her. "It leads to an enclosed courtyard, and from there it's only a few steps to the street."

Chapter Fourteen

Getting away from the church unseen wasn't difficult. Getting into the private wing of the palace was. Charles's personal guards were well-trained, and the man on sentry duty was most unwilling to allow the king to be disturbed in the middle of the night by people who demanded entrance through a small side door that led directly to the royal apartments.

"Come back in the morning," said the guard, "and present yourself at the main entrance. Explain your business, and you'll be conducted to Charles." With that, the guard slammed the door shut in their faces.

"You don't understand!" Fardulf shouted, pounding on the door. "I am a deacon of the church of St. Peter and a respectable man. I bring news of vital importance to Charles. You must admit me!"

"Fardulf, calm yourself," Dominick ordered.

"Our errand is urgent!" Fardulf exclaimed.

"Do you think I don't know that?" Dominick placed a restraining hand on Fardulf's shoulder. "Stand back, and allow me to speak with the guard."

Dominick rapped briskly on the door. When the annoyed guard jerked it open again, Dominick spoke at once, talking right over the the guard's command to stop making so much noise. In a firm voice Dominick stated his name and title for a second time and was insisting that he must see the king promptly when Charles himself appeared. The king was barefoot and wearing only a pair of trousers evidently donned so hastily that he kept them up by holding them to his waist with one hand.

"What in the name of heaven is all this noise?" Charles demanded. "Dominick, is that you? Why are you here so late? Come in and tell me what's wrong."

"Count Dominick, you must leave your sword outside," said the guard.

"Never mind," Charles said brusquely. "Let him in."

The guard stood back to let Dominick and his companions file through the small entry hall into a slightly larger room.

When Charles saw Gina, he quickly fastened the drawstring on his trousers and accepted a short cloak the guard handed to him. With the cloak slung over his shoulders to cover the upper half of his body, Charles ran his fingers through his pale hair. Thus prepared, though still barefoot and bare chested, he faced his unexpected visitors with the regal dignity that was natural to him, a dignity that did not require costly robes or a golden crown.

Fardulf was so overcome that he fell to his knees before Charles.

"Well, Dominick?" Charles quirked an eyebrow at the younger man and awaited an explanation.

"My lord, with your permission, I'd like the guard to remain with us while Fardulf speaks," Dominick said. "I don't believe we have been followed from St. Peter's church, but if we have, there will be two of us ready to defend you."

"Why should I need defending?" Charles asked, his tall body suddenly still, his handsome face alert.

"I will let Fardulf explain," Dominick said, turning to the deacon. "Now is the time to tell your story. When you are finished, Gina and I will add what we know of the matter. On your feet, man."

"Fardulf is something of a hero, my lord," Gina added, seeing how the deacon trembled and wanting to encourage him. "Go on, Fardulf."

"It was my turn to rise early and light the candles before Matins," Fardulf began, and he recounted the events of that night from his personal point of view. He ended by showing the king his torn robe, and then thanked Dominick and Gina for their aid. "They told me I must come to you at once, my lord, so here I am."

"Did you recognize any of the traitors?" Charles asked in a voice so low and calm that it was possible to imagine he wasn't at all upset by what he had learned.

Unless one looked into his eyes. The usually warm and humorous blue gaze of the king of the Franks had turned hard as stone. Seeing that look, Gina knew the conspirators were going to pay dearly for their treacherous scheme.

"I never saw their faces," said Fardulf. "All of them kept their hoods pulled well forward. It was almost as if they wanted to remain hidden even from each other, though it was plain that they were old comrades. I believe I did recognize one of the voices I heard, but I cannot accuse any man of such dastardly intentions unless I am absolutely certain of his guilt."

"I'll not blame you for being scrupulous," Charles said. "If you see or hear anything that definitely puts a name to any of those faceless figures, come to me again and tell me of it. I will not forget what you have done, Fardulf."

"It was no more than my duty," Fardulf responded, standing very straight.

Charles ordered his guard to see Fardulf to the door by which he had entered and to find a man-at-arms to escort the deacon safely back to the church.

"Now that we are alone," Charles said, looking from Dominick to Gina, "I will hear the rest of it. I am sure there is more than Fardulf knows. That's why you wanted him to speak first, isn't it? He said the conspirators mentioned young Pepin."

"I believe Pepin is nothing more than a pawn to them," Gina said quickly.

"Have you proof of that assertion?" Charles asked, turning his cold blue stare on her.

"He loves you!" Gina cried.

"Love can lead to terrible crimes," Charles said. "Dominick, I will hear you first, then Gina."

Dominick began to speak, starting with Pepin's unexpected arrival at Feldbruck and his attempt to convince Dominick to join the conspiracy.

"Pepin feels slighted in favor of his more able-bodied brothers," Dominick concluded his account. "He believes you do not love him, and his sense of honor was sorely wounded when he was declared a bastard and then, later, when you ordered Carloman rebaptised as Pepin. Even so, he insisted to me that the worst punishment he wants to see inflicted upon you is confinement to a monastery. When I warned him that the traitors would most certainly take your life, he was horrified. I doubt if he has yet considered the inevitable end of the plot, which is that once he has served his purpose, he will have to be killed, too."

"Furthermore," Gina said, breaking into Dominick's remarks on Pepin's behalf, "Pepin has that dreadful Father Guntram talking at him all day, every day, constantly scolding and criticizing and forever lecturing him. It's enough to drive anyone to desperate measures."

"Fastrada recommended Father Guntram as Pepin's tutor and spiritual advisor," Charles said. "She has every faith in the priest."

"The queen hates Pepin," Gina stated flatly. "Did you know she met with Father Guntram yesterday?"

"That is impossible. Father Guntram is with Pepin, and they are still a day's journey away from Regensburg."

"Pepin may be a day's journey away. Father Guntram was here, in the palace. I saw him with the queen," Gina insisted.

Charles stared at her again for a long moment, those blue eyes boring into her. Gina returned his gaze without fear. Then he said, "Tell me everything you know of this matter of the plot."

She did as he ordered, confirming Dominick's story and Deacon Fardulf's tale and adding her own feminine impressions of the situation, hoping Charles would not discount them. She also spoke bluntly of Pepin's feelings about Fastrada and said she thought Pepin was justified in disliking the queen. Gina didn't think Charles would be angry with her for being honest. Surely he knew what kind of person Fastrada was.

"There is a general feeling of resentment against the queen," Dominick said quietly when Gina was finished.

"I have heard the complaints about Tassilo's fortune," Charles retorted impatiently. "I do not want to hear them repeated yet again."

"It isn't just the treasure," Dominick said. "I thought it was, until I came to Regensburg and began to listen to what your nobles are saying amongst themselves. Fastrada is too selfish and cruel to ever exercise power fairly. While you were away in Bavaria, and Fastrada ruled in your name, she undertook the ruin of all who disagreed with her on any subject. Nor did she cease her machinations after you returned home."

Dominick halted there, not mentioning what Fastrada had tried to do to him. The sharp look he gave Gina warned her to say nothing of his marriage and divorce. After a moment of reflection,

Gina decided he was right. If Dominick brought up his own situation, Charles could dismiss his observations, claiming he had a personal complaint against the queen.

But Gina feared that Dominick's remarks would make no difference. Charles was emotionally attached to his wife, and he wasn't likely to institute divorce proceedings just because his nobles didn't like her.

"For the moment, let us concentrate on forestalling the plot against me," Charles said. "That is the most urgent issue. Can either of you put names to any of those hidden faces?"

"I don't know any of them," Gina said, glad that she couldn't speak the words that would condemn any man to certain death.

"Before tonight, as a result of all the questions I've been asking, I know the names of two of the men involved," Dominick said, his face grim with the realization of what he was doing. "The gathering at the church altar confirmed what I had previously learned. One of the names mentioned was that of Count Gerold of Konz. The man who spoke Gerold's name was his cousin and best friend, Lord Utred."

"So." Charles's face was as solemn as Dominick's, and his voice was steady. "Noblemen who have fought by my side, whom I counted as friends, men whom I have honored with lands and titles, now choose to betray me to my death. Dominick, find a man-at-arms. I have commands to give."

Before Gina and Dominick left the palace near dawn, Charles had ordered his palace guards to surround the church of St. Peter, to keep it secure and to see that the priests were safe. A troop of men-at-arms who were directly attached to Charles, rather than to any of his nobles, was sent into the streets of Regensburg to maintain order. And Charles had sent a message to the church in which he stated that he would definitely be attending morning prayers.

"I must show myself," Charles said when Dominick protested that last decision. "We cannot keep news of the plot secret for more than a few hours. You know as well as I do how quickly rumors fly. One of those rumors will certainly be that I have been slain. My public appearance will put an end to such speculation and reduce the fear of violence."

With his calm insistence they had to be satisfied, for Charles refused to alter his decision.

"All will be well," he said, bidding them good night.

"I am so glad this night is almost over," Gina said when she and Dominick had returned to his house and were alone in his bedchamber. "When I realized what was going on in that church, I was sure we were both going to be murdered.

"We can rest easy now," she said, putting her arms around Dominick's waist. "Thanks to Fardulf, and to us, the villains will be caught." She didn't add what they both knew, that the villains would be brought to trial and those found guilty of plotting against Charles would be publicly executed. She wished she and Dominick could be on their way back to Feldbruck before the trial began.

She certainly didn't want to witness any executions. For the moment, all she wanted to do was hold Dominick tight and forget her earlier fears.

"I ought to be angry with you," he said, laying his cheek against her hair. "It was incredibly foolish of you to follow me."

"I know." She snuggled closer to him. "But when I saw you sneaking out of the house, I was sure you were going into danger. I couldn't let you go alone."

"What a remarkable woman you are." He put a finger under her chin so he could tilt her face upward and kiss her.

Passion flared suddenly, burning all the hotter after the the peril they had been through together. The realization that they were safe after facing death added a special savor to the moment. Gina tore her mouth from Dominick's and reared back in his arms to look at him. She caught his face between her hands, studying him as if she had never seen him before, seeing the molten silver of his eyes and the sensual longing in his parted lips. They were standing so close that she was immediately aware of the swift hardening of his manhood.

"Dominick," she whispered.

His lips curved in a smile of understanding, a very masculine acknowledgment that she was his to take, when and how he wanted. He began to remove her clothing. It wasn't done in haste, but he didn't dawdle, either, and his smooth, deliberate movements intensified the desire that was building inside Gina.

Dominick's attention was so intensely concentrated on her that she would have to have been a

231

marble statue not to respond. Gina was not a piece of stone; she was a woman in a world that was still new and intriguing to her, and Dominick was the most fascinating man she'd ever known. He was a rare and heady combination of irreproachable honor and earthy passion, of practical common sense and breathtaking romance. He was also the one man she had ever been able to trust for more than a single hour.

Dominick caressed her breasts as he claimed her mouth, touching her as if he could not get enough of her, as if she was everything he wanted or needed, and as if he was determined to imprint himself on all her senses.

Gina was well past the time when she was shy of him. She returned every caress and handled his masculinity with tender firmness. It was wonderful to hear Dominick's moans of pleasure as she stroked and fondled him, and it was wildly exciting to her to watch him grow larger and harder. His unashamed desire for her stirred a warmth deep within her, a yearning that left her weak and trembling. He knew it; he was attuned to her every wish, and he did not make her wait much past the moment when she began to fear she would go mad with wanting.

"Come here." He placed his hands on her hips and sat her down on top of him, impaling her, holding her there when she cried out in surprise as his hardened length filled her. She knew what he was doing, but she had never experienced it before, never sat astride a man who wanted her and who had made her desire him. Like everything else about Dominick's lovemaking, the sensation was glorious, and the freedom he granted her to move as she wished only intensified her response.

The sole complaint she could possibly have made was that her climax came upon her too quickly. Ah, but with Dominick to touch her in secret places, to rear upward and kiss her with laughter on his lips, the incredible peak of pleasure continued on and on, until Gina was limp and damp with perspiration. She fell across Dominick's chest, weeping and gasping. He held her that way until she was completely recovered.

She wanted to say she loved him. Only a last, lingering hint of insecurity left over from her previous life prevented her from speaking the words. In the course of that long and dangerous night she had been called courageous, and foolishly brave, and she did trust him, yet still she lacked the courage to open her heart completely.

At mid morning, while Gina and Dominick were breaking their fast, Ella rushed into the hall, breathless with excitement.

"I was at the market," Ella said, "when I noticed a boat tying up at one of the docks, and who do you think was aboard? Pepin and Father Guntram. It certainly took them long enough to get here, didn't it?"

"I'm going to the palace. Pepin will need a friend," Dominick said, rising from the table. He gave Gina a serious look and spoke with great firmness. "You are to remain at home today."

With that he was gone, calling to Harulf to come with him, shouting at Benet to saddle two horses.

"Ha!" Gina said, setting her mug of watered

wine down with a thud. "If Dominick imagines I am going to remain here and miss the next act of this drama while he is at the palace, right in the middle of things, then he is sadly mistaken."

"He didn't even wait long enough for me to tell him the rest of the news," Ella said.

"You mean there's more?" Gina grinned. "Sit down and tell me. Here, have some wine and bread."

"Just a little wine, thank you. I ate earlier, with Harulf." Ella gulped down a mouthful of wine, then began talking. "A plot against the king's life has been uncovered. They are saying in the marketplace that more than a dozen nobles have fled Regensburg, and that Charles has sent troops to find them and bring them back for trial." She paused, looking at Gina as if expecting a comment.

"Oh, my," Gina said as innocently as she could manage. "Word does travel quickly, doesn't it?"

"A man I spoke to told me the queen is involved," Ella said.

"I doubt that," Gina responded. "Why would Fastrada want Charles murdered, when her position depends on keeping him alive?" She could understand how such a rumor would start, though. A lot of people hated Fastrada enough to try to link her to the plot. Fastrada must know it, too, which meant she would be busy trying to direct suspicion away from herself and onto anyone she considered an enemy.

"Dominick," Gina said. "She won't miss this chance to do him harm."

"What?" Ella gave her a puzzled look.

"I am beginning to think like a Frankish noblewoman," Gina said. "Finish your wine, Ella. We are going to the palace."

"But Dominick said for you to stay here."

"Where I come from, women don't obey men," Gina said. "I will wear my red dress this morning."

Chapter Fifteen

"Ansa," Gina said, stopping the young woman in the center of the great hall, "have you seen Count Dominick?"

"Always you ask the same question," Ansa responded. She looked around the hall, where the Frankish nobles and their ladies stood about in groups, heads together, talking in low voices. "Never have I heard so much gossip, or so many wild rumors, either. No, I have not seen Dominick. Could he be with the men Charles has sent to round up the traitors? That is where my betrothed, Fulrad, has gone."

"I don't think Dominick is with Fulrad," Gina said. "Perhaps he is with Charles."

"Fastrada is with Charles," Ansa told her. "Here

comes Lady Adalhaid. She may have news, though if she has, it's surely bad. How serious she looks."

Having noticed Gina, Lady Adalhaid made her way across the hall. Her face was pale, and her mouth was set in a hard line.

"I have been looking for you," Lady Adalhaid said to Gina without offering any polite greeting first. "Ansa, you may leave us."

"Not I," said Ansa, her eyes gleaming with anticipation. "Lady Adalhaid, have you heard a new rumor? Has there been a battle between the traitors and Charles's men? Was anyone killed?"

"There was a battle?" cried a young fellow who was standing near enough to hear what Ansa said. "And men killed in it? Oh, I must tell my friends." He rushed to a group of boys and girls who looked as if they were barely into their teens and began talking in an animated way.

"Now see what you've done, you thoughtless creature!" Lady Adalhaid exclaimed, fixing Ansa with a cold glare. "Take yourself over to those children immediately and explain to them that there has been no battle, that you were merely asking a question with no care for what you were saying. And do not let me catch you engaging in gossip again!"

The instant Ansa was out of hearing, Lady Adalhaid caught Gina's arm and leaned close, speaking in hushed tones.

"I am so glad to see you here. Fastrada is with Charles."

"That's what Ansa said."

"Did she tell you Fastrada's declared purpose for going to her husband? No, of course she didn't.

That foolish girl doesn't have a serious thought in her head."

"Why are you so disturbed?" Gina asked.

"Because Fastrada is attempting to convince Charles that Dominick is involved in this dreadful, treasonous plot."

"She won't succeed. Charles knows better." But a cold chill crept over Gina. The fear that had driven her from Dominick's house to the palace became a hard knot in her chest, making it difficult to breathe.

"Don't you be as foolish as Ansa," Lady Adalhaid said, assuming a stern expression. "I took you for a more intelligent woman than that. Fastrada is determined to ruin Dominick, and she will use any opportunity that presents itself. What better way to destroy the man who dared to criticize her to her face than to see him convicted of treason? If she has her way, Dominick will be executed and his lands confiscated—and those lands will then very likely be handed over to Fastrada or to one of her arrogant relatives."

"Why do you care?" Gina asked, adding suspicion to her fear.

"Fastrada's first scheme against Dominick spoiled my child's life." Lady Adalhaid's whisper was harsh with fiercely repressed emotion. "Were Hiltrude wed to any other nobleman, what she did on Fastrada's orders would almost certainly have meant her death. When Dominick learned that Hiltrude was acting as the queen's agent, he could have beaten her, could have arranged an accident that killed her, but he did not. He never laid a hand on Hiltrude. He let her leave Feldbruck, and he

239

took upon himself the blame for their divorce. For that, I owe Dominick a deeper debt of gratitude than I can ever repay. I will do anything to help him, so long as nothing I say or do endangers Hiltrude."

"You are saying that you don't want to tell Hiltrude's story to Charles."

"At the moment, his thoughts are entirely on the plot to murder him," Lady Adalhaid said. "That is perfectly understandable. There will come a time when I can tell him about Hiltrude, but it is not now. Gina, there must be something I can do for Dominick."

"First, we have to be sure of what Fastrada is saying to Charles. We can't counter her accusations until we know what they are. By the way, have you seen Dominick?"

"Not this morning," Lady Adalhaid said.

"Excuse me a moment." Gina beckoned to Ella, who was standing a short distance away. "Ella, I want you to ask questions of the servants and the men-at-arms. Do it very discreetly. Try to discover if anyone has seen Dominick and, if so, where he is."

"He said he was coming to the palace to see Pepin," Ella reminded her.

"Yes, I know, but no one has mentioned Pepin to me. I wonder if the nobles here know he has reached Regensburg? Find out as much as you can without arousing suspicion. Then come and report to me in private."

"I will. I'll try to find Harulf, too. I haven't seen him here at the palace." Ella started for the main entrance of the great hall.

"Now," Gina said to Lady Adalhaid, "we are going to enlist a witness whose words on Dominick's behalf no one will doubt, and then we are going to join Charles and Fastrada."

"We cannot walk in on them when they are in private together," Lady Adalhaid protested.

"Just watch me," said Gina. Grabbing Lady Adalhaid's elbow, she all but dragged the noblewoman out of the great hall by the side door, then through the maze of rooms to the garden courtyard, and thence to Alcuin's office.

Happily, he was there, sitting at his desk, hunched over a sheet of parchment on which he was writing industriously. He did not look up until Gina cleared her throat.

"I have been expecting you," Alcuin said. He laid down his quill pen and got to his feet.

"I am sure you have sources of information unknown to me," Gina said, "so I won't waste time telling you what you already know. Are you willing to help us save Dominick from Fastrada?"

"I am." Alcuin responded without hesitation. He looked at Gina's hand on Lady Adalhaid's arm and raised his eyebrows.

"It seems I have no choice in the matter," Lady Adalhaid said with some asperity, answering Alcuin's unspoken question.

"What would you have us do, Lady Gina?" Alcuin asked.

"Go with me to Charles's apartments, and speak the truth as you know it," she said.

"That I will most willingly do." Alcuin came around the desk to join the two women. "Gina, I promise you, Lady Adalhaid will not run away if you release her. I suspect she has her own, long-delayed, reasons for joining us." Alcuin gestured toward the door.

With the king's scholarly friend and Lady Adal-haid flanking her, Gina passed the guards at the door to the royal apartments without question.

"No need to announce us," Alcuin said to one of the sentries. "We will see ourselves in."

The guard threw open the door, and they entered Charles's private reception room. At the far end of the room Fastrada faced Charles, with her back toward the newcomers.

"I tell you that while he was still at Feldbruck, Dominick held a secret meeting with Pepin," Fastrada declared, sounding angry and completely confident of her facts. "They held a long, private conversation during which Pepin set forth his plan to remove you from the throne. The next day they separated, and each man then traveled to Regensburg so as to be present when their fellow conspirators struck at you."

"I find it difficult to believe that Dominick is involved," Charles said. "He revealed the plot to me."

His glance flickered from his wife's face to Gina, Lady Adalhaid, and Alcuin. Immediately, without indicating that he had seen them, Charles returned his full attention to Fastrada, who raised her voice and spoke again.

"Dominick's revelations were a ruse, a clever stratagem intended to allay your suspicions," Fastrada exclaimed. "Dominick betrayed you when he joined Pepin's wicked scheme while they were at Feldbruck together, and then he betrayed Pepin when he came to you to tell you of the plot.

Dominick is twice a deceiver. The penalty for treason is death. Dominick must be executed!"

Silence fell while Charles stared at his wife as if uncertain what to say next. He glanced toward Alcuin, and Fastrada whirled around, gasping when she saw who stood just inside the doorway.

"What are you doing here?" she demanded of Gina.

"How can you possibly know what Dominick and Pepin discussed in private?" Gina asked, for she had noticed the flaw in Fastrada's accusations.

"You have no right to question me!" Fastrada exclaimed.

"Answer Lady Gina," Charles said to her.

"Charles, you cannot doubt what I say!" Fastrada cried.

"How did you know the content of a private conversation?" Charles persisted.

"I—I was told by a reliable source," Fastrada said. "There can be no mistake."

" 'A reliable source,' " Gina repeated. "That is a phrase I've heard many times before, in my own ti—before I came to Francia. It's a phrase that is almost always used to mask a lie or to distort the truth.

"In this case," Gina continued, speaking directly to Charles, knowing he'd already heard the story from Dominick, "the truth is that Pepin and Dominick did speak together at Feldbruck. I noticed Father Guntram eavesdropping on their private conversation. He and I both heard what was said."

Behind Gina, Lady Adalhaid gasped. Out of the corner of her eye Gina saw Alcuin clasp his hands together as if in prayer.

"Lady Gina," Charles asked, "are you admitting

your own complicity in the plot against me?"

"No, sir," Gina answered. "I am saying the queen knew about the meeting at Feldbruck because Father Guntram told her of it. That must have been what they were discussing when I saw them in the courtyard, at a time when Father Guntram supposedly hadn't come to Regensburg yet."

"That is a lie!" Fastrada cried. "Charles, don't you see that this woman is Dominick's spy as well as his concubine?"

"Lady Gina is speaking the truth," Alcuin said, his quiet voice cutting across Fastrada's strident tones. "I also saw the queen speaking with Father Guntram."

"No!" Fastrada screeched. "Charles, you cannot believe these vicious slurs against me. This creature who calls herself a noblewoman cannot deny that Pepin and Dominick met secretly at Feldbruck."

"I do not deny it," Gina said. "Unlike you, I have the benefit of having heard what they actually said, rather than what a malicious priest reported. I heard Pepin's deep distress because he has been led to believe his father does not love him. He repeatedly insisted that when the conspiracy was carried out, no harm should come to the king. My opinion is that Pepin imagined he would gain his father's full attention at last and that when he was king, his father would listen to his feelings about the slights that have been visited upon him for years."

"Your opinion means nothing!" Fastrada yelled, starting toward Gina with fingers outstretched like claws.

"Stop, Fastrada." Charles's hand came down on

his wife's shoulder, halting her advance on Gina. "Lady Gina, you have so far neglected to tell us what Dominick's response was to the suggestion that he should join the plot."

"Dominick tried to make Pepin see what a foolish idea the plan was," Gina said. She couldn't understand what game Charles was playing at the moment, but she was willing to go along with it. "He insisted the other nobles involved were so untrustworthy that Pepin should not believe the promises they made to him. Later, Dominick told me he would never join any group that was trying to remove you from the throne.

"We came to Regensburg to seek out concrete evidence of the plot and who was involved in it— evidence so solid it could not be denied by the conspirators, evidence that Dominick could then present to you. We uncovered bits and pieces of the story, hints of coming trouble, but no facts reliable enough for us to tell you about them—until Dominick and Deacon Fardulf overheard the noblemen in the church last night. Fardulf was there purely by accident, as he explained to you. Dominick was there because he was following one of the men he suspected. You know about that, too, sir. Dominick told you everything he was able to learn about the conspiracy."

"Fastrada was never involved in the scheme," Charles said, sounding as if he was seeking reassurance.

"No, she was not," Gina said at once. "Such an involvement would not be in her best interests. However, she does hate Pepin, and she hates Dominick almost as much." Gina took a long breath to give herself a moment in which to reflect. Then she plunged on, risking much for Dominick's sake, and risking making an enemy of Lady Adalhaid.

"I'm not surprised that Fastrada is trying to include Dominick among the traitors," Gina said. "She tried to ruin him once before, when she used one of her ladies-in-waiting as a spy against him."

"This is ridiculous!" Fastrada cried.

Charles regarded his wife with a cold gaze. Then he looked at Lady Adalhaid, who had gone white as chalk. Gina could see understanding spreading across the king's handsome features. His hand on Fastrada's shoulder tightened noticeably.

"Is this true?" Charles asked Lady Adalhaid. "Is that why Fastrada was so insistent that Hiltrude should marry Dominick?"

"Tell him," Gina urged when Lady Adalhaid hesitated. "It's Hiltrude's best chance for freedom and safety. If she is harmed now, Charles will know who is to blame."

"Yes, my lord," Lady Adalhaid said. "Hiltrude was such a poor spy that Dominick soon found her out. I do believe he sent her to Chelles in the belief that she would be safe from the queen as long as she was in the convent where your own sister resides."

"I'll have your heads for this!" Fastrada screamed, writhing against the firm hold Charles was keeping on her shoulder.

"Alcuin, ladies, I thank all of you for coming to me," Charles said. He appeared to be perfectly calm, not the least bit flustered or angered by what he had heard, though Fastrada continued to squirm in his grip and to mutter threats against Gina and Lady Adalhaid. "Now I wish to speak with my wife, alone." His nod toward the door was an unmistakable dismissal.

"Please, sir," Gina said, "I beg you to remember that Dominick has always been completely loyal to you."

"He is a damned traitor!" Fastrada yelled.

"And Pepin loves you," Gina added to Charles.

"That dim-witted monster!" Fastrada screeched. "That spawn of a concubine! That hideous troll!"

"Sir," Lady Adalhaid said to Charles, "I humbly entreat you to consider who is the true monster."

"Go now," Charles commanded as Fastrada let out another threatening shriek. "Leave us, all of you."

Gina and Lady Adalhaid left the chamber, followed a few seconds later by Alcuin, who had paused for a final word with Charles. Fastrada uttered a high-pitched scream of rage. Gina could hear the murmur of Charles's voice. It sounded as though he was moving away from the doorway, perhaps to a more private room somewhere farther inside the royal apartments, and as if Fastrada was following, berating him as she went. Alcuin nodded at the guard, who closed the door.

"Oh, Gina," Lady Adalhaid exclaimed into the sudden quiet, "I pray you have not made matters worse for my dear Hiltrude."

"I think not," said Alcuin. "Charles admires courage, and Gina has just displayed a remarkable degree of it, so we may be certain that Charles will consider with care everything she has said. Charles loathes injustice. Whatever he decides to do about

Hiltrude, she will be well protected from now on."

"I just hope I've helped Dominick," Gina said. "And Pepin, too."

"Whatever that misinformed young man thinks," Alcuin said, "Charles does love Pepin and has often worried over his future."

"He should tell Pepin that."

"Perhaps he will," Alcuin said, "*now*."

"I am not sure I will ever forgive you," Lady Adalhaid said to Gina. "You carried me off to the royal apartments under false pretenses. I was to speak for Dominick, and you knew I did not want to mention Hiltrude." She looked so angry that Gina retreated a few paces before daring to respond to her heated remarks.

They were standing in the middle of the flowery courtyard, having paused to catch their breath and calm themselves in the same spot where only the day before Gina had observed Father Guntram and Fastrada in secret conversation. To Gina, it seemed like a year since that hour.

Alcuin had retreated to his office to continue his work of translating the Bible. Claiming that his students frequently visited him there, he promised to let Gina know anything he heard about Dominick's situation or about Charles's intentions toward the conspirators.

"Actually, as far as Hiltrude is concerned, I believe our talk with Charles turned out rather well," Gina said. "I think her chances of getting out of Chelles are greatly improved."

"I pray you are right." Lady Adalhaid's eyes filled with tears. "You cannot know how frightened I have been for Hiltrude during these last years. First I feared Dominick's reaction if he learned why she was apparently so eager to marry him. Then I was afraid of the queen's long reach, even when Hiltrude was supposedly safe at Chelles. My daughter is all I have." She wiped a tear off her pale cheek.

"I wish I had a mother who cared about me as much as you care about Hiltrude," Gina said.

"Haven't you?" Lady Adalhaid looked at her in surprise.

"My parents are both dead," Gina said flatly, clearly indicating she would say no more on the subject.

"I didn't know." Lady Adalhaid clasped Gina's hands. "I am sorry. But now you have Dominick to care about you."

"Unless Fastrada finds a way to have him executed."

"We cannot let that happen."

Gina had never been blessed with an aunt or an older female friend. She saw in Lady Adalhaid's eyes that she possessed such a friend now.

They returned to the great hall together to find the nobles still gossiping. There were some new arrivals, among them Dominick's half brother.

"Good day to you, Count Bernard," Lady Adalhaid said coldly when the young man approached them.

"Here's an odd pairing," said Bernard, looking from Lady Adalhaid to Gina. "Whoever would expect the two of you to become bosom companions? Have you heard the latest news?"

He was so smug, so self-satisfied that Gina

regarded him warily, certain the news he spoke of was something to do with Dominick, and it probably wasn't good. He was hoping to make her beg for it, too; she could tell by the way he was smiling. She longed to snarl an insult at him, but where Dominick was concerned she had no pride.

"What news?" she asked, almost expecting him to respond as the bullies of her childhood used to do, by inquiring why she wanted to know and what she'd give in return. She wished she had nerve enough to slap his face and wipe the smirk off it.

"Yes, what news?" demanded Lady Adalhaid, speaking so crisply that Bernard looked at her in surprise. "What do you know that is so dreadfully important?"

"Pepin Hunchback has arrived in Regensburg," Bernard announced.

"Really?" Lady Adalhaid regarded him as if he were a worm on which she was about to step. "What of it?"

"He has been arrested."

"Indeed?" drawled Lady Adalhaid with remarkable coolness.

Gina's heart was in her throat. She made a snap decision to let Lady Adalhaid handle Count Bernard. Lady Adalhaid could manage a man like Bernard with greater skill than Gina, frightened as she was for Dominick's sake, could hope to muster. That way, Gina wouldn't have to try to drag information about Dominick out of his brother. Because this *was* about Dominick. Bernard was too confident, too sure of his inside knowledge, for his big news to be about anyone but Dominick.

Lady Adalhaid let Bernard stand there waiting

for some further response from her until he could bear it no longer. Gina wouldn't have been as patient. She was ready to grab the big oaf and shake what he knew out of him well before Bernard finally gave in and began to talk.

"The Hunchback is confined to his room here at the palace," Bernard said. "It's special consideration because he's the king's son. The other conspirators won't be treated as well. But then, they won't have to wait long before they are brought to trial. Plans are already being made."

"I understand the others have fled," Lady Adalhaid said, sounding as if she were terribly bored by the whole business.

"Most of them have gone. A few were rounded up here at Regensburg." Bernard smiled at Gina. "Dominick was easy to find. He was with Pepin when Pepin was arrested. The two are being held together. They will die together, too."

Gina could tell there was no point in arguing with him. Bernard didn't want to hear that Dominick wasn't part of the conspiracy. She was curious, however, about his reaction to what he assumed would be his brother's fate.

"If Dominick is charged and convicted," Gina said, forcing the hateful words off her tongue, "won't that reflect badly on you?"

"Why should it? Fastrada will see to it that I remain in Charles's good graces. Besides, Dominick is nothing to me."

"He's your brother!"

"He is a bastard!" Bernard shouted. In a quieter tone he said, "Our father loved him better than me."

"I don't believe this. How can a grown man be so

childish? Bernard, you inherited everything from your father."

"By law, not by love," Bernard said. "Now, by law, Dominick will die. And I am glad of it."

He stalked away, leaving Gina with her mouth open in astonishment.

"Jealousy can twist and pervert a man's heart," said Lady Adalhaid. "Fastrada is an expert at playing on the weaknesses of men. You have just witnessed an example of her work."

She didn't mention Charles. She didn't have to. Gina understood what Lady Adalhaid did not say. And her fears for Dominick grew more desperate.

"My lady!" Ella hurried across the hall, interrupting Gina's disturbing thoughts. "I have learned where Dominick is. He insisted on remaining with Pepin. The guards said that in that case, they'd have to arrest him, too."

"Then what Dominick's brother told us was only half true," Gina responded. "Were you able to find Harulf?"

"Yes, and he has orders from Dominick. You and I are to leave the palace and return to Dominick's house. Harulf will escort us there and see to it that we are kept safe. Dominick also sent a message through Harulf to tell you not to worry."

"How can I not worry?" Gina muttered. "Ella, just let me tell Lady Adalhaid that we are leaving." When she turned, she noticed a weeping maidservant speaking to Lady Adalhaid.

"What's wrong?" Gina exclaimed, seeing the noblewoman white and shaking. "What has happened? Not bad news from Hiltrude?"

"As far as I know, Hiltrude is well," Lady Adalhaid said. "I pray that you and Alcuin were correct in believing that Charles will see to her safety. No, the immediate problem is that I have been turned out of my room."

"What?"

"As one of Fastrada's most senior ladies-in-waiting, I have for some years occupied a small room in the queen's apartments so I can be quickly available to her if she requires my presence. This is Imma, my maidservant, who is commanded by the queen to inform me that I have been dismissed as one of her ladies and must quit the palace at once."

"Fastrada doesn't waste any time, does she?" The cold knot in Gina's chest tightened still more. If Fastrada could get rid of one of her most important ladies so easily, even after what had been said in the royal apartments less than an hour ago, then she obviously still held a strong grip on Charles's emotions. Which meant Dominick was in serious trouble. If Fastrada turned her sexual charms on her husband, she might be able to convince him that, despite what Dominick, Gina, and Fardulf had told him, Dominick really was involved in the plot against him.

Fastrada might find a way to circumvent Charles's precautions for Hiltrude, too. That dire possibility, Gina admitted to herself, was her sole doing. If she had kept quiet, Hiltrude wouldn't have been mentioned at all, and she'd stay at Chelles, forgotten in all the excitement of a treasonous conspiracy. There was just one way Gina could think of to make up for what she had done. She could provide shelter to Lady Adalhaid. She felt certain Dominick would approve.

"Lady Adalhaid, I want you and your maid to move to Dominick's house," Gina said. "We have plenty of space. I'll sleep in Dominick's room, and you may have mine. Unless, of course, you'd rather have nothing more to do with me, or with Dominick. I'll understand if you feel that way. I have caused a lot of trouble for you." She held her breath, hoping that Lady Adalhaid would agree to the invitation, while knowing she had to give the distraught woman a chance to refuse.

"I gladly accept your offer," Lady Adalhaid said. "To tell the truth, being dismissed from Fastrada's service is a great relief. I have spent too many years biting my tongue and trying to be polite to her, when I really wanted to scratch her eyes out. I stayed with her in the hope that she'd make a mistake and provide me with the opportunity to rescue Hiltrude. But she never has. Fastrada is too clever to make mistakes."

"Sooner or later, everyone slips up," Gina said. "Especially a person who is playing as many dangerous games with people's lives as Fastrada is. We ought to be going. Can I help you with your packing?"

"Imma did most of it before she came to find me," Lady Adalhaid said. "But we will require two or three men to carry my boxes and baskets to Dominick's house."

"Ella, will you ask Harulf to find a few men?" Gina said.

"Imma, come with me." Ella put an arm around the weeping maid and led her away.

"I am so sorry about this," Gina said to Lady Adalhaid.

"My only regret is that if we are refused admittance to the palace, we won't know the latest news," Lady Adalhaid responded.

"No one has told me I can't return here," Gina said, "and I've noticed that Ella is very clever about picking up useful information. We won't be as isolated as you fear."

Chapter Sixteen

In late afternoon Alcuin sent a note to Gina to inform her that she, too, was henceforth refused entry to the palace.

"He promises to keep me informed of any developments having to do with Dominick's situation, or Pepin's," Gina said, reading the letter to Lady Adalhaid. "Listen to this. 'Charles perceives two separate problems, and he will deal with them individually. First and most important is the conspiracy. Only after the traitors have been tried and punished will Charles consider his wife's misbehavior.'"

"Why can't he see that Fastrada's greed and her cruel character are partly the cause of the conspiracy?" cried Lady Adalhaid in exasperation.

"He is bound to her emotionally and sexually. Even I, who have known them for little more than a week, can see that," Gina said. As she spoke, she folded Alcuin's letter. "At least we have a contact inside the palace. While we try to think of a way to help Dominick, Alcuin will keep us up to date on what is happening."

They didn't need a correspondent within the palace to learn what happened next. All of Regensburg was talking about the noble traitors who were tracked to Ratisbon and arrested there, and who were being transported back to court for trial. Rumor said Queen Fastrada was so horrified by the plot against Charles that she was insisting at every opportunity that all of those involved, without exception, must be put to death.

"It isn't just Dominick she wants dead," Lady Adalhaid said upon hearing the latest story. "Fastrada has strong personal reasons for hating every man among them, for each of them has, at one time or other, spoken out against her. She never forgets or forgives a slight."

"Now she will have her revenge," Gina said. "Not to mention all the lands and titles those nobles held, which will revert to the crown and have to be redistributed. She will influence the decisions on who will get those lands and titles, won't she?"

"You are learning." Lady Adalhaid responded to Gina's remarks with a bitter smile. "All the same, while I sympathize with anyone who dislikes Fastrada and her ruthless methods, treason is unforgivable and deserves the death sentence."

"Only if a man is truly guilty," Gina said. "We both know Dominick isn't guilty."

"Just so," Lady Adalhaid agreed.

* * *

In Pepin's small room in the palace, he and Dominick were cramped for space even when they were alone. When Father Guntram was there, which he was for the better part of each day, the walls began to close in on Dominick until he would have given all he owned for a single hour out of doors in fresh air and sunshine, with Father Guntram far away and preferably gagged so he couldn't talk.

"It is a wicked sin to wish for your father's death," Father Guntram intoned for the eighth time that day. His hand was on Pepin's head, keeping the young man on his knees with his head bowed in a posture that the most uncaring observer could see was painful.

"I have never wanted my father's death," Pepin said. It was the same response he had uttered again and again during the last three days.

Every fiber of Dominick's being strained to seize the heartless priest by the neck of his cassock and haul him away from Pepin. Dominick's fists ached from the effort he was exerting to keep from smashing them into Father Guntram's face, over and over, until the priest agreed to stop tormenting Pepin.

In spite of the anger that almost choked him, Dominick still had sense enough left to know that attacking Father Guntram was the worst thing he could possibly do. Aside from the crime of hitting a priest, which Dominick did not want on his conscience, Father Guntram would take any act of violence as proof of Dominick's guilt, and he'd carry the tale to Charles. Or to Fastrada, which would be worse. So Dominick sat at the foot of Pepin's narrow bed and stared at the rolled-up pallet that he spread on the floor to sleep on at night, and he pretended he didn't care what the priest was saying.

"Come, Pepin, confess your sins," Father Guntram urged. "You, too, Dominick. Confess and be shriven. Go to your deaths with hearts and souls made pure by honest repentance."

"What death?" Dominick asked, lifting his head to stare the priest in the eye. "I haven't done anything wrong. Neither has Pepin." That wasn't exactly true of Pepin, but Dominick wasn't going to admit that to a man who gave the Holy Church a bad name.

"You, a bastard, have much to repent," said Father Guntram, releasing his hold on Pepin's head to turn his fiery gaze on Dominick.

"I cannot change the circumstances of my birth," Dominick replied. Then he stopped listening and let the priest's words roll over him unheeded. He could bear the accusations, and with Father Guntram busy scolding him, Pepin would have a rest.

Dominick allowed his mind to wander to more pleasant subjects than Father Guntram or the approaching trial. He thought of Feldbruck, where the midsummer harvest was likely just beginning. In his mind he could see the mountains, the green forest, and the buildings tucked within the palisade—his home, the place he had earned with his strong sword arm and his blood. Lately, whenever he thought of Feldbruck, he saw Gina in the garden, sitting on the little stone bench, waiting for him.

He was trained to be a warrior, a man of steel

and blood and violence, yet the image dearest to his heart was no longer a battle scene but the picture of a slender young woman with short, dark curls sitting beneath a tree with shimmering green leaves. When she saw him, she would rise and hold out her arms. . . .

"Confess your crimes and be saved," Father Guntram cried, his raised voice interrupting Dominick's daydream.

"I have committed no crimes," Dominick said. "Quite the opposite. I tried to prevent a crime from being committed."

"Every man sins," Father Guntram insisted.

"Mine are venial sins," Dominick said, "which I will confess to my own priest when I see him again. You are not that priest."

"Blasphemy!"

"What is? To point out the obvious fact that you are not my priest?" Dominick stretched, making the movement look as languid and lazy as possible. "I have nothing to say to you, Father Guntram."

The priest drew a deep breath, a warning to Dominick that he was preparing to begin yet another lengthy exhortation on the subject of sins that were crimes against one's liege lord as well as against heaven.

"Excuse me," a new voice interrupted from the doorway.

"Alcuin, I'm glad to see you." Dominick was on his feet, a welcoming hand extended to the tall, stoop-shouldered cleric.

"What business have you with these sinful men?" Father Guntram demanded in his usual rude manner.

"Actually, my errand is with you," Alcuin said, turning a bland smile on the priest. "Queen Fastrada requests that you attend her. 'As soon as possible' were the exact words she used."

"I shall return, Pepin." Father Guntram spoke to the top of Pepin's bent head. "Use this interval to consider all I have said to you. Repent of your wickedness. When I do return, I expect to hear a full confession of your sins." Without a word of thanks to Alcuin for bearing the queen's message, he left the room.

"I could better consider what he has said," Pepin muttered, "if only he didn't say so much. I can't recall most of it."

"That's because he repeats himself," Dominick said, and he bent to help Pepin to his feet. "Father Guntram has only two speeches. I think I have both memorized. I'll drill you on them if you like."

"No, thank you." With a groan Pepin tried to straighten his back. "Bless you, Alcuin, for interrupting."

"Speaking of sins, I am now guilty of a lie designed to remove Father Guntram for a little while. Are you being well treated?" Alcuin asked.

"Yes, aside from Father Guntram's constant attendance," Pepin said. "Please, I beg of you, don't tell me he means well or that he is attempting to save my immortal soul. *He* has told me so too many times for the words to hold any meaning for me."

"My boy, you did plot against your father," Alcuin said sadly.

"But Dominick did not! Can't you explain that to Charles and convince him to release Dominick?" Pepin asked.

"I have tried. So has Lady Gina. Dominick, I have disturbing news to impart."

"Don't tell me Gina has been arrested?" Dominick's hand went to his side, where his sword hilt would be if the weapon weren't safely at his house, left there because swords were not worn at the palace.

"Not Gina," Alcuin said. "She and Lady Adalhaid are together, well guarded by Harulf and your other men-at-arms and well served by that delightful and intelligent girl, Ella."

"Good." Dominick ran his hands over the stubble on his jaw, wishing he could take a bath and shave. "What bad news, then?"

"Your brother, Bernard, has been implicated in the plot against Charles. He is being arrested at this moment."

"Bernard?" Dominick scarcely knew whether to burst into laughter at the sheer lunacy of the charge or to become seriously worried. "Bernard is Fastrada's man. She will protect him."

"It was Fastrada who denounced Bernard to Charles."

"What?" Dominick gaped at Alcuin. "In heaven's name, why?"

"I gather Bernard did or said something to annoy Fastrada. It's easy enough to do."

"So she is sending him to trial for treason?" Dominick shouted. "The woman is mad! If Charles lets her do this, so is he!"

"Keep your voice down," Alcuin warned. Frowning, he looked from Dominick to Pepin and back again. "The situation becomes more serious by the moment. Both of you must guard every word you speak, particularly when Father Guntram is present. Do not confess, for Guntram will most likely not abide by the sacred seal of the confessional. He is too ambitious, too eager to gain Fastrada's favor. Do not provide evidence that will surely be used against you when you come to trial."

"Am I to be tried?" Dominick asked, knowing what the answer must be and prepared to hear his belief confirmed.

"Yes." Alcuin bit off the single word as if speaking it hurt his tongue.

"What of Deacon Fardulf?"

"Fastrada has been attempting to convince Charles that Fardulf was a party to the meeting of traitors, and that after it ended he began to fear the consequences."

"So he protected himself by rushing off to Charles and telling what he knew," Dominick finished. "That version is not true. Gina and I both were in the church and saw how roughly Fardulf was treated. At first he didn't want to go to Charles. He was afraid for his life."

"The Church will protect Fardulf, and the truth will eventually be known," Alcuin said.

"You do see what is happening, don't you?" Pepin exclaimed. "Fastrada has found the perfect opportunity to destroy anyone who ever spoke against her, or who even just irritated her. She will use the conspiracy as a way to have all her enemies declared traitors."

"How can Charles be a party to such viciousness?" Dominick asked. "It's not like him. He has always been a reasonable man. If he refused to execute Duke Tassilo after all Tassilo did, including plotting against his life, then how can he justify a death sentence on anyone who has been arrested solely on Fastrada's instigation?"

"I do wonder how far Fastrada will go," Alcuin said, "and when Charles will decide she has over-stepped the power a queen of Francia rightfully holds."

"Not soon enough for Dominick and me," said Pepin. "By the time my father finally comes to his senses, we will be dead."

"I will never be able to thank you adequately for what you're doing," Gina said to Alcuin. "This could prove dangerous for you."

"My safety is irrelevant," Alcuin said. "It is a matter of justice, and justice is the concern of every man and woman, whatever the cost may be."

It was late evening, and they were in the now-familiar garden courtyard. The only light came from a few stars and from the open door of the corridor that led to Alcuin's office.

"I asked Charles to join me after he was finished meeting with his councillors," Alcuin said, explaining the arrangements he had made. "I used a freshly translated chapter of the Book of Genesis as an excuse, saying I wanted him to read a portion of it and give me his opinion on certain passages. I think he was glad to know he'll have an hour when he won't feel compelled to think about the trial tomorrow."

"Where is Fastrada?"

"She has taken to her room, claiming a severe headache."

"More likely she just wants a bit of privacy so

she can dream up a few new ways to make decent people miserable."

"I cannot think the queen is a happy woman," Alcuin said in a dry tone that made Gina look sharply at him. She couldn't see his face, just his tall shape looming beside her in the shadows.

"Baloney! That woman loves to be nasty."

"Baloney?" Alcuin mispronounced the word and laughed softly.

"It's a kind of sausage."

"Thank you, Gina."

"For what?"

"You have just provided a few moments in which *I* did not have to think about the trial. It's a relief to enjoy a small joke and laugh." Alcuin touched her shoulder lightly. "We should go to my office now. Charles will be joining us soon."

In fact, they waited almost an hour for him, and when the king of the Franks arrived, he looked weary. When he saw Gina, his handsome face creased into a scowl.

"Alcuin, you tricked me," Charles said reproachfully.

"Not at all," Alcuin said. "I do have the transla-tion I spoke of, and I would appreciate hearing your comments on it. I admit, I did promise Lady Gina you would listen to her petition first."

"As I said, a trick." Charles sighed, looking at Gina. "I have just finished speaking with another woman, a lady I have known since I was a young man, who came to me to plead for the life of her son and to tell me she suspects that Pepin has been used and manipulated in this business."

"I'm glad to know there is someone else who sees

the conspiracy as Dominick and I do," Gina said. She was about to launch into her plea for Dominick's life when Charles spoke again.

"I will tell you what I told Lady Elza. There is enough evidence to sentence almost every one of them to death. They have been remarkably careless in their treason. When their houses were searched my agents found documents, letters and lists, stating names. A more clever group of men would have seen to it that even the smallest bit of incriminating parchment was destroyed."

Gina stared at him, knowing Dominick's house had not been searched and trying to figure out what that meant. Was it because Charles knew Dominick wasn't among the traitors, or was Dominick's name on one of those lists because he was Pepin's longtime friend and, thus, guilty by association? Not knowing what evidence, if any, Charles possessed about Dominick, still she was compelled to continue fighting for him.

"You cannot possibly believe Dominick has ever wished you ill," she declared in a firm voice. "He owes everything to you—his lands, title, and his position."

"The same could be said about most of the other men under arrest," Charles responded.

"Dominick told me once that you were like a second father to him."

"One of the conspirators is a son of my own body. If Pepin could betray me, why not a foster son?"

"If you know anything at all about men, you must know that Dominick is honest. For heaven's sake, he came to you and warned you about the plot!"

"It has been suggested to me that Dominick and Deacon Fardulf were originally part of the plot, that they revealed it to me only after they realized it could not succeed, and that they did so in hope of saving themselves."

"You saw Fardulf's condition the night we told you of the plot, and you saw his torn robe."

"Fardulf could easily have torn his own robe, or Dominick could have torn it for him."

"That meek, innocent soul was manhandled by a gang of ruffians. In a church!" Gina exclaimed. Outraged by what Charles had said, she spoke without considering the consequences of her words. "I came to the palace tonight, planning to get down on my knees and plead with you for Dominick's life because I thought you were an intelligent, reasonable man. If you have allowed Queen Fastrada to corrupt your mind until you believe anything that vicious, spiteful, spoiled brat tells you about a person you *know* is honest, then you are not the man I thought you were. You are not the man the Franks believe you to be, not the man they honor as their king."

She had gone too far, and she knew it. That was not the way to speak to a king, especially when she wanted something from him. She saw Alcuin's disapproving expression and knew she had blown her chance to change Charles's mind.

And yet, she could not bring herself to apologize. She wasn't sorry for what she had said. Charles needed to hear the truth about Fastrada from someone who wasn't a courtier with a personal agenda to advance, or a traitor. She hoped she had made an impression on him, though she feared that Charles already knew what kind of wife he had and that, for some private, perverse reason, he wasn't going to stop her.

Charles didn't look angry over Gina's harsh words. He just stood there with his arms folded across his chest, watching her closely. She made one more attempt.

"Dominick is completely innocent of treason," she insisted. "So is Deacon Fardulf. You cannot believe Fastrada's lies against them."

"What I believe or do not believe," Charles said, "will become known at the trial tomorrow. I will not discuss this matter with you any longer. You have my leave to depart, Lady Gina."

There was no way she could protest or attempt to make him listen to a new plea. If she tried, she'd only hurt Dominick's case. The sole action left to her was a polite withdrawal.

"Thank you for listening to me," Gina said to Charles. To Alcuin she added, "I am sorry I've caused you trouble."

"You haven't," Alcuin said. "Go now."

She did. When she left the palace grounds she found Harulf waiting for her at the gate where she had left him. To his questions about the success of her mission she could only respond that she didn't know what effect her pleas had had on Charles. She did not begin to weep until she was alone in Dominick's room.

Chapter Seventeen

The trial was held in the great hall of the palace. Charles sat in a simple wooden chair on a raised dais. He was clad in his usual outfit of undecorated woolen tunic and trousers, though for this solemn occasion he also wore his golden crown. His council, his secretaries, and a few clerics, including Alcuin, stood near him, ready to provide opinions or advice should he require either.

At one side of the hall, sitting in a row on benches, were the men Charles had appointed as judges, who were to listen to the case and offer a verdict. On the opposite side of the hall, at some distance from Charles, Fastrada was seated on a gilded chair, her ladies clustered around her. The queen's face was hard, and her blue eyes glittered when she looked at the accused men.

Heavily armed guards were everywhere, pressing the spectators back so that they were forced to stand against the walls. The accused were surrounded so closely that Gina couldn't help wondering if Charles had heard rumors of a plan for an escape, or of another attempt on his life, even at this late hour. Still, security wasn't perfect; she and Ella had been able to sneak into the palace by a servants' entrance that Ella knew, and no one had stopped them as they made their way to the hall. Both of them wore cloaks with the hoods pulled up, as did quite a few other people, and none of them was required to lower his hood.

The men who were to be tried all sat on stools in the center of the hall. Pepin was in the front row, and he kept a defiant face lifted toward his father. He and all the others wore rumpled clothing, their hair was uncombed, and they were unshaven. Dominick sat on the stool next to Pepin, and next to him was Bernard. That surprised Gina. She couldn't imagine why Bernard would choose a seat next to his despised half brother. But then, perhaps seating was assigned, and Bernard hadn't been given a choice.

From Gina's point of view, familiar as she was with television and newspaper coverage of drawn-out twentieth-century legal proceedings, it was astonishing that a trial of such vital importance to Francia should be so simple and so quickly arranged.

Charles acted as the presiding judge. As soon as everyone directly involved in the trial was seated, he called the first witness, who was Deacon Fardulf.

Fardulf repeated the same story that he, Dominick, and Gina had told Charles on the night they overheard the conspirators. Fardulf was a compelling witness, describing in vivid detail how roughly he had been treated, and eliciting murmurs of sympathy when he spoke of his shame at having been completely disrobed before the holy altar. His account of hastening to the palace to reveal the details of the conspiracy was corroborated by Charles himself.

"You made so much noise," Charles said, "that I threw on a few clothes and hurried to the anteroom to see what was wrong. There I found you arguing with the guard who was posted at my door that night. At my request, you told the story you have just recounted here. Thank you, good deacon. I will not forget your efforts on my behalf. You are excused."

"A moment, my lord, if it please you," Fardulf cried. "As you know, Count Dominick of Feldbruck was also in the church of St. Peter that night. It was he who convinced me to speak to you when I was too terrified to comprehend what my true duty was, and he who escorted me safely to your presence when I feared the conspirators would accost me as soon as I left the church. Yet today I see Count Dominick seated among the traitors. My lord, I must speak out. Count Dominick is not a traitor. He risked his life so that I could tell you what I had heard."

"Thank you, Deacon Fardulf," Charles said. "You may go." He spoke in the commanding, kingly way he used only occasionally, the voice that left no room for refusal.

Fardulf retreated after casting a frightened look

at Dominick, who smiled his thanks for the deacon's efforts on his behalf.

The next witness was the man-at-arms who had been guarding the door to the king's apartments on the night in question. He confirmed Fardulf's tale of arriving well after midnight, with Fardulf highly agitated and in a state of disarray and with Count Dominick and another, cloaked, person in attendance.

The man-at-arms was followed by the captain of the palace guards, who described the long search for and capture of the traitors presently on trial, except for the few who were arrested in Regensburg. Then it was Charles's turn to speak again.

"I have read the documents seized from the accused," Charles said. "They reveal a plan to murder me and place my eldest son, Pepin, on the throne. Among those documents was a list that included all the men before us today. There can be no doubt of their guilt.

"Has any one of the accused aught to say in his own defense?" Charles asked, raising his voice.

Several men did rise from their stools to make statements. A few proclaimed that Duke Tassilo was still the rightful ruler of Bavaria, not Charles of Francia. Some complained of the way the by-now infamous treasure seized from Duke Tassilo had been handed over to Fastrada. Others denounced Fastrada for refusing to accept the counsel of the nobles appointed to advise her while Charles was away at war.

"My lord, the queen exerts a wicked and baleful influence over you!" one noble cried. "She is an evil woman, whom you must cast aside if you want to prevent future rebellions."

It was a bold statement, and Gina marvelled at the nobleman's courage, until she realized that all of the accused expected to be sentenced to death, their nearest kin permanently confined to convents or monasteries. With their fates already sealed, they dared to speak what was in their hearts, and doubtless in the hearts of many other Franks.

"You have heard the accusations, and you have heard the accused speak freely," Charles said to the row of judges. "Take counsel together, and announce your verdict."

The judges looked at one another, nodded, and exchanged a word or two. Then they stood, one by one, to pronounce their decision. The verdict was unanimous. All of the accused were found guilty, and all were sentenced to death. The hall was silent as people waited to learn whether Charles would be merciful to any of the condemned men.

Gina stood with both hands clapped over her mouth to keep herself from crying out at the injustice of Dominick's being included among the condemned. She was only distantly aware of Ella's arms around her waist, as if the faithful girl feared Gina would faint without that support. As for Dominick, he sat immobile, his gaze fixed on Charles. Knowing that anything she might try to do would only make matters worse for Dominick, Gina resorted to prayer. She prayed as she had never prayed before, and she heard Ella's whispered prayer as an echo of her own.

Charles looked around the hall, from council to clerics and priests, to the guards and the condemned. His gaze rested on his queen for a long moment, and Gina saw his shoulders rise and fall, as if he was heaving a great sigh. Then he spoke to the conspirators.

"You have heard the sentence. I am disposed to clemency toward only a few of you, for most of you knew exactly what you were doing when you deliberately plotted the death of a ruler to whom you had freely pledged your allegiance. By Frankish custom and law, your lives are now forfeit to me, as are all the lands you hold."

He began the ritual of naming each man, his sad and heavy voice clearly speaking of his regret at the loss of men upon whom he had depended, many of whom he had counted among his friends. When a name was called, that man rose, and Charles spoke his punishment. Most were to be hanged or beheaded. One by one the guards led them out of the hall, to be confessed, shriven, and then to meet their fates with no delay. A few who were elderly and not likely to live much longer were to be sent into exile. They, too, were taken out at once, for they were commanded to leave Regensburg before the sun had set.

The number of men seated on the stools grew smaller and smaller, and Fastrada's smile grew wider and wider.

"Hugh of Montraive," Charles called. One of the younger nobles who was in the front row near Pepin stood to face the king. But suddenly there was an alteration in the deadly routine.

"My lord, I wish to speak!" cried Hugh.

"Your opportunity has passed," Charles said. "Your sentence has been decided."

"It's not for myself I want to be heard, but for Pepin, who will not speak for himself. He and I were at the palace school as boys and have been friends ever since. Pepin loves you and longs for you to love him." Before he could say anything more, Charles cut him off.

"Be silent, Hugh." Those three words brought to a quick end the plea of Hugh of Montraive. But instead of pronouncing the young man's sentence, Charles spoke to Pepin. "I have been told repeatedly that you believe I do not love you and that, in return, you do not bear the affection due to me as your parent. I tell you now, before these witnesses, that I do love you, and always have. I grieve for your affliction, but I cannot cure it, nor am I able to change the way Frankish nobles regard physical incapacity. Because of that ingrained prejudice, which you have repeatedly faced throughout your life, I cannot understand why you believed that a band of lying traitors would permit you to rule over them for more than a few weeks.

"Pepin, you should have followed the advice I gave you years ago and taken holy orders," Charles continued. "I would have seen you made abbott of whatever religious house you chose, there to achieve wealth and power beyond the dreams of most men."

"I do not want to become a priest!" Pepin shouted, jumping awkwardly to his feet. "Why can't you understand that? Why won't you listen to what I say?"

"Ah, Pepin, my son, my dear son." Charles shook his head sadly. "Why can't you understand that I have always had your best interests at heart?"

"Pronounce my sentence," Pepin said. "Only, I beg you, spare Hugh, who did no more than carry a few messages for me. And release Dominick, who was never involved in the conspiracy. He pleaded with me not to lend myself to it, but I refused to listen. Both of these men love you almost as much as I do."

"Pepin," Charles said, motioning his son to silence, "out of my great love for you, I will set aside the death sentence. Instead, you are to be scourged with whips. Forty lashes will be laid upon your back. As soon as you have recovered, you will profess your vows as a priest. Afterward, you are to be returned under guard to Prum, there to live for the rest of your life."

"*No!*" Fastrada was on her feet, fists clenched in fury. "Pepin deserves to die! Give him to the headsman's axe! Order him drawn and quartered, torn apart by wild horses, for what he has done. Let his blood be spilled. Let his body parts be fixed upon spears and displayed in every town in Francia!"

"Sit down, Fastrada." Charles spoke in a cold way that made Gina shiver to hear him. "It is my right, and not yours, to decide Pepin's fate.

"Hugh of Montraive." Charles's voice cut across Fastrada's renewed protests. "Based upon the statement just given by my son Pepin, and the plea made on your behalf by your mother, who knows you very well, I believe you were not fully aware of the extent of the plot against me. All the same, you must be punished for not revealing to me the little you did know. In the same hour in which Pepin is scourged, and in the same place, you will receive ten lashes on your back. Thereafter, I grant you two days for recovery in the custody of your mother. On the third day you will be escorted by six of my men-at-arms to the nearest seaport in Francia, where you will be placed aboard a ship bound for Northumbria.

"From the day you sail," Charles continued, "you are forbidden ever to set foot in Francia again, under pain of instant death. Nor may your body, your bones, or your heart ever be returned to Francia for burial. Your exile is complete and permanent. Do you understand the provisions of your sentence?"

"I do, my lord, and I thank you for your clemency." The young man bowed his head. He and Pepin were escorted out of the hall.

"Charles, you must listen to me!" Fastrada shouted. "All of them must be executed, including Pepin. Only then can you be safe. Only then can I and my daughters sleep without fear for our lives."

"I told you to sit down," Charles said. "Now I demand your silence." He sent his wife a glance so filled with loathing that Fastrada, seeing it, actually obeyed Charles's order. Her mouth agape, Fastrada sank back into her chair and spoke no more.

Now only Dominick and Bernard were left to be sentenced. Dominick was on his feet, and Gina held her breath, hoping he would make an appeal that would move Charles to declare him not guilty. When he began to speak, Gina groaned, for Dominick wasn't pleading for his own life.

"My lord," Dominick said to Charles, "I ask your mercy for my brother, Bernard, who was never in any way involved with the conspiracy. Bernard's only crime is that, after years of faithful service to Queen Fastrada, she suddenly and without cause took an irrational dislike to him. There is no shred of proof to link Bernard to the traitors."

"I don't want help from you!" Bernard snarled at Dominick.

"Instead of quarreling with your brother, you ought to thank him," Charles said. "Bernard of Salins, I sentence you to perpetual exile, upon the same terms I imposed on Hugh of Montraive. The lands you inherited from your father are confiscated and will be distributed elsewhere. I grant your mother one week to vacate your former lands. You are to be gone from Regensburg before the sun sets."

"Yes, my lord." Bernard stood very straight, but Gina could see he was shaking with outrage. She suspected that knowing he owed his life to Dominick was to Bernard a harder punishment than the loss of his lands or exile.

"Dominick of Feldbruck," Charles said, "I will deal with you later, after I have considered several possible punishments I have in mind."

"Am I to remain in confinement?" Dominick asked.

"You are free to return to your house," Charles answered. "However, you may not leave Regensburg without my express permission, and you may not ride a horse. A man-at-arms will follow you at all times. If you attempt to escape, you will be brought back and executed immediately."

"My lord, you have my word that I will not disobey the restrictions you have set upon me," Dominick said.

"In that case, when you enter your house, the man-at-arms will stand guard at the door, thus leaving you your privacy," Charles said. "I will summon you when I have decided on your punishment."

"Well, Bastard," said Bernard in a loud voice, "now you have what you've always wanted. Salins will be yours."

"I do not know what my punishment will be," Dominick responded quietly to his brother's challenging tone. "But I do not need, nor do I covet, Salins. Even if it were offered to me, I would not accept it. I have Feldbruck, which I earned with my own two hands and my sword."

"You always were a noble fool," said Bernard, a wealth of scorn in his tone.

"Have a care, Bernard," Charles interrupted, "lest I change my decision and include you among those to be executed." Rising from his chair, he gazed around the hall with a sad, solemn expression.

"I thank you for rendering a thoughtful decision in this most difficult matter," he said to the judges. "You are dismissed. The trial is ended."

Charles turned and walked out of the hall without sparing the slightest glance for Fastrada, who was not troubling to hide her fulminating anger at the way justice had been administered.

With only Dominick and Bernard left of all the prisoners, most of the guards were gone, and the spectators began to move more freely about the hall. Gina started forward to where Dominick was standing. Ella dutifully followed at her heels.

"Where will you go, brother?" Dominick asked Bernard.

"You are not my brother, Bastard." Bernard's

spine had stiffened noticeably at Dominick's use of the word. Still, he answered the question. "I will go to Spain, to try my luck fighting for the Moslems. I, too, have a strong sword arm. Before I'm done, I'll win a larger prize than Feldbruck or Salins."

"I wish you well." Dominick would have embraced him, but Bernard pushed him away.

"Don't touch me, Bastard. I still have some standards left." Turning on his heel, Bernard marched out of the hall.

"Isn't he the gracious one?" Gina said, coming up to Dominick.

"Bernard is angry at having lost his inheritance as the result of Fastrada's whim," Dominick said mildly.

"You got the better part of your father's legacy, you know," Gina said. "He gave you something more valuable than worldly goods. He taught you how to make your own way in the world, how to be a decent, honest man. I don't think Bernard ever learned those lessons."

"Perhaps he will now," Dominick replied, "now that *he* is landless, friendless, and forced to make his own way."

A swish of silk skirts and the scent of heavy jasmine perfume alerted them that Fastrada was approaching. Gina and Dominick turned together to face her.

"Your half brother is more fortunate than you will be," Fastrada said to Dominick. "Before this week is over, I intend to see to it that you are tortured until you scream for mercy. Then I'll have you drawn and quartered while I watch. When you are dead, your precious Gina will be next. After that I'll see to Hiltrude, whom you thought to protect by sending her to a secure convent, and Lady Adalhaid, who betrayed me to Charles at Gina's behest. All of them will die in excruciating pain."

"Will that make you happy?" Gina asked.

"I will writhe in exquisite pleasure while you are shrieking in agony," the queen responded with a brilliant and lovely smile.

"Are you sure you can convince Charles to allow what you want?" Having heard Ella's gasp of horror at the queen's words and wanting to reassure the girl, Gina spoke with a flippant humor she did not really feel. Fastrada's outspoken fascination with bloodshed and death left Gina feeling queasy.

"Charles adores me," Fastrada declared with perfect confidence. "He will do whatever I want." She turned her back on them and stalked out of the hall.

"Is she deaf, dumb, and blind?" Gina asked. "Didn't she notice the way Charles was looking at her, or hear the way he spoke to her?"

"Perhaps she sees and hears only what she wants to see and hear," Dominick said. "Unfortunately, it is possible that she's correct about her influence over Charles. He is a lusty man."

"But not a stupid man. I can't help wondering if he has been giving Fastrada the rope to hang herself."

"She would never do that. Suicide is a mortal sin," Dominick responded.

"It's just an expression I learned long ago," Gina said. "It sounds different in Frankish. Dominick, shall we go home now?"

"Yes." He draped an arm over her shoulders. "I want a bath, I want to shave, and then I want you."

"In that order? Well, now I know where I stand in your list of priorities." That sentence was also different in Frankish. She didn't often make such mistakes these days. When she heard Dominick's chuckle and Ella's giggle, Gina decided her language errors didn't matter. But she couldn't forget Fastrada's threats, and she didn't fool herself into believing that Dominick had forgotten, either.

Chapter Eighteen

Upon seeing Dominick walk into his house as if he hadn't a care in the world, a weeping Lady Adalhaid flung herself into his arms and began to kiss him.

"My prayers have been answered!" she cried. "I knew Charles would never condemn an innocent man to death."

"Dominick hasn't been publicly exonerated yet," Gina explained. "He is confined to Regensburg, there is a guard outside the door to prevent him from running away, and Charles is going to call him back later to pronounce his sentence."

"I don't understand," said Lady Adalhaid.

"Neither do I, but the delay means that Fastrada will now have time to work on Charles—and she won't be working for Dominick's benefit." Seeing how pale the older woman had become, Gina decided not to repeat the queen's threats against Lady Adalhaid and Hiltrude. Lady Adalhaid looked worn out. Gina knew she hadn't slept for days, for she had been worrying over Dominick's fate as if her daughter's life depended on his well-being. As, perhaps, it did. Fastrada had implied as much with her taunt that she would have Hiltrude killed once Dominick was dead.

"If you ladies will be good enough to excuse me," Dominick said, "I am for the bathhouse. I am not fit to be in your presence until I am clean." Gently he freed himself from Lady Adalhaid's embrace. Then, after calling for one of the manservants to bring hot water, he headed for the back door.

"Go to him," Lady Adalhaid said to Gina.

"What?" Gina responded with surprise to the intense quality in the older woman's voice.

"When Dominick wakened this morning, assuming he slept at all last night, he believed he would die before the day ended," Lady Adalhaid explained. "He still may die; we cannot know what Fastrada will convince Charles to do to Dominick. But for the moment, he is a living, healthy man." She began to push Gina toward the back of the house, emphasizing each word with a gentle shove. "Do—not—waste—precious—time."

"You are a very strange woman," Gina declared.

"Do you think so?" As if she was offended, Lady Adalhaid began to draw herself up in noble pride until Gina impulsively hugged her.

"I meant that you are the most unusual ex-mother-in-law I have ever met, because Dominick is so fond of you, and you obviously love him,"

Gina said. "You are also a good friend to me. I will take your advice."

Pausing only long enough to kiss Lady Adalhaid on the cheek and then toss her cloak to Ella, Gina hurried off to the bathhouse.

It was considerably smaller than the bathhouse at Feldbruck, though it, too, was built next to the kitchen so hot water didn't have to be carried very far. There were no windows. A pair of fat candles burned in dishes set on a shelf. A small metal mirror was propped on the shelf, a razor waiting beside it.

Dominick was already in the steaming water, scrubbing his hair with soap he scooped out of a wooden bowl. The old sheet that lined the tub dripped water onto the floor as Dominick splashed.

Gina shut the door quietly, then kicked off her shoes and pulled her gown over her head. Dominick still hadn't noticed her. He was humming softly, a tune she didn't recognize.

She wished she were clever enough to think of something witty to say about the way he had come through the trial with his skin intact. She couldn't do it. She thought of all the men who were being hanged or beheaded even as she stood there listening to Dominick hum a silly tune and watching as he poured a pitcher of rinse water over his head. She thought of the women who loved the men who were dying, and who could never hold them again, and she shivered, knowing Lady Adalhaid was both correct and wise. While Dominick remained alive and relatively free, they could still be together.

She wanted that. The strength of her longing turned her knees to jelly. What she felt for Dominick was more than simple physical desire, more than lust for a handsome and virile man. Dominick's heart called to her own heart. Without him, she would survive, as she had survived before she knew him, but she would be lost. In any century. In any country. And that certainty terrified her.

She started for the tub. Dominick saw her and stretched out a soapy hand, the cheerful, honest smile she so loved to see lighting his face.

"Have you come to help me bathe?" he asked, waving at the lightweight linen shift that was her only remaining garment. A few soap bubbles flew off his hand to float slowly toward the floor, shining in the candleglow as they drifted downward.

"Am I overdressed for the occasion?" Gina asked. There, she had discovered a light touch after all. She saw his smile deepen at her teasing question.

"Slightly," he responded. "But it's a minor problem, and one I can easily overcome." He reached for the hem of her shift.

"In my days at the royal court I have learned decorum." She took a backward step, putting herself beyond his grasp. While she was with him she was going to continue to be lighthearted, charming, cheerful. She wasn't going to say a word about the trial or about the fate that could await him if Fastrada got her claws into Charles and talked him into doing something terrible.

"You have always been decorous," Dominick said, grinning so she would know he remembered moments when she had been anything but. "However, I am only a rude, unmannerly warrior."

288

He rose out of the tub, splashing water and soapsuds onto wallboards and floor planks, and seized Gina around the waist as if he really was a marauding soldier and she no more than his helpless victim. When he sank back into the water, he pulled Gina in with him, silencing her shriek of surprise with his warm mouth.

She thought she was drowning, not sure whether she was above water or below it, until she realized that Dominick was reclining in the tub and she was on top of him with her soaked shift floating upward and threatening to smother her. Dominick tore his lips from hers long enough to rip off the sodden linen and toss it to the floor.

"I see what you mean," Gina gasped. "No manners at all. A cold-blooded warrior. A man of steel."

"Not cold," he corrected her. "My blood is hot. But steel, yes. Forged in passion."

Taking her hand, he guided it to the hard, flaring evidence of his desire. And while she caressed him, he let his wet hands slide along her body, touching every sleek curve from her shoulders to her toes. He explored her as if during the past few days he had feared they would never be together again, as if he was memorizing every inch of her in case they were torn apart forever and what they were doing in the bathhouse was going to have to last for all eternity. His intense concentration communicated itself to Gina, threatening to demolish her attempt at lightheartedness.

Still, there were amusing aspects to their lovemaking. The tub really wasn't large enough to hold two people. Dominick sat with his back and shoulders against one side and his knees slightly drawn up. Gina was forced to straddle him, a position that made it easy for him to reach every part of her but limited her access to his more intimate areas, unless she wanted to duck her head under the water and keep it there for a while.

Then again, she held a very important part of Dominick in her hand, and he didn't seem to mind the restrictions of a cramped space. He kissed her lips and eyelids and nose. He nibbled at her throat and shoulders and lifted her a little so he could lavish attention on her breasts.

"I must taste of soap," she said, pushing closer to his searching mouth.

"You are as sweet as honey," he murmured.

Below the water, her fingers became busier on him, until Dominick leaned back, a blissful expression spreading over his face.

"Now!" he breathed, his hands still teasing her breasts, making her whimper with delight. "This instant, Gina, or I will disappoint both of us."

"You could never disappoint me." But she could see that he had endured enough of her sensual tormenting. She rose on her knees until his hardness probed at her warmth, and then she impaled herself on him, leaning forward to kiss him as he filled her.

His arms clutched her, and she felt his hips lift once, twice. She heard his cry of release just before she was swept into a state of joy so intensely sweet that she imagined she was melting, running into the water, floating there, suspended in unending pleasure.

She drifted thus for a long, lovely time, until

Dominick's renewed kisses brought her back to the reality of rapidly cooling bathwater and thigh and calf muscles aching from being forced into an unnatural position for too long. Still, Gina discovered that she didn't mind being uncomfortable as long as Dominick was with her.

"I have missed you sorely these last days," he murmured, his lips against hers.

"I don't know what I'd do without you." Gina wound her fingers into his wet hair. "I never want to find out, either. Oh, dear, that doesn't sound right. At critical moments I lose most of my ability to speak fluent Frankish."

"I comprehend your meaning." Dominick placed a finger on her lips to silence her self-criticism. "I think you understand me, too, for much lies unspoken within my heart and must remain there until I know what Charles intends for me."

"I cannot believe he will order your execution." She paused for a moment, choking on that terrible word. "If he were planning to, he'd have done it today, along with the other men he sentenced." She stopped talking again when Dominick's arms tightened around her, and she rested her head on his broad shoulder.

Gina expected Dominick to be sent into exile. It wasn't fair—his loyalty to his king should have earned him a reward, not punishment—but exile was far preferable to death. She began to calculate their chances of reaching Feldbruck if they were to flee from Regensburg now. Once at Feldbruck, perhaps they could locate the opening in his room, the gateway between the centuries. They could escape to New York together.

She wasn't sure Dominick would agree to such a plan. He had refused the suggestion once, while they were still at Feldbruck, and he was so honorable that he'd probably believe it his duty to remain where he was and accept whatever Charles decided to do to him. But, assuming that she could convince him to flee to New York, and assuming they were able to travel across time without becoming separated, what kind of life could Dominick create for himself there? He was an eighth-century Frankish warrior and landowner, hardly a good fit for America at the end of the twentieth century. He was too accustomed to command ever to fit into the restrictions of the modern armed forces. Moreover, he knew nothing of computers or modern technology; he didn't even know about electricity.

The qualities Dominick did understand—honor, valor, trustworthiness, loyalty—were attributes her world desperately needed but probably wouldn't accept from someone like him. For Dominick was a man perfectly suited to his own time and place, and, therefore, he belonged exactly where he was. With a sigh of regret Gina concluded that she couldn't expect him to escape with her, not even to save his own life.

"You are cold," Dominick said, kissing her forehead. "Come, we will go to my room. I want to make love to you again, and we have occupied this place too long. Others will want to use it. It's only polite of us to leave."

"There, you see?" she said, forcing a laugh. "I knew it. You aren't a rude, unmannerly warrior, after all."

* * *

In late afternoon three days after the trial Charles sent a man-at-arms to inform Dominick that he was to present himself at the king's private apartments immediately following Charles's return from morning prayers the next day.

"Lady Adalhaid and Lady Gina are to accompany you," the man-at-arms added. "An escort will be sent for you."

"Charles is going to send all of us into exile," Lady Adalhaid guessed when Gina and Dominick found her in the great hall and told her the news. "Either that, or he will send you away, Dominick, and order Gina and me into convents for the rest of our lives."

"Perhaps Ella can get a message to Alcuin," Gina suggested. "He may be able to tell us what is going on."

"No." Dominick's firm refusal put a prompt end to that notion. "Alcuin has done more than enough for me over the last weeks. I will not require more of his friendship. If he angers Charles, his own position could be in jeopardy, and I won't do that to him."

"Surely Alcuin could never be in danger of losing his place at court?" Lady Adalhaid cried.

"We do not know what has been happening since the trial," Dominick said, "or who has spoken to Charles."

Fastrada.

None of them mentioned the queen's name aloud, yet her malicious presence pervaded the hall as they looked at one another.

"Well," said Lady Adalhaid with a briskness that

could not conceal her fear, "I must decide what to wear tomorrow and give a few instructions to Imma."

"Are we to sit here like mice caught in a trap?" Gina asked when she and Dominick were alone.

"In honor, there is nothing else we can do," Dominick responded. "I owe obedience to Charles. However, you do not. If you wish, I will order Harulf and Ella to help you leave Regensburg."

"Don't be silly," she snapped at him, her own fears threatening to overcome her. She told herself to be strong, as Lady Adalhaid was. As Dominick was. "Charles has ordered me to appear, too. Even if I could go without endangering Harulf and Ella, I wouldn't desert you. Or Lady Adalhaid. Tomorrow morning, we go to the palace together, and whatever Charles has planned for us, we face it together."

Dominick made no verbal response to her emotional declaration. He just took her into his arms and held her close. They were still embracing when Ella returned from a late-day foray to the marketplace. Her basket was loaded with a large fish fresh from the river, a duck that was intended for dinner on the morrow, and several bottles of wine from far western Francia.

"I have news," Ella said, handing her purchases to the cook, who, upon hearing Ella's voice, had come into the hall to collect them.

"What news?" Dominick asked.

"Lady Gisela has come for a visit."

"Has she?" Dominick murmured.

It seemed to Gina that Dominick suddenly became quiet and withdrawn, as if deep in thought. Not so the cook, who spoke over her shoulder as she headed back to the kitchen.

"Aha!" said the cook. "That'll show Fastrada who really matters. And none too soon, either. I say it serves her right."

"What is she talking about?" Gina asked as soon as the kitchen door closed.

"Lady Gisela is Charles's sister," Dominick answered. "He loves her dearly and she visits him often. Fastrada is jealous of their affection."

"Wait a minute," Gina said. "I remember Hedwiga mentioning Lady Gisela. It was right after I arrived at Feldbruck. Doesn't she live at Chelles? The same place where Hiltrude lives?"

"The same," Dominick said.

"In that case, we must tell Lady Adalhaid at once. She will want to contact Lady Gisela to find out how Hiltrude is and perhaps send a message to her. And Lady Gisela ought to be warned about Fastrada's threats against Hiltrude." She started for the door to Lady Adalhaid's chamber.

"Wait, Gina," Dominick ordered.

"What do you mean, wait?" Puzzled by his abrupt command, she turned to face him, to explain her intensions more fully. "If we are all sent off into exile tomorrow, this may be Lady Adalhaid's last chance to contact her daughter. Surely you realize what this opportunity will mean to her. After her unswerving support of you and her kindness to me, we owe her this information."

"Do you trust me?" Dominick asked.

"Of course, I trust you, more than I have ever trusted anyone in my entire life."

"Then believe that I know what I am doing. Say

nothing to Lady Adalhaid about Lady Gisela's presence in Regensburg. Nor you, either, Ella," he added, looking at the serving girl. "I will speak to the cook and be sure she refrains from gossiping when Lady Adalhaid or Imma are present."

"Yes, Dominick," said Ella.

"Good. Gina?" Dominick regarded her with a question in his eyes.

"I don't agree with you," Gina said, "but because I trust you, I'll go along with what you are asking. I won't tell Lady Adalhaid."

"Thank you," Dominick said.

"I'll expect an explanation later," Gina added.

Dominick's only response to that statement was a mysterious look.

For their evening meal they ate the fish Ella had bought, and they drank some of the wine. They all retired early, and Dominick spent several hours making tender love to Gina until she lay beside him limp and satisfied. But she couldn't sleep, and she couldn't stop wondering why Dominick had placed such an unreasonable restriction on her when he must have known what it would mean to Lady Adalhaid to have word of her daughter, or to be able to write a note to Hiltrude in the certain knowledge that it would be delivered when Lady Gisela returned to Chelles.

Chapter Nineteen

It was obviously going to be a private trial, as opposed to the public spectacle of five days ago. Gina wasn't sure whether she ought to be encouraged or frightened as the man-at-arms who was the leader of their escort conducted her, Dominick, and Lady Adalhaid into a reception room inside Charles's personal apartments.

"Wait here," the guard instructed, leaving them alone to stare at the hangings on the walls and the simple wooden stools and tables.

The quiet was ominous. Gina could hear her own heart beating. Lady Adalhaid grabbed her hand and held it tightly. On Gina's other side, Dominick stood very straight and still, his face set as if he was prepared to deal with any enemy.

One of the wall hangings was drawn aside to

reveal a doorway, through which Charles entered. Gina thought she caught the sound of urgent whispers from behind him, but they were cut off when the heavy tapestry fell back into place. She gave her full attention to the king of the Franks, who appeared remarkably solemn and imposing. She feared that was not a good sign. Charles was usually smiling, ready with a handclasp and a pleasant word. The man who took his seat in the only chair in the room was a stern ruler with an unwelcome task to perform.

"Seat yourselves," Charles said, indicating the stools.

Gina didn't like stools. They made her feel uneasy, unbalanced, and they were almost always built too low to offer any comfort. She preferred a chair with a back she could lean against if she required support, and arms to grasp if she needed to hang on to something solid. She had the feeling she was going to want to hang on tight during the next hour or so. Nevertheless, she couldn't refuse the king's command. She crouched down on the nearest stool.

"Some time ago, when we spoke in private," Charles said, looking from Gina to Lady Adalhaid, "I was told a story I found so difficult to believe that I decided to investigate it more thoroughly. Until that day I had no inkling of any devious intentions directed toward Count Dominick. But if the story was true, then Dominick did have a motive for despising me and for promoting my removal and death."

"I have never conspired against you," Dominick declared firmly.

"I have called you here in order to prove your loyalty," Charles said. Raising his voice, he called out, "Gisela, please join us."

Once again the wall hanging was pulled aside.

"My dear lady." Dominick went to his knees before the woman who entered. He took both her hands in his and kissed them. "I rejoice to see you once more."

"On your feet, Dominick," Gisela said, pulling one hand free so she could brush it across his fair hair. "You have much to explain."

In her gown of deep red silk, wearing gold bracelets on either arm and several rings, Gisela did not look at all like a nun. Only the cross set with garnets that hung on a heavy gold chain around her neck suggested a religious vocation. She was almost as tall as her brother and close to Charles in age. Their features were remarkably similar, though Gisela's hair was a shade or two darker, braided and swept to the top of her head in the current style and held in place with several jeweled combs.

"My lady!" cried Lady Adalhaid, rising from her stool to curtsy to Gisela. "I beg you to tell me if my daughter is well."

"See for yourself," said Gisela, laughing. "Come out, Hiltrude, and embrace your mother." At her command the hanging was drawn back a third time.

"Oh!" Lady Adalhaid gasped, her hands fluttering to her breast. Then she stretched out her arms to the young woman who rushed forward to embrace her. "Hiltrude, my dearest! My heart! I thought never to see you again in this world. Oh, let me look at you. Are you well? Are you safe? Why are you here? What is the meaning of this unexpected visit?" That last question was addressed to Charles, who sat regarding with a sharp eye the scene being played out before him.

Gina took advantage of the opportunity to get off her uncomfortable stool and stand as the others were doing. She gazed in fascination at Dominick's former wife, though all she could see at the moment was the back of a gray wool dress, for Hiltrude was completely surrounded by her mother's arms.

"Within an hour after you and Lady Gina revealed Hiltrude's spying to me," Charles said to Lady Adalhaid, "I sent a rider to Chelles at top speed. He carried a letter to my sister, in which I asked Gisela to come to Regensburg at once, bringing Hiltrude with her. As you can see by their presence here today, they wasted no time in answering my request.

"Dominick, this is why I postponed your sentencing," Charles continued. "There were many souls proclaiming your honesty, including Alcuin, Deacon Fardulf, and these ladies here, among others. Only one loud voice constantly repeated that you were guilty. I harbored no doubts about the other men who stood trial for treason. They received their just sentences. But I found it difficult to believe that you were involved."

"I never was," Dominick stated. "Sir, I love and honor you. There is but one person in this affair whom I despise." The two men locked glances for a long moment, and it was Charles who looked away first.

"Lady Hiltrude," Charles said, "I want to know the entire truth of your marriage to Count Dominick."

"Sir, what do you mean?" Visibly trembling, Hiltrude detached herself from her mother's embrace.

At last Gina could take a good look at her. Hiltrude was not an especially pretty girl, having light brown hair worn in two tight braids and unremarkable gray eyes. Nor did her simple gray dress enhance her sturdy figure. Yet there was something of Lady Adalhaid's elegance in Hiltrude's posture and movements, and, like her mother, she had a tendency to turn pale at moments of stress. Her cheeks were colorless now.

"Speak honestly," Charles ordered her. "Tell me everything."

"I . . . I . . . oh, sir!" Hiltrude bit her lip and glanced nervously around the room. "Is the queen ill? I've not seen her since coming to Regensburg."

"Nor will you see her until after you have told me what I want to know," said Charles. "Fastrada is not here. She will not interrupt us, nor will she influence what you say."

Gina couldn't stand the tension any longer. Lady Adalhaid was so white and was shaking so hard that Gina was afraid she'd have a heart attack. Gisela had withdrawn from the group before Charles to stand at her brother's side. Dominick was frowning and looking like a thundercloud about to burst into a violent storm. Gina couldn't tell what his feelings about Hiltrude were, but she could see that the poor young woman was scared half to death. Very deliberately, she moved to stand next to Hiltrude, and put a supporting arm across her shoulders.

"Tell him what he wants to know," Gina instructed in a fierce tone. "Your mother was afraid to speak out until I maneuvered her into a position where she had no choice, and now I think she's glad she spoke. Charles needs to know what happened."

"Who are you?" Hiltrude's gray eyes met Gina's steady gaze.

"She is a friend," said Lady Adalhaid. "Moreover, Gina is right. Hiltrude, you must stop being afraid. Your life—all our lives—depend upon your honesty now."

There followed a brief silence, during which Hiltrude took several deep breaths, and Gina could feel her trembling. Then Hiltrude lifted her chin and looked directly at Charles.

"Shortly after I first came to court, I was appointed as one of the queen's ladies," Hiltrude said. "Queen Fastrada was more friendly to me than I expected. I was, after all, only an ignorant young girl, and I was very flattered by her attentions. One day she told me that she wanted me to marry Count Dominick. I asked why, because I knew she did not like him. Dominick had criticized her before others, and Fastrada took great offense at that. She told me I was to marry Dominick and then spy on him, to discover any facts that could be used against him and report them to her. She was determined to ruin him for what he'd said about her. At first, I refused."

"Go on," Charles urged when Hiltrude paused to wipe her eyes.

"Queen Fastrada said if I didn't do what she wanted, she would have my mother killed under circumstances that would make her appear to be an evil woman."

"What circumstances?" asked Charles.

"She was going to arrange for my mother and Count Audulf to die together as if in a lovers' suicide pact." Hiltrude's voice sank so low as she pronounced those last words that Charles leaned forward in his chair to hear better.

"Are you speaking of Audulf of Birnau?" Charles asked. "The same young man to whom you were originally betrothed?"

"Yes," Hiltrude whispered. "The idea was that my mother would appear to be the lover of my betrothed. Thus, the two people I love most in the world would be seen to have betrayed me in the most disgraceful fashion. Furthermore, as suicides, neither of them could be buried in consecrated ground, nor could they receive the prayers or blessings of the Church. They would be condemned to the fires of Hell forever. I could not let that happen. I had to obey the queen."

Charles sat back, looking as if someone had struck him. Gisela put a hand on his shoulder.

"Merciful heaven!" exclaimed Lady Adalhaid. "Hiltrude, child, why didn't you tell me?"

"I was so afraid," Hiltrude said. "I know you, Mother. You would have confronted the queen and made a great commotion. But I knew they weren't idle threats. Your life was in danger. So was Audulf's. I had to do what Fastrada wanted."

"And so you married Dominick," said Charles.

"Yes. Dominick was always kind to me. He

never—" Hiltrude gulped back tears. She still had not looked directly at Dominick. "He never hurt me, and he seemed to understand that my heart lay elsewhere. He was even kind when he discovered my attempts to spy on him. I am a very poor spy, my lord."

"Dominick," Charles said, "you ought to have told me when you learned what Hiltrude was doing."

"I begged him not to!" Hiltrude cried. "Everyone in Francia knows how much you love Fastrada. I didn't think you'd believe anything against her. I had obeyed her and married Dominick, but I hadn't been able to learn anything that would be helpful to Fastrada, so I still feared for my mother's life, and for Audulf's, and for Dominick's, too. I am ashamed of what I did to Dominick, and I was glad when he found me out and said he would not remain married to a woman he could not trust."

"But you divorced him," said Charles. Then he nodded. "I understand. He thought you would be safe at Chelles."

"And so I have been," Hiltrude said.

"Yet I have been told on good authority that you have no taste for conventual life." Charles gave Hiltrude a sharp look.

"No," Hiltrude responded. She sent a quick little smile in the direction of Charles's sister. "Lady Gisela knows me well. I wish I could have married Count Audulf."

"Would Audulf have you now, do you think?" Charles asked.

"I don't know," Hiltrude said with a sigh. "I

haven't seen or spoken to Audulf since the day my forthcoming marriage to Dominick was announced.

"No doubt the young man's heart was broken," Charles said.

"Perhaps," Hiltrude responded sadly. "I know mine was."

Charles sat for a few moments as if meditating. Hiltrude leaned against Gina. Lady Adalhaid put an arm around her daughter so the three of them stood together, facing Charles. As he watched them his eyes began to sparkle. He motioned to Gisela, who bent to hear his whispered words. Gisela nodded and retreated behind the wall hanging.

"It is possible, Lady Hiltrude," Charles said after a few more minutes of silence, "that I can provide a remedy for your unhappiness."

Gisela returned just then, and Gina began to wonder how many people were hidden on the other side of the doorway behind the tapestry, for with the king's sister came a short, wiry man with a cap of unruly black curls. To Gina's eyes he possessed at least some Italian blood, for his most outstanding features were a fine Roman nose and dark, flashing eyes.

The newcomer stopped short when he beheld Hiltrude—and at the sight of him, Hiltrude went limp between her mother and Gina.

"What have you done to her?" cried the young man, and he snatched Hiltrude from her companions to hold her against his bosom as if she were a delicate treasure. He appeared oblivious to the fact that Hiltrude was several inches taller than he and, by the look of them, ten pounds or so heavier.

"I do believe the unexpected sight of you has made her lightheaded," Charles said, regarding the couple. "Count Audulf, I suggest that you take Hiltrude for a long, reviving horseback ride, during which I expect you come to an agreement with her."

"My lord," the young man began to protest, but he ceased when Hiltrude stirred in his arms.

"Audulf?" Hiltrude's rather large, square hand stroked his tanned cheek. "Is it really you?"

"I can see I was not wrong about you two," Charles said, forestalling Audulf's response to his lady's question. "I trust Alcuin will be able to locate a copy of your original betrothal contract somewhere among the palace archives, so there will be no difficulty there, and no reason for delay.

"Count Audulf, this is my command: Heed it well. You and Lady Hiltrude will marry in the great hall tomorrow morning, after which we will all proceed to the church of St. Peter, where your vows will be properly blessed by a priest. I want no doubts raised later about the legality of your marriage or the legitimacy of your future children, of whom, I suspect, there will be many. Your marriage feast will be celebrated at midday tomorrow, in the great hall. After the last two weeks, it is a pleasure to have a joyful occasion to contemplate." He sat gazing upon the young couple with a pleased expression.

"My lord," said Dominick, "with your permission, Lady Hiltrude is welcome to join her mother at my house for this last night before her marriage. I believe Lady Gina has several available gowns from which Hiltrude may choose her wedding dress."

"Oh, yes, gladly," said Gina, barely repressing a giggle at the arrangement Dominick was suggesting. "I am sure Ella and Imma will be happy to re-alter something that is appropriate for a bride to wear."

"Go on, children." Charles waved Hiltrude and Audulf away. "Enjoy yourselves today. Soon enough your lives will turn serious again."

They required no more urging. With Audulf's arm around Hiltrude's waist they left by the tapestry-covered doorway.

"Charles," said Gisela, "it's cruel of you to keep Dominick in suspense any longer."

"As always, your advice is good." Charles nodded his agreement. "Dominick, I assure you, I have never suspected you of involvement in that detestable plot, though I deliberately waited to tell you so until after I had heard Hiltrude's testimony. For reasons I am not ready to divulge as yet, I still do not want anyone else to suspect that I am aware of your innocence. Therefore, I ask all three of you to swear that you won't reveal what I have just said. Tomorrow will be taken up with Hiltrude's very happy wedding. On the following day, I will meet with you again. Have I your word that you will maintain a scrupulous silence on the subject until then?"

"I swear it," Dominick said at once.

"So do I," said Gina.

"And I," Lady Adalhaid said. "Sir, I thank you with all my heart for the way you have made my beloved girl so happy."

* * *

"Well," Gina said when the three of them had been dismissed and were outside the palace gate, "what do you make of all that?"

"You have just seen why Charles is a great king," Lady Adalhaid declared. "He has given me back my daughter and has assured her safety."

"That's not what I meant," Gina said, aware that Lady Adalhaid wasn't paying attention to much of anything but her daughter's wedding.

But Dominick was listening. He put his mouth close to Gina's ear and spoke softly, so only she could hear.

"What I make of it," Dominick said, "is that Charles is setting a trap for Fastrada. And we are the bait."

"I can't believe it," Ella whispered to Gina. "You invited Dominick's former wife to stay here, and you are going to provide her wedding gown? Have you gone mad?"

"Hush," Gina cautioned with a quick look in the direction of Lady Adalhaid, who was at the other side of the hall telling Imma what had happened at the palace. "I don't want her to hear you and feel uncomfortable."

"What about your feelings?" Ella cried. "I can't imagine what Hedwiga would say about this!"

"With Lady Adalhaid already staying here, Dominick thought it only right to give her some time alone with her daughter. Hiltrude has been through a lot."

Ella made a rude sound, then said, "I know how she treated Dominick when they were married, how cold she was to him. You are much too generous."

"You don't know everything," Gina said, "and I can't tell you all the details. I will just say that Fastrada was behind much of Hiltrude's unhappiness." It was a statement calculated to arouse Ella's sympathy toward Hiltrude. Gina was by now familiar enough with the way Dominick's household operated to know that Ella would quickly tell the cook, and within an hour all the servants and men-at-arms would be united in favor of Hiltrude against Fastrada. The one unalterable certainty among Dominick's people was that every one of them hated the queen. It wasn't going to take a special order from Dominick to keep Hiltrude's presence in his house a secret.

Gina also trusted the universal feminine fascination with weddings to keep the household occupied and less apt to gossip.

"There is one of Hiltrude's gowns that I haven't worn yet," Gina said. "It's the pale blue silk. I think it will be easy to open and then resew the side seams. Let's ask Lady Adalhaid what she thinks."

And Gina's assumption about the power of nuptials to preoccupy women was soon proven correct. She and Lady Adalhaid, along with Ella and Imma, spent several pleasant hours talking about brides they had known while they carefully pulled out Hedwiga's stitches—and saved the thread, something Gina hadn't thought of—so that when Hiltrude returned from her ride with Audulf, the gown was ready to be refitted on its original owner and resewn.

Since Gina still couldn't sew a decent seam, she left the other women at that point and went in search of Dominick. She found him in his bedchamber in private conversation with Count Audulf, and what she heard when she pushed open the unlatched door left her speechless.

"What are you saying?" exclaimed Audulf. "Are you telling me you never consummated the marriage?"

"How could I, when Hiltrude was unable to hide her terror?" Dominick responded. "At first I thought her fear was directed toward me. Only later, after I discovered her futile attempts at spying, did I learn it was Fastrada she feared."

"But that means you were never legally married." Audulf stared at Dominick in astonishment. "You didn't need a divorce. You could have demanded an annulment."

"The divorce was for Hiltrude's protection, and yours. If the marriage were annulled, she would be expected to return to court and resume her position as the queen's lady," Dominick said. "Surely Hiltrude has explained to you by now how Fastrada threatened her. The arrangement she and I agreed to in private allowed her to retire to Chelles, as other divorced ladies do. I have told you all of this, Audulf, so you will be forewarned that the bride you take tomorrow is a virgin, and you will treat her accordingly, with the patience and gentleness that any innocent girl deserves."

"What a wedding gift you've given me." Audulf sounded as if he was about to cry. "How can I ever thank you for your goodness toward my love?"

"You can repay me by treating Hiltrude kindly and by respecting her mother, who would gladly give her life in order to keep Hiltrude safe."

"I will," Audulf promised, clasping Dominick's hand. "No one but you, Hiltrude, and I will ever know she comes to me untouched by any man. I think it best if the queen never learns of this."

"I agree," Dominick said.

Gina wiped away the tears that were spilling down her cheeks. The gesture caught the attention of both men at the same instant.

"Don't worry," Gina said. "I won't tell anyone. I'm sorry I intruded. I was looking for Dominick and overheard by accident."

"It doesn't matter," Dominick said. "I was going to tell you tomorrow, after the wedding, after Hiltrude was safely married to Audulf and away from Regensburg, out of Fastrada's reach."

"Thank you again, Dominick," Audulf said. "If ever you need anything, all I have is yours to command."

"Then I command you to be happy," Dominick said, and he sent the young man on his way.

"I do wish," Gina said when she and Dominick were alone, "that we didn't have to tiptoe around to avoid upsetting a spoiled queen."

"We won't be tiptoeing tomorrow. Fastrada is going to be at the wedding."

"Yes. It's sure to be an interesting occasion." Gina looked directly into Dominick's eyes. "You never slept with Hiltrude." It wasn't a question. She knew what he'd said to Audulf was the simple truth.

"How could I take a weeping, cowering young girl to my bed?" he asked.

"You never loved Hiltrude." Gina put her hands on his broad shoulders.

"No." Dominick's arms slid around her waist. "I gave Hiltrude her own room, hoping the separation would allay her fears. Of course, it didn't, because I wasn't the true source of her constant terror."

"That's why Ella thought Hiltrude was afraid to have children. Because she slept apart from you." Gina kissed his chin.

"It's also how I discovered she was spying on me. I found her in my room, a place where she had no excuse to be, rummaging through my belongings." His hands slipped upward until his palms rested against the sides of her breasts.

"Just as you once found me," she whispered, moving nearer.

"I soon learned what you were doing in my room," he murmured as he began nibbling at her earlobe. "Now I must ask you, why have you come to my room today?"

"To find you. Because I missed you. I didn't expect Audulf to be here, but I am glad I heard what you said to him."

"Are you?" His mouth caressed her throat, and Gina's heart began to beat faster.

"May I suggest that you latch the door securely this time?" she said. "You don't want anyone else coming in, do you?"

"No." He backed her against the door and pinned her there with his body while he fastened the latch. "Definitely not. I prefer one woman at a time, and of all the women in Regensburg, I prefer you." His mouth scorched hers until Gina was grateful for the door supporting her back. Without it she'd be a puddle on the floor, every bone in her body liquified by Dominick's passionate heat.

He lifted her high in his arms, and Gina put her hands on his shoulders to look down at him. Then he lowered her, very slowly, until she was fully aware of his hard and eager need of her. He carried her to his bed and undressed her as if he was unwrapping a wonderful gift, but Gina knew he was the real gift, an honest man who would never force an unwilling woman or take any woman without tender feelings on his part. And when, toward the end, their passion turned wild and fierce and Dominick no longer restrained himself, she knew he was the only man she would ever want.

Chapter Twenty

Fastrada knew about the wedding, and she knew Audulf was to be the bridegroom; she just didn't know the name of the bride. Gina learned later that Charles had promised her a delightful surprise.

Thus, Fastrada came to the great hall robed in cloth of gold and glittering with jewels and took her seat on the dais beside Charles's chair, which was unoccupied at the moment. Her ladies, also finely gowned for the occasion, arranged themselves to one side of the queen.

She hadn't yet noticed Dominick in the crowd or the discreet little group around him. Ella and Imma blended easily into the background, for servants were always to be found in the hall, and Harulf looked just like all the other men-at-arms. Gina and Lady Adalhaid stood behind the protective width of Dominick's shoulders, and they kept Hiltrude well hidden between them.

After the courtiers were assembled, Charles arrived, accompanied by Gisela, Alcuin, and Audulf.

"This young man comes before us to be wed," Charles announced, laying a hand on Audulf's shoulder. "If the bride and her mother will step forward, Alcuin will read the marriage contract."

A suspenseful moment passed, during which Fastrada looked around the hall in open curiosity. Then Lady Adalhaid took Hiltrude's hand and led her toward the dais.

In her pale blue silk dress, with her hair piled up in the fashionable topknot style and decorated with two of Lady Adalhaid's gold combs, Hiltrude looked remarkably pretty. Her cheeks were flushed with color, and she moved toward Audulf with easy, smiling grace.

Gina's gaze flashed from Hiltrude to Fastrada. She didn't think the queen recognized her erstwhile pawn at first. But Fastrada did know Lady Adalhaid, and her beautiful face swiftly assumed a fearsome expression. Gina noticed how the queen's fingers clenched the arms of her chair. Fastrada must have realized by then who the bride was, but she sat as if transfixed while Alcuin, parchment scroll in hand, moved to stand facing the young couple.

Alcuin began to read from the scroll while Gina watched unconcealed fury mounting in the queen. The marriage contract noted that Hiltrude's original dowry, her inheritance from her father, had been turned over to Chelles when she entered that convent and could not be returned to her. In place of that dowry Charles conferred a large estate on Hiltrude, which was given, the contract stated, in return for faithful service to Francia. In obedience to Frankish custom Audulf granted a portion of his estate to his bride, thus completing Hiltrude's transformation into a great heiress.

Charles and Gisela smiled benignly at the bride and groom as Alcuin beckoned to a servant to bring a small table, ink, and quill pen so the copies of the contract could be witnessed and signed. The king and his sister were the first to sign after the bride and groom. Next, Lady Adalhaid took up the pen and bent over the parchment.

"Count Dominick, Lady Gina," Alcuin called out, "will you come forward and make your marks?"

At those words Fastrada's head whipped around so she was no longer watching the bridal party. Instead, she regarded Gina with cold malevolence.

Gina's heart was pounding, but she wasn't going to let the queen know it. Keeping a smile pasted on her face, she approached the table where the marriage contract lay. Alcuin handed her the pen. Gina had never used a quill before, had never even used an old-fashioned fountain pen. She saw Charles's name written in the shape of a cross, and Gisela's neat letters in the new writing style Alcuin was promoting. She noticed that on one copy Hiltrude's signature was marred by an ink splatter, probably the result of nervousness. Gina made up her mind that *she* was not going to add a sloppy signature. She dipped the point of the quill into the ink bottle and began to write her name.

Gina of New York. The pen skimmed across

parchment three different times, and not a drop of extraneous ink spotted any of the documents. Gina smiled at Alcuin in triumph. She could have sworn he winked at her.

As Dominick took the quill from her and leaned down to sign his name as the last of the witnesses, Gina stepped back and looked around. That was when she saw Fastrada rising slowly to her feet. The queen's baleful glare moved from Gina to Dominick, and on to Charles, who she must have known was responsible for what was happening.

"How dare you?" Fastrada demanded in a low, venomous tone. "Dominick of Feldbruck, a traitor and Hiltrude's former husband, to be a witness to her remarriage? This is an outrage! No priest will bless a marriage so witnessed. The contract is illegal. This so-called marriage is a sham."

Dominick calmly finished signing the contract, and Alcuin's servant began to sprinkle sand over the damp ink.

"Did you hear me?" Fastrada screeched at Charles. "What are you thinking to lend your consent to this abomination? Every bishop of the Church will condemn you for it. The pope will declare the marriage invalid. Hiltrude is making herself into a concubine, not a wife."

"Sit down, Fastrada," Charles ordered in a terrible voice.

Confronting his furious wife, he heaved a great sigh. The sound, as well as the expression on his face, reminded Gina forcefully of the sigh she had observed after Fastrada's loud scene during the trial of the traitors. Comprehension flooded over Gina, allowing her to understand the full meaning of what she was seeing. That first, earlier sigh had been the moment when Charles relinquished his marriage to Fastrada for the sake of the Frankish realm. Fastrada's unregal behavior in the present moment merely confirmed him in his decision.

Fastrada didn't know it yet. Caught up in her anger and confident of her influence over her husband, she still thought she held Charles in the palm of her hand—or the heat of her bed—as she had held him for ten long years.

Then Gina saw the grief etched on Charles's handsome face, and noticed how quickly it was hidden, and she knew he loved Fastrada still, in spite of all her wickedness. Charles would hide his deepest feelings, and he would go on—for he truly was the good ruler that Dominick and Lady Adalhaid believed him to be—but he'd go on without Fastrada. Her days of power and influence were over.

The revealing moment ended quickly, and then Charles was kissing Hiltrude on both cheeks and congratulating Audulf. A few minutes later they were all trooping out of the palace and along the road to St. Peter's church for morning prayers and to hear the marriage blessed.

As if she had never uttered her loud complaints about the marriage arrangements—or perhaps in expectation of yet another emotional scene when her prediction came true and a blessing on the marriage was refused—Fastrada took her place beside Charles at the head of the procession. Already Gina could detect the cool formality in Charles's manner toward his wife. She wondered how long it would be before Fastrada was aware of it. The woman was no fool; she'd figure it out quickly. And when she did, she'd see to it that someone else paid for her misdeeds.

Contrary to Fastrada's passionate declaration, there was no problem at all at the church, and after the new marriage was blessed by Father Theodulf, the head priest at St. Peter's, morning prayers proceeded smoothly. The queen stood quietly at Charles's side, a glowering presence who could not dampen the innocent joy of either the bride or the bridegroom. When the wedding party returned to the great hall, Fastrada claimed a sudden headache and retired to her chambers before the feast began. A surprising number of her ladies chose to remain in the hall.

"They remind me of politicians," Gina said to Dominick. "They can spot a loser a mile away, and they don't want to be associated with one. They're probably making secret bets on whether or not Charles will pack Fastrada off to a convent."

The wedding feast was over by early afternoon, and the guests waved Audulf and Hiltrude off on their journey from Regensburg to Audulf's home at Birnau.

An hour or so later, back at Dominick's house, Lady Adalhaid sank down upon a bench, leaned her shoulders against the wall, put her feet on a nearby stool, and tossed down the large goblet of wine Gina handed her. Then she expelled a long breath and held out the goblet to be refilled.

"Just like every other mother of the bride, once the wedding is over," Gina said, teasing her.

"You were remarkably kind to my girl. I won't

forget it," Lady Adalhaid responded. Turning her attention to Dominick, she said, "You did invite me to remain here for as long as I like. However, I have no desire to stay near a court where Fastrada is. I will impose upon your hospitality only until our meeting with Charles tomorrow. On the day after, unless Charles has other plans for me, I will leave Regensburg and go to live at the country house near Trier that was settled on me when I married Hiltrude's father. I do think I ought to allow the young people some time to be alone before I visit them," she added with a wistful smile.

"You are always welcome in my home, whether here or at Feldbruck," Dominick told her, and he sounded as if he really meant it.

Gina couldn't work up much concern over the meeting with Charles. He had been so kind to Hiltrude and so obviously annoyed about Fastrada's scheming that Gina was convinced he wasn't going to punish either Dominick or herself. She believed Charles was planning to grant Dominick permission to return to Feldbruck. She would go with him, back to his peaceful estate with its views of mountains and forest and stream. She could hardly wait to see it all again.

She didn't think it the least bit strange that there were no guards sent from the palace to escort them to Charles, as there had been since the treasonous plot was revealed and Dominick placed under house arrest. But the plot was over, the traitors were punished, and things were returning to normal in Regensburg. There was no longer any danger, though a nobleman usually wanted an

attendant or two. Dominick called on Harulf to act
as their escort.

Leaving their maidservants at the house, Gina,
Lady Adalhaid, and the two men set out for their
appointment with the king. This time they weren't
heading for the main palace gate. Instead, they
took the street that ended at the square in front of
St. Peter's church. At one side of the square was
the palace entrance Gina and Dominick had used
with Deacon Fardulf, which provided a direct
route to Charles's private apartments.

They had reached the square and were starting
across it when Gina noticed Fardulf also crossing
the square, headed for the front door of the church.
She waved to him, and Fardulf waved back.

"Good morning, my lady," Fardulf called.

Then, in a split second, the deacon's smile of
greeting changed to a fearful look, and he abruptly
altered his direction.

"No!" Fardulf shouted, breaking into a run and
heading directly for Gina. "Beware! Dominick—no!"

At first, Gina was perplexed by Fardulf's peculiar
actions. It wasn't until she heard Lady Adalhaid's
cry of terror and spun around to ask what was happening that she saw the horsemen bearing down
on them. She hadn't heard their hooves on the
damp, muddy street, but Fardulf had seen them
and had guessed at once what they intended.

There were at least six heavily armed men,
though from the instant she first saw them everything was so confused that Gina couldn't be sure of
their exact number. She did notice that each horseman was wearing a rounded metal helmet with a
noseguard that effectively disguised his identity.

Even as she began to wonder why they were all riding so fast through the center of a busy town, and whether they were going to swerve in time to miss her and her companions, she realized that the horsemen were heading directly toward Dominick's group—and that they had no intention of changing direction. They were set upon riding down every person who stood in their path.

The other pedestrians in the square scattered fast, heading for doorways or the church steps to get out of the way of the charging hooves.

Dominick was basically unarmed, having only his eating knife thrust through his belt in obedience to the rule forbidding swords to be worn within the palace confines. Harulf, who expected to await his master outside the palace entrance, was armed with both sword and knife. Gina and Lady Adalhaid carried with them the dainty eating knives that ladies used, worn in decorated sheaths at their belts. In no way were those paltry weapons a match for the flashing broadswords in the hands of the onrushing horsemen.

"Run, Gina!"

She heard Dominick shouting and tried to do what he commanded, only to discover that her feet would not obey her brain. She heard Fardulf yelling and panting for breath as he raced toward her. Then the horsemen were upon them in a clamorous rush, and Gina looked up at the gleaming edge of a raised broadsword that was mere seconds away from descending on her head.

Suddenly, everything went into slow motion. Gina saw Dominick slash with his knife at the hindquarters of the horse carrying the man about to kill her. The animal reared upward, unseating its rider. Dominick caught Gina around the waist and pulled her away, hurling her into Fardulf's arms.

"Take her to the church!" Dominick shouted, and he turned to meet the next horseman.

Gina heard Lady Adalhaid screaming and saw the unhorsed rider who had tried to kill her raising his sword again, this time over her friend. Without thinking she pulled the eating knife from her belt and jabbed at the assailant's sword arm.

He was wearing chainmail that reached only to his elbows, and she struck his forearm. It was enough. He cursed, dropped his sword, and whirled on her, cold blue eyes furious. When he saw Fardulf in his clerical robes beside her, the man turned to retrieve his sword.

"Lady Gina, please," Fardulf coaxed, tugging at her sleeve, "come to the church as Count Dominick ordered."

"I can't leave Dominick!" she cried. "Let me go, Fardulf!" She pulled away from the deacon, seeking the one man who mattered to her.

Dominick and Harulf were shoulder to shoulder, fighting off the horsemen as best they could, but Gina saw that it was hopeless. Their opponents were too many, and there was no way for barely armed men on foot, no matter how brave they were, to win against well-armed, mounted warriors.

So much shouting and violent action could not go unnoticed for long, and, after the many disruptions of recent weeks, the king's guards were bound to investigate any suspicious uproar. Or perhaps one of the fleeing pedestrians had reached the main gate of the palace and there sounded the alarm.

Without warning a band of men-at-arms erupted around the corner of the palace wall. They were on foot, wearing chainmail, with their swords drawn and ready for battle, and they wasted no time setting upon the horsemen. There were so many men-at-arms that hope blossomed in Gina's bosom. Surely sheer numbers would overcome the advantage the attacking riders had so far held over their opponents. She saw horsemen dragged from their mounts to fight on foot, while the riderless horses reared and neighed in panic, thus adding to the noise and confusion. In the resulting tangle of men and horses, Gina lost sight of Dominick.

"Gina, you're bleeding." Lady Adalhaid caught her arm and held on with a tight grip. "We must get to the church. We can take shelter there. Fardulf, help me with her."

Fardulf stopped trying to argue with Gina and grabbed her other arm, pulling her in the direction of the church. Both he and Lady Adalhaid were bleeding.

"Dominick!" Gina gasped. "Where is he? I can't leave him."

"Dominick is well able to take care of himself in a battle," Lady Adalhaid said. "Do as he wants, so he doesn't have to worry about you."

Reluctantly, knowing Lady Adalhaid was right, Gina allowed herself to be drawn toward the church entrance. They climbed the wide, shallow steps, pausing when they reached the door. While Fardulf was pulling on the heavy handle, Gina looked back to where the fighting continued. From her vantage point three steps above the square she had a good view.

She spotted a man in a bright blue tunic lying face down in the middle of the square. The burly man who stood over him, still laying about with his sword though covered with blood, was unmistakably Harulf—Harulf, who was valiantly protecting his master's body with his own. But was that master dead or alive?

"Dominick!" Gina screamed. Lady Adalhaid and Deacon Fardulf together were not strong enough to hold her. Breaking away from their restraining hands, she headed straight for Dominick, dodging among the combatants, leaping over a motionless body, barely escaping the downward slash of a rearing horse's hooves.

"Dominick!" She was kneeling beside him, touching his shoulder, noting the blood that stained his tunic and afraid to turn him over lest she inflict greater damage by moving him. She couldn't feel any pulse in his neck, and she couldn't tell whether he was breathing or not.

"How is he?" Harulf was squatting beside her, his blood-smeared sword still in his right hand.

"I don't know." Gina caught her breath, repressing a sob. She was *not* going to cry, not while she cherished a hope of helping Dominick. "Why is it suddenly so quiet?"

"The battle's over," Harulf said. Raising his voice, he called, "Bring a litter at once! Count Dominick is wounded."

They had to move him, of course. He couldn't remain there in the square, with his face in the mud. The men-at-arms were accustomed to such duty. As gently as they could, they rolled Dominick over onto his back on the litter. One of his arms slipped off the litter, to dangle lifelessly until Gina lifted his hand and laid it on his chest. His lips were blue. Gina could feel her heart breaking, quickly and silently, yet she must have appeared calm, for the men-at-arms were asking her where they were to take Dominick. She couldn't speak to answer them.

"Take him to the church," said Fardulf in a firm voice. The usually timid deacon then proceeded to prove himself the hero Gina had once insisted he was, and a competent organizer of weary men and women, as well. "There is an infirmary in the priests' lodging house, where there is room enough to take in the wounded or the sick. We have no patients at present, so it will be private. We will need a guard at the door to protect Count Dominick and his companions from further attack. Someone should notify the king of what has happened. The bodies will have to be removed from the square and their identities established. Charles will want to know who did this."

"I can guess who's to blame, and so can you," said Harulf. To the officer who was leading the men-at-arms he added, "Let's do as the good deacon says. Dominick needs immediate care, and the ladies are both hurt. I don't think we ought to risk carrying Dominick down that narrow street to his house. There may be more men waiting for us along the way, in case we escaped the attack and decided to run for home."

"Any wounded man is welcome to use the services of the infirmary," Fardulf said to the officer. "That includes the attackers, for Christian charity requires us to aid anyone who suffers, regardless of the cause. Besides, there is a purely practical consideration. Charles is going to want those men in good health when he interrogates them."

With this the commanding officer agreed, and he issued his orders. Half a dozen men-at-arms surrounded Dominick and his friends, another group began to pick up the wounded and the dead, while a third contingent was sent to round up the horses and see to their welfare. Finally, the officer left to report the incident to Charles.

Lady Adalhaid was swaying on her feet. Blood dripped from a gash on her forehead. When she crumpled toward the steps, Harulf, himself blood soaked, simply caught her by an arm and a leg, slung her unceremoniously over his shoulder, and marched through the church door after Fardulf, who was leading the way.

So numb was Gina in the aftermath of violence, and so fearful that Dominick was dying if not already dead, that she saw nothing the least bit amusing in the way Harulf was carrying the elegant court lady as if she were a sack of dried beans.

Chapter Twenty-one

The infirmary was a white-walled, quiet place with a row of narrow beds for the patients. According to Fardulf, the infirmarer, whose name was Brother Anselm, was skilled with herbal remedies and could neatly sew up almost any wound. He was also shorthanded, so he was willing to allow Gina and Fardulf to assist him once their own wounds were bandaged.

"You are the fortunate ones," Brother Anselm said. "Fardulf, this gash on your upper arm is but a shallow flesh wound. It ought to heal quickly." He finished tying a cloth around Fardulf's arm. "Go yourself, good deacon, or send one of the guards you've brought here, and inform Father Theodulf of what has happened. Ask if he will release some of the younger priests and deacons from their duties so they may come and help us here. Then return, yourself, I beg you. We will want all the help that Father Theodulf will allow us."

While Brother Anselm spoke to Fardulf, he was cleaning and bandaging the wound on Gina's shoulder.

"I have put an herbal poultice on it," he explained. "Now you may begin to assist me."

"I think Count Dominick's injuries are the most urgent," Gina told him somewhat impatiently, for she thought Brother Anselm should have seen to Dominick at once and let herself and Fardulf wait.

Dominick had been laid on one of the beds, and Harulf, though still bleeding from his own wounds, was busy cutting off his master's tunic to reveal the damage beneath the blue wool.

"When we moved him to bring him here, he started to breathe again," Harulf said, sending an encouraging glance in Gina's direction. "See? His lips aren't blue anymore."

"He's been stabbed in his side," Brother Anselm said. He pressed on the flesh that surrounded the gash just under Dominick's left ribs, then moved on to touch a bruised area a little higher. "One, and possibly two, ribs have been broken. They can be bound tightly until they heal. That's a minor concern. It's the open wound that worries me."

"Did the sword thrust open his guts?" Harulf asked, not mincing words. "If so, he'll swell up and die, for no man can survive such a wound."

Gina couldn't move for shock. She was incapable of uttering a single word of objection to what Harulf had just said. The gash in Dominick's side was only three or four inches wide, yet in a world without antibiotics or sterile instruments it could mean the death of a strong and vital man.

Brother Anselm examined the wound more closely, putting his nose right against the torn area to smell the flesh beneath, then poking his fingers into the opening until Gina gagged and had to look the other way.

"I don't think his innards have been opened," Brother Anselm declared. "I will wash the wound with wine and water, and then I'll sew it closed, after which we can only pray to the Good Lord for Count Dominick's recovery."

"Just a minute," Gina said. She'd had time to recover from her initial shock, and she was now prepared to do whatever was necessary to help Dominick to survive. She supposed prayer was a good idea, though it certainly wasn't the first defense against a raging infection. She didn't know much about twentieth-century medicine; in fact, most of what she knew was derived from television shows, and she wasn't sure how accurate her information was. But she did know one thing beyond dispute.

"Cleanliness is absolutely essential," she said to Brother Anselm. "I want to watch while you boil the needle and thread you are going to use. Your hands are to be scrubbed with the strongest soap you have. And you are going to clean that wound thoroughly before you start sewing it."

"As always before repairing an open cut, I will cleanse the area with cool water infused with herbs and wine." Brother Anselm spoke as if he was addressing a hysterical woman who needed calming so he could then get on with his work.

"If the wine comes from a freshly opened bottle it will likely act as a mild disinfectant," Gina said, trying to sound as if she knew whereof she spoke. "But any water that touches that wound is going to be boiled first. Any herbs you use will also be washed first in freshly boiled water."

"I have years of experience in these matters," Brother Anselm protested.

"I am not questioning your skill," Gina said. "I am merely telling you how these problems are handled in my country, where only rarely do the doctors lose a patient from a simple wound like Dominick's."

"Really?" Brother Anselm frowned, looking doubtful. "I must tell you that in Francia, death is a common outcome when the area between ribcage and groin has been opened."

"All the more reason for you to try my methods." Gina's mouth was dry with fear. She wasn't sure how much longer she could continue the argument. Then Harulf added his male authority to Gina's insistence.

"We will treat Dominick as Lady Gina suggests," Harulf declared with great firmness. "If he dies, she and I will take the blame."

"It's not a matter of blame," Brother Anselm responded. "The will of the Lord will determine whether Count Dominick lives or dies."

"If that be so, then where is the harm in trying a new treatment?" Harulf asked.

"Very well," Brother Anselm said, casting a sympathetic look at Dominick's inert form. "I do confess, I am curious about the effects of such excessive cleanliness. Harulf, hold this compress

over the wound and press hard to stop the bleeding. Come with me, Lady Gina, and show me the
methods of the physicians of your country."

He led her to a little room off the infirmary,
where a vile-smelling concoction was simmering
over a charcoal brazier. Lined up neatly on shelves
around the room were the herbal medicines that
Brother Anselm said he made himself or with the
help of two assistants. At the moment, those two
younger men were attending to the wounded men-
at-arms from the palace, and to the horsemen who
had attacked Dominick and his friends.

Lady Adalhaid, who was resting on one of the
beds, was complaining of a severe headache,
which was being treated with moist cloths dipped
in cool water infused with lavender and mint. The
cut on her forehead had stopped bleeding, and she
didn't appear to have any other injuries.

Gina observed all this activity while she was
overseeing Brother Anselm's preparations. When
the threaded needle and the knife he was going to
use had boiled for what Gina guessed was twenty
minutes, she placed the pot on a linen-covered
tray. Brother Anselm added to the tray a bowl of
clean herbs and a bottle of wine he had just
opened, along with a pile of clean linen bandages.
Gina carried the tray to the infirmary and set it on
a stool.

Having done all she could to try to prevent infection, Gina nodded, and Brother Anselm began to
repair the gash in Dominick's side. Dominick was
so deeply unconscious that he did not waken or
move or even moan. He just lay there on the bed
that was stained with his blood and the mud that

had been on his clothing. Harulf had finally removed all of his garments and had slipped a clean piece of linen under him beneath the area of the wound. Only a cloth draped across Dominick's loins covered his nakedness.

Gina watched everything Brother Anselm did and tried to keep herself from becoming sick. She counted each stitch in Dominick's flesh, telling herself she was responsible for seeing to it that Brother Anselm did his very best, so Dominick would have a chance to heal. She was forced to admit that Brother Anselm knew what he was doing. He drew the edges of the wound together so skillfully that she knew there would be only minor scarring—assuming that Dominick lived.

"There." Brother Anselm cut the thread with the sterilized knife and packed the fresh, cleaned herbs over the wound. He laid a piece of folded linen on top of the herbs. "I'll wrap a bandage around him to keep the compress in place. I can do no more."

"Thank you," Gina said when he was finished, and stretched out both her hands to him.

"I must see to the other patients," Brother Anselm said, as if embarrassed by her gratitude. "Harulf, come and let me tend to your injuries. You've been standing too long; that's why you are so pale."

"Go on, Harulf. I'll stay with Dominick," Gina said. She thought his pasty, clammy-looking skin was more the result of watching Brother Anselm work on Dominick than of standing. All the same, Harulf ought to sit down.

Left alone with Dominick, Gina pulled a stool to

his bedside and sat on it. Dominick appeared to be breathing normally, but he gave no indication of returning consciousness. The skin was drawn tight over his finely chiseled features, and when she took his hand it was limp.

"Wake up," she whispered. "Stay with me, Dominick. Please, I need you."

There was no response. Nevertheless, Gina continued to speak to him. She had read somewhere that unconscious patients who recovered had reported hearing all that was said in their vicinity. She wasn't going to let Dominick think he had been abandoned. She held his hand and spoke softly into his ear until she was interrupted by a man-at-arms.

"My lady, the king wishes to speak with you. I am ordered to conduct you to him."

She had been sitting on the stool for so long that she stumbled when she tried to get up. The man-at-arms caught her by the waist and stood her on her feet, then removed his hands at once.

"I will stay with Dominick while you're gone." Harulf, scrubbed and bandaged, stepped forward. "Lady Gina, you and I know who must be behind that dastardly attack. Charles needs to know, too. I trust you will not hesitate to speak the queen's name."

"I will do whatever is necessary to protect Dominick," Gina said. "Don't leave him alone for a moment. And keep talking to him."

Charles's private audience chamber was by now becoming familiar to Gina. She scowled with impatience as she looked around the simply furnished room with its woven wall hangings. When Charles appeared a few moments after she arrived and invited her to sit, she refused the offer.

"I prefer to remain on my feet, thank you." She bit off the words, fighting against the righteous anger that was beginning to flood over her.

"How is Dominick?" Charles asked.

"Brother Anselm has done his best, but no one knows whether Dominick will live or die." She couldn't be polite; she snapped her response at him, and Charles looked taken aback at her rudeness.

"And Lady Adalhaid?" he asked after a moment or two of uncomfortable silence. "How is she?"

"She appears to be recovering quickly from a head wound. So is Deacon Fardulf recovering from his wounds, and Harulf, and I. I don't know how many of your men-at-arms, or of the attackers, will recover, or how long it will be before any of your men are well enough to go back on duty. Does that answer all your questions?"

"I do regret this incident." Charles spoke rather mildly, considering Gina's provocative attitude.

"Incident?" she repeated, flinging the word back in his face. "It was a deliberate attack on a party that was unarmed!"

"Has no one told you that the six men-at-arms I sent to escort you and Dominick and Lady Adalhaid to me were set upon and killed before they could reach you?" Charles asked.

"No," Gina said, more politely. "I didn't know. We assumed that you believed Regensburg so safe that no armed escort was necessary. That's why only Harulf was with us. If it weren't for Deacon Fardulf, who saw the horsemen coming, we'd have had no warning at all. The four of us would be dead, just like your men-at-arms."

"I am sorry."

"Sorry isn't enough." Gina paused, struck by a sudden question. "Who would dare attack the king's men? Don't tell me there are still traitors on the loose who weren't rounded up weeks ago?"

"The killers were guards attached to Fastrada's service. I assume the men who attacked you were also Fastrada's."

Gina's jaw dropped in amazement that Charles would admit it. She stared at the man, at one of the greatest kings in history, who couldn't control his own wife.

"That's lovely," she said when she could speak again. "Just lovely. Dominick told me he thought you were setting a trap for Fastrada and using us as bait."

Charles did not respond. He looked at her with a sad expression on his face but not one bit of guilt or regret that she could see.

"Your clever little scheme almost killed the finest man I have ever known. How could you do such a thing?" Gina's anger and her fear for Dominick rose beyond her power to control them. She didn't care who Charles was, how great or how famous in history. "Dominick is completely loyal to you, and you knew that when you set him up. You ought to be ashamed of yourself! Instead of endangering the lives of people who love and respect you, why don't you stop that conniving, vicious wife of yours?"

"I have done so," Charles said. "I understand your outrage, Gina, for I, too, love Dominick. He has been like a son to me."

It was on the tip of Gina's tongue to tell him that he hadn't treated Dominick much like a son, when she thought of Pepin. Charles wasn't always kind to his sons.

"An hour ago," Charles said, "I dismissed all Fastrada's servants and guards, all her ladies-in-waiting. Every person who is loyal to her has left the palace. I have sent every man and woman of them home, except for a few who are on their way to convents or monasteries. They will be replaced by people who are responsible directly to me."

"It's a bit late for housecleaning," Gina said, unwilling to relent an inch, not when Dominick lay near death because of Fastrada's hatred. "While you're mentioning people loyal to Fastrada, where is Father Guntram? I haven't seen him since before the trial. I hope you haven't sent him back to Prum, to rant and rave at poor Pepin for the rest of his life."

"No," Charles responded with a bitter twist to his mouth. "I deeply regret giving Pepin into the care of that cold-hearted priest. Father Guntram is on his way to Rome, carrying a message from me to the pope. One of the men-at-arms charged with seeing to his safety also bears a message, in which I ask the Holy Father to assign Father Guntram to a post beyond the borders of Francia.

"Soon I will begin to travel around Francia again," Charles told her. "In recent years I have neglected the first duty of a king, which is to listen to his people and make the best decisions for them."

"I am sure the common folk will be thrilled to see you and Fastrada," Gina retorted with all the sarcasm she could muster.

"Fastrada will remain in Regensburg when I leave," Charles said. "Later, if she so wishes, I will grant her permission to move to Worms when the new palace there is finished, or to Mainz, if she prefers. But she will travel with me no more. I no longer reside with Fastrada."

"Are you planning to divorce her?" Gina found it difficult to believe.

"I cannot. The Church has declared any marriage that has been blessed by a priest to be indissoluble," Charles said. He took a breath before continuing, and Gina could only guess how difficult his marital situation was for him.

"For the sake of the love I once bore Fastrada, and because I love the two daughters she has given me, I will not humiliate her in public," Charles said. "From this hour onward, I will not speak of what she has done."

"You will need an explanation for why she isn't with you any longer," Gina reminded him. "People are bound to ask questions."

"I will simply claim that she is too ill to accompany me. Fastrada has always been in delicate health, and she is known to dislike travel, so no other excuse will be necessary."

"Why are you telling me all of this?"

"I never intended for Dominick or you or Lady Adalhaid to be hurt," Charles said. "You deserved to know why I put you in danger, and since Dominick is too sorely wounded to come to me, I have chosen to tell you the truth. I swear you to secrecy, Gina. Never reveal what I have said in this room."

"I refuse to keep something so important from Dominick," she exclaimed.

"I expected that response from you." Charles smiled at her, his charming, bewitching smile that could almost always convince strong men and brave-hearted women to do whatever he asked of them. "When Dominick is well enough, you have my permission to tell him, in strictest privacy, what I have just told you. Is that acceptable to you?"

"It is," she said, relenting just a little. "*If* Dominick recovers, I will tell him, and only him." She saw Charles wince at the emphasis she put on the word *if,* and she understood that he did regret the harm done to all those who had been caught up in his plan to trap Fastrada in one last, vicious scheme that she would be unable to deny. Perhaps in the future Charles would think twice before allowing a wife or lover to run amok with too much unsupervised power.

The wound in Dominick's side began to heal with only a slight degree of infection. Brother Anselm adhered scrupulously to Gina's directions about using only boiled water to wash the area, and he replaced the bandage with clean linen every day.

A far more frightening problem than the wound was the fact that Dominick did not regain consciousness. He lay like a man already dead, his only sign of life the regular expansion of his chest as he drew breath.

Gina began to appreciate the benefits of the medical advances of her own century as she seldom had before. Dominick was wasting away, and they were unable to get either food or fluids into him. Brother Anselm warned her that if they tried,

Dominick could choke to death, for in his present condition he was incapable of swallowing. Gina would gladly have given her right arm for a nurse with intravenous equipment and the sterile fluids that would keep Dominick alive until he could eat and drink again.

"If he revives," said Brother Anselm, "it will be weeks before he is fully recovered. All too often patients who remain unconscious for so long never entirely regain their wits. I wish there were more that I could do for him. Beyond keeping him clean and comfortable, all I can suggest is prayer."

Gina wanted to scream out her fear and frustration. She restrained herself, because she knew Brother Anselm was treating Dominick as best he could. He was a kindly man, wise in the medicine of his own time and place, but his learning wasn't adequate to Dominick's injuries.

During those days of constant fear, if the infirmary ceiling had opened up to show Gina a way to return to New York, she would have seized Dominick in her arms and tried to carry him into the twentieth century with her. Once there, she'd have taken him to the nearest hospital and demanded that he be treated, no matter what the expense. She'd sell her body or her soul, if necessary, to pay for Dominick's recovery.

But the ceiling never opened. Dominick remained in his stuporous condition, and Gina began to lose hope.

She and Harulf and Lady Adalhaid took turns sitting with him. Both Harulf and Lady Adalhaid insisted that Gina must return to Dominick's house each day for at least a few hours, to bathe and sleep and change her clothes, so she could return to her nursing duties refreshed.

"When Dominick wakens," Lady Adalhaid said one afternoon, "he won't be cheered to see you looking haggard and starving. Attend to your clothes and your hair, Gina. Keep up your appearance for Dominick's sake."

They were in the hall at Dominick's house, and Gina had just shoved her plate of food aside. Lady Adalhaid pushed the full plate back to Gina, who regarded it with distaste and a growing sense of incipient nausea.

"Keep up my sagging spirits, you mean," Gina said, swallowing hard.

"What's wrong with that?" asked Lady Adalhaid. "It's what I forced myself to do for all those sad years when Hiltrude was living at Chelles and dared not leave there. My faith and hope were rewarded. So will yours be."

"Dominick's condition is different from Hiltrude's."

"She was in danger for her life. So is Dominick. Eat, Gina." It was said with the firm resolve of a determined mother.

"I am so glad you postponed returning to Trier," Gina said. "I don't know what I'd do without you."

Lady Adalhaid's hand closed over hers, and suddenly Gina couldn't hold back the tears any longer. She began to sob uncontrollably. Lady Adalhaid put her arms around Gina, pulled the younger woman's head onto her shoulder, and sat there holding her, letting Gina cry until she was too drained to continue.

"I think you needed that," Lady Adalhaid said,

releasing her. "Now, eat a little, drink some wine, and then take a nap. I am going to the infirmary to relieve Harulf, but Ella and Imma will be here if you need anything. I am sure you will be more cheerful when you see Dominick later this evening."

"How can I ever thank you?"

"It's I who owe a debt to you." Lady Adalhaid caught Gina's face between her hands and kissed her forehead. Then she stepped back and wagged a finger at Gina. "Now, go to sleep."

"Yes, Mama." As soon as she realized what she'd said, Gina caught her breath, uncertain how Lady Adalhaid would react.

Lady Adalhaid chuckled. "I always did want another daughter," she said. "You'll do nicely, provided you develop a habit of following my instructions."

The sun was setting when Gina reached the infirmary. She had slept well and had eaten again before leaving the house, and, to her surprise, she was feeling more hopeful.

But the moment she walked into the infirmary, her heart sank. Lady Adalhaid was helping Brother Anselm wring out a wet sheet, which they then spread out over Dominick's exposed body.

"What's wrong now?" Gina cried, hurrying to the bedside.

"Count Dominick has developed a severe fever," Brother Anselm explained. "We are attempting to lower it by cooling him. This is the accepted treatment, my lady. Please do not tell me a fever is treated differently in your country."

"I won't," Gina said. "Is there any ice available?"

"Earlier in the season there would have been. We keep blocks of ice stacked in the buttery. Unfortunately, the weather has been so warm of late that all the ice has melted. There is none left at the palace, either. I have asked."

"Then I guess you're doing the best you can for him." Gina sat on the stool beside Dominick's bed and took his hot, dry hand in hers. "His breathing is so noisy."

"An inflammation has settled in his chest." Brother Anselm was so serious that Gina at once perceived what the real trouble was. Dominick had developed pneumonia. That was why he was struggling for breath, why he had such a high fever. In the eighth century, no medicine existed to cure it.

"Perhaps if we prop him up on several pillows, he can breathe more easily," she suggested in desperation.

"It cannot hurt him." Brother Anselm sounded as if he didn't think Gina's idea would be much help, either. Nevertheless, he went around the infirmary collecting spare pillows from the vacant beds. Most of the men brought in after the battle in the square had recovered enough to leave, whether to their barracks to finish their recuperations, or to cells to await sentencing for their attack on Dominick. Two of the wounded men had died. There were plenty of pillows available for Dominick.

They lifted him until he was sitting almost upright, and Gina thought the change in position did ease his breathing a little.

"I could fan him," she said. "That will increase the effect of the wet sheets."

"A good thought," said Brother Anselm. "I will send to the palace for some fans."

"That's something useful I can do," Lady Adalhaid said. "I know most of the court ladies. I'll have no trouble finding fans."

"The sheet will need redampening every hour," Brother Anselm said to Gina. "Either I or one of my assistants will return to help you."

"You are very good to us," Gina said, overcome by the man's willingness to do whatever would help Dominick.

"Caring for the sick and wounded is my life's work," Brother Anselm responded. "My skill is a gift I offer to God's service. I only wish I were successful more often."

"No one could try harder than you do. I don't mean to criticize your methods, Brother Anselm. It's just that I'm so worried."

"I understand," said the infirmarer, and he excused himself to join his brothers for prayers in the church.

Left alone with Dominick, Gina dampened a small cloth with cool water and placed it on his forehead. Lady Adalhaid returned with several fans and an elderly woman.

"Lady Madelgarde knows Dominick," explained Lady Adalhaid. "She has volunteered to help us."

The three of them fanned Dominick's body for several hours, pausing only long enough to sprinkle water on the sheet or to dip the whole thing into a tub of cool water and wring it out with Brother Anselm's aid. Toward midnight Gina noticed how her companions were wilting with fatigue.

"Lady Adalhaid," Gina said, "I am going to give you the same advice you gave to me earlier today. Eat something, drink a little wine, and sleep. You cannot continue to nurse Dominick if you fall ill."

"I'll see to it," said Lady Madelgarde. "Come along, Adalhaid. I don't want to hear a word of protest. You are spending the rest of the night with me, in my room at the palace. It will be quiet there; a surprising number of the queen's ladies have left. I promise to tell you all the rumors about that interesting situation." Lady Madelgarde put an arm around her friend and led her away.

Chapter Twenty-two

The infirmary was silent. A few lamps here and there threw flickering brightness onto the white walls and the ceiling. The remaining patients were all asleep. Only Dominick's labored breathing and the distant voices of priests and lay brothers chanting the first holy office of the new day broke the stillness.

Gina continued to fan Dominick while holding his hand. Slowly she lowered her head until her cheek rested on his hand, and the fan ceased to move. The arm she had been using to wave it lay across Dominick's abdomen. As her eyelids drifted shut, Gina's last waking thought was that all the wet cloths and fanning were producing some effect, for the hand she was holding seemed a little cooler.

Dominick drew a long, shuddering breath. Gina

came bolt upright, wide awake in an instant, her heart pounding in fear.

"Gi . . . na." Dominick's voice was so weak she almost didn't hear it the first time he spoke. "Gina?"

"I'm here." She fought back tears. Her fingers on his forehead, his open eyes, told her all she needed to know, what she had hoped for since seeing him lying in the square. "You're awake. The fever has broken. You're getting better."

"I'm cold."

"Of course you are. We've been trying to cool you off ever since sunset."

"Thirsty . . ." His eyelids began to close.

"Don't you dare leave me again!" she cried. "Stay awake, Dominick. I'll find some water and a cup."

After days of Gina's repeated insistence on the medicinal boiling of water, Brother Anselm had taken to keeping a large, covered pitcher of it on a nearby table to use when washing Dominick's wound. There was also a bottle of wine, recently opened and recorked to keep it clean and free of insects. Gina mixed water and wine in a cup and held it to Dominick's lips.

"Weak," he murmured, sipping.

"Do you mean yourself or the drink?" she asked, trying to tease him when what she really wanted to do was throw her arms around him and hold on tight while she bathed him in tears of relief.

"Both," he answered. "Cold, too. I dreamed I was floating in an icy lake. Bed's wet. Unmanly." He sounded thoroughly disgusted.

"Oh, it's not that," she said, torn between laughter and weeping. "We've been keeping you wet to bring down the fever. It worked, too. Your mattress is soaked, but it's thanks to us, not you, I promise. As soon as the singing stops, I'll find Brother Anselm and ask him to help me move you to a dry bed. Then we'll feed you."

"No need to wait for the priests," said a familiar masculine voice. "I will move Dominick."

Startled, Gina looked up into the blue eyes of the king of the Franks.

"I couldn't sleep," Charles said. "It's a recent affliction. I'm sure you understand the cause. I came to see how Dominick is faring."

"Well enough," Dominick answered for himself before Gina could speak. "I can stand up to walk to another bed." He made as if to rise, then collapsed back against the pillows.

"You look and sound as weak as a newborn kitten," Charles said to him. "I forbid you to try to get out of bed on your own. Lady Gina, tell me exactly where the wound is, so I don't tear it open again when I lift him."

"Let me dry him first," Gina said, "and prepare the bed next to this one." She wasn't going to raise any protest about the king helping her to move Dominick. In her opinion, Charles owed a serious debt to both of them.

Charles waited patiently while she uncovered Dominick and used a towel on him. He was so thin, his muscles wasted from dehydration and from days of lying in bed, and his cheeks were pale as ashes above the blond beard that had grown while he was too sick to shave. But he was awake, and, as far as she could tell, he was in his right mind, so she wasn't going to worry about anything else for the moment.

The bed next to Dominick's was made up with

clean sheets and a quilt, in case a patient arrived unexpectedly. All Gina had to do was turn back the covers and pile up a few dry pillows to keep Dominick's head elevated.

When she was ready, Charles lifted Dominick into his brawny arms as if the indomitable warrior weighed no more than a baby, and laid him down again with great tenderness.

"What has happened to you is, in some measure, my doing," Charles said, looking down at Dominick while Gina pulled up the quilt. "I give you my word, nothing like it will ever happen again."

There came the hurried sound of sandaled feet entering the infirmary, and then a pair of gasps. Brother Anselm and one of his assistants had arrived. Both men halted abruptly when they recognized Charles.

"Sir," exclaimed Brother Anselm, "I am surprised to see you here."

"It's clear to me you've performed a blessed service in your care of Dominick," Charles said. "You and your assistants have my deep thanks, Brother Anselm. I won't forget what you've done.

"Dominick," Charles went on, turning back to the man on the bed, "when you are feeling strong enough, Gina will answer all your questions. I don't want to tire you further, so I'll bid you a good night's rest."

"Good night, my lord," said Brother Anselm, looking somewhat flustered as Charles departed. "Lady Gina, what has happened in my absence?"

"As you see, the fever broke, and Dominick is awake. He complained of being cold, so we moved him to a dry bed."

"I am amazed and confounded," said Brother Anselm, shaking his head as he observed Dominick.

"Why should you be?" asked his assistant. "Our prayers have been answered. Even as we knelt in the church, praying for Count Dominick's recovery, he awakened. It's a miracle!"

"He won't be awake for long if we don't feed him," Gina said, afraid that all the priests and brothers would come traipsing into the infirmary to have a look at the miracle man and, by their well-meant but tiring attentions, drive Dominick back into a state of unconsciousness.

"Broth," said Brother Anselm, meeting Gina's warning look. "I recommend freshly boiled chicken broth, served in a clean bowl."

"I want meat," Dominick said.

"Perhaps a bit of day-old bread crumbled into the broth," Brother Anselm suggested in a conciliatory way.

"Perfect," Gina responded with a smile so bright that both brothers blinked at her.

"Meat," Dominick muttered.

"Broth," Brother Anselm repeated, and he departed for the kitchen to find some.

"Are you all deaf?" asked Dominick. "I want meat!"

"That's a sure sign of recovery," said the assistant brother. "Every man becomes difficult as soon as he begins to feel better. If he tries to get out of bed or calls for his sword, just yell for me, Lady Gina. I'll be seeing to the other patients."

"I am not being difficult," Dominick said. "I'm just hungry."

"You have been very sick," Gina told him, "and

351

you will remain weak for some time yet, so do as Brother Anselm advises. He's a fine physician."

"What happened to me?" Dominick asked. "I know where I am, but why am I here?"

"We were attacked by Fastrada's people," Gina began. Hoping to keep him lying quietly in bed, at least until Brother Anselm returned, she told him all of it, including Charles's decision to keep Fastrada under what amounted to house arrest, with her loyal attendants removed from court. She decided the almost-empty infirmary was private enough to satisfy Charles's restrictions on repeating the sordid tale.

"Dominick, you saved my life," Gina ended her story. "You attacked a gigantic war horse with an eating knife. I never imagined such bravery existed in this world."

"Were you hurt?" he asked, holding her fingers in a surprisingly tight grip.

"Only a minor wound that's well on its way to healing," she said. "So are Lady Adalhaid and Harulf and Deacon Fardulf all recovered. Assuming you recover completely, the only lasting injury will be Charles's broken heart—unless, after the past few weeks, he finds that his heart was only bruised rather badly, not broken beyond repair."

"I want to go home," Dominick said.

"Well, unless you are willing to travel through the streets of Regensburg in a litter," she told him, knowing he would never consent to that mode of transportation, "you will have to stay here in the infirmary for a few more days, until we can build up your strength."

"I mean, home to Feldbruck."

"It will be quite a while before you are well enough to make that long journey," she said.

"If I were at Feldbruck, I'd recover more quickly."

"I'm sure you would. Getting you there is the problem."

"I want you beside me every night."

"Oh, Dominick." She was about to kiss him, until she saw Brother Anselm approaching with a tray on which rested a bowl of steaming broth and a chunk of bread.

Though he claimed to be hungry, Dominick was able to swallow only a small amount of the broth before he fell into a deep sleep.

"It's natural slumber," Brother Anselm assured Gina when she expressed renewed concern. "He will recover now; I'm sure of it. We will feed him each time he wakens."

Gina remained with Dominick, holding his hand and watching him sleep until Harulf arrived just after dawn to take his shift of nursing his master.

"Don't disturb him too much," Gina instructed after telling Harulf the good news. "Brother Anselm says he needs to sleep."

"So do you," said Harulf, seeing her yawn.

He had brought Eric, another of Dominick's men-at-arms, to escort her through the early-morning streets. Once at home, Gina stripped off her gown, fell into bed, and slept till Ella wakened her in late afternoon.

Dominick's condition improved so rapidly that no more than a single day passed before he was complaining about being confined. Harulf got him out of bed and supported him as he tried to walk about the infirmary. He walked a little farther each day, wearing the tunic and trousers Harulf brought him, though he still spent most of his time lying on his bed.

"Harulf is bringing another man-at-arms tomorrow," Dominick said to Gina one evening. "They will take turns helping me. You won't have to spend so many hours sitting here."

"I don't mind sitting with you."

"I mind it. The time has come for me to begin working to regain my strength, and I will need men, not women, to assist me."

"Of course, my lord," she said, trying to hide her hurt feelings from him. She left his bedside quickly, before she could burst into tears.

Brother Anselm's assistant, who was close enough to overhear the conversation, stopped her headlong flight to offer a sympathetic explanation. "Dominick's impatience is simply what Brother Anselm warned you would happen. It's all part of his recovery. However, I am concerned about your health," said the assistant. "You are pale and wan. Haven't you been eating and sleeping, as you should?"

"I've been too worried about Dominick to care about eating or sleeping."

"Are you ever light-headed?" The assistant's eyes were sharp as he regarded her.

"Occasionally," she admitted. "I'm sure it's due simply to the stress and strain of recent weeks."

"That could be the reason. However, I grew up in a large family, with older sisters, and I do wonder . . ." The assistant paused, as if considering how to phrase what he wanted to say. "My lady, there are certain women's problems that it would be most improper of me to discuss with an unmarried lady. If you feel ill, I would advise you to speak to Lady Adalhaid."

"Thank you. I'll do that."

But she didn't have a chance to speak with her friend, for Dominick decided he wasn't going to stay cooped up in the infirmary any longer. One afternoon, without having mentioned his plans to Gina or Lady Adalhaid, he bid Brother Anselm and his assistants farewell and walked to his house, arm-in-arm with Harulf and Eric.

By the time he reached his front door, Dominick's companions were practically carrying him, and there was an untidy masculine scramble to get him undressed and into his bed before he disgraced his manhood by fainting.

"I feel recovered already," Dominick announced, and he promptly lapsed into sleep.

"He does that a lot lately after he has exerted himself," Harulf said to Gina. "Brother Anselm assures us he will grow stronger with regular exercise."

"Thank you for that valuable bit of medical information." Gina's response was so sharp that Harulf departed from the bedchamber as fast as he decently could. Hands planted on her hips, Gina glanced around the garment-strewn chamber, her gaze coming to rest on Dominick's sleeping form. "He does look peaceful," she said to Lady Adalhaid.

"Let him be," Lady Adalhaid responded. "Let him do as he wants, and don't protest. He's not a child you can keep under your control. It's time for Dominick to be about manly business again."

"Well, he won't want me sleeping here until he's fully restored to health. Do you mind if I move in with you for a while?"

"Of course not. It won't be for long."

The next morning Dominick began working out with his sword. Every day thereafter he and Harulf and the other men-at-arms gathered in the open yard behind the house to practice. At midday Dominick's companions carried him to the bathhouse, where they soaped and rinsed him, then dragged him to his room and tossed him into bed to sleep till evening.

Following Lady Adalhaid's advice, Gina bit her tongue on the objections she longed to make about this harsh regimen. She told herself that Dominick was eating well and sleeping long hours. She could see his progress. The debilitated muscles in his torso and arms were beginning to fill out again as his body regained its taut, sleek contours. His cheeks were no longer hollow.

There came a day when he bathed himself without help after his workout and only needed to lean on Harulf's shoulder to get from bathhouse to bedchamber. Two days later, he did it all on his own. His face and upper body were tanned, and his blond hair was bleached in streaks from the long hours he spent in the sun. Eric shaved off his beard for him and trimmed his overgrown hair. By the end of his first week at home Dominick was beginning to look like the man Gina had met at Feldbruck. But he still treated her as if she was of no importance to him.

Brother Anselm came to see him, and, after a private examination to which Gina was not invited, he declared that Dominick was almost fully recovered.

"And much sooner than I expected, too," Brother Anselm said to Gina after Dominick excused himself to go horseback riding with Harulf and Eric. "But then, when he was carried into the infirmary,

I didn't really expect him to live. I have learned from you, Lady Gina. Hereafter I will follow the methods of the physicians of your country and use only boiled water and newly decanted wine to wash open wounds. I still intend to include a great deal of prayer, of course."

"Good idea. You want to cover all the bases," Gina said. As usual, her twentieth-century slang came out quite differently in Frankish, and she and Brother Anselm both laughed, though he couldn't possibly know why her speech was occasionally so odd.

Gina was surprised to learn there was no charge for all the time Brother Anselm and his assistants had spent caring for Dominick, nor for the use of his bed in the infirmary.

"Secular physicians and barber-surgeons charge fees," Brother Anselm explained. "Ours is charitable work, for the glory of God."

"But surely you deserve something in return," Gina protested.

"Will you feel less indebted if I tell you that Count Dominick has made an extremely generous donation to the infirmary, which is to be used for food and supplies to treat the poor souls who come to us?"

"Yes, it would help. Thank you for telling me." Dominick hadn't told her. In fact, he seldom bothered to speak to her. He didn't have time, for his every waking hour was taken up with masculine pursuits. He was hunting again, often riding into the forest with Charles and his nobles.

"It was fun while it lasted," Gina said tartly to Lady Adalhaid. "Now he doesn't need me any longer. Perhaps he's tired of me. There's no mystery left."

"Oh, you foolish girl! You and Dominick are about to embark upon the greatest of all mysteries." Lady Adalhaid burst into laughter. "Haven't you guessed why Dominick has been working so hard? It's because he wants to come to you a whole, strong man. His pride won't allow him to offer his weakling self to you."

"Is that so?" Gina stabbed her needle through the seam she was mending. There was always so much sewing to be done. Clothes were seldom thrown out; they were repaired or remade and worn again till the cloth in them was reduced to rags, which were then used for cleaning. "So, Dominick imagines I prefer brute muscles and sunburned skin to—to—"

"To a man who is pale and weak from long illness," Lady Adalhaid finished for her. "Just so, my dear. It's the way men think. You will never change a man's opinion on the subject of physical strength, so don't try."

"Is that motherly advice you're giving me?"

"Take it as you will. I suppose Dominick did tell you that Charles wants to see us tomorrow morning?"

"*Count* Dominick hasn't said a word to me since he wished me a good day early this morning."

"I was afraid of that. Wear the red silk dress tomorrow. I'll lend you some of my jewelry."

"Oh, my lady!" exclaimed Ella, rushing into Lady Adalhaid's chamber and plopping down on a stool. "Wait till you hear the latest gossip. Everyone in the marketplace is talking about it."

"Now what?" asked Gina. She noticed Lady Adalhaid's disapproving glance at Ella, but Gina was weary of sewing, and she didn't want to discuss Dominick any longer.

"Well," said Ella, obviously bursting with the news, "you know that Queen Fastrada hasn't been seen in public since the day of Hiltrude's wedding. Now everyone is saying that she has taken to her bed. That's why she sent so many of her attendants away. It's because she has stopped participating in court functions, so she doesn't need as many ladies around her."

"Very sensible," said Lady Adalhaid in a tone that made Gina look hard at her. Nothing in Lady Adalhaid's expression betrayed any knowledge of the truth of Fastrada's situation—except for the twinkle in Lady Adalhaid's eyes.

"And now," Ella continued, "Charles intends to depart from Regensburg two days hence. He is to make a grand royal progress throughout Francia. And Fastrada won't be going!"

"Really?" said Gina, keeping her eyes fixed on her sewing.

"Don't you see what it all means?" cried Ella. When neither woman responded, she said, "The rumor is that Fastrada is with child again. That's why she stays in bed. She's sick every morning. It's clear she's hoping for a son this time, and she won't jeopardize the baby by travelling."

Again, neither woman said a word.

"I'm going to tell Imma and the cook," Ella said, sounding offended by the lack of interest in her gossip.

"Do you think it's true?" Gina asked as soon as Ella was gone.

"With Fastrada, almost anything is possible, but frankly, I doubt it," said Lady Adalhaid. "My friend, Lady Madelgarde, knows all the court news. During that night I spent with her, she recounted everything that had happened since Fastrada banished me from the palace. Madelgarde claims that Charles has been living a celibate life ever since the plot to unthrone him was discovered."

"But he wasn't celibate before that time, and Fastrada was very demonstrative toward him in public. I'm thinking of the night when you and I first met." Gina frowned. "Wouldn't it be just like Fastrada to produce a son and use the baby to worm her way back into Charles's good graces?"

"I consider it highly unlikely that she is with child. Despite Charles's constant attentions during the first ten years of their marriage, Fastrada was able to conceive only two daughters. Ella has made a great deal out of a few rumors. I don't think we need to worry about Fastrada any longer." Lady Adalhaid suddenly stopped talking, looking guilty. Then she broke into a naughty grin. "Besides, I would never dream of uttering a single word on so delicate a topic. Neither should you. Such gossip is for servants."

"Right," Gina said, and they both went back to their sewing.

Once again Gina, Dominick, and Lady Adalhaid stood in Charles's private audience chamber. He kept them waiting, and when he finally appeared, Alcuin was with him.

"Dominick, I am glad to see you looking so well," Charles said in a jovial way, as if he hadn't seen Dominick on the previous day, when they went hunting together. "Lady Adalhaid, I understand you are planning to return to Trier."

"As soon as I take my leave of you, my lord," she

said. "I have only stayed so long to help nurse Dominick back to health."

"And a fine job you did. Perhaps too fine." Charles looked from Lady Adalhaid to Dominick to Gina, and on her his gaze rested. "Lady Adalhaid, if you depart from Regensburg, there will be a scandal."

"I beg your pardon?" Lady Adalhaid looked as if she was about to burst into laughter.

"How can you leave a lovely young woman and such a handsome, vigorous young man to live alone in the same house?" Charles asked, his gaze still on Gina. "Lady Adalhaid, you know as well as I do what everyone in Regensburg will say about that arrangement. No, it will not be seemly for you to leave. Lady Gina requires a chaperone."

"I do not!" Gina exclaimed, annoyed that they were talking about her as if she weren't present. "I've never had a chaperone in my life."

"But you have," said Alcuin. "That is what Lady Adalhaid has been to you since shortly after you came to Regensburg."

"She's my friend," Gina said.

"All the better," Charles told her. "Since she is your friend, surely you cannot want to prevent her from returning to the home she so loves?"

"What's going on here?" Gina demanded. "Dominick, do you know what these people are up to?"

"No, I do not," he said, frowning, "but I suspect we are about to learn. Lady Adalhaid, never tell me you intend to take Gina to Trier with you? I won't allow it."

"*You* won't allow it?" Gina turned on him. "I'll go wherever I please. *You*, who won't give me the time of day lately, have no right to tell me what to do."

"I haven't invited Gina to Trier," Lady Adalhaid said. "Nor will I."

"I thought you were my friend!" Gina cried in complete confusion.

"There is only one solution." Charles's voice rose above the others', who were all talking at once. "It is my duty to protect maidens from the depredations of men."

Gina was going to tell Charles that she wasn't a maiden and that if he didn't know it he was blind and deaf, but something in his blue gaze made her keep her mouth shut and listen to his next words.

"Count Dominick," Charles said, speaking very formally, "I hereby command you to marry Lady Gina. The ceremony will take place early tomorrow morning. Father Theodulf has agreed to bless the union during morning prayers. I regret to say I cannot provide a wedding feast here at the palace, as I will be leaving Regensburg directly after morning prayers end. Lady Adalhaid, you will then be free to leave also, though I trust you will rejoin my court before too long."

"Of course I will. Thank you for *everything*."

The way Lady Adalhaid made her thanks convinced Gina that she and Charles, together, had planned the interview and, for reasons of their own, had decided that Gina and Dominick must marry.

She was going to refuse. It wasn't right to go through a marriage ceremony pretending that all was well, when she wasn't sure Dominick really cared about her, and, furthermore, she didn't know how long she could stay in the eighth century. With a chill in her heart and a sudden, queasy rolling of her stomach, she recalled the way the ceiling of

Dominick's room at Feldbruck had opened, and the way she had almost been sucked into that long, dark tunnel. She was certain the same thing would happen again, and, when it did, she might not be able to escape.

"I can't," she said.

"What?" Charles was frowning at her.

She had never been frowned at by a king before and it was truly frightening. Gina stared back at him, knowing she was in for a major battle and fearing she wouldn't be strong enough to hold out against his will, because, deep in her heart, she wanted to obey his command. She wanted so much to marry Dominick and live with him to the end of their lives. But she couldn't. It wouldn't be fair to him.

"Gina," Alcuin said, "look at me."

She did, meeting his honest gaze and knowing that he was the only person in the room other than Dominick who understood her predicament.

"I advise you to do as Charles orders," Alcuin said. "Obey the urging of your heart."

"You know why I can't," she said.

"I know why you must."

Alcuin's cryptic statement left Gina so puzzled and nervous that her stomach began to churn.

"Gina," Dominick said, taking her hand, "marry me. Please. I insist on it."

Not *I love you and I can't live without you.* Just *I insist on it.*

"What a typical Frankish male you are!" she exclaimed, and she heard Lady Adalhaid's distinctive throaty chuckle.

"Marry me," Dominick repeated with an intensity that suggested he might have some inkling of what was going through her mind. "Say yes."

"Yes?" All her doubts were in that single word, making it into a question. She promised herself that, after they got out of that cursed audience chamber, she was going to talk to Dominick without the interference of well-meaning friends, and she'd remind him why it wasn't a good idea for them to marry. For the moment, she just wanted to get away from Charles. She hadn't fully realized how manipulative the king of the Franks could be beneath his relaxed, easygoing exterior.

"Good." Charles was beaming his approval on them. "I'll let you go now. I'm sure all of you have a great deal to accomplish in preparation for tomorrow. Alcuin will meet with you about the marriage contract."

"Contract?" Gina said. "I don't have any property. No dowry. I guess that means no wedding."

"On the contrary," said Charles. "I am settling upon you the estate of one of the exiled traitors. Vincona isn't a very large estate, but the farmland is rich. So you now have a dowry in Lombardy."

"Lombardy?" Gina cried. "You mean it's in Italy?" She wanted to add, *Are you crazy?*, but Dominick was thanking Charles for her, and by the time she had a chance to say anything at all, Charles had dismissed them.

Lady Adalhaid went off to bid farewell to Lady Madelgarde and her other friends.

Gina and Dominick spent an hour in Alcuin's office while he and Dominick discussed the terms of their marriage contract. Gina agreed to whatever the men suggested. It didn't matter what the contract said. She couldn't marry Dominick.

Chapter Twenty-three

"I shouldn't have to explain it to you," Gina said.

Dominick had sent Harulf home, so the two of them were walking unattended beside the Danube. Sunlight glittered on the blue water. Tree leaves rustled in a gentle breeze. A few puffy clouds drifted overhead. The grass was springy beneath their feet. Altogether it was a perfect summer day.

Gina's heart was aching.

"You know," she said, stopping so she could turn to face Dominick, "ever since I met you, I've been pulled one way and then the other. I don't know what to think or whether you care about me or not. I can't take it anymore."

"Are you saying that you want to return to New York?" His face was grim. His strong hands gripped her shoulders so tightly that her bones hurt. "Look me in the eye and tell me the truth. I will have nothing but honesty from you. I deserve that much, after you've refused my offer of marriage despite the king's order and despite the fact that Alcuin is even now dictating the final terms of our marriage contract to one of his secretaries."

"It wasn't an offer of marriage, it was Charles's command."

"Stop quibbling," he ordered. "Answer me truthfully."

She couldn't tear her eyes away from his hard gaze, and she knew if she didn't speak what was in her heart, she'd regret it for the rest of her life. No, she'd regret it for all eternity.

"The truth is, if I were given a choice of returning to the twentieth century or of staying here with you," she said, "I would choose to stay with you."

"Then marry me."

"Don't you understand? I may not have a choice. I don't know how long I will stay in this time. What if I marry you tomorrow morning, and I'm taken back to the twentieth century tomorrow night? Or the day after? Or on the day when we return to Feldbruck and I walk into your bedchamber?"

"I am willing to take the risk," he said. "I want to seize whatever time heaven grants us to be together. We can move to a different bedchamber at Feldbruck. There is a large room on the second level that I have never used because my needs were those of an ordinary warrior."

"There is nothing ordinary about you," she said, thinking of the grueling work he had undertaken to restore his health and strength.

"The room is bare of all furniture," Dominick

said. "Would you like to see to the decorating yourself? My storerooms are full, or you may take furniture from the other rooms if you like."

"Pale blue walls," she murmured, daring to dream for just a brief moment, though she knew dreams were futile. "Is blue wall paint possible in this time?"

"Anything is possible with you, my love."

"A rug on the floor, a couple of chairs with thick cushions—what did you say?"

"Anything is possible."

"No, I mean after that."

"I called you my love."

"You love me?" she exclaimed, uncertain whether to believe him or not. But why would he lie? Dominick never lied to her.

"I thought you knew," he said.

"How do you expect me to know something like that when no one has ever—until now—?" She halted, still not quite able to believe he had actually spoken the words she wanted to hear from him.

"Let me say it straight out, so there will be no chance of misunderstanding." Using the name she had written on the marriage contract, he said, "Gina of New York, I love you."

"Oh, Dominick." She saw him in blurry fashion, for her eyes were swimming with happy tears. "I love you, too. It wasn't until I met you and began to learn what a fine, honest man you are that I was able to understand what real love is."

"Nor did I ever love," he said, "until the morning I first looked into your beautiful green eyes."

"But you did love before I came to Francia," she protested. "You love Charles and Alcuin and Pepin.

You love Lady Adalhaid, even if she was once your mother-in-law, and I think you did love Hiltrude, too."

"Say, rather, I respect Lady Adalhaid. And for a brief time I was fond of Hiltrude in the way I would care for a young and innocent sister."

"For heaven's sake, Dominick, you even love your miserable brother!"

"Bernard would insist that you refer to him as my half brother," Dominick corrected her.

"You probably treat Bernard's mother nicely, too."

"That is more difficult," Dominick said wryly. "And never did I love any of the people you have mentioned with the kind of passionate, enduring love I feel for you. Gina, you are my whole heart and soul. I will love you until I die. And if we are ever torn apart as you fear, I will pray ceaselessly that we will find each other again in the next world, so we can spend eternity together."

"That's not fair to you," she whispered, making one last objection for the sake of her conscience and his future happiness.

"I don't care," he said. "Please, Gina, marry me. It is the deepest desire of my heart, what I want above all else in this lifetime."

"It's what I want, too," she said, capitulating to the love in his eyes. Silently she vowed to do everything she could to make him happy for as long as they were together. "All right. If you are willing to take the chance, then so am I. I will marry you, Dominick."

He was still holding her by her shoulders, but now he pulled her closer, and his hands slid across her back, until she was right up against him. She lifted her face to him, and his lips caressed hers, sweetly, softly. Gina whimpered, and Dominick deepened the kiss, exploring her mouth until she went limp with desire and hung on to his shoulders to keep herself from falling.

"That was only a promise, for the future," he said.

"No." She pressed closer, recalling the frightening days when she had feared he'd have no future. "Dominick, please, kiss me again. Then take me home right away. I want to be as close to you as two people can be. I've missed you so." It wasn't just his physical closeness she had missed; it was his deep tenderness and the expression on his face in the last seconds before his pleasure seized him in a whirlwind that always—*always*—included her.

"I hope you understand," he said, "that in this century a wife is expected to obey her husband in all things." With that cool statement he took his hands from her and stood back.

Her eyes opened wide in hurt surprise, and she reacted with irritation bordering on anger. "I wouldn't depend on that if I were you," she said.

"I am about to issue my first order." He actually shook a finger just in front of her nose.

"You aren't my husband yet," she reminded him. "Where I come from, women have rights."

"So have Frankish women, as you very well know. My order is that, from this moment until nightfall, we will not speak of any unpleasant subject, nor of any unkind or unloving person."

"Oh. I think I can live with that."

"See how easy it is to obey me? Here is your

reward." Before Gina could respond to his teasing comments, Dominick kissed her again, this time so thoroughly that she was rocked to her very toes.

"Now," he said, releasing her, "we will walk along the river and talk and make plans as if we have forever to be together. For it may be that we have."

"Walk and talk," she said. "Is that another order?"

"It is a desperate scheme," he responded with solemnity, "intended to prevent me from dragging you back to my house and into my bedchamber as you requested. It will be difficult to restrain myself when I am burning for you and you admit that you also desire me, but I would like to wait until tomorrow, until you are officially my wife, before we lie together again. Then, on our wedding night, we will celebrate a new beginning."

"You are, without a doubt, the most remarkable man I have ever known," she said, touching his face tenderly. *And the greatest optimist in the face of uncertainty*, she added silently.

Gina wore a green silk gown to her wedding, another of Hiltrude's dresses with the seams taken in so it would fit her. She was no longer without jewelry of her own, for on their return from their walk along the Danube, Dominick had presented her with a necklace of heavy gold links set with green stones.

"I ordered Charles's jeweler to make it for you soon after we came to Regensburg," he said. "There's a ring, too. You will see that tomorrow."

Dominick set out for the palace early on the day of the wedding, attended by all his men-at-arms except for the two who were to escort Gina and the other women.

"That's a good thing," said Ella, bustling about. "Imma and I are going to clean Dominick's chamber and put clean sheets on the bed for tonight. Cook is preparing a lovely meal for you that you can serve yourselves. The rest of us will carry our midday feast to the riverbank and enjoy it there."

Lady Adalhaid was wearing her traveling garments. Her belongings were packed, and she and Imma were to depart from Regensburg as soon as Charles left.

"Let me say farewell now," Lady Adalhaid said just before they were scheduled to mount and ride to the wedding. She embraced Gina warmly, kissing her on both cheeks.

"Don't say good-bye," Gina whispered, her throat suddenly too tight for normal speech. "Visit us at Feldbruck, and I hope we will meet at court, too. Dominick tells me that he is required to attend Charles periodically."

"I will travel to Feldbruck," Lady Adalhaid responded with a sly smile, "for the birth of your first child. I think you will want someone there to counteract Hedwiga's bossiness."

"That would be lovely. But who knows when, or if, I will have a child?" Gina's cheeks warmed at the thought of what she and Dominick would do later in the day, which could, of course, result in a baby, but she forgot her momentary embarrassment when she heard Lady Adalhaid's next, puzzling statement, which bore no apparent connection to what she had just said.

"Lady Madelgarde assures me most positively

that Fastrada is not with child. Apparently Fastrada was greatly distressed when the evidence presented itself right on schedule. She knew a pregnancy was her last hope of holding on to Charles's affections, for he surely will not lie with her again.

"As for you, let me see now." Lady Adalhaid held up her hands and began, rather ostentatiously, to count on her fingers. "As near as I can tell, it will be in late January or early February. If I visit Hiltrude and Audulf at Birnau for the Christmas festivities and travel on to Feldbruck immediately thereafter, I ought to reach you with sufficient time to spare. Is that arrangement acceptable to you?"

"What are you implying?" Gina asked. "Even if I were to conceive tonight—well, it's early August. How could I possibly have a child in January?"

Lady Adalhaid didn't answer. She merely chuckled, making that throaty sound Gina liked to hear, and regarded Gina out of smiling eyes.

"Unless," Gina said, realization slowly dawning, "you are trying to tell me that I'm already pregnant. But how can that be?"

"I suppose it happened in the usual way," Lady Adalhaid responded with dry humor. "I assume that you and Dominick were lying together before you left Feldbruck, which is why he kept you in his house here in Regensburg, rather than sending you to the women's quarters at the palace. That was a wise decision in many ways. I began to consider the possibility when I noticed that you were pale, with circles under your eyes, and you ate little. Your bosom has grown larger. Haven't you noticed how snug the tops of your dresses are?"

"I developed circles under my eyes because I wasn't sleeping much while I was so worried about Dominick," Gina said. "That's why I haven't been eating." Yet in the back of her mind lay the tantalizing memory of a brief conversation she'd had at the infirmary.

"There is a final, conclusive detail," Lady Adalhaid said. "Since you first arrived at Feldbruck, you've not had a single monthly flow."

"How can you possibly know something like that?" Gina cried, dumbfounded.

"Ella noticed. She told Imma, who then told me. Servants always know these things, sometimes before their masters or mistresses do."

Of course Ella had noticed. At Feldbruck she and Gina routinely spread out the laundry together, including the cloths the women used each month. Gina recalled being glad not to have to use and reuse the same cloths and hoping she'd return to New York before she needed such supplies. Then, with the journey to Regensburg and all the excitement there, she'd forgotten about the matter entirely.

"Brother Anselm's assistant told me he thought I had a female problem of some kind, and he said I ought to speak to you about it," Gina admitted. "I was so concerned about Dominick that that conversation slipped my mind until now."

"There, you see?" Lady Adalhaid chuckled again. "How can you doubt what even a lay brother has noticed? Why do you think I went to Charles and insisted that you and Dominick marry quickly?"

"You told Charles I'm having a baby? Before you said anything to me?"

"Of course not. I wouldn't do that. I only told him that you and Dominick were deeply in love and deserved to marry but that I feared you would refuse him if he asked because you lacked a dowry. I knew Charles could easily remedy that problem."

"You've been arranging my life behind my back!" Gina cried.

"I have been doing what any loving foster parent would do," Lady Adalhaid replied, unruffled by the accusation. "I perceive that you are frightened about the future. It's natural, you know. Any bride who's not a half-wit is worried on her wedding day, and to learn on the same day that you are to have a child must be somewhat disturbing."

"That's putting it mildly," Gina said, horrified by the possibility that she might be returned to the twentieth century while pregnant, leaving Dominick to wonder forever about the gender and the well-being of their child, and leaving her far from his love and tender support.

"You do want to marry Dominick, don't you?" Lady Adalhaid began to look worried. "I'm sure I'm not mistaken in thinking you love him."

"I love him with all my heart and soul." It was a simple statement of truth that put the uncertain future into perspective. "I want to marry Dominick and live with him for the rest of my life."

"Well, then, we ought to start for the palace before he begins to think you've run away and deserted him," Lady Adalhaid said, teasing. "He would come after you, you know."

"I know," Gina said, love and hope and fear all mingling together in her heart. "If it were possible to follow me to the end of time, Dominick would."

* * *

Gina did like the simplicity of a Frankish wedding. In the presence of Charles and his courtiers, but with Fastrada absent, Alcuin read out the terms of their marriage contract. Gina's dowry of Vincona in Lombardy was given to Dominick to administer. Since he held only Feldbruck, having no lesser properties to bestow on her as a marriage gift, the contract stated that, in the event of Dominick's death without heirs of his body, Vincona would become Gina's property, to do with as she wished, so she would not be destitute when Feldbruck was returned to Charles to give to a new count.

After they both agreed to the terms, Dominick slid onto Gina's finger a simple gold band into which a green stone was deeply set. The top of the stone was rounded, and it shone with a soft glow. Gina couldn't tell whether it was an emerald or some other kind of gem. It didn't matter. She touched the ring and looked into Dominick's eyes and blinked away tears of happiness.

As soon as all the copies of the contract were signed and witnessed, the entire court went to morning prayers at St. Peter's. Gina was pleased to see Deacon Fardulf, Brother Anselm, and his two assistants among the attending clergymen. All four of them congratulated Dominick and Gina after the service and after Father Theodulf had formally blessed the union.

"All that's left is to say good-bye!" exclaimed Lady Adalhaid, laughing and crying at the same time as she embraced Dominick. "I will see you again in January," she whispered into Gina's ear.

"Dominick," Charles said as they all stood on the church steps, waiting for the king to depart so they could leave without being disrespectful, "my wedding gift to you is temporary remission of your military service to me. You will require time to recover from your recent wounds and also to put the estate at Vincona into order. Nor would I deprive a new bride of her husband's company. I will see you at the Mayfield next spring. You will receive the usual notice of when and where it's to be held and how many fighting men you are to bring with you. Lady Gina, you are always welcome to join the other ladies who attend the Mayfield assembly with their husbands."

Charles clasped Dominick's hand and kissed Gina on both cheeks. Then he was gone, mounted on his favorite steed and riding out of Regensburg surrounded by his loyal nobles and their ladies. He was so tall that Gina could easily distinguish him in the crowd.

Dominick latched the bedchamber door and turned toward his new wife, noting the nervousness she could not conceal. Gina was behaving like a skittish virgin. He couldn't understand it; he was sure he had banished the last of her qualms about the act of love some time ago, and they had settled the final differences between them on the previous day. Perhaps there was another reason.

"I am completely restored to health," he said.

"I know." She backed away from him. "The room looks nice."

"It's lovely." He made a quick assessment of the

clean sheets, neatly turned down and awaiting them, and of the large pitcher crammed full of flowers that sat atop his clothing chest.

"The servants were considerate to leave us alone," Gina said.

"I suggested it." He took another step forward.

"I didn't know." Gina took another step backward.

"Enough, Gina." He caught her by the shoulders. "I did not come to my own bedchamber to stalk quarry. What's wrong?"

"Can't a girl be nervous on her wedding night?"

"It's midday, and we have done this before, several times. Though, I grant you, there is a special solemnity to this occasion." He wished he were capable of understanding a woman's mind. He knew of no man who could. Gina was a greater mystery than most women. From the first moment, she had baffled and intrigued him. He was sure she was hiding something from him now, though he couldn't think what it might be. She had told him everything about her past, and he knew she was completely honest.

"We have the rest of our lives to learn to know each other," he murmured, as if to convince himself.

"If we're lucky," she said. Then she rephrased the thought. "If heaven wills it."

"Surely heaven will not take you from me now." Dominick knew he couldn't wait much longer to possess her. More than a month of abstinence was too long for any man to endure, especially a man who knew what joys awaited him in Gina's embrace. Fire surged through his veins.

"Wife," he said, "my beloved wife," and he bent to taste her lips.

"There is something I ought to tell you," she said, sounding uncertain.

"I want to know, but later. Let it wait." He silenced her attempt to speak again by claiming her mouth, and by moving closer, so she could feel his arousal. To his surprise, she actually resisted for a moment. Then she surrendered, melting against him, and his heart beat harder in triumph. Her mouth opened to his pressure, and Dominick let his tongue surge into her, establishing a rhythm he would very soon continue with another eager part of himself that was already throbbing insistently.

For him, it had been this way since the day Gina fell into his bed at Feldbruck. He remembered waking, sure that he was being attacked, and tossing her onto her back to hold her down. Even then, his body had instantaneously reacted to her. Even then, when he'd thought she was an enemy, a spy for the queen, he couldn't resist her. Now that he knew her better, Gina's allure was increased tenfold.

She was clinging to him, sighing softly, her green eyes shining with moisture.

"Gina? Why are you crying?"

"Because it hurts to love this much," she whispered. "Whatever happens, wherever I am, I will always love you. But, Dominick—"

"Hush. You are going to stay with me." He couldn't bear to think she wouldn't.

"I wish I could be so certain," she said.

Dominick kissed her again, to reassure her and himself.

Slowly they undressed each other. When she stood naked before him, Dominick smiled in appreciation of her womanly beauty. She had gained weight since coming to Francia. No one could call her sickly or ill-nourished now. Her arms and legs were gracefully rounded, and her breasts were fuller than when he had first known her. She was everything a man could desire in a woman. But most of all he loved her independent spirit that was bold enough to challenge a king, and her unique way of looking at life.

While he was gazing at her in rapt enjoyment, Gina had been assessing him. She ran her hands along his shoulders, feeling the newly hard muscles of his upper arms.

"You do appear to be almost completely recovered," she said, her fingertips skimming lightly over the scar on his side.

"There is still one place that aches," he said.

"I'm sorry." She took her hands away. "I shouldn't have touched your wound."

"Not there." She was becoming nervous again, and he could tell he was going to have to act quickly to calm her. "Here." He caught her hand and guided it to his rigid manhood.

"Oh." She touched him with gentle, trembling fingers, and Dominick almost went to his knees as a wave of desire surged through him.

Fortunately, they were standing right next to the bed. He wasn't going to have to pick her up; he didn't think he could, not when he was shaking and half-mad with longing. He put his arms around her and exerted a slight downward pressure. They fell onto the bed together. He was on top of her, and it was pure bliss to be pressed against her soft skin and sweet curves, from knee to shoulder.

Gina appeared startled by his sudden action, and he could see she was still oddly nervous.

Exerting severe self-control, he rolled off her, lifted her legs onto the bed, and lay down beside her. Then he began to kiss her, starting at her forehead and slowly working his way down toward her toes. By the time he reached her breasts, her nervousness was gone, and when he finally, after a long, delicious interval, arrived at her knees, she was whimpering and begging for more.

He made her wait. There was one area he had deliberately omitted from his attentions. Not until he was working his way back up her lovely body did he pause and separate her creamy thighs and touch the liquid center of her.

"Dominick!" She reared upward, clutching at his shoulder with one hand and grabbing his hair with the other. "Please, come to me. Now!"

As he had known it would be, it was worth the wait, worth taking the time to gentle her, though he had feared more than once during the last half hour that he'd shatter into a thousand pieces.

He settled over her, and she lifted her hips to meet him. The ecstasy on her face was all the reward he needed. But there were even greater rewards for his patience. He thrust into Gina's tight warmth, offering her his manhood, his heart, all that he was or ever would be. And in return she gave him a rapture beyond anything he had previously experienced, and a fulfillment that bound them together forever.

Hours later, in the blue twilight, with the stars just beginning to shine, Gina revealed her last secret.

"A child?" he said, laying a tender hand on her abdomen.

"An heir for Feldbruck."

"Not only an heir. A child born of love." In reverent homage to a mystery as old as humankind, Dominick bent his head and kissed the place beneath which their child grew.

"I hope this doesn't mean you'll neglect me until after January," she said with a wistful smile.

"Oh, no. I am not meant to be a monk." He wasn't quite sure whether she was teasing him or not, so he chose the only course open to a joyfully overwhelmed husband and proved he had no intention of neglecting her. With infinite care, he made love to her all over again.

Chapter Twenty-four

By the time they reached Feldbruck, it was harvest season. Grain lay gold in the fields, where Dominick's tenants were cutting it, and there was early snow on the lower mountains, the ones that lost their icy cover during the warm summer.

Gina noticed the happiness on Dominick's face and understood his emotions, for she shared them. She put out a hand, reaching across the space between their horses to touch him.

"I'm home, too," she said as his fingers laced with hers. "So long as you are with me, this is where I belong."

Arno, the steward, was at the door of the reception room to meet them, with Hedwiga by his side.

"Welcome. I wish both of you happiness in your marriage!" Hedwiga cried. It took less than ten seconds after Dominick lifted the cloak from Gina's shoulders for the chatelaine to notice her new mistress's rounded shape. "Ah, what a joy! What good news for Feldbruck! I must begin at once to sew little clothes. But you are still too thin, Gina. I can see I'll have to fatten you up a bit."

"I'm fine just as I am," Gina said, laughing. "I have never felt healthier or happier."

Nothing would deter Hedwiga. In spite of Gina's repeated assurances, to which Dominick added his confident remarks, the chatelaine began to list all the herbal potions she was planning to mix for Gina to drink regularly.

"For now, all Gina requires is a nap," Dominick said firmly.

"I understand." Hedwiga's manner suggested that she thought something more romantic than a nap was on Dominick's mind. "The moment Arno read your message to me, I ordered the maidservants to clean your room and make up your bed. They will be taking your baggage there and unpacking it for you. It won't take long, I'm sure, and then you may lie down and rest."

"No!" Gina cried in alarm. "Not Dominick's room. I want my old room back."

"A new wife always moves to her husband's bedchamber," Hedwiga proclaimed.

"Actually," Dominick said, putting a protective arm around Gina, "we have decided not to use my room any longer. I think it's time to move into the largest bedchamber, the one the former owner of Feldbruck used."

"That does make good sense." Hedwiga nodded her approval. "Now that you're married, you will need more space, and with a baby coming, you'll probably want a cradle in there and a chest to hold the little shirts and all those small towels to keep him dry. I will order the room cleaned and furniture moved in there at once. In the meantime, Gina, you may nap in Dominick's old room. It will be quiet there. Nothing will disturb you."

"I'm not so sure of that," Gina muttered.

"Wait, Hedwiga." Dominick's arm around Gina tightened. "The new room is to be Gina's personal project, and you are to obey her orders about the painting and the furniture. For now, have the maids open the windows to air it out, and tell them to sweep the floor. Later, after Gina has slept for a while, you may show her the furniture in the storerooms and allow her to choose what she wants. Send Wulfric to her, too, so she can tell him what color she prefers on the walls."

"Of course." Hedwiga submitted to Dominick's instructions with good grace.

"For now," Dominick continued, "have fresh sheets put on the bed in Gina's old room, so she can rest there."

"I'll see to it at once." Hedwiga left in the direction of the great hall and the kitchen, where most of the maidservants were to be found.

Watching her go, Gina reflected ruefully that Lady Adalhaid was right about Hedwiga. The chatelaine was a managing kind of woman. In her first weeks at Feldbruck, Gina had been so confused that she welcomed Hedwiga's bossiness, for it had often saved her from making stupid mistakes out of ignorance. But now Gina was more acclimated to the time in which she was living, and she wanted to make her own decisions on domestic matters. She had no intention of swallowing Hedwiga's herbal medicines unless she decided for herself that she would benefit from them and that they wouldn't harm her baby. She wasn't going to eat mountains of food, either.

Gina knew Dominick would always back her up in a dispute with Hedwiga, but he couldn't be at her side every moment of each day. His duties as count of Feldbruck kept him busy; already Arno was describing a problem with one of the tenant farmers and telling Dominick about a broken drain in the barracks where the men-at-arms lived. It was clear to Gina that she was going to have to find a diplomatic way to deal with Hedwiga.

At present, though, all she wanted was a nap, so when Ella came to inform her that her old bedroom was ready, Gina made her excuses to Dominick and Arno and hurried to the second level of the house. There she let Ella help her off with her clothes and accepted a clean linen shift. Then Gina climbed into bed with a contented sigh.

She was asleep almost before the door shut behind Ella, and she slept until late afternoon. Someone had been in recently to check on her, for there was warm water in the pitcher on the table, a clean linen towel, and a bowl of soap.

Gina washed, then looked around for her comb. Her hair had grown several inches since she'd been in Francia, so she could no longer arrange it by just running her fingers through it. She needed her wooden comb, and she wanted a fresh dress to replace the dusty, travel-strained gown Ella had taken away to clean. She also wanted her light house shoes instead of boots. The only garment left to her was the shift she was wearing. Her comb and all her clothes were in Dominick's room, taken there at Hedwiga's order.

She opened the bedroom door and peered into the corridor. The house was so quiet that Gina recognized the late-afternoon lull, when everyone was finishing up chores before the evening meal.

She laid a hand on her rounded abdomen while she tried to decide whether to make a dash to Dominick's room to grab a dress and her comb. She didn't want to wait for Dominick to appear so she could ask him to run the errand for her. She couldn't go below wearing only her shift to locate a maid who would do for her what she was perfectly capable of doing for herself. If she yelled down the stairs for someone to come to her, Hedwiga would probably assume the worst and arrive with half a dozen maidservants and a few men to pick her up and carry her back to bed. And then Hedwiga would start issuing orders, and she'd force Gina to swallow some noxious herbal brew, and she would probably never thereafter believe that Gina was able to take care of herself.

By far the best way to deal with Hedwiga would be for Gina to appear downstairs freshly washed and dressed and in command of her position as the new mistress of Feldbruck.

Viewed from that perspective, Gina really didn't have a choice. She was going to have to enter Dominick's room.

"I'll be quick," she told herself. "I'll only stay for a minute or two, and if anything strange happens, I can leave at once."

She didn't allow herself time to think twice. If she stopped to mull over her decision, she'd be too scared to carry it out. Barefoot, wearing only her shift, she tiptoed down the hall to Dominick's room.

She opened the door all the way and left it wide open, so she would have a quick exit available. Except for the addition of the clothing chest from her room, Dominick's bedchamber was unchanged since the last time she had been in it. When she opened her clothing chest she discovered there weren't many dresses available. Apparently, Ella had taken all the gowns worn at Regensburg to the laundry, to be spot-cleaned with fuller's earth, then aired and ironed if necessary.

Gina plucked a plain, lightweight blue wool gown from the chest and grabbed her shoes, then looked around for her comb. It lay on the table under the window. She hurried across the room to pick it up.

She paused to look out at the mountains and the forest, now mellowing from summer greens into muted autumn shades.

"No wonder Dominick loves Feldbruck," she murmured. "It's so beautiful here."

She hadn't yet seen the larger bedchamber they were to occupy together, and as she headed for the door and the corridor beyond, she wondered if the view was similar to the one from this room. She hoped so, for Dominick's sake. He liked to look at the mountains; she thought he derived some of his strength from their solid presence.

She was just a few steps away from the door when the ceiling opened.

It happened suddenly and silently, in the time between two heartbeats. Sensing that something was changed, Gina stared upward into a long, dark tunnel with no light at all to be seen in it. And she experienced again the dreadful sucking sensation, as if she was being drawn upward, off her feet, into the air, toward darkness.

"No!" She wasn't close enough to the door to grab it and hold on, nor could she reach the bed-frame. No other object in the room offered a hand-hold or the weight to keep her at floor level, thus forestalling the inevitable. "No, please, don't do this."

In the terrifying silence that surrounded her she struggled to keep her feet firmly planted on the wooden floor, even as she acknowledged that she wasn't going to succeed. She was on her toes. Then she was in the air. She saw her dress, shoes, and comb hit the floor, and she caught her breath on a panic-stricken sob.

"Gina? Where are you?" Dominick's beloved voice sliced through the eerie stillness.

"I said no!" Gina began to fight more vigorously against what was happening, waving her arms and legs like a frantic swimmer, trying to return to the floor and to Dominick. "I won't go! You can't make me leave. I belong here. There's nothing for me back there. This is my home. Dominick is my love. Do you hear me? *I won't go!*"

"Gina!" Dominick was in the room, flinging his arms around her legs, using his weight to try to pull her down to his level.

His efforts weren't working. Both of them were being pulled upward with an inexorable force.

"Stop it! Leave us alone!" Gina screamed into the darkness of the tunnel. Then, realizing that neither her pleas nor Dominick's strength was making a difference, she shouted at him, "Dominick, let me go! Save yourself!"

"Wherever you go, I go, too," Dominick said, sounding remarkably calm. "I will not be parted from you."

They had reached the gaping opening in the ceiling, and they hung there for a moment, suspended in time and place. Gina looked down at Dominick, who was clasping her knees in a grip so tight that she thought her bones would break. She touched his hair and tried to bend toward him, so she could kiss him one last time. To her despair, she couldn't quite reach him.

"Oh, Dominick, I love you." There was nothing else to say, nothing else that mattered, not in the entire world, not in all eternity.

"I love you, Gina. I always will. Nothing can separate us. Nothing!"

With a clap like loud thunder, the hole in the ceiling closed. Abruptly released from its pull, Gina and Dominick tumbled through the air to land on his bed.

"Are you hurt?" Dominick gathered her into his arms, holding her tightly, as if he feared she'd be pulled away from him.

"No," she said in a shaking voice. "I'm just scared out of my wits. Let's get out of this room right away, before that thing comes back."

Dominick didn't get up and make for the still-open door. Instead, he lay back on the bed, so he could look up at the unblemished ceiling. He kept

Gina firmly against his heart, and she let her head fall onto his chest until she felt a bit more steady.

"I don't think we will see that gateway through time again," Dominick said. "It is possible that our refusal to be separated is what vanquished it."

"I'm not taking any chances." Pushing away from him, Gina sat up. She sent a fast, shuddering glance toward the ceiling, then turned her attention to Dominick. "I will never set foot in this room again. I don't want anyone else to come in here, either. That includes you. Especially you."

"Agreed." Dominick sat up, too. "We don't need this room. I'll have it closed up, and I will personally lock the door and keep the key in my possession. Unless, of course, someone we don't like comes to visit. Then I may open it again."

"It isn't funny," Gina said.

"No? Then explain to me why I suddenly feel like laughing uproariously, like running barefoot through the forest, like taking you up to the attic to make passionate love to you again."

"I have no objection to laughter, or to making love," she said, "but I don't think I'm in any shape to run anywhere." She placed a hand on her abdomen.

"We've won," Dominick said. "I'm certain of it. Whatever the force was that brought you to me, I cannot believe it will separate us now."

"Alcuin did tell me once that he believes I will remain in this time so long as I am linked to you."

"Here is a link that can never be broken," he said, laying his hand over hers, over the place where the child they had engendered out of love was growing.

Dominick kissed his wife again. When, after a long and increasingly warm period of time he broke off the kiss and looked upward, he saw a small, star-shaped area in the ceiling, just where the opening to the tunnel had been. It pulsed twice, with an intense golden glow, and then it vanished.

Dominick grinned. Not wanting to alarm Gina, he said nothing about what he had just seen. He helped her to her feet, making sure that she wasn't trembling any longer. Then he took her hand and led her out of his old bedchamber. When they were both standing in the corridor, he closed the door very firmly behind them and locked it.

Author's Note

Part of the fun of writing historical fiction lies in the opportunity to combine actual events with make-believe characters. Gina, Dominick and his people at Feldbruck, Lady Adalhaid, Hiltrude, and Father Guntram are all fictional characters. However, the plot against Charles and the trial that followed its discovery did occur in the year 792, for the reasons Pepin explains to Dominick.

The plotters were overheard by Deacon Fardulf, as I describe, though he did not have the help of a Gina or a Dominick, and after the traitors abused him, he was forced to make his way unprotected to the palace to reveal what he had learned. Fardulf's loyalty was well rewarded by Charles, who from then on kept a watchful eye on the deacon's progress through the Church hierarchy.

Every historian who mentions Charles's fourth wife, Fastrada, speaks of her incredible beauty. No one has anything good to say of her character. The Frankish queens of this period were in charge of the treasury, and they ruled the land while their husbands were away fighting wars. Fastrada's misuse of the power entrusted to her was so outrageous that I actually toned down her character for this book, to make her more believable. The lady was addicted to intrigue, with most of her schemes aimed at ruining anyone who dared to cross her. There is no question that she loathed Pepin Hunchback and tried to convince Charles to have him sentenced to death at the treason trial.

Charles had always been an overindulgent husband to Fastrada. He even remained at home with her for several years, rather than touring his lands or waging war along the borders of Francia, as he usually did in the summer seasons. But *something* happened between them during or shortly after Pepin's trial. It's tempting to speculate, as I do in this book, that Charles had reached the limit of his patience with his temperamental, bloody-minded wife but didn't want to divorce her, because a divorce would create problems with the Church, which was at that time tightening the rules on marriage and divorce.

Whatever the truth of his marital circumstances, before the end of that summer Charles was on the move, travelling around Francia as the king was expected to do, and he left Fastrada behind. From then on he seldom visited her. Two years later, in A.D. 794, when Fastrada fell ill and died, Charles was not with her. He did provide a funeral suitable for a queen and buried her at the Church of St. Alban at Mainz.

Three months after Fastrada's death Charles married his fifth and final wife, Luitgarde. According to the historians, she was a sweet, gentle noblewoman who quickly restored the loving family relationships and domestic harmony that Charles found necessary for his happiness.

As for Pepin Hunchback, he lived on quietly in the monastery at Prum for twenty years after his trial, until he died a natural death.

Readers may write to Flora Speer at: P.O. Box 270347, West Hartford, CT 06127-0347. Please include a stamped, self-addressed envelope if you require a reply.

A Love
Beyond
Time
Flora Speer

Accidentally thrust back to the eighth century, Mike Bailey falls from the sky and lands near Charlemagne's camp: Knocked senseless by the crash, he can't remember his name, but no shock can make his body forget how to respond when he awakes to the sight of an enchanting angel on earth. Headstrong and innocent, Danise chooses to risk spending her life cloistered in a nunnery rather than marry for any reason besides love. Unexpectedly mesmerized by the stranger she discovers unconscious in the forest, Danise is quickly roused by an all-consuming passion—and a desire that will conquer time itself.

___52326-4 $5.50 US/$6.50 CAN

Dorchester Publishing Co., Inc.
P.O. Box 6640
Wayne, PA 19087-8640

Please add $1.75 for shipping and handling for the first book and $.50 for each book thereafter. NY, NYC, and PA residents, please add appropriate sales tax. No cash, stamps, or C.O.D.s. All orders shipped within 6 weeks via postal service book rate. Canadian orders require $2.00 extra postage and must be paid in U.S. dollars through a U.S. banking facility.

Name_____
Address_____
City_____ State_____ Zip_____
I have enclosed $_____ in payment for the checked book(s).
Payment <u>must</u> accompany all orders. ❏ Please send a free catalog.
CHECK OUT OUR WEBSITE! www.dorchesterpub.com

Destiny's Lovers
FLORA SPEER

She is utterly forbidden, a maiden whose golden purity must remain untouched. Shunned by the villagers because she is different, Janina lives with loneliness until she has the vision—a vision of the man who will come to change everything. His life spared so that he can improve the blood lines of the village, the stranger is expected to mate with any woman who wants him. But Reid desires only one—the virginal beauty who heralds his mysterious appearance among them. Irresistibly drawn to one another, Reid and Janina break every taboo as they lie tangled together by the sacred pool.

___52281-0 $5.50 US/$6.50 CAN

Love Just in Time

Flora Speer

After discovering her husband's infidelity, Clarissa Cummings thinks she will never trust another man. Then a freak accident sends her into another century—and the most handsome stranger imaginable saves her from drowning in the canal. But he is all wet if he thinks he has a lock on Clarissa's heart. After scandal forces Jack Martin to flee to the wilds of America, the dashing young Englishman has to give up the pleasures of a rake and earn his keep with a plow and a hoe. Yet to his surprise, he learns to enjoy the simple life of a farmer, and he yearns to take Clarissa as his bride. But after Jack has sown the seeds of desire, secrets from his past threaten to destroy his harvest of love.

___52289-6 $5.50 US/$6.50 CAN

Love ONCE & FOREVER
FLORA SPEER

Laura has traveled here, to this time before the moon has come to circle the earth, to embrace Kentir beneath the violet-and-ochre brilliance of the Northern Lights. In his gray-blue gaze, she sees the longing he cannot hide. His lips seek hers and find them. In his kiss she tastes the warmth of amber wine and the urgency of manly desire. She drinks deeply, forgetting that for them there can be no past, no future; for he is of a time that is ending, while she belongs to one that has yet to begin. Closing her eyes to the soft shadows of the lantern lights, she gives herself to him, determined to live out her destiny in this one precious night.

___52291-8 $5.99 US/$6.99 CAN

Dorchester Publishing Co., Inc.
P.O. Box 6640
Wayne, PA 19087-8640

Please add $1.75 for shipping and handling for the first book and $.50 for each book thereafter. NY, NYC, and PA residents, please add appropriate sales tax. No cash, stamps, or C.O.D.s. All orders shipped within 6 weeks via postal service book rate. Canadian orders require $2.00 extra postage and must be paid in U.S. dollars through a U.S. banking facility.

Name_____
Address_____
City_____State_____Zip_____
I have enclosed $_____ in payment for the checked book(s).
Payment <u>must</u> accompany all orders. ❑ Please send a free catalog.
CHECK OUT OUR WEBSITE! www.dorchesterpub.com